I0688782

A Simple Creed

A Simple Creed

A Classic Tale of Friendship and Betrayal

Trevor Schindeler

Rock's Mills Press
Oakville, Ontario
2020

Published by
Rock's Mills Press
www.rocksmillspress.com

Copyright © 2020 by Trevor Schindeler
All rights reserved. No part of this book may be reproduced in any form or
by any electronic or mechanical means, including information storage and
retrieval systems, without the permission in writing from the publisher, except
by a reviewer, who may quote brief passages in a review.

This book is a work of fiction. Names, characters, places, and incidents are
products of the author's imagination or are used fictitiously. Any resemblance
to actual events or locales or persons, living or dead, is entirely coincidental.

This work is an abridged retelling of *Oliver Twist,* which was first published by
Charles Dickens as a serial from 1837 to 1839.

For my parents,
Mid and Fred Schindeler

Chapter 1
Birth in a Workhouse

Among other public buildings in a certain town, which for many reasons it will be prudent to refrain from mentioning, and to which I will assign no fictitious name, there is one anciently common to most towns, great or small—to wit, a workhouse; and in this workhouse was born; on a day and date which I need not trouble myself to repeat, inasmuch as it can be of no possible consequence to the reader, in this stage of the business at all events; the item of mortality who is the subject of this biography.

For a long time after it was ushered into this world of sorrow and trouble, by the parish surgeon, it remained a matter of considerable doubt whether the child would survive to bear any name at all: in which case it is somewhat more than probable that these memoirs would never have appeared; or, if they had, that being comprised within a couple of pages, they would have possessed the inestimable merit of being the most concise and faithful specimen of biography extant in the literature of any age or country.

Although I am not disposed to maintain that being born in a workhouse is, in itself, the most fortunate and enviable circumstance that can possibly befall a human being, I do mean to say that in this particular instance it was the best thing for Oliver Twist that could possibly have occurred. The fact is that there was considerable difficulty in inducing Oliver to take upon himself the office of respiration—a troublesome practice, but one which custom has rendered necessary to our easy existence; and for some time he lay gasping on a little flock mattress, rather unequally poised between this world and the next: the balance being decidedly in favour of the latter. Now, if during this brief period, Oliver had been surrounded by careful grandmothers, anxious aunts, experienced nurses, and doctors of profound wisdom, he would most inevitably and indubitably have been killed in no time. There being nobody by, however, but a pauper woman, who was rendered rather misty by an unwonted allowance of beer; and a parish surgeon who did such matters by contract; Oliver and Nature fought out the point between them. The result was that, after a few struggles, Oliver breathed, sneezed, and proceeded to advertise to the inmates of the workhouse the fact of a new burden having been imposed upon the parish, by setting up as loud a cry as could reasonably have been expected from a male infant who had not been possessed of that very useful appendage, a voice, for a much longer space of time than three minutes and a quarter.

As Oliver gave this first proof of the free and proper action of his lungs, the patchwork coverlet which was carelessly flung over the iron bedstead, rustled; the pale face of a beautiful young woman rose feebly from the pillow; and a faint voice imperfectly articulated the words, 'Let me see my child and die.'

The surgeon had been sitting with his face turned towards the fire, giving the palms of his hands a warm and a rub alternately. As the young woman spoke he rose, and advancing to her bed, said, with more kindness than might have been expected of him:

'Oh, you must not talk about dying yet.'

'Lor bless her dear heart, no!' interposed the nurse, hastily depositing in her pocket a green glass bottle, the contents of which she had been tasting in a corner with evident satisfaction. 'Lor bless her dear heart, when she has lived as long as I have, sir, and had thirteen children of her own, and all on 'em dead except two, and them in the wurkus with me, she'll know better than to take on in that way, bless her dear heart! Think what it is to be a mother, there's a dear young lamb, do.'

Apparently this consolatory perspective of a mother's prospects failed in producing its due effect. The patient shook her head, and stretched out her hands towards the child.

The surgeon deposited the infant in her arms. She imprinted her cold white lips passionately on its forehead; passed her hands over her face; gazed wildly around; shuddered; fell back—and died. They chafed her breast, hands, and temples; but the blood had stopped forever. They talked of hope and comfort. They had been strangers too long.

'It's all over, Sally!' said the surgeon at last.

'Ah, poor dear, so it is!' said the nurse, picking up the cork of the green bottle, which had fallen out on the pillow, as she stooped to take up the child. 'Poor dear!'

'You needn't mind sending for me if the child cries,' said the surgeon, putting on his gloves with great deliberation. 'It's very likely that he *will* be troublesome. Give it a little gruel if it is.' He put on his hat, and, pausing by the bedside on his way to the door, added, 'She was a good-looking girl, too; where did she come from?'

'She was brought here last night,' replied the nurse, 'by the overseer's order. She was found lying in the street. She had walked some distance, for her shoes were worn to pieces; but where she came from, or where she was going to, nobody knows.'

The surgeon leaned over the body, and raised the left hand. 'The old story,' he said, shaking his head; 'no wedding-ring, I see. Ah! Goodnight!'

The medical gentleman walked away to dinner; and the nurse, having once more applied herself to the green bottle, sat down on a low chair before the fire, and proceeded to dress the infant.

What an excellent example of the power of dress young Oliver Twist was! Wrapped in the blanket which had hitherto formed his only covering, he might have been the child of a nobleman or a beggar; it would have been hard for the haughtiest stranger to have assigned to him his proper station in society. But now that he was enveloped in the old calico robes which had grown yellow in the same service, he was badged and ticketed, and fell into his place at once—a parish child—the orphan of a workhouse—the humble, half-starved drudge—to be cuffed and buffeted through the world—despised by all, and pitied by none.

Oliver cried lustily. If he could have known that he was an orphan, left to the tender mercies of church-wardens and overseers, perhaps he would have cried the louder.

On that same day, yea at that very same hour, in a dank alley behind a public-house in Little Saffron Hill, a week's journey away, a white furred dog died giving birth to a litter of five mongrel puppies. A girl of six years sat beside the dog sobbing and stroking its fur. A boy twice her years, and big for his age, stood over her. 'Hush up and move away,' he said to her. One by one, the boy picked up each of the puppies and inspected it closely. Four of the puppies he tossed aside. The fifth, a white one with a black patch over one eye, he placed into a pocket and took away home.

In an upper room of that same public-house an infant boy was proudly named Jack; after his father who would be arrested, convicted, and hung by the neck until dead within a fortnight.

Chapter 2
Mr. Bumble

For the next eight or ten months, Oliver was the victim of a systematic course of treachery and deception. He was brought up by hand; that is, without the comfort and sustenance provided by a mother's breast. The hungry and destitute situation of the infant orphan was duly reported by the workhouse authorities to the parish authorities. The parish authorities inquired with dignity of the workhouse authorities, whether there was no female then domiciled in 'the house' who was in a situation to impart to Oliver Twist the consolation and nourishment of which he stood in need. The workhouse authorities replied with humility, that there was not. Upon this the parish authorities magnanimously and humanely resolved that Oliver should be 'farmed;' or, in other words, that he should be dispatched to an asylum for orphans some three miles off, where twenty or thirty other juvenile offenders against the poor-laws rolled about the floor all day, without the inconvenience of too much food or too much clothing, under the parental superintendence of a widow, who received the culprits at and for the consideration of sevenpence-halfpenny per small head per week. Sevenpence-halfpenny's worth per week is a good round diet for a child; a great deal may be got for sevenpence-halfpenny, quite enough to overload its stomach, and make it uncomfortable. The said matriarch was a woman of wisdom and experience; she knew what was good for children: and she had a very accurate perception of what was good for herself. So, she appropriated the greater part of the weekly stipend to her own use, and consigned the rising parochial generation to even a shorter allowance than was originally provided for them: thereby finding in the lowest depths a yet deeper well; and proving herself a very great experimental philosopher.

Everybody knows the story of another experimental philosopher who had a great theory about a horse being able to live without eating, and who demonstrated it so well, that he had got his own horse down to a straw a day, and would unquestionably have rendered him a very spirited and rambunctious animal on nothing at all, if he had not died, four-and-twenty hours before he was to have had his first comfortable bit of air. Unfortunately for the experimental philosophy of the female to whose protecting care Oliver Twist was delivered over, a similar result usually attended the operation of *her* system; for at the very moment when a child had contrived to exist upon the smallest possible portion of the weakest possible food, it did perversely happen in eight and a half cases out of ten, either that it sickened from want and cold, or fell into the fire from neglect, or got half-smothered by accident; in any one of which cases, the miserable little being was usually summoned into another world, and there gathered to the fathers it had never known in this.

Occasionally, when there was some more than usually interesting inquest upon a parish child who had been overlooked in turning up a bedstead, or inadvertently scalded to death when there happened to be a washing—though the latter accident was very scarce, anything approaching a washing being a rare occurrence on the farm—the jury would take it into their heads to ask troublesome questions, or the parishioners would rebelliously affix their signatures to a remonstrance. But these impertinences were speedily checked by the evidence of the surgeon, and the testimony of the beadle; the former of whom had always opened the body and found nothing inside (which was very probable indeed), and the latter of whom invariably swore whatever the parish wanted (which was very self-devotional). Besides, the board made periodical pilgrimages to the farm, and always sent the beadle the day before, to say they were coming. The children were neat and clean to behold when *they* went; and what more would the people have!

The parish, of course, provided for the religious instruction of the orphans. Every Sunday children age six and up would troop over to the local church for a special children's service; as regular congregants objected to associating with them. There they were taught that all men are sinners, and especially boys, but that if they were good and did as they were told then they might, through the grace of God, be saved and go to Heaven.

It cannot be expected that this system of farming would produce any very extraordinary or luxuriant crop. Oliver Twist's twelfth birthday found him somewhat diminutive in stature, and decidedly small in circumference. But nature or inheritance had implanted a good sturdy spirit in his breast. It had had plenty of room to expand, thanks to the spare diet of the establishment; and perhaps to this circumstance may be attributed his having any twelfth birthday at all. Be this as it may, however, it was his twelfth birthday, and he was keeping it in the coal-cellar with a select party of two other young gentleman, who, after participating with him in a sound thrashing, had been locked up for atrociously presuming to be hungry, when Mrs. Mann, the good lady of the house, was unexpectedly startled by the apparition of Mr. Bumble, the beadle, striving to undo the wicket of the garden gate.

'Goodness gracious! Is that you, Mr. Bumble, sir?' said Mrs. Mann, thrusting her head out of the window in well-affected ecstasies of joy. '(Mary, take Oliver and them two brats upstairs, and wash 'em directly.)—My heart alive! Mr. Bumble, how glad I am to see you, surely!'

Now, Mr. Bumble was a fat man, and a choleric; so, instead of responding to this open-hearted salutation in a kindred spirit, he gave the little wicket a tremendous shake, and then bestowed upon it a kick which could have emanated from no leg but a beadle's. A beadle might be but a minor parish officer of the mighty Church of England, charged with tasks too lowly for clergy, but the sinecure provided a grand three cornered cocked hat, a handsome gold-laced coat, and a sturdy cane of which Mr. Bumble was justly proud.

'Lor, only think,' said Mrs. Mann, running out,—for the three boys had been removed by this time,—'only think of that! That I should have forgotten that the gate was bolted on the inside, on account of them dear children! Walk in, sir; walk in, pray, Mr. Bumble, do, sir.'

Although this invitation was accompanied with a curtsey that might have softened the heart of a church warden, it by no means mollified the beadle.

'Do you think this respectful or proper conduct, Mrs. Mann,' inquired Mr. Bumble, grasping his cane, 'to keep the parish officers a-waiting at your garden gate, when they come here upon parochial business with the parochial orphans? Are you aweer, Mrs. Mann, that you are, as I may say, a parochial delegate, and a stipendiary?'

'I'm sure Mr. Bumble, that I was only a telling one or two of the dear children as is so fond of you, that it was you a-coming,' replied Mrs. Mann with great humility.

Mr. Bumble had a great idea of his oratorical powers and of his importance. As he had displayed the one and vindicated the other, he relaxed.

'Well, well, Mrs. Mann,' he replied in a calmer tone; 'it may be as you say; it may be. Lead the way in, Mrs. Mann, for I come on business, and have something to say.'

Making her way over and around several filthy, ill-clothed children; Mrs. Mann ushered the beadle into a small parlour with a brick floor; placed a seat for him; and officiously deposited his cocked hat and cane on the table before him. Mr. Bumble wiped from his forehead the perspiration which his walk had engendered, glanced complacently at the cocked hat; and smiled. Yes, he smiled. Beadles are but men; and Mr. Bumble smiled.

'Now don't you be offended at what I'm a-going to say,' observed Mrs. Mann, with captivating sweetness. 'You've had a long walk, you know, or I wouldn't mention it. Now, will you take a little drop of something, Mr. Bumble?'

'Not a drop, not a drop,' said Mr. Bumble, waving his right hand in a dignified, but placid manner.

'I think you will,' said Mrs. Mann, who had noticed the tone of the refusal, and the gesture that had accompanied it. 'Just a little drop, with a little cold water, and a lump of sugar.'

Mr. Bumble coughed.

'Now, just a leetle drop,' said Mrs. Mann, persuasively.

'What is it?' inquired the beadle.

'Why, it's what I'm obliged to keep a little of in the house, to put into the blessed infants' tonic, when they ain't well, Mr. Bumble,' replied Mrs. Mann as she opened a corner cupboard, and took down a bottle and a glass. 'It's gin. I'll not deceive you, Mr. B. It's gin.'

'Do you give the children tonic, Mrs. Mann?' inquired Bumble, following with his eyes the interesting process of mixing.

'Ah, bless 'em, that I do, dear as it is,' replied the matron. 'I couldn't see 'em suffer before my very eyes, you know sir.'

'No,' said Mr. Bumble, approvingly; 'no, you could not. You are a humane woman, Mrs. Mann.' (Here she set down the glass.) 'I shall take an early opportunity of mentioning it to the board, Mrs. Mann.' (He drew it towards him.) 'You feel as a mother, Mrs. Mann.' (He stirred the gin-and-water.) 'I—I drink your health with cheerfulness, Mrs. Mann;' and he swallowed half of it.

'And now about business,' said the beadle, taking out a leathern pocketbook. 'The child who was half-baptized Oliver Twist is twelve years old today.

'Bless him!' interposed Mrs. Mann, inflaming her left eye with the corner of her apron.

'And notwithstanding an offered reward of ten pounds, which was afterwards increased to twenty pounds. Notwithstanding the most superlative, and, I may say, supernat'ral exertions on the part of this parish,' said Bumble, 'we have never been able to discover who is his father, or what was his mother's settlement, name, or con—dition.'

Mrs. Mann raised her hands in astonishment; but added, after a moment's reflection, 'How comes he to have any name at all, then?'

The beadle drew himself up with great pride, and said, 'I inwented it.'

'You, Mr. Bumble!'

'I, Mrs. Mann. We name our foundlings in alphabetical order. The last was an S,—Swubble, I named him. This was a T,—Twist, I named *him*. The next one as comes will be Unwin, and the next Vilkins. I have got names ready made to the end of the alphabet, and all the way through it again, when we come to Z.'

'Why, you're quite a literary character, sir!' said Mrs. Mann.

'Well, well,' said the beadle, evidently gratified with the compliment; 'perhaps I may be. Perhaps I may be, Mrs. Mann.' He finished the gin-and-water, and added, 'Oliver being now too old to remain here, the board has determined to have him back into the house to earn his keep. I have come out myself to take him there. So let me see him at once.'

'I'll fetch him directly,' said Mrs. Mann, leaving the room for that purpose. Oliver having had by this time as much of the outer coat of dirt which encrusted his face and hands, removed as could be scrubbed off in one washing, was led into the room by his benevolent protectress.

'Make a bow to the gentleman, Oliver,' said Mrs. Mann.

Oliver made a bow, which was divided between the beadle on the chair and the cocked hat on the table.

'Oliver,' asked Mr. Bumble, 'do you know what today is?'

'Yes,' replied Oliver, timidly, 'Tuesday.'

'True enough,' admitted Mr. Bumble, stifling a laugh. Catching himself, he continued speaking with his most majestic voice, 'It is also your twelfth birthday, time for you to part from this place and join other lads yur age in town. 'So, will you come along with me?'

Oliver was about to say that he would go along with anybody with great readiness, when, glancing upwards, he caught sight of Mrs. Mann, who had got behind the beadle's chair, and was shaking her fist at him with a furious expression. He took the hint at once, for the fist had been too often impressed upon his body not to be deeply impressed upon his recollection.

'Can *she* go with me?' inquired poor Oliver.

'No, she can't,' replied Mr. Bumble. 'But she'll come and see you sometimes.'

This was no very great consolation to the child. Young as he was, however, he had sense enough to make a feint of feeling great regret at going away. It was no very difficult matter for the boy. Hunger and recent ill-usage are great assistants if you have a need to look forlorn.

'What about Johnny and wee Ricky?' asked Oliver, referring to his long-time companions. 'Can they come? They're nearly twelve, they is.'

'You impertinent boy!' exclaimed Mr. Bumble. 'They will be transferred when they come of age, and not before.'

Mrs. Mann gave Oliver a thousand embraces, and what he wanted a great deal more, a piece of bread and butter, lest he should seem too hungry when he got to the workhouse. With the slice of bread in his hand, and the little brown-cloth parish cap on his head, Oliver was then led away by Mr. Bumble from the wretched home where one kind word or look had never lighted the gloom of his infant years. And yet he felt the agony of childish grief as the cottage gate closed after him.

Wretched as were the little companions in misery Oliver was leaving behind, they were the only friends he had ever known; and a sense of his loneliness in the great wide world sank into his heart for the first time.

Mr. Bumble walked on with long strides; little Oliver, firmly grasping his gold-laced cuff, trotted along beside him—inquiring at the end of every quarter of a mile whether they were 'nearly there.' To these interrogations, Mr. Bumble returned very brief and snappish replies; for the temporary blandness which gin-and-water awakens in some bosoms had by this time evaporated, and he was once again a beadle.

Oliver had not been within the walls of the workhouse a minute when Mr. Bumble handed him over to the first woman he saw, which happened to be old Sally, and continued on his way to attend to more important matters. Sally took his hand, and led him away towards the boys' quarters.

'Does ya have a name?' asked Sally. 'Mr. Bumble's not one for making introductions.'

'Oliver,' replied Oliver.

'Oliver Twist? asked Sally, with more enthusiasm that might be expected.

'Yes,' confirmed Oliver.

'I knew yur mum,' said the old woman. 'She was an Angel, she was.'

'No!' retorted Oliver, vehemently.

'No?' queried Sally.

'No,' confirmed Oliver, 'she *is* an Angel, and I hope to see her someday if I am good in heart and deed.

At this point in their conversation Mr. Bumble returned, looking harried; and, telling Oliver it was a board night, informed him that the board had said he was to appear before it forthwith.

Not having a very clearly defined notion of what a live board was, Oliver was rather astounded by this intelligence, and was not quite certain whether he ought to laugh or cry. He had no time to think about the matter, however; for Mr. Bumble gave him a tap on the head, with his cane, to wake him up, and another on the back to make him lively; and bidding him to follow, conducted him into a large whitewashed room, where eight or ten fat gentlemen were sitting around a table. At the top of the table sat Mr. Limbkins; a particularly fat gentleman with a very round, red face. He happened to occupy an armchair rather grander and higher than the rest and, on account of this, was oft times addressed with the honorific of 'chairman.'

'Bow to the board,' said Bumble. Oliver rubbed his eyes, and still seeing no board but the table, fortunately bowed to that.

'What's your name, boy?' asked the chairman.

Oliver was startled by the sight of so many gentlemen, which made him pause; and the beadle gave him another tap behind, which made him jump. These two causes made him answer in a low and hesitating voice; whereupon a gentleman in a white waistcoat said he was a fool. This was a capital way of raising Oliver's spirits, and putting him quite at his ease.

'Boy,' said the chairman, 'listen to me. You know you're an orphan, I suppose?'

'What's that, sir?' inquired poor Oliver.

'The boy *is* a fool—I thought he was,' said the gentleman in the white waistcoat.

'Hush!' said the gentleman who had spoken first. 'You know you've got no father or mother, and that you were brought up by the parish, don't you?'

'Yes, sir,' replied Oliver, sullenly.

'What are you irritated about?' inquired the gentleman in the white waistcoat. And to be sure it was very extraordinary. What *could* the boy be irritated about?

'I hope you say your prayers every night,' said another gentleman in a gruff voice; 'and pray for the people who feed you, and take care of you—like a Christian.'

'Yes, sir,' answered the boy. The gentleman who spoke last was unconsciously right. It would have been very like a Christian, and a marvellously good Christian too, if Oliver had prayed for the people who fed and took care of *him*. But he hadn't, because nobody had taught him.

'Well! You have come here to be educated, and taught a useful trade,' said the red-faced chairman.

'So you'll begin to pick oakum tomorrow morning at six o'clock,' added the surly one in the white waistcoat.

To acknowledge receipt of both these blessings in the one simple process of picking oakum—picking apart old ropes to salvage the long stringy hemp fibers, an occupation reserved for the youngest male inmates in the workhouse—Oliver bowed low by the direction of the beadle, and was then hurried away to a large ward, where, on a rough hard bed, he willed himself to sleep. What a novel illustration of the tender laws of England! They let the paupers go to sleep!

Poor Oliver! He was unaware, as he lay sleeping in happy unconsciousness of all around him, that the board had that very day arrived at a decision which would exercise the most material influence over all his future fortunes. But they had. And this was it:—

The members of this board were very sage, deep, philosophical men; and when they came to turn their attention to the workhouse, they found out at once, what ordinary folks would never have discovered – that the poor people liked it! It was a regular place of public entertainment for the poorer classes; a tavern where there was nothing to pay; a public breakfast, dinner, tea, and supper all the year round; a brick and mortar paradise, where it was all play and no work.

'Oho!' said the board, looking very knowing; 'we are the fellows to set this to rights; we'll stop it all, in no time.' So, they established the rule that all poor people should have the alternative (for they would compel nobody, not they), of being starved by a gradual process in the house, or by a quick one out of it. With this view, they contracted with the waterworks to lay on an unlimited supply of water; and with a granary to periodically supply small quantities of oatmeal; and issued three meals of thin gruel a day, with an onion twice a week, and half a bread roll on Sundays. They made a great many other wise and humane regulations, having reference to the ladies, which it is not necessary to repeat; kindly undertook to divorce poor married people, in consequence of the great expense of a suit in Doctors' Commons; and, instead of compelling a man to support his family, as they had theretofore done, took his family away from him, and made him a bachelor! There is no saying how many applicants for relief, under these last two heads, might have started up in all classes of society, if it had not been coupled with the workhouse; but the board were long-headed men, and had provided for this difficulty. The relief was inseparable from the workhouse and the gruel; and that frightened people.

In the months following Oliver Twist's return, the system was in full operation. It was rather expensive at first, in consequence of the increase in the undertaker's bill, and the necessity of taking in the clothes of all the paupers, which fluttered loosely on their wasted, shrunken forms, after a week or two of gruel. But the number of workhouse inmates got thin as well as the paupers; and the board members were in ecstasy. Oliver was unsure as to which emotion he felt most, joy or sorrow, when his friend Johnny soon followed in his footsteps.

The room, in which the boys were fed, was a large stone hall, with a copper pot at one end; out of which the master of the workhouse, Mr. Slout, dressed in an apron for the purpose and assisted by one or two pauper women, ladled the gruel at mealtimes.

Of this festive composition each boy was allotted one shallow bowl, and no more—except on occasions of great public rejoicing, when he had two ounces and a quarter of bread besides. The bowls never wanted washing. The boys polished them with their spoons till they shone again; and when they had performed this operation (which never took very long, the spoons being nearly as large as the bowls), they would sit staring at the copper, with such eager eyes, as if they could have devoured the very bricks on which it sat; employing themselves, meanwhile, in sucking their fingers most assiduously, with the view of catching up any stray splashes of gruel that might have been cast thereon. Boys generally have excellent appetites. Oliver Twist and his companions suffered the tortures of slow starvation for three months. At last they got so voracious and wild with hunger, that one boy christened Stephen, who was tall for his age, and hadn't been used to this sort of thing (for his father had kept a small cook-shop), hinted darkly to his companions that, unless he had another basin of gruel *per diem*, he was afraid he might some night happen to eat Johnny, who slept next him. Stephen had a wild, hungry eye; and the others implicitly believed him.

A council was held; lots were cast as to who should walk up to the master after supper that evening, and ask for more; and it fell to Johnny. Upon receiving this news Johnny collapsed in a heap of arms and legs sprawled upon the floor. Oliver look down at his young friend and up at his colleagues, and then resolutely volunteered to take on Johnny's assignment.

The evening arrived, and the boys took their places. Mr. Slout, proudly attired in his cook's uniform, stationed himself at the copper; his pauper assistants ranged themselves behind him; the gruel was served out; and a long grace was said over the short commons. The gruel disappeared; the boys whispered to each other, and winked at Oliver; while his next neighbours nudged him. Child though he was, he was desperate with hunger, and reckless with misery. He rose from the table; and advancing to the master, basin and spoon in hand, said, somewhat alarmed at his own temerity:

'Please, sir, I want some more.'

The master was a fat, healthy man; but he turned very pale. He gazed in stupefied astonishment upon the small rebel for some seconds, and then clung for support to the copper. The assistants were paralysed with wonder, the boys with fear.

'What?' said the master at length, in a faint voice.

'Please, sir,' repeated Oliver, 'I want some more.'

The master aimed a blow at Oliver's head with the ladle, pinioned him with his arms, and shrieked aloud for the beadle.

The board members were sitting in solemn conclave when Mr. Bumble rushed into the room in great excitement, and addressing the gentleman in the highchair, said:

'Mr. Limbkins, I beg your pardon, sir! Oliver Twist has asked for more!'

There was a general start. Horror was depicted on every countenance.

'For *more*!' said Mr. Limbkins. 'Compose yourself, Bumble, and answer me distinctly. Do I understand that he asked for more, after he had eaten the supper allotted by the dietary?'

'He did, sir,' replied Bumble.

'That boy will be hung,' said the gentleman in the white waistcoat. 'I know that boy will be hung.'

Nobody contradicted the gentleman's prophetic opinion. An animated discussion took place. Oliver was ordered into instant confinement; and a bill was next morning pasted on the outside of the gate, offering a reward of five pounds to anybody who would take Oliver Twist off the hands of the parish. In other words, five pounds and Oliver Twist were offered to any man or woman who wanted an apprentice to any trade, business, or calling.

'I never was more convinced of anything in my life,' said the gentleman in the white waistcoat, as he knocked at the gate and read the bill next morning—'I never was more convinced of anything in my life, than I am that that boy will come to be hung.'

As I purpose to show in the sequel whether the white waistcoated gentleman was right or not, I should perhaps mar the interest of this narrative (supposing it to possess any at all), if I ventured to hint, just yet, whether the life of Oliver Twist had this violent termination or no.

Chapter 3
An Apprenticeship

For a week following the commission of the impious and profane offence of asking for more, Oliver remained a close prisoner in the dark and solitary room to which he had been consigned by the wisdom and mercy of the board. It appears at first sight not unreasonable to suppose, that if he had entertained a becoming feeling of respect for the prediction of the gentleman in the white waistcoat, he would have established that sage individual's prophetic abilities, once and for ever, by tying one end of his pocket handkerchief to a hook in the wall, and attaching himself to the other. To the performance of this feat, however, there was one obstacle: namely, that pocket handkerchiefs being decided articles of luxury, had been, for all future times and ages, removed from the noses of paupers by the express order of the board, in council assembled, solemnly given and pronounced under their hands and seals. There was still the greater obstacle of Oliver's youth and childishness. By day he braved his bitter situation, but come the long dismal night; he spread his hands over his eyes to shut out the darkness, and, crouching in a corner, tried to sleep; ever and anon waking with a start and tremble, and drawing himself closer and closer to the wall as if to feel, even in its cold hard surface, a protection from the gloom and loneliness which surrounded him.

Let it not be supposed by the enemies of 'the system' that, during the period of his solitary incarceration, Oliver was denied the benefit of exercise, the pleasure of society, or the advantages of religious consolation. As for exercise, it was nice cold weather, and he was allowed to perform his ablutions every morning under the pump, in a stone yard, in the presence of Mr. Bumble; who prevented his catching cold, and caused a tingling sensation to permeate his frame, by repeated applications of the cane. As for society, he was carried every other day into the hall where the boys dined, and there sociably flogged as a public warning and example. And as for being denied the advantages of religious consolation, he was kicked into the same room every evening at prayer-time and there permitted to listen to, and console his mind with, a general supplication of the boys containing a special clause, therein inserted by authority of the board, in which they entreated to be made good, virtuous, contented, and obedient, and to be guarded from the sins and vices of Oliver Twist: whom the supplication distinctly set forth to be under the exclusive patronage and protection of the powers of wickedness, and a sinner direct from the manufactory of the very Devil himself.

It chanced one morning, while Oliver's affairs were in this auspicious and comfortable state, that Mr. Gamfield, chimney-sweep, was winding his way down High Street, deeply cogitating in his mind his ways and means of paying certain arrears of rent, for which his landlord had become rather pressing. Mr. Gamfield's most sanguine estimate of his finances could not raise them within full five pounds of the desired amount; and, in a species of arithmetical desperation, he was alternately cudgelling his brains and his donkey, when passing the workhouse, his eyes encountered the bill on the gate.

'Wo—o!' said Mr. Gamfield to the donkey.

The donkey was in a state of profound abstraction; wondering, probably, whether he was destined to be regaled with a cabbage-stalk or two when he had disposed of the two sacks of chimney soot with which the little cart was laden; so, without noticing the word of command, he plodded onward.

Mr. Gamfield growled a fierce imprecation on the donkey generally, but more particularly on his eyes; and, running after him, bestowed a blow on his head, which would inevitably have beaten in any skull but a donkey's. Then, catching hold of the bridle, he gave his jaw a sharp wrench, by way of gentle reminder that he was not his own master; and by these means stopped him in his tracks. The chimney-sweep then gave him another blow on the head, just to stun him till he came back again. Having completed these arrangements, he walked up to the gate to read the bill.

The gentleman with the white waistcoat was standing at the gate with his hands behind him, after having delivered himself of some profound sentiments in the boardroom. Having witnessed the little dispute between Mr. Gamfield and the donkey, he smiled joyously when that person came up to read the bill, for he saw at once that Mr. Gamfield would provide exactly the sort of apprenticeship that Oliver Twist wanted. Mr. Gamfield smiled, too, as he perused the document; for five pounds was just the sum he had been wishing for; and, as to the boy with which it was encumbered, Mr. Gamfield, knowing what the dietary of the workhouse was, well knew he would be a nice small pattern, just the very thing for cleaning the insides of register stoves. So, he spelt the bill through again, from beginning to end; and then, touching his fur cap in token of humility, accosted the gentleman in the white waistcoat.

'This here boy, sir, wot the parish wants to 'prentis off,' said Mr. Gamfield.

'Ay, my man,' said the gentleman in the white waistcoat, with a condescending smile. 'What of him?'

'If the parish vould like him to learn a right pleasant trade, in a good 'spectable chimbley-sweepin' bisness,' said Mr. Gamfield, 'I wants a 'prentis, and I am ready to take him.'

'Walk in,' said the gentleman in the white waistcoat. Mr. Gamfield having lingered behind, to give the donkey another blow on the head, and another wrench of the jaw, as a caution not to run away in his absence, followed the gentleman with the white waistcoat into the room where Oliver had first seen him.

'It's a nasty trade,' said Mr. Limbkins, when Gamfield had again stated his wish.

'Young boys have been smothered in chimneys before now,' said another gentleman.

'That's acause they damped the straw afore they lit it in the chimbley to make 'em come down again,' said Gamfield; 'that's all smoke, and no blaze; vereas smoke ain't o' no use at all in making a boy come down, for it only sinds him to sleep, and that's wot he likes. Boys is wery obstinit, and wery lazy, gen'l'men, and there's nothink like a good hot blaze to make 'em come down vith a run. It's humane too, gen'l'men, acause, even if they've stuck in the chimbley, roasting their feet makes 'em struggle to extricate theirselves.'

The gentleman in the white waistcoat appeared very much amused by this explanation, but his mirth was speedily checked by a look from Mr. Limbkins. The board then proceeded to converse among themselves for a few minutes, but in so low a tone, that the words 'saving of expenditure,' 'looked well in the accounts,' 'have a printed report published,' were alone audible. These only chanced to be heard, indeed, on account of their being very frequently repeated with great emphasis.

At length the whispering ceased; and the members of the board, having resumed their seats and their solemnity, Mr. Limbkins said:

'We have considered your proposition, and we don't approve of it.'

'Not at all,' said the gentleman in the white waistcoat.

'Decidedly not,' added another member.

As Mr. Gamfield did happen to labour under the slight imputation of having bruised three or four boys to death already, it occurred to him that the board had, perhaps, in some unaccountable freak, taken it into their heads that this extraneous circumstance ought to influence their proceedings. It was very unlike their general mode of doing business, if they had; but still, as he had no particular wish to revive the rumour; he twisted his cap in his hands, and walked slowly from the table.

'So you won't let me have him, gen'l'men?' asked Mr. Gamfield, pausing near the door.

'No,' replied Mr. Limbkins; 'at least, as it's a nasty business, we think you ought to take something less than the premium we offered.'

Mr. Gamfield's countenance brightened as, with a quick step, he returned to the table, and said:

'What'll you give, gen'l'men? Come! Don't be too hard on a poor man. What'll you give?'

'I should say three pound ten was plenty,' said Mr. Limbkins.

'Ten shillings too much,' said the gentleman in the white waistcoat.

'Come!' said Gamfield; 'say four pound, gen'l'men. Say four pound and you've got rid of him for good and all. There!'

'Three pound ten,' repeated Mr. Limbkins, firmly.

'Come! I'll split the difference, gen'l'men, urged Gamfield. 'Three pound fifteen.'

'Not a farthing more,' was the firm reply of Mr. Limbkins.

'You're desperate hard upon me, gen'l'men, said Gamfield, wavering.

'Pooh! Pooh! Nonsense!' said the gentleman in the white waistcoat. 'He'd be cheap with nothing at all as a premium. Take him, you silly fellow! He's just the boy for you. He wants the stick now and then; it'll do him good; and his board needn't come very expensive, for he hasn't been overfed since he was born. Ha! ha! ha!'

Mr. Gamfield gave an arch look at the faces round the table, and, observing a smile on all of them, gradually broke into a smile himself. The bargain was made. Mr. Bumble was at once instructed that Oliver Twist and his indentures of apprenticeship were to be conveyed before the magistrate, for signature and approval that very afternoon.

In pursuance of this determination, little Oliver, to his astonishment, was released from bondage, and ordered to put himself into a clean shirt. He had hardly achieved this very unusual gymnastic performance, when Mr. Bumble brought him, with his own hands, a basin of gruel, and the holiday allowance of two and a quarter ounces of bread. At this tremendous sight, Oliver began to tremble; thinking, not unnaturally, that the board must have determined to kill him for some useful purpose, or they never would have begun to fatten him up in this way.

'Don't shake so, Oliver, but eat your food and be thankful,' said Mr. Bumble, in a tone of impressive pomposity. 'You're a-going to be made a 'prentice of, Oliver.'

'A 'prentice, sir?' asked the child, cautiously.

'Yes, Oliver,' said Mr. Bumble. 'The kind and blessed gentlemen who are so many parents to you, Oliver, when you have none of your own, are a-going to 'prentice you; and to set you up in life, and make a man of you; although the expense to the parish is three pound ten!—three pound ten, Oliver! seventy shillings—one hundred and forty sixpences!—and all for a naughty orphan which nobody can't love.'

As Mr. Bumble paused to take breath, after delivering this address in an awful voice, tears of happiness began to roll down the poor child's face.

'Come,' said Mr. Bumble, somewhat less pompously, for it was gratifying to his feelings to observe the effect his eloquence had produced; 'Come, Oliver! Wipe your eyes with the cuffs of your jacket, and don't cry into your gruel; that's a very foolish action, Oliver.' It certainly was, for there was quite enough water in it already.

On their way to the magistrate, Mr. Bumble instructed Oliver that all he would have to do would be to look very happy, and say, when the gentleman asked him if he wanted to be apprenticed, that he should like it very much indeed; both of which injunctions Oliver promised to obey: as Mr. Bumble threw in a gentle hint, that if he failed in either particular, there was no telling what would be done to him. When they arrived at the courthouse, he was shut up in a little room by himself, and admonished by Mr. Bumble to stay there until he came back to fetch him.

There the boy remained, with a palpitating heart, for half an hour. At the expiration of which time Mr. Bumble thrust in his head, unadorned with the cocked hat, and said aloud:

'Now, Oliver, my dear, come to the gentlemen.' As Mr. Bumble said this, he put on a grim and threatening look, and added, in a low voice, 'Mind what I told you, you young rascal!'

Oliver gazed innocently at Mr. Bumble's face at this somewhat contradictory style of address; but that gentleman prevented his offering any remark thereupon, by leading him at once into an adjoining room, the door of which was open. It was a large room, with a great window. Behind a desk sat two old gentlemen with powdered heads, one of whom was reading the newspaper; while the other was perusing, with the aid of a pair of tortoise-shell spectacles, a small piece of parchment which lay before him. Mr. Limbkins was standing in front of the desk on one side, and Mr. Gamfield, with a partially washed face, on the other; while two or three rough-looking men, in top-boots, were lounging about.

The old gentleman with the spectacles gradually dozed off, over the little bit of parchment; and there was a short pause, after Oliver had been stationed by Mr. Bumble in front of the desk.

'This is the boy, your worship,' said Mr. Bumble.

The old gentleman who was reading the newspaper raised his head for a moment, and pulled the other old gentleman by the sleeve; whereupon, the last mentioned old gentleman woke up.

'Oh, is this the boy?' asked the old gentleman.

'This is him, sir,' replied Mr. Bumble. 'Bow to the magistrate, my dear.'

Oliver roused himself, and made his best obeisance. He had been wondering, with his eyes fixed on the magistrates' powdered hair, whether all boards were born with that white stuff on their heads, and were boards from thenceforth on that account.

'Well,' said the old gentleman, 'I suppose he's fond of chimney sweeping?'

'He dotes on it, your worship,' replied Bumble, giving Oliver a sly pinch to intimate that he had better not say he didn't.

'And he *will* be a sweep, will he?' inquired the old gentleman.

'If we was to bind him to any other trade tomorrow, he'd run away simultaneous, your worship,' replied Bumble.

'And this man that's to be his master—you, sir—you'll treat him well, and feed him, and do all that sort of thing,—will you?' said the old gentleman.

'When I says I will, I means I will,' replied Mr. Gamfield, doggedly.

'You're a rough speaker, my friend, but you look an honest, open-hearted man,' said the old gentleman, turning his spectacles in the direction of the candidate for Oliver's premium, whose villainous countenance was a regular stamped receipt for cruelty. But the magistrate was half-blind and half-childish, so he couldn't reasonably be expected to discern what other people did.

'I hope I am, sir,' said Mr. Gamfield, with an ugly leer.

'I have no doubt you are, my friend,' replied the old gentleman, fixing his spectacles more firmly on his nose, and looking about him for his inkstand.

It was the critical moment in Oliver's fate. If the inkstand had been where the old gentleman though it was, he would have dipped his pen into it and signed the indentures; and Oliver would have been bound to Mr. Gamfield for seven hard years, presuming he survived that long. But, as it chanced to be immediately under his nose, it followed, as a matter of course, that he looked all over his desk for it, without finding it; and happened, in the course of his search, to look straight before him encountering for the first time the terrified face of Oliver Twist, who, despite all of the admonitory looks and pinches of Bumble, was regarding the repulsive countenance of his future master with a mixed expression of horror and fear, too palpable to be mistaken even by a half-blind magistrate.

The old gentleman stopped, laid down his pen, and looked from Oliver to Mr. Limbkins, who attempted to take snuff with a cheerful and unconcerned aspect. 'My boy!' said the old gentleman, 'you look alarmed. What is the matter?'

'Stand a little away from him, Beadle,' said the other magistrate, laying aside the paper, and leaning forward with an expression of interest. 'Now, boy, tell us what's the matter, don't be afraid.'

Oliver saw his chance and, looking up, implored the gentlemen to order him back to the workhouse, or to some other dungeon, rather than send him away with that dreadful man.

'Well!' said Mr. Bumble, raising his hands and eyes with most impressive solemnity—'well! of all the artful and designing orphans that I ever did see, Oliver, you are one of the most bare-facedest.'

'Hold your tongue, Beadle,' said the second old gentleman, when Mr. Bumble had given vent to this compound adjective.

'I beg your worship's pardon,' said Mr. Bumble, incredulous of having heard aright. 'Did your worship speak to me?'

'Yes. Hold your tongue.'

Mr. Bumble was stupefied with astonishment. A beadle ordered to hold his tongue! A moral revolution!

The old gentleman in the tortoise-shell spectacles looked at his companion, who nodded significantly. 'We refuse to sanction these indentures,' he said tossing aside the piece of parchment as he spoke.

'I hope,' stammered Mr. Limbkins—'I hope the magistrates will not form the opinion that the authorities have been guilty of any improper conduct, on the unsupported testimony of a mere child.'

'The magistrates are not called upon to pronounce any opinion on the matter,' said the second old gentleman sharply. 'Take the boy back to the workhouse, and treat him kindly. He seems to want it.'

That same evening, the gentleman in the white waistcoat most positively and decidedly affirmed, not only that Oliver would be hung, but added that he would be drawn and quartered into the bargain. Mr. Bumble shook his head with gloomy mystery, and said he wished that Oliver might come to some good; whereunto Mr. Gamfield replied, that he wished he might come to him; which, although he agreed with the beadle in most matters, would seem to be a wish of a totally opposite description.

The next morning the public were more once informed that Oliver Twist was again To Let, and that five pounds would be paid to anybody who would take possession of him.

Chapter 4
Mr. and Mrs. Sowerberry

In great families, when an advantageous place cannot be obtained, either in possession, reversion, remainder, or expectancy, for a young man who is growing up, it is a very general custom to send him to sea. The board, in imitation of so wise and salutary an example, took counsel together on the expediency of shipping Oliver Twist off in some small trading vessel bound to some good unhealthy port. This suggested itself as being the very best thing that could possibly be done with him; the probability being that the skipper would flog him to death, in a playful mood, some day after dinner, or would knock his brains out with an iron bar; both pastimes being, as is pretty generally known, very favourite and common recreations among gentlemen of that class. The more the case presented itself to the board, in this point of view, the more manifold the advantages of the step appeared; so, they came to the conclusion that the only way of providing for Oliver effectually was to send him to sea without delay.

Mr. Bumble had been despatched to make various preliminary inquiries, with the view of finding out some captain or other who wanted a cabin boy without any friends; and was returning to the workhouse to communicate the result of his mission, when he encountered, just at the gate, no less a person than Mr. Sowerberry, the parochial undertaker.

Mr. Sowerberry was a tall gaunt, large-jointed man, attired in a suit of threadbare black, with darned cotton stockings of the same colour, and shoes to answer. His features were not naturally intended to wear a smiling aspect, but he was in general rather given to professional humour. His step was elastic, and his face betokened inward pleasantry, as he advanced to Mr. Bumble and shook him cordially by the hand.

'I have taken the measure of the two women that died last night, Mr. Bumble,' said the undertaker.

'You'll make your fortune, Mr. Sowerberry,' said the beadle, as he thrust his thumb and forefinger into the proffered snuffbox of the undertaker; which was an ingenious little model of a patent coffin. 'I say you'll make your fortune, Mr. Sowerberry,' repeated Mr. Bumble, tapping the undertaker on the shoulder, in a friendly manner, with his cane.

'Think so?' said the undertaker in a tone which half admitted and half disputed the probability of the event. 'The prices allowed by the board are very small, Mr. Bumble.'

'So are the coffins,' replied the beadle, with precisely as near an approach to a laugh as a great official ought to indulge in.

Mr. Sowerberry was much tickled at this—as of course he ought to be—and laughed a long time without cessation. 'Well, well, Mr. Bumble,' he said at length, 'there's no denying that, since the new system of feeding has come in, the coffins are something narrower and more shallow than they used to be; but we must have some profit, Mr. Bumble. Well-seasoned timber is an expensive article, sir; and all the iron handles come, by canal, from Birmingham.'

'Well, well,' said Mr. Bumble, 'every trade has its drawbacks. A fair profit is, of course, allowable.'

'Of course, of course,' replied the undertaker; 'and if I don't get a profit upon this or that particular article, why, I make it up in the long-run, you see—he! he! he!'

'Just so,' said Mr. Bumble.

'Though I must say,' continued the undertaker, resuming the current of observations which the beadle had interrupted—'though I must say, Mr. Bumble, that I have to contend against one very great disadvantage—which is that all the stout people go off the quickest. The people who have been better off, and have paid parish rates for many years, are the first to sink when they come into the house. And let me tell you, Mr. Bumble, that three or four inches over one's calculation makes a great hole in one's profits; especially when one has a family to provide for, sir.'

As Mr. Sowerberry said this with the becoming indignation of an ill-used man, and as Mr. Bumble felt that it rather tended to convey a reflection on the honour of the parish, the latter gentleman thought it advisable to change the subject. Oliver Twist being uppermost in his mind, he made the boy his theme.

'By-the-bye,' said Mr. Bumble, 'you don't know anybody who wants a boy, do you? A parochial 'prentis, who is at present a deadweight—a millstone, as I may say, round the parochial throat! Liberal terms, Mr. Sowerberry, liberal terms!' As Mr. Bumble spoke, he raised his cane to the bill above him, and gave three distinct raps upon the words 'five pounds'; which were printed thereon in Roman capitals of gigantic size.

'Gadso!' said the undertaker, taking Mr. Bumble by the gilt-edged lapel of his official coat; 'that's just the very thing I wanted to speak to you about. You know—dear me, what a very elegant button this is, Mr. Bumble! I never noticed it before.'

'Yes, I think it rather pretty,' said the beadle, glancing proudly downwards at the large brass buttons which embellished his coat. 'The die is the same as the parochial seal—the Good Samaritan healing the sick and bruised man. The board presented it to me on New Year's morning, Mr. Sowerberry. I put it on, I remember, for the first time, to attend the inquest into that reduced tradesman, who died in a doorway at midnight.'

'I recollect,' said the undertaker. 'The jury brought in, "Died from exposure to the cold, and want of the common necessaries of life," didn't they?'

Mr. Bumble nodded.

'And they made it a special verdict, I think,' said the undertaker, 'by adding some words to the effect, that if the relieving officer had -'

'Tush! Foolery!' interposed the beadle. 'If the board attended to all the nonsense that ignorant jurymen say, they'd have enough to do.'

'Very true,' said the undertaker; 'they would indeed.'

'Juries,' said Mr. Bumble, grasping his cane tightly, as was his wont when working into a passion—'juries is ineddicated, vulgar, grovelling wretches.'

'So they are,' agreed the undertaker.

'They haven't no more philosophy nor political economy about 'em than that,' said the beadle, snapping his fingers contemptuously.

'No more they have,' acquiesced the undertaker.

'I despise 'em,' said the beadle, growing very red in the face.

'So do I,' rejoined the undertaker.

'And I only wish we'd a jury of the independent sort, in the house for a week or two,' said the beadle; 'the rules and regulations of the board would soon bring their spirit down for 'em.'

'Let 'em alone for that,' replied the undertaker. So saying, he smiled, approvingly; to calm the rising wrath of the indignant parish officer.

Mr. Bumble lifted off his cocked hat, took a handkerchief from the inside of the crown, wiped from his forehead the perspiration which his rage had engendered, fixed the cocked hat on again, and, turning to the undertaker, said in a calmer voice: 'Well, what about the boy?'

'Oh!' replied the undertaker; why, you know, Mr. Bumble, I pay a good deal towards the poor rates.'

'Hem!' said Mr. Bumble. 'Well?'

'Well,' replied the undertaker, 'I was thinking that if I pay so much towards 'em, I've a right to get as much out of 'em as I can, Mr. Bumble; and so—and so—I think I'll take the boy myself.'

Mr. Bumble grasped the undertaker by the arm and led him into the building. Mr. Sowerberry was closeted with the board for five minutes; and it was arranged that Oliver should go to him that evening 'upon lik-ing'—a phrase which means, in the case of a parish apprentice, that if the master finds, upon a short trial, that he can get enough work out of a boy without putting too much food into him, he shall have him for a term of seven years to do what he likes with.

When little Oliver was taken before 'the gentlemen' that evening, and informed that he was to go that night as general house-lad to a coffin-maker's; and that if he complained of his situation, or ever came back to the parish again, he would be sent to sea, there to be drowned, or knocked on the head, as the case might be, he evinced so little emotion, that they, by common consent, pronounced him a hardened young rascal, and ordered Mr. Bumble to remove him forthwith.

Now, although it was very natural for the board to consider in a state of virtuous astonishment and horror the smallest token of strength of feeling on the part of anybody; they were rather put out by the lack of emotion in this particular instance. However, the simple fact was that Oliver, far from possessing too little feeling, possessed rather too much, but was a fair way towards being reduced to a state of brutal stupidity and sullenness by the ill usage he had received. He heard the news of his destination, in perfect silence; and, having had his luggage put into his hand—which was not very difficult to carry, inasmuch as it was all comprised within the limits of a brown paper parcel, about half a foot square by three inches deep—he pulled his cap over his eyes; and once more attaching himself to Mr. Bumble's coat cuff, was led away by that dignitary to a new scene of suffering.

For some time, Mr. Bumble drew Oliver along, without notice or remark; for the beadle carried his head very erect, as a beadle always should, and, it being a windy day, little Oliver was completely enshrouded by the skirts of Mr. Bumble's coat as they blew open, and disclosed to great advantage his flapped waistcoat and plush brown knee-breeches. As they drew near to their destination, however, Mr. Bumble thought it expedient to look down, and check to see if the boy was in good order for inspection by his new master, which he accordingly did, with a fit and becoming air of gracious patronage.

'Oliver!' said Mr. Bumble, looking sternly down at his young charge.

'Yes, sir?' replied Oliver, with some trepidation.

'Pull that cap off your eyes, and hold up your head,' exclaimed Mr. Bumble. 'Look smart!', he added for good measure.

Oliver did what was asked of him and then, once more taking hold of Bumble's coat cuff, continued to walk on with him in silence.

The undertaker, who had just put up the shutters of his shop, was making some entries in his daybook by the light of a most appropriately dismal candle, when Mr. Bumble entered.

'Aha!' said the undertaker, looking up from the book, and pausing in the middle of a word; 'is that you, Bumble?'

'No one else, Mr. Sowerberry,' replied the beadle. 'Here! I've brought the boy.' Oliver bowed.

'Oh! that's the boy, is it?' said the undertaker, raising the candle above his head, to get a better view of Oliver. 'Mrs. Sowerberry! will you have the goodness to come here a moment, my dear?'

Mrs. Sowerberry emerged from a little room behind the shop, and presented the form of a short, thin, squeezed-up woman, with a vixen's countenance.

'My dear,' said Mr. Sowerberry, deferentially, 'this is the boy from the workhouse that I told you of.' Oliver bowed again.

'Dear me!' said the undertaker's wife, 'he's very small.'

'Why, he *is* rather small,' replied Mr. Bumble, looking at Oliver as if it were his fault that he was no bigger; 'he is small. There's no denying it. But he'll grow, Mrs. Sowerberry—he'll grow.'

'Ah! I dare say he will,' replied the lady pettishly, 'on our food and our drink. I see no savings in parish children, not I; for they always cost more to keep than they're worth. However, men always think they know best. There! Get downstairs, little bag o' bones.' With this, the undertaker's wife opened a side door, and pushed Oliver onto a steep flight of stairs down to a stone cellar, damp and dark, forming the ante-room to the coal-cellar, and denominated 'the kitchen'; wherein sat a slatternly girl, in shoes worn down at the heel, and blue woolen stockings very much out of repair.

'Here, Charlotte,' said Mrs. Sowerberry, who had followed Oliver down, 'give this boy some of the cold bits that were put by for the dog. He hasn't come home since morning, so he may go without 'em. I dare say the boy isn't too dainty to eat 'em—are you, boy?'

Oliver, whose eyes had glistened at the mention of meat, and who was trembling with eagerness to devour it, replied in the negative; and a plateful of cold leftovers was set before him.

I wish some well-fed philosopher, whose meat and drink turn to gall within him, whose blood is ice, and whose heart is iron, could have seen Oliver Twist clutching at the dainty morsels of food that the dog had neglected. I wish he could have witnessed the horrible avidity with which Oliver tore the bits asunder with all the ferocity of famine. There is only one thing I should like better—and that would be to see the Philosopher making the same sort of meal himself, with the same relish.

'Well,' said the undertaker's wife, when Oliver had finished his supper—which she had regarded in silent horror, and with fearful premonitions of his future appetite—'have you done?' There being nothing eatable within his reach, Oliver replied in the affirmative.

'Then come with me,' said Mrs. Sowerberry, taking up a dim and dirty lamp, and leading the way upstairs; 'your bed's under the counter. You don't mind sleeping among the coffins, I suppose? But it doesn't much matter whether you do or you don't, for you can't sleep anywhere else. Come—don't keep me here all night!'

Oliver lingered no longer, but cautiously followed his new mistress.

Chapter 5
Mister Noah Claypole

Oliver, being left to himself in the undertaker's shop, set the lamp down on a workman's bench, and gazed about him with a feeling of awe and dread which many people a good deal older than he will be at no loss to understand. An unfinished coffin on black trestles, which stood in the middle of the shop, looked so gloomy and death-like that a cold tremble came over him every time his eyes wandered in the direction of the dismal object—from which he almost expected to see some frightful form slowly rear its head to drive him mad with terror. Against the wall were arranged, in regular array, a long row of elm boards cut in the same shape; looking in the dim light like high-shouldered ghosts with their hands in their breeches pockets. Coffin plates, elm chips, bright headed nails, and shreds of black cloth, lay scattered on the floor; and the wall behind the counter was ornamented with a lively representation of two mourners in very stiff collars, on duty at a large private door, with a hearse drawn by four black steeds, approaching in the distance. The shop was close and hot, and the atmosphere seemed tainted with the smell of coffins. The recess beneath the counter in which his flock mattress was thrust looked like a grave.

Nor were these the only dismal feelings which depressed Oliver. He was alone in a strange place; and we all know how chilled and desolate the best of us will sometimes feel in such a situation. The regret of recent separation from his workhouse friends was fresh in his mind. The boy had no friend to chat with, no confidant to confide in, no companion to console him, and no comrade to complain to. He missed Ricky most of all; the absence of his friendly, well remembered face weighed heavily on his heart.

Oliver was awakened in the morning by a loud kicking at the shop-door; which, before he could huddle on his clothes, was repeated, in an angry and impetuous manner, about twenty-five times. As Oliver began to undo the chain, the legs desisted, and a voice began.

'Open the door, will yer?' cried the voice which belonged to the legs which had kicked at the door.

'I will, directly, sir,' replied Oliver, undoing the chain, and turning the key.

'I suppose yer the new boy, ain't yer?' said the voice through the key-hole.

'Yes, sir,' replied Oliver.

'How old are yer?' inquired the voice.

'Twelve, sir,' replied Oliver.

'Then I'll whop yer when I get in,' said the voice; 'you just see if I don't, that's all, my work'us brat!' and, having made this obliging promise, the voice began to whistle.

Oliver had been subjected too often to the process to which the very expressive monosyllable just recorded bears reference, to entertain the smallest doubt that the owner of the voice, whoever he might be, would redeem his pledge most honourably. He drew back the bolts with a trembling hand, and opened the door.

For a second or two, Oliver glanced up the street, and down the street, and over the way, impressed with the belief that the unknown, who had addressed him through the keyhole, had probably walked a few paces off to warm himself; for nobody did he see but a big charity-boy, sitting on a post in front of the house, eating a slice of bread and butter, which he cut into wedges, the size of his mouth, with a clasp-knife, and then consumed with great dexterity.

'I beg your pardon, sir,' said Oliver, at length, seeing that no other visitor made his appearance; 'did you knock?'

'I kicked,' replied the charity-boy.

'Did you want a coffin, sir?' inquired Oliver, innocently.

At this the charity-boy looked monstrous fierce, and said that Oliver would want one before long if he cut jokes with his superiors in that way.

'Yer don't know who I am, I suppose, Work'us?' said the charity-boy, in continuation, descending from the top of the post, meanwhile, with edifying gravity. In an erect position, the boy stood a good foot taller than Oliver.

'No, sir,' rejoined Oliver.

'I'm Mister Noah Claypole,' said the charity-boy, 'and you're under me. Take down the shutters, yer idle young ruffian!'

With this, Mr. Claypole administered a kick to Oliver, and entered the shop with a dignified air, which did him great credit. It is difficult for a large-headed, small-eyed youth, of lumbering make and heavy countenance, to look dignified under any circumstances; but it is more especially so when superadded to these personal attractions are a red nose and yellow leather breeches.

Oliver, having taken down the shutters, (and broken a pane of glass in his effort to stagger away beneath the weight of the first one to a small court at the side of the house in which they were kept during the day), was graciously assisted by Noah; who, having consoled him with the assurance that 'he'd catch it,' condescended to help him. Mr. Sowerberry came down soon after. Shortly afterwards, Mrs. Sowerberry appeared, and Oliver, having 'caught it' in fulfilment of Noah's prediction, followed that young gentleman down the stairs to breakfast.

'Come near the fire, Noah,' said Charlotte. 'I saved a nice little bit of bacon for you from master's breakfast. Oliver, shut that door at Mister Noah's back, and take them bits that I've put out on the cover of the bread-pan. There's your tea; take it away to that box, and drink it there, and make haste, for they'll want you to mind the shop. D'ye hear?'

'D'ye hear, Work'us?' said Noah Claypole.

'Lor, Noah!' said Charlotte, playfully, 'what an odd creature you are! Why don't you let the boy alone?'

'Let him alone!' said Noah. 'Why everybody lets him alone enough, for the matter of that. Neither his father nor his mother will ever interfere with him. All his relations have let him have his own way pretty well. Eh, Charlotte? He! he! he!'

'Oh, you odd soul!' said Charlotte, bursting into a hearty laugh, in which she was joined by Noah; after which, they both looked scornfully at poor Oliver, as he sat shivering on the box in the coldest corner of the room, and ate the stale pieces which had been specially reserved for him.

Noah was a charity-boy, but not a workhouse orphan. No chance-child was he, for he could trace his genealogy all the way back to his parents, who lived hard by; his mother being a washerwoman, and his father a drunken soldier, discharged with a wooden leg, and a diurnal pension of twopence-halfpenny and an unstatable fraction. The shop-boys in the neighbourhood had long been in the habit of branding Noah, in the public streets, with the ignominious epithets of 'leathers,' 'charity,' and the like; and Noah had borne them without reply. But, now that fortune had cast in his way a nameless orphan, at whom even the meanest could point the finger of scorn, he lashed out at him with interest. This affords charming food for contemplation. It shows us what a beautiful thing human nature sometimes is, and how impartially the same amiable qualities are developed in the finest lord and the dirtiest charity-boy.

Oliver had been sojourning at the undertaker's some three weeks or a month, and Mr. and Mrs. Sowerberry—the shop being shut up—were taking their supper in the little back parlour, when Mr. Sowerberry, after several deferential glances at his wife, said:

'My dear -' He was going to say more; but with Mrs. Sowerberry looking up, with a peculiarly unpropitious aspect, he stopped short.

'Well,' said Mrs. Sowerberry, sharply.

'Nothing, my dear, nothing,' said Mr. Sowerberry.

'Ugh, you brute!' said Mrs. Sowerberry.

'Not at all, my dear,' said Mr. Sowerberry, humbly. 'I thought you didn't want to hear, my dear. I was only going to say -'

'Oh, don't tell me what you were going to say,' interposed Mrs. Sowerberry. 'I am nobody; don't consult me, pray. I don't want to intrude upon your secrets.' As Mrs. Sowerberry said this, she gave a hysterical laugh, which threatened violent consequences.

'But, my dear,' said Sowerberry, 'I want to ask your advice.'

'No, no, don't ask mine,' replied Mrs. Sowerberry, in an affecting manner; 'ask somebody else's.' Here, there was another hysterical laugh, which frightened Mr. Sowerberry very much. This is a very common and much approved matrimonial course of treatment, which is often very effective. It at once reduced Mr. Sowerberry to begging, as a special favour, to be allowed to say what Mrs. Sowerberry was most curious to hear. After a short altercation of less than three-quarters of an hour's duration, the permission was most graciously conceded.

'It's only about young Twist, my dear,' said Mr. Sowerberry. 'A very good-looking boy, that, my dear.'

'He need be, for he eats enough,' observed the lady.

'There's an expression of melancholy in his face, my dear,' resumed Mr. Sowerberry, 'which is very interesting. He would make a delightful mute, my love.' Mr. Sowerberry, like all undertakers, hired professional mourners or mutes to attend funeral processions to ensure that the dearly departed were suitably escorted to their graves; the more prominent the deceased, the more numerous the mutes.

Mrs. Sowerberry looked up with an expression of considerable wonderment at Mr. Sowerberry's suggestion. Mr. Sowerberry remarked it; and without allowing time for any observation on the good lady's part, proceeded to say:

'I don't mean a regular mute to attend grownup funerals, my dear, but only for children's practice. It would be very new to have a mourner in proportion, my dear. You may depend upon it, it would have a superb effect.'

Mrs. Sowerberry, who had a good deal of taste in the undertaking way, was much struck by the novelty of this idea; but, as it would have been compromising her dignity to have said so under existing circumstances, she merely inquired, with much sharpness, why such an obvious suggestion had not presented itself to her husband's mind before? Mr. Sowerberry rightly construed this as an acquiescence in his proposition. It was speedily determined, therefore, that Oliver should be initiated at once into the mysteries of the trade; and, with this objective in view, that he should accompany his master on the very next occasion of his services being required.

The occasion was not long in coming. Half an hour after breakfast the next morning, Mr. Bumble entered the shop; and, supporting his cane against the counter, drew forth his large leathern pocketbook, from which he selected a small scrap of paper, which he handed over to Sowerberry.

'Aha!' said the undertaker, glancing over it with a lively countenance; 'an order for a coffin, eh?'

'For a coffin first, and a parochial funeral afterwards,' replied Mr. Bumble, fastening the strap of the leathern pocketbook, which, like himself, was very corpulent.

'Bayton,' said the undertaker, looking from the scrap of paper to Mr. Bumble. 'I never heard the name before.'

Bumble shook his head, as he replied, 'Obstinate people, Mr. Sowerberry; very obstinate. Proud, too, I'm afraid, sir.'

'Proud, eh?' exclaimed Mr. Sowerberry with a sneer. 'Come, that's too much.'

'Oh, it's sickening,' replied the beadle. 'Unnatural, Mr. Sowerberry!'

'So it is,' acquiesced the undertaker.

'We only heard of the family the night before last,' said the beadle, 'and we shouldn't have known anything about them then, except only that a woman who lodges in the same house made an application to the parochial committee for them to send the parochial surgeon to see a woman as was very bad. He had gone out to dinner; but his 'prentice—who is a very clever lad, very clever indeed—sent 'em some medicine in a shoe polish bottle, off-hand.'

'Ah, there's promptness,' said the undertaker.

'Promptness, indeed!' replied the beadle. 'But what's the consequence; what's the ungrateful behaviour of these rebels, sir? Why, the husband sends back word that the medicine won't suit his wife's complaint, and so she shan't take it—says she shan't take it, sir! Good, strong, wholesome medicine, as was given with great success to two Irish labourers and a coalheaver, only a week before—sent 'em for nothing, with a shoe polish bottle included,—and he sends back word that she shan't take it, sir!'

As the atrocity presented itself to Mr. Bumble's mind in full force, he struck the counter sharply with his cane, and became flushed with indignation.

'Well,' said the undertaker, 'I ne—ver—did -'

'Never did, sir!' ejaculated the beadle. 'No, nor nobody never did; but now she's dead, we've got to bury her; and that's the direction; and the sooner it's done the better.'

Thus saying, Mr. Bumble put on his cocked hat wrong side first, in a fever of parochial excitement, and flounced out of the shop.

'Why, he was so angry, Oliver, that he forgot even to ask after you!' said Mr. Sowerberry, still looking at the beadle as he strode down the street.

'Yes, sir,' replied Oliver, who had carefully kept himself out of sight during the interview; and who was shaken at the mere recollection of the sound of Mr. Bumble's voice.

He needn't have taken the trouble to shrink from Mr. Bumble's glance, however; for that functionary, on whom the prediction of the gentleman in the white waistcoat had made a very strong impression, thought that now that the undertaker had Oliver upon trial, the subject was better avoided until such time as he should be firmly bound for seven years, and all danger of his being returned upon the hands of the parish should be thus effectually and legally overcome.

'Well,' said Mr. Sowerberry, taking up his hat, 'the sooner this job is done, the better. Noah, look after the shop. Oliver, put on your cap, and come with me.' Oliver obeyed, and followed his master on his professional mission.

They walked on for some time, through the most crowded and densely inhabited part of the town; and then, striking down a narrow street more dirty and miserable than any they had yet passed through, paused to look for the house which was the object of their search. The houses on either side were high and large, but very old, and tenanted by people of the poorest class: as their neglected appearance would have sufficiently denoted, without the concurrent testimony afforded by the squalid looks of the few men and women who, with folded arms and bodies half-doubled, occasionally skulked along. A great many of the tenements had shopfronts; but these were closed fast, and mouldering away, only the upper rooms being inhabited. Some houses which had become insecure from age and decay, were prevented from falling into the street by huge beams of wood reared against the walls, and firmly planted in the road; but even these crazy dens seemed to have been selected as the nightly haunts of some homeless wretches, for many of the rough boards which supplied the place of door and window, were wrenched from their positions, to afford an aperture wide enough for the passage of a human body. The gutter was stagnant and filthy. The very rats, which here and there lay putrefying in its rottenness, were hideous with famine.

There was neither knocker nor bell-handle at the open door where Oliver and his master stopped; so, groping his way cautiously through the dark passage, and bidding Oliver keep close to him and not be afraid, the undertaker mounted to the top of the first flight of stairs. Stumbling against a door on the landing, he rapped at it with his knuckles.

It was opened by a young girl of thirteen or fourteen. The undertaker at once saw enough of what the room contained to know that it was the apartment to which he had been directed. He stepped in, and Oliver followed him.

There was no fire in the room; but a man was crouching, mechanically, over the empty stove. An old woman, too, had drawn a low stool to the cold hearth, and was sitting beside him. There were some ragged children in another corner; and in a small recess, opposite the door, there lay upon the ground something covered with an old blanket. Oliver shuddered as he cast his eyes toward the place, and crept involuntarily closer to his master; for though it was covered up, the boy felt that it was a corpse.

The man's face was thin and very pale; his hair and beard were grizzly; his eyes were bloodshot. The old woman's face was wrinkled; her two remaining teeth protruded over her lower lip; and her eyes were bright and piercing. Oliver was afraid to look at either her or the man. They seemed so like the rats he had seen outside.

'Nobody shall go near her,' said the man, starting fiercely up, as the undertaker approached the recess. 'Keep back! Damn you, keep back, if you've a life to lose!'

'Nonsense, my good man,' said the undertaker, who was pretty well used to misery in all its shapes. 'Nonsense!'

'I tell you,' said the man, clenching his hands, and stamping furiously on the floor—'I tell you I won't have her put into the ground. She couldn't rest there. The worms would worry her—not eat her—she is so worn away.'

The undertaker offered no reply to this raving; but, producing a tape from his pocket, knelt down for a moment by the side of the body.

'Ah!' said the man, bursting into tears, and sinking on his knees at the feet of the dead woman; 'kneel down, kneel down, kneel round her, every one of you, and mark my words! I say she was starved to death. I never knew how bad she was till the fever came upon her; and then her bones were starting through the skin. There was neither fire nor candle; she died in the dark—in the dark! She couldn't even see her children's faces, though we heard her gasping out their names. I begged for her in the streets; and they sent me to prison. When I came back, she was dying; and all the blood in my heart has dried up, for they starved her to death. I swear it before the God that saw it! They starved her!' He twined his hands in his hair; and, with a loud scream, rolled grovelling upon the floor, his eyes fixed, and foam gushing from his lips.

The terrified children cried bitterly; but the old woman, who had hitherto remained as quiet as if she had been wholly deaf to all that passed, menaced them into silence. Having unloosened the neck tie of the man, who still remained extended on the ground, she tottered towards the undertaker.

'She was my daughter,' said the old woman, nodding her head in the direction of the corpse; and speaking with an idiotic leer, more ghastly than even the presence of death in such a place. 'Lord, Lord! Well, it *is* strange that I who gave birth to her, and was a woman then, should be alive and merry now, and she lying there, so cold and stiff! Lord, Lord!— to think of it; it's as good as a play—as good as a play!' As the wretched creature mumbled and chuckled in her hideous merriment, the undertaker turned to go away.

'Stop, stop!' said the old woman in a loud whisper. 'Will she be buried tomorrow, or next day, or tonight? I laid her out; and I must walk, you know. Send me a large cloak—a good warm one, for it is bitter cold. We should have cake and wine, too, before we go! Never mind; send some bread—only a loaf of bread and a cup of water. Shall we have some bread, dear?' she said eagerly, catching at the undertaker's coat, as he once more moved towards the door.

'Yes, yes,' said the undertaker, of course. Anything, everything.' He disengaged himself from the old woman's grasp; and, drawing Oliver after him, hurried away.

The next day (the family having been meanwhile relieved with a half loaf of bread and a piece of cheese, left with them by Mr. Bumble himself) Oliver and his master returned to the miserable abode; where Mr. Bumble had already arrived, accompanied by four men from the workhouse, who were to act as bearers. Old black cloaks had been thrown over the rags of the old woman and the man; and the bare coffin, having been screwed down, was hoisted on the shoulders of the bearers, and carried into the street.

'Now, you must put your best leg foremost, old lady!' whispered Sowerberry in the old woman's ear; 'we are rather late, and it won't do to keep the clergyman waiting. Move on, my men—as quick as you like!'

Thus directed, the bearers trotted on under their light burden; and the two mourners kept as near to them as they could. Mr. Bumble and Sowerberry walked at a good smart pace in front; and Oliver, whose legs were not so long as his master's, ran by his side.

There was not so great a necessity for hurrying as Mr. Sowerberry had anticipated, however; for when they reached the obscure corner of the churchyard in which the nettles grew, and where the parish graves were made, the clergyman had not arrived; and the clerk, who was sitting by the vestry room fire, seemed to think it by no means improbable that it might be an hour or so, before he came. So they put the coffin on the brink of the grave; and the two mourners waited patiently in the damp clay, with a cold rain drizzling down, while the ragged boys whom the spectacle had attracted into the churchyard played a noisy game of hide-and-seek among the tombstones, or varied their amusements by jumping backwards and forwards over the coffin. Mr. Sowerberry and Bumble, being personal friends of the clerk, sat by the fire with him, and read the paper.

At length, after a lapse of something more than an hour, Mr. Bumble, and Sowerberry, and the clerk, were seen running towards the grave. Immediately afterwards the clergyman appeared, putting on his ecclesiastical surplice as he came along. Mr. Bumble then thrashed a boy or two, to keep up appearances; and the reverend gentleman, having read as much of the burial service as could be compressed into four minutes, gave his surplice to the clerk, and walked away again.

'Now, George!' said Sowerberry to the grave-digger, 'fill up!'

It was no very difficult task, for the grave was so full that the uppermost coffin was within a few feet of the surface. The grave digger shovelled in the earth; stamped it loosely down with his feet; shouldered his spade; and walked off, followed by the boys, who murmured very loud complaints at the fun being over so soon.

'Come, my good fellow!' said Bumble, tapping the man on the back. 'They want to shut up the yard.'

The man, who had never once moved since he had taken his station by the grave side, started, raised his head, stared at the person who had addressed him, walked forward for a few paces, and fell down in a swoon. The crazy old woman was too much occupied in bewailing the loss of her cloak (which the undertaker had taken off), to pay him any attention; so they threw a can of cold water over him, and when he came to, saw him safely out of the churchyard, locked the gate, and departed on their different ways.

'Well, Oliver,' asked Sowerberry, as they walked home, 'how do you like it?'

'Pretty well, thank you, sir,' replied Oliver, with considerable hesitation. 'Not so very much, sir.'

'Ah, you'll get used to it in time, Oliver,' said Sowerberry. 'Nothing when you *are* used to it, my boy.'

Oliver wondered, in his own mind, whether it had taken a very long time for Mr. Sowerberry to get used to it? But he thought it better not to ask the question; and walked back to the shop, thinking over all he had seen and heard.

Chapter 6
A Murderous Villain

The month's trial being over, Oliver was formally apprenticed, and thereby indentured under the law to Mr. Sowerberry until the fifth month of his nineteenth year; much to Mr. Bumble's pleasure.

It was a nice sickly season just at this time. In commercial phrase, coffins were looking up; and, in the course of a few weeks, Oliver acquired a great deal of experience. The success of Mr. Sowerberry's ingenious speculation exceeded even his most sanguine hopes. The oldest inhabitants recollected no period at which measles had been so prevalent, or so fatal to infant existence; and many were the mournful processions which little Oliver headed, in a hat-band reaching down to his knees, to the indescribable admiration and emotion of all the mothers in the town. As Oliver accompanied his master in most of his adult expeditions, too, in order that he might acquire that equanimity of demeanour and full command of nerve which was essential to a finished undertaker, he had many opportunities of observing the beautiful resignation and fortitude with which some strong-minded people bear their trials and losses.

For instance: when Sowerberry had an order for the burial of some rich old lady or gentleman, who was surrounded by a great number of nephews and nieces, who had been perfectly inconsolable during the previous illness, and whose grief had been wholly irrepressible even on the most public occasions, they would be as happy among themselves as need be—quite cheerful and contented; conversing together with much freedom and gaiety as if nothing whatever had happened to disturb them. Husbands, too, bore the loss of their wives with the most heroic calmness. Wives adorned themselves with flowers and jewels to honour their husbands, as if, so far from grieving in the garb of sorrow, they had made up their minds to render themselves as becoming and attractive as possible. It was observable, too, that ladies and gentlemen who were in passions of anguish during the ceremony of interment, recovered almost as soon as they reached home, and became quite composed before the tea-drinking was over. All this was very pleasant and improving to see; and Oliver beheld it with great admiration.

That Oliver Twist was moved to resignation by the example of these good people, I cannot, although I am his biographer, undertake to affirm with any degree of confidence; but what I can most distinctly say is that for many months he continued to suffer under the domination and ill-treatment of Noah Claypole; who used him far worse than before, now that his jealousy was roused by seeing the new boy promoted to the black stick and hatband, while he, the old one, remained stationary in the muffin-cap and leathers. Charlotte treated him ill, because Noah did; and Mrs. Sowerberry was his decided enemy because Mr. Sowerberry was disposed to be his friend; so, between these three on one side, and a glut of funerals on the other, Oliver was not altogether as comfortable as a hungry pig would be if he was shut up, by mistake, in a granary.

And now I come to a very important passage in Oliver's history; for I have to record an act, slight and unimportant perhaps in appearance, but which indirectly produced a material change in all his future prospects and proceedings.

One day Oliver and Noah had descended into the kitchen at the usual dinner hour, to banquet upon a small joint of mutton—a pound and a half of the worst end of the neck—when Charlotte being called out of the room, there ensued a brief interval of time, which Noah Claypole, being hungry and vicious, decided that he could not possibly devote himself to a worthier purpose than aggravating and provoking young Oliver Twist.

Intent upon this innocent amusement, Noah put his feet up on the tablecloth; and pulled Oliver's hair; and twitched his ears; and expressed his opinion that he was a 'sneak'; and furthermore announced his intention of coming to see him hanged, whenever that desirable event should take place; and entered upon various other topics of petty annoyance, like the malicious and ill-conditioned charity-boy that he was. But, as none of these taunts produced the desired effect of making Oliver cry, Noah attempted to be more facetious still; and in his attempt did what many small wits, with far greater reputations than Noah, sometimes do to this day when they want to be funny—he got rather personal.

'Work'us,' asked Noah, 'how's your mother?'

'She's dead,' replied Oliver, 'don't you say anything about her to me!'

Oliver's colour rose as he said this; he breathed quickly; and there was a curious working of his mouth and nostrils, which Mr. Claypole thought must be the immediate precursor to a violent fit of crying. Under this impression he returned to the charge.

'What did she die of, Work'us?' asked Noah.

'Of a broken heart, some of our old nurses told me,' replied Oliver, more as if he was talking to himself than answering Noah. 'I think I know what it must be to die of that!'

'Tol de rol lol lol, right fol lairy, Work'us,' said Noah, as Oliver's emotions strengthened. 'What's set you a snivelling now?'

'Not *you*,' replied Oliver, sharply.

'Oh, not me, eh?' sneered Noah.

'No, not *you*,' repeated Oliver. 'There; that's enough. Don't say anything more to me about her; you'd better not!'

'Better not!' exclaimed Noah. 'Well! Better not! Work'us, don't be impudent. *Your* mother, too! She was a nice 'un she was. Oh, Lor!' And here Noah nodded his head expressively, and curled up as much of his small red nose as muscular action could collect together for the occasion.

'Yer know, Work'us,' continued Noah, emboldened by Oliver's silence, and speaking in a jeering tone of affected pity—of all tones the most annoying—'yer know, Work'us, it can't be helped now; and of course yer couldn't help it then; and I am very sorry for it; and I'm sure we all are, and pity yer very much. But yer must know, Work'us, yer mother was a regular right-down bad 'un.'

'What did you say?' inquired Oliver, looking up very quickly.

'A regular right-down bad 'un, Work'us,' replied Noah, coolly. 'And it's a great deal better, Work'us, that she died when she did, or else she'd have been hard labouring in Bridewell, or transported to the colonies, or hung; which is the most likely of all, isn't it?'

Crimson with fury, Oliver jumped up; overthrew the chair and table; seized Noah by the throat; shook him in the violence of his rage, till his teeth chattered in his head; and, collecting his whole force into one heavy blow, knocked him to the ground.

A minute ago, the boy had looked to be a quiet child, the mild creature that harsh treatment had made him. But his spirit was roused at last; the cruel insult to his dead mother had set his blood on fire. His breast heaved; his attitude was erect; his eye bright and vivid; his whole person changed, as he stood glaring over his cowardly tormentor who now lay crouching at his feet, and defied him with an energy he had never known before.

'He'll murder me!' blubbered Noah. 'Charlotte! missis! Here's the new boy a-murdering me! Help! help! Oliver's gone mad! Char—lotte!'

Noah's shouts were responded to by a loud scream from Charlotte, and a louder scream from Mrs. Sowerberry; the former of whom rushed into the kitchen by a side door, while the latter paused on the staircase till she was quite certain that it was consistent with the preservation of human life to come further down.

'Oh, you little wretch!' screamed Charlotte, seizing Oliver with the utmost force, which was equal to that of a moderately strong man in particularly good training. 'Oh, you little un-grate-ful, mur-der-ous, hor-rid villain!' And between every syllable, Charlotte gave Oliver a blow with all her might, accompanying it with a scream, for the benefit of society.

Charlotte's fist was by no means a light one; but, lest it should not be effectual in calming Oliver's wrath, Mrs. Sowerberry plunged into the kitchen, and assisted by holding him with one hand, while she scratched his face with the other. Seeing this favourable state of affairs, Noah rose from the ground and pummelled Oliver from behind.

This was rather too violent exercise to last long. When all three were all wearied out, and could tear and beat no longer, they dragged Oliver, struggling and shouting but nothing daunted, into the coal cellar and locked him up. This being done, Mrs. Sowerberry sunk into a chair and burst into tears.

'Bless her, she's going off!' said Charlotte. 'A glass of water, Noah, dear. Make haste!'

'Oh! Charlotte,' said Mrs. Sowerberry, speaking as well as she could, through a deficiency of breath, and a sufficiency of cold water, which Noah had poured over her head and shoulders. 'Oh! Charlotte, what a mercy we have not all been murdered in our beds!'

'Ah! mercy indeed, ma'am,' was the reply. 'I only hope this'll teach master not to have any more of these dreadful creatures, that are born to be murderers and robbers from their very cradle. Poor Noah! He was all but killed, ma'am, when I come in.'

'Poor fellow!' said Mrs. Sowerberry, looking piteously on the charity-boy.

Noah, whose top waistcoat button might have been somewhere on a level with the crown of Oliver's head, rubbed his eyes with the inside of his wrists while this commiseration was bestowed upon him, and performed some affecting tears and sniffs.

'What's to be done!' exclaimed Mrs. Sowerberry. 'Your master's not at home; there's not a man in the house; and he'll kick that door down in ten minutes.' Oliver's vigorous plunges against the bit of timber in question rendered this occurrence highly probable.

'Dear, dear! I don't know, ma'am,' said Charlotte, 'unless we send for a police officer.'

'Or the millingtary,' suggested Mr. Claypole.

'No, no,' said Mrs. Sowerberry, bethinking herself of Oliver's old friend. 'Run to Mr. Bumble, Noah, and tell him to come here directly, and not to lose a minute; never mind your cap! Make haste! You can hold a knife to that black eye, as you run along. It'll keep the swelling down.'

Noah stopped to make no reply, but started off at his fullest speed; and it very much astonished the people who were out walking, to see a charity-boy tearing through the streets pell-mell, with no cap on his head, and a clasp-knife at his eye.

Chapter 7
The Drubbing

Noah Claypole ran along the streets at his swiftest pace, and paused not once for breath, until he reached the workhouse gate. Having rested here, for a minute or so, to collect a good burst of sobs and an imposing show of tears and terror, he knocked loudly at the wicket; and presented such a rueful face to the aged pauper who opened it, that even he, who saw nothing but rueful faces about him at the best of times, started back in astonishment.

'Why, what's the matter with you, boy?' asked the old pauper.

'Mr. Bumble! Mr. Bumble!' cried Noah, with well-affected dismay, and in tones so loud and agitated that they not only caught the ear of Mr. Bumble himself, who happened to be hard by, but alarmed him so much that he rushed into the yard without his cocked hat—which is a very curious and remarkable circumstance, showing that even a beadle, acted upon by a sudden and powerful impulse, may be afflicted by a momentary loss of self-possession and forgetfulness of personal dignity.

'Oh, Mr. Bumble, sir!' said Noah, 'Oliver, sir,—Oliver has -'

'What? What?' interposed Mr. Bumble, with a gleam of pleasure in his metallic eyes. 'Not run away; he hasn't run away, has he, Noah?'

'No, sir, no. Not run away, sir, but he's turned wicious,' replied Noah. 'He tried to murder me, sir; and then he tried to murder Charlotte; and then the missis. Oh! what dreadful pain it is! Such agony, please, sir!' And here, Noah writhed and twisted his body into an extensive variety of eel-like positions; thereby giving Mr. Bumble to understand that, from the violent and bloodthirsty attack by Oliver Twist, he had sustained severe internal injury and damage, from which he was, at that moment, suffering the acutest torture.

When Noah saw that the intelligence he communicated perfectly paralysed Mr. Bumble, he imparted additional effect thereunto by bewailing his dreadful wounds ten times louder than before; and, when he observed a gentleman in a white waistcoat crossing the yard, he was more tragic in his lamentations than ever, rightly conceiving it highly expedient to attract the notice and rouse the indignation of the gentleman aforesaid.

The gentleman's notice was very soon attracted; for he had not walked three paces, when he turned angrily round, and inquired what that young cur was howling for, and why Mr. Bumble did not favour him with something which would render the series of vocal exclamations so designated an involuntary process?

'It's a poor boy from the free-school, sir,' replied Mr. Bumble, 'who has been nearly murdered—all but murdered, sir,—by young Twist.'

'By Jove!' exclaimed the gentleman in the white waistcoat, stopping short. 'I knew it! I felt a strange presentiment from the very first, that that audacious young savage would come to be hung!'

'He has likewise attempted, sir, to murder the female servant,' said Mr. Bumble, with a face of ashy paleness.

'And his missis,' interposed Mr. Claypole.

'And his master, too, I think you said, Noah?' added Mr. Bumble.

'No; he's out, or he would have murdered him,' replied Noah. 'He said he wanted to.'

'Ah! Said he wanted to; did he, my boy?' inquired the gentleman in the white waistcoat.

'Yes, sir,' replied Noah. 'And please, sir, missis wants to know whether Mr. Bumble can spare time to step up there, directly, and flog him—'cause master's out.'

'Certainly, my boy; certainly,' said the gentleman in the white waistcoat, smiling benignly, and patting Noah's head, which was about three inches higher than his own. 'You're a good boy—a very good boy. Here's a penny for you. Bumble, just step up to Sowerberry's with your cane, and see what's best to be done. Don't spare him, Bumble.'

'No, I will not, sir,' replied the beadle, adjusting the wax-end which was twisted round the bottom of his cane for the purpose of parochial flagellation.

'Tell Sowerberry not to spare him either. They'll never do anything with him without stripes and bruises,' said the gentleman in the white waistcoat.

'I'll take care, sir,' replied the beadle. And the cocked hat and cane having been by this time adjusted to their owner's satisfaction, Mr. Bumble and Noah Claypole betook themselves with all due speed to the undertaker's shop.

Here the position of affairs had not at all improved. Sowerberry had not yet returned, and Oliver continued to kick, with undiminished vigour, at the cellar-door. The accounts of his ferocity as related by Mrs. Sowerberry and Charlotte, were of so startling a nature, that Mr. Bumble judged it prudent to parley before opening the door. With this view he gave a kick at the outside, by way of prelude; and, then, applying his mouth to the keyhole, said, in a deep and impressive tone:

'Oliver!'

'Come; you let me out!' replied Oliver, from the inside.

'Do you know this here voice, Oliver?' said Mr. Bumble.

'Yes,' replied Oliver.

'Ain't you afraid of it, sir? Ain't you a-trembling while I speak, sir?' said Mr. Bumble.

'No!' replied Oliver, boldly.

An answer so different from the one he had expected to elicit, and was in the habit of receiving, staggered Mr. Bumble not a little. He stepped back from the keyhole; drew himself up to his full height; and looked from one to another of the three bystanders, in mute astonishment.

'Oh, you know, Mr. Bumble, he must be mad,' said Mrs. Sowerberry. 'No boy in half his senses could venture to speak to you so.'

'It's not Madness, ma'am,' replied Mr. Bumble, after a few moments of deep meditation. 'It's meat!'

'What?' exclaimed Mrs. Sowerberry.

'Meat, ma'am, meat,' replied Bumble, with stern emphasis. 'You've over-fed him, ma'am. You've raised an artificial soul and spirit in him, ma'am, unbecoming a person of his condition; as the board, Mrs. Sowerberry, who are practical philosophers, will tell you. What have paupers to do with soul or spirit? It's quite enough that we let 'em have live bodies. If you had kept the boy on gruel, ma'am, this would never have happened.'

'Dear, dear!' ejaculated Mrs. Sowerberry, piously raising her eyes to the kitchen ceiling, 'this comes from being liberal!'

The liberality of Mrs. Sowerberry to Oliver, had consisted of a profuse bestowal upon him of all the dirty odds and ends which nobody else would eat; so there was a great deal of meekness and self-devotion in her voluntarily remaining under Mr. Bumble's heavy accusation, of which, to do her justice, she was wholly innocent, in thought, word, and deed.

'Ah!' said Mr. Bumble, when the lady brought her eyes down to earth again; 'the only thing that can be done now, that I know of, is to leave him in the cellar for a day or so till he's a little starved down; and then to take him out, and keep him on gruel all through the apprenticeship. He comes of a bad family. Excitable natures, Mrs. Sowerberry! Both the nurse and doctor said that his mother had made her way here against difficulties and pain that would have killed any well-disposed woman weeks before.'

At this point of Mr. Bumble's discourse, Oliver, just hearing enough to know that some allusion was being made to his mother, recommenced kicking with a violence that rendered every other sound inaudible. Sowerberry returned at this juncture. Oliver's offence having been explained to him, with such exaggerations as the ladies thought best calculated to rouse his ire, he unlocked the cellar-door in a twinkling, and dragged his rebellious apprentice out by the collar.

Oliver's clothes had been torn in the beating he had received; his face was bruised and scratched; and his hair scattered over his forehead. The angry flush had not disappeared, however, and when he was pulled out of his prison, he scowled boldly at Noah, and looked quite undismayed.

'Now, you are a nice young fellow, ain't you?' said Sowerberry, giving Oliver a shake and a box on the ear.

'He called my mother names,' replied Oliver.

'Well, and what if he did, you ungrateful little wretch?' said Mrs. Sowerberry. 'She deserved what he said, and worse.'

'She didn't,' said Oliver.

'She did,' said Mrs. Sowerberry.

'It's a lie!' said Oliver.

Mrs. Sowerberry burst into a flood of tears.

This flood of tears left Mr. Sowerberry no alternative. If he had hesitated for one instant to punish Oliver most severely, it must be quite clear to every experienced reader that he would have been, according to all precedents in disputes of matrimony established, a brute, an unnatural husband, an insulting creature, a base imitation of a man, and various other agreeable characters too numerous for recital within the limits of this chapter. To do him justice, he was, as far as his power went—it was not very extensive—kindly disposed towards the boy; perhaps because it was his interest to be so; perhaps because his wife disliked him. Her flood of tears, however, left him no recourse; so he at once gave him a drubbing, which satisfied even Mrs. Sowerberry herself, and rendered Mr. Bumble's subsequent application of the parochial cane rather unnecessary. For the rest of the day, he was locked up in the kitchen, in company with a pump and a slice of bread. That night Mrs. Sowerberry, after making various remarks outside the door, by no means complimentary to the memory of his mother, looked into the room, and, amidst the jeers and pointing of Noah and Charlotte, ordered him upstairs to his dismal bed.

It was not until he was left alone in the silence and stillness of the gloomy workshop of the undertaker that Oliver gave way to the feelings which the day's treatment may be supposed likely to have awakened in a young child. He had listened to their taunts with a look of contempt; he had borne the lash without a cry: for he felt that pride swelling in his heart which would have kept down a scream to the last, though they had roasted him alive. But now, when there were none to see or hear him, he fell upon his thin bed and, thinking of his mother, began to weep.

For a long time, Oliver remained motionless in this attitude. The candle was burning low in the socket when he rose to his feet. Having gazed cautiously around him, and listened intently, he gently undid the fastenings of the door and looked abroad.

It was a cold, dark night. The stars seemed, to the boy's eyes, farther from the earth than he had ever seen them before; there was no wind; and the sombre shadows thrown by the trees upon the ground, looked gloomy and deathlike, from being so still. He softly reclosed the door; and having availed himself of the expiring light of the candle to tie up in a handkerchief the few articles of wearing apparel he had, he sat himself down upon a bench to wait for morning.

With the first ray of light that struggled through the crevices in the shutters, Oliver rose, and again unbarred the door. After one quick look back—one moment's pause of hesitation—he closed the door behind him and was in the open street.

He looked to the right and to the left, uncertain whither to fly. He remembered having seen wagons, as they went out, toiling up the hill. He took the same route, and arrived at a footpath across the fields which he knew, after some distance, led out again onto the road. He struck out onto the path and walked quickly on.

Oliver well remembered that he had trotted along this same footpath beside Mr. Bumble when first escorted back to the workhouse from the farm. His way lay directly in front of the cottage. His heart beat quickly when he bethought himself of this, and he half resolved to turn back. He had come a long way though, and should lose a great deal of time by doing so. Besides, it was so early that there was very little fear of his being seen; so he walked on.

He reached the cottage. As there was no appearance of its inmates stirring at that early hour Oliver stopped, and peeped into the garden. Alas, a child was weeding one of the little beds. The boy stopped his gentle toiling, raised his pale face, and disclosed the features of Oliver's long-time companion Ricky. Oliver felt glad to have chanced upon a friendly face before he continued on his flight from his apprenticeship, the workhouse, his place of birth, and from everyone and everything he had ever known. Though younger than himself, Ricky had long been Oliver's best friend and playmate. They had been beaten, and starved, and shut up together many and many times.

'Hush!' said Oliver, as the boy ran to the gate, and thrust his thin arms between the rails to greet him. 'Is anyone up?'

'Nobody but me,' replied Ricky.

'You mustn't say you saw me, Ricky,' said Oliver. 'I am running away. They beat me and ill-use me, Ricky. I am going to seek my fortune some long way off. I don't know where. How pale you are!'

'I heard the doctor tell them I was dying,' whispered Ricky, with a faint smile. 'I am very glad to see you, Oliver; but don't stop, don't stop!'

'No, no, only to say goodbye to you,' replied Oliver. 'I shall see you again, Ricky. I know I will! You will be strong and healthy!'

'I hope so,' replied Ricky. 'After I am dead, but not before. I know the doctor must be right, Oliver, because I dream so much of Heaven, and Angels, and kind faces that I never see when I am awake. Hug,' said Ricky, climbing up the low gate, and flinging his arms round Oliver's neck. 'Goodbye, Oliver! God bless you!'

The blessing was only from a young boy's lips, but it was the first that Oliver had ever heard invoked upon his head. Through all of the struggles, sufferings, troubles and changes he subsequentially endured, he never once forgot it.

Chapter 8
Jack Dawkins

Oliver reached the stile at which the footpath terminated, and once more gained the highroad. It was eight o'clock now. Though he was nearly five miles away from his town, he ran and hid behind hedges, by turns, till noon, fearing that he might be pursued and overtaken. Then he sat down to rest by the side of a milestone, and began to think, for the first time, about where he had better go and try to live.

The stone by which he was seated, bore, in large characters, an intimation that it was just seventy miles from that spot to London. The name awakened a new train of ideas in the boy's mind.

London!—that great place!—nobody, not even Mr. Bumble, could ever find him there! He had often heard the old men in the workhouse, too, say that no lad of spirit need want in London; and that there were ways of living in that vast city, which those who had been raised up in country parts had no idea of. It was the very place for a homeless boy, who must die in the streets unless someone helped him. As these things passed through his thoughts, he jumped upon his feet, and again walked forward.

He had diminished the distance between himself and London by full four miles more, before he recollected how much he must undergo ere he could hope to reach his place of destination. As this consideration forced itself upon him, he slackened his pace a little, and meditated upon his means of getting there. He had a crust of bread, a coarse shirt, and two pairs of stockings in his bundle. He had a penny too—a gift of Sowerberry's after some funeral in which he had acquitted himself more than ordinarily well—in his pocket. 'A clean shirt,' thought Oliver, 'is a very comfortable thing; and so are two pairs of darned stockings; and so is a penny; but they are small helps to a sixty-five mile walk in winter time.' But Oliver's thoughts, like those of most other people, although extremely ready and active to point out his difficulties, were wholly at a loss to suggest any feasible mode of surmounting them; so, after a good deal of thinking to no particular purpose, he shifted his little bundle over to his other shoulder, and trudged on.

Oliver walked twenty miles that day, and all that time tasted nothing but the crust of dry bread, and a few draughts of water which he begged at the cottage doors by the roadside. When the night came he turned into a meadow, and, creeping close under a hayrick, determined to lie there till morning. He felt frightened at first, for the wind moaned dismally over the empty fields, and he was cold and hungry, and more alone than he had ever felt before. Being very tired with his walk, however, he soon fell asleep, and forgot his troubles.

He felt cold and stiff when he got up next morning, and so hungry that he was obliged to exchange the penny for a small loaf, in the very first village through which he passed. He had walked no more than twelve miles when night closed in again. His feet were sore, and his legs so weak that they trembled beneath him. Another night passed in the bleak damp air, made him worse, and when he set forward on his journey the next morning he could hardly crawl along.

He waited at the bottom of a steep hill till a stagecoach came up, and then begged of the outside passengers; but there were very few who took any notice of him; and even those told him to wait till they got to the top of the hill, and then watched to see how far he could run for a halfpenny. Poor Oliver tried to keep up with the coach a little way, but was unable to do it, by reason of his fatigue and sore feet. When the outside passengers saw this, they put their halfpence back into their pockets again, declaring that he was an idle young dog, and didn't deserve anything. The coach rattled away, and left only a cloud of dust behind.

In some villages, large painted boards were erected, warning all persons who begged within the district that they would be sent to jail. This frightened Oliver very much, and made him glad to get out of those villages with all possible expedition. In others, he would stand about the inn-yards, and look mournfully at every one who passed; a proceeding which generally terminated in the landlady's ordering one of the post-boys who were lounging about to drive that strange boy out of the place, for she was sure he had come to steal something. If he stopped at a farmer's house, ten to one but they threatened to set the dog on him; and when he showed his nose in a shop, they talked about the beadle, which brought Oliver's heart into his mouth—very often the only thing he had there for many hours together.

In fact, if it had not been for a good-hearted turnpike-man, and a benevolent old lady, Oliver's troubles would have been shortened by the very same process which had put an end to his mother's: in other words, he would most assuredly have fallen dead upon the King's highway. But the turnpike-man shared a meal of bread and cheese with him; and the old lady, who had a shipwrecked grandson wandering barefoot in some distant part of the earth, took pity upon the poor orphan, and gave him what little she could afford—and more – together with kind and gentle words of compassion that warmed Oliver's soul and gave him courage. How solicitous some people could be!

While meditating upon these and other thoughts, Oliver happened to hear a dreadful moan emanate from behind some low bushes. His first impulse was to quicken his pace and not look back. However, as further moans informed him that they did not emanate, as he first supposed, from some demon or fiend but, rather, from someone who was crying out in pain; he peered over the bushes to determine the source of the lament. Oliver saw a fully-grown man, with a scraggly three day growth of beard, sitting on the ground wearing a blood soaked handkerchief wrapped around his head which covered one eye. He was gingerly holding his right ankle. While such a fearsome sight might have frightened a less experienced boy, Oliver had seen many similarly bruised and battered gentlemen come into the workhouse.

'What's the matter, sir?' asked Oliver.

'Bloody ankle!' exclaimed the stranger. 'Twisted it.'

'Can I be of any assistance, sir?' asked Oliver.

This question appeared to stump the stranger, and, for some moments, he just sat there on the ground looking up at Oliver. He couldn't recall anyone else asking him such a confounding question. At last he answered:

'I suppose you can,' said the stranger, pulling out a bulging leather purse and removing a coin. 'Here's a shilling,' he said, placing it in Oliver's hand. 'Go to that village yonder and purchase me a joint of cooked ham and some bottles of beer. Bring them back smart like. Mind you don't wander off with me shilling. Wouldn't be healthy for you. Come back directly, prompt like, without yakking to no one.'

Oliver fairly ran all the way to the village and, in the first shop he encountered, placed the shilling on the counter and asked the proprietor for the requested joint of ham and two bottles of beer. These items were soon placed on the counter next to the shilling.

'Anything else?' asked the shopkeeper.

This question dumbfounded Oliver who, having lived off of the generosity of the parish his entire life, had only just recently made his first purchase. He had no concept of the value of a shilling or the possibility of demanding change. Oliver's utmost, and perhaps only, concern was to ensure that the bloody stranger sitting in the ditch was not displeased with the execution of his duties.

'What might you suggest?' asked Oliver.

The shopkeeper looked around and then placed several apples and carrots and a half-loaf of bread on the counter.

'That'd work out even,' said the shopkeeper, knowing he had easily made the best of the deal.

'Good,' replied Oliver, scooping the groceries onto his shirt front which he held out like a sack.

Not having any genuine expectation of seeing Oliver again, the stranger had allowed himself to succumb to the comfort provided only by sleep. He woke with a start and flashed a long knife when Oliver suddenly sat beside him.

'Never startle a man who'd be sleeping!' said the stranger, 'not if ye want to see tomorrow'.

The stranger then spied the provisions Oliver had brought and broke into a large grin. 'Well done my little friend, well done!' said the stranger. 'Join me in this banquet you've spread out. You look like you could do with some nourishment yurself.'

It being well past sunset by the time the two friends had finished their meal, Oliver and the stranger lay down where they were and fell asleep. Come dawn, Oliver found himself alone and a half shilling richer. Still feeling strong from the feast he had gorged upon the previous evening, he put many miles between himself and the workhouse that day.

Early on the seventh morning after he had left his native place, Oliver limped slowly into the little town of Barnet. The window-shutters were closed; the street was empty; not a soul had awakened to the business of the day. The sun was rising in all its splendid beauty; but the light only served to show the boy his own lonesomeness and desolation, as he sat, with bleeding feet and covered with dust, upon a doorstep.

By degrees, the shutters were opened; the window blinds were drawn up; and people began passing to and fro. A few stopped to gaze at Oliver for a moment or two, or turned around to stare at him as they hurried by; but none relieved him, or troubled themselves to inquire how he came to be there. He had no heart to beg. So, there he sat.

He had been crouching on the step for some time, wondering at the great number of public-houses (every other house in Barnet was a tavern, large or small); gazing listlessly at the coaches as they passed through, and thinking how strange it seemed that they could do, with ease, in a few hours, what it had taken him a whole week of courage and determination beyond his years to accomplish; when he was roused by observing that a boy, who had passed him carelessly some minutes before, had returned, and was now surveying him most earnestly from the opposite side of the road. He took little heed of this at first; but the boy remained in the same attitude of close observation for so long, that Oliver raised his head, and returned his steady look. Upon this, the boy crossed over; and, walking up close to Oliver, said:

'Hullo! my covey, what's the row?'

The boy who addressed this inquiry to the young wayfarer was about his own age and size, but was the cockiest, most self-confident boy that Oliver had ever seen. While he had a pleasant, friendly face, and bright, intelligent eyes; he was as dirty a juvenile as one would wish to see, and had about him all of the airs and manners of a man. His hat was stuck on the top of his head so lightly, that it threatened to fall off every moment—and would have done so, very often, if the wearer had not had a knack of every now and then giving his head a sudden twitch, which brought it back to its old place again. He wore a man's coat, which reached nearly to his heels. He had turned the cuffs back, half-way up his arm, to get his hands out of the sleeves, apparently with the ultimate view of thrusting them into the pockets of his corduroy trousers; for there he kept them. He was, altogether, as arrogant and swaggering a young gentleman as ever stood four feet ten, or something less, in boots.

'Hullo, my covey! What's the row?' repeated this strange young gentleman to Oliver.

'I am very hungry and tired,' replied Oliver, 'I have walked a long way. I've been walking for seven days.'

'Walking fur sivin days!' repeated the young gentleman. 'Oh, I see. Beak's order, eh? But,' he added, noticing Oliver's look of surprise, 'I suppose you don't know what a beak is, my flash companion.'

Oliver mildly replied that he had always heard a bird's mouth described by the term in question.

'My eyes, how green!' exclaimed the young gentleman. 'Why, a beak's a madgst'rate; and when you walk by a beak's order, it's not straight forerd, but always a-going up, and niver a-coming down agin. Was you never on the mill?'

'What mill?' inquired Oliver.

'What mill!—why, *the* mill—the mill as takes up so little room that it'll work inside a Stone Jug; and always goes better when the wind's low with people, than when it's high; acos then they can't get workmen. But come,' said the young gentleman; 'you want grub, and you shall have it. I'm at low-water-mark myself, only one bob and a magpie; but *as* far *as* it goes, I'll fork out and stump. Up with you on your pins. There! Now then! Morrice!'

Assisting Oliver to rise, the young gentleman took him to an adjacent shop, where he purchased a sufficiency of ready-dressed ham and a loaf of bread, or, as he himself expressed it, 'a fourpenny bran!' the ham being kept clean and preserved from dust, by the ingenious expedient of making a hole in the loaf by pulling out a portion of the crumb, and stuffing it therein. Taking the bread under his arm, the young gentleman turned into a small public-house, and led the way to a tap-room in the rear of the premises. Here a pot of beer was brought in, at the direction of the mysterious youth; and Oliver, falling to, at his new friend's bidding, made a long and hearty meal, during the progress of which the strange boy eyed him from time to time with great attention.

'Going to London?' asked the strange boy, when Oliver had at length concluded.

'Yes.'

'Got any lodgings?'

'No.'

'Money?'

'No.'

The strange boy whistled; and put his arms into his pockets, as far as the big coat-sleeves would let them go.

'Do you live in London?' inquired Oliver.

'Yes. I do, when I'm at home,' replied the boy. 'I suppose you want some place to sleep in tonight, don't you?'

'I do, indeed,' answered Oliver. 'I have not slept under a roof since I left the country.'

'Don't fret your eyelids on that score,' said the young gentleman. 'I've got to be in London tonight; and I know a 'spectable old gentleman as lives there, wot'll give you lodgings for nothink, and never ask for the change—that is, if any gentleman he knows interduces you. And don't he know me? Oh, no! Not in the least! By no means. Certainly not!'

The young gentleman smiled, as if to intimate that the latter fragments of discourse were playfully ironical; and finished the beer as he did so.

This unexpected offer of shelter was too tempting to be resisted, especially as it was immediately followed up by the assurance that the old gentleman referred to would doubtless provide Oliver with a comfortable place, without loss of time.

This led to a more friendly and confidential dialogue; from which Oliver discovered that his friend's name was Jack Dawkins, and that he was an apprentice and *protégé* of the elderly gentleman before mentioned.

Mr. Dawkins's appearance did not say a vast deal in favour of the comforts which his patron's interest obtained for those whom he took under his protection. He had a rather flighty and dissolute mode of conversing, and furthermore avowed that among his intimate friends he was better known by the pseudonym 'The Artful Dodger.' Oliver concluded that, being of a dissipated and careless turn, the moral precepts of his benefactor had hitherto been thrown away upon him. Nevertheless, Oliver, not being in a position to make demands upon his host, resolved to cultivate the good opinion of his young friend, and of the older gentleman of whom he spoke, as quickly as possible.

As Dawkins objected to their entering London before nightfall, it was nearly eleven o'clock when they reached the turnpike at Islington. They crossed from the Angel onto St. John's Road, struck down the small street which terminates at Sadler's Wells Theatre; through Exmouth Street and Coppice Row; down the little court by the side of the workhouse; across the classic ground which once bore the name of Hockley-in-the-Hole; thence into Little Saffron Hill; and so into Saffron Hill the Great, along which the Dodger scudded at a rapid pace, directing Oliver to follow close at his heels.

Although Oliver had enough to occupy his attention in keeping sight of his leader, he could not help bestowing a few hasty glances on either side of the way as he passed along. A dirtier or more wretched place he had never seen. The street was very narrow and muddy, and the air was impregnated with filthy odours. There were a good many small shops; but the only stock in trade appeared to be heaps of children, who, even at that time of night, were crawling in and out at the doors, or screaming from the inside. The sole places that seemed to prosper, amid the general blight of the place, were the public-houses; and in them, the lowest orders of society were wrangling with might and main. Covered ways and yards, which here and there diverged from the main street, disclosed little knots of houses, where drunken men and women were positively wallowing in filth; and from several of the door-ways great ill-looking fellows were cautiously emerging, bound, to all appearance, on no very well-disposed or harmless errands.

The wild riot of unfamiliar sights and sounds and the scores of narrow, meandering avenues, streets, roads, and lanes, bewildered Oliver, and he quickly lost track of the route they were taking. To him all of the streets looked very much alike and he wondered, on occasion, if they had not actually traversed the same crooked, crowded lane more than once. He was just about to ask if they still had far to go when, at the bottom of a hill, his conductor caught him by the arm and pushed open the door of a house near Field Lane. After drawing Oliver into the passage, he closed it again behind them.

'Now, then!' cried a voice from below, in reply to a whistle from the Dodger.

'Plummy and slam!' was the reply.

This seemed to be some watchword or signal that all was right; for the light of a feeble candle gleamed on the wall at the remote end of the passage; and a man's face peeped out, from where a balustrade of the old kitchen staircase had been broken away.

'There's two of you,' said the man, thrusting the candle farther out, and shielding his eyes with his hand. 'Who's the t'other one?'

'A new pal,' replied Jack Dawkins, pulling Oliver forward.

'Where'd he come from?'

'Greenland. Is Fagin upstairs?'

'Yes, he's a sortin' hankies. Up with you!' The candle was drawn back, and the face disappeared.

Oliver, groping his way with one hand, and having the other firmly grasped by his companion, ascended with much difficulty the dark and broken stairs, which his conductor mounted with an ease and expedition that showed he was well acquainted with them. He threw open the door of a backroom, and drew Oliver in after him.

The walls and ceiling of the room were perfectly black with age and dirt. There was a small table before the fire; upon which were a candle, stuck in a ginger-beer bottle, two or three pewter pots, a loaf and butter, and a plate. In a frying-pan, which was on the fire, and which was secured to the mantelshelf by a string, some sausages were cooking; and standing over them, with a toasting-fork in his hand, was a very old and shrivelled man, whose villainous-looking and repulsive face was obscured by a quantity of matted hair. He was dressed in a greasy flannel gown, with his throat bare; and seemed to be dividing his attention between the frying-pan and the clothes-horse, over which a great number of silk handkerchiefs were hanging. Several rough beds made of old sacks, were huddled side-by-side on the floor. Seated round the table were four or five boys, none older than the Dodger, smoking long clay pipes, and drinking spirits with the air of middle-aged men. These all crowded about their associate as he whispered a few words to the old man, and then turned round and grinned at Oliver; as did the old man himself, toasting-fork in hand.

'This is him, Fagin,' said Jack Dawkins, 'my friend, Oliver Twist.'

The old man grinned, and, making a low obeisance to Oliver, took him by the hand, and hoped he should have the honour of his intimate acquaintance. Upon this the young gentlemen with the pipes came round him, and shook both his hands very hard, especially the one in which he held his little bundle. Another young gentleman was very anxious to hang up his cap for him; and yet another was so obliging as to put his hands into Oliver's pockets, in order that, as he was very tired, he might not have the trouble of emptying them himself when he went to bed. These civilities would probably be extended much farther, but for the liberal exercise of Fagin's toasting-fork on the heads and shoulders of the affectionate youths who offered them.

'We are very glad to see you, Oliver—very,' said Fagin. 'Dodger, take off the sausages; and draw a tub near the fire for Oliver. Ah, you're a-staring at the handkerchiefs! eh, my dear. There are a good many of 'em, ain't there? We've just took 'em out, ready for the wash; that's all, Oliver—that's all. Ha! ha! ha!'

The latter part of this speech was hailed by a boisterous shout from all the hopeful pupils of the merry old gentleman. In the midst of which they went to supper.

Oliver ate his share, and Fagin then mixed him a glass of hot gin-and-water; telling him he must drink it off directly, because another gentleman wanted the tumbler. Oliver did as he was desired. Immediately afterwards he felt himself gently lifted onto one of the sack beds; and then he sank into a deep sleep with Fagin watching gentle over him.

'Such a handsome lad you are,' thought Fagin. 'I knows people who'd be smitten by a face such as yours. Oh, the fiddles you could play. I knows too people who'd pay generously to make your acquaintance. You're worth a small fortune, you are.'

Chapter 9
Fagin

It was late the next morning when Oliver awoke from a long sound sleep. There was no other person in the room but the old man, who was boiling some coffee in a saucepan for breakfast, and whistling softly to himself as he stirred it round and round with an iron spoon. He would stop every now and then to listen, when there was the least noise below; and, when he had satisfied himself, he would go on whistling and stirring again as before.

Although Oliver had roused himself from sleep, he was not thoroughly awake. There is a drowsy state, between sleeping and waking, when you dream more in five minutes with your eyes half open, and yourself half conscious of everything that is passing around you, than you would in five nights with your eyes fast closed, and your senses wrapped in perfect unconsciousness. At such times, a mortal knows just enough of what his mind is doing to form some glimmering conception of its mighty powers, its bounding from earth and spurning time and space, when freed from the restraint of its corporeal associate.

Oliver was precisely in this condition. He saw Fagin with his half-closed eyes, heard his low whistling, and recognised the sound of the spoon grating against the saucepan's sides; and yet the self-same senses were mentally engaged, at the same time, in busy action with almost everybody he had ever known.

When the coffee was done, the old man drew the saucepan to the fireplace hob; and, standing in an irresolute attitude for a few minutes, as if he did not well know how to employ himself, turned round and looked at Oliver, and called him by his name. He did not answer, and was to all appearances asleep.

After satisfying himself upon this head, Fagin stepped gently to the door, which he fastened. He then drew forth, as it seemed to Oliver, from some trap in the floor, a small box, which he placed carefully on the table. His eyes glistened as he raised the lid, and looked in. Dragging an old chair to the table, he sat down, and took from it a magnificent gold watch, sparkling with jewels.

'Aha!' said Fagin, shrugging up his shoulders, and distorting every feature with a hideous grin. 'Clever dogs! Clever dogs! Staunch to the last! Never told the old parson where they were. Never peached upon old Fagin! And why should they? It wouldn't have loosened the knot, or kept the drop up a minute longer. No, no, no! Fine fellows! Fine young fellows!'

With these, and other muttered reflections of the like nature, the old man once more deposited the watch in its place of safety. At least half a dozen more were severally drawn forth from the same box and surveyed with equal pleasure; besides rings, brooches, bracelets, and other articles of jewellery, of such magnificent materials, and costly workmanship, that Oliver had no idea even of their names.

Having replaced these trinkets, Fagin took out another, so small that it lay in the palm of his hand. There seemed to be some very minute inscription on it; for the old man laid it flat upon the table, and shading it with his hand, pored over it, long and earnestly. At length he put it down, as if despairing of success; and, leaning back in his chair, muttered:

'What a fine thing capital punishment is! Dead men never repent; dead men never bring awkward stories to light. Ah, it's a fine thing for the trade! Five of 'em strung up in a row, and none left to play booty, or turn white-livered!'

As Fagin uttered these words, his bright dark eyes, which had been staring vacantly before him, fell on Oliver's face. The boy's eyes were fixed on his in mute curiosity; and, although the recognition was only for an instant—for the briefest space of time that can possibly be conceived—it was enough to show the old man that he had been observed. Although he was quite unaware of the fact, Oliver's precarious trajectory through life had suddenly changed, and not necessarily for the better.

Fagin closed the lid of the box with a loud crash; and, laying his hand on a bread knife which was on the table, started furiously up. He trembled very much though; for, even in his terror, Oliver could see that the knife quivered in the air.

'What's that?' said the old man. 'What do you watch me for? Why are you awake? What have you seen? Speak out, boy! Quick—quick! for your life.'

'I wasn't able to sleep any longer, sir,' replied Oliver, meekly. 'I am very sorry if I have disturbed you, sir.'

'You were not awake five minutes ago?' questioned Fagin, scowling fiercely at the boy.

'No—no, indeed!' replied Oliver.

'Are you sure?' cried Fagin, with a still fiercer look than before, and a threatening attitude.

'Upon my word I was not, sir,' replied Oliver, earnestly. 'I was not, indeed, sir.'

'Tush, tush, my dear!' said the old man, abruptly resuming his old manner, and playing with the knife a little, before he laid it down; as if to induce the belief that he had caught it up in mere sport. 'Of course I know that, my dear. I only tried to frighten you. You're a brave boy. Ha! ha! you're a brave boy, Oliver!' Fagin rubbed his hands with a chuckle, but glanced uneasily at the box notwithstanding.

'Did you see any of these pretty things, my dear?' asked Fagin, laying his hand upon it after a short pause.

'Yes, sir,' replied Oliver.

'Ah!' said the old man, turning rather pale. 'They—they're mine, Oliver; my little property. All I have to live upon in my old age. The folks call me a miser, my dear—only a miser; that's all.'

Oliver thought the old gentleman must be a decided miser to live in such a dirty place, with so many watches; but, thinking that perhaps his fondness for the Dodger and the other boys cost him a good deal of money, he only cast a deferential look at the old man, and asked if he might get up.

'Certainly, my dear—certainly,' replied the old gentleman. 'Stay. There's a pitcher of water in the corner by the door. Bring it here; and I'll give you a basin to wash in, my dear.'

Oliver got up, walked across the room, and stooped for an instant to raise the pitcher. When he turned his head the box was gone.

He had scarcely washed himself, and made everything tidy, by emptying the basin out of the window, agreeably to the old man's directions, when the Dodger returned, accompanied by a very sprightly young friend, whom Oliver had seen smoking on the previous night, and who was now formally introduced to him as Charley Bates. The four sat down to breakfast on the coffee and the hot rolls and ham which the Dodger had brought home in the crown of his hat.

'Well,' said Fagin, glancing slyly at Oliver, and addressing himself to the Dodger, 'I hope you've been at work this morning, my dears?'

'Hard,' replied the Dodger.

'As nails,' added Charley Bates.

'Good boys, good boys!' said Fagin. 'What have you got, Dodger?'

'A couple of wallets,' replied that young gentleman.

'Lined?' inquired the old gentleman, with eagerness.

'Pretty well,' replied the Dodger, producing two wallets; one green, and the other red.

'Not so heavy as they might be,' said Fagin, after looking at the insides carefully; 'but very neat and nicely made. Ingenious workman, ain't he, Oliver?'

'Very indeed, sir,' said Oliver. At which Mr. Charles Bates laughed uproariously; very much to the amazement of Oliver, who saw nothing to laugh at in anything that had passed.

'And what have you got, my dear?' said Fagin to Charley Bates.

'Hankies,' replied Master Bates, at the same time producing four monogramed silk handkerchiefs which were, at that time, all the rage amongst fashionable Londoners.

'Well,' said the old miser, inspecting them closely; 'they're very good ones—very. You haven't marked them well, though, Charley; so the marks shall be picked out with a needle, and we'll teach Oliver how to do it. Shall we, Oliver, eh? Ha! ha! ha!'

'If you please, sir,' said Oliver.

'You'd like to be able to make silk handkerchiefs as easy as Charley Bates, wouldn't you, my dear?' asked Fagin.

'Very much indeed, if you'll teach me, sir,' replied Oliver.

Master Bates saw something so exquisitely ludicrous in this reply that he burst into another laugh; which laugh, meeting the coffee he was drinking, and carrying it down some wrong channel, very nearly terminated in his premature suffocation.

'He is so jolly green!' said Charley, once he recovered, as an apology to the company for his impolite behaviour.

The Dodger said nothing, but he smoothed Oliver's hair down over his eyes, and said he'd know better by-and-by; upon which the old gentleman, observing Oliver's colour mounting, changed the subject by asking whether there had been much of a crowd at the execution that morning? This made Oliver wonder more and more; for it was plain from the replies of the two boys that they had both been there; and he naturally wondered how they could possibly have found time to be so very industrious.

'Five hung at Newgate for break'n, enter'n!' exclaimed the Dodger.

'The Artful and me work 'ard every day to avoid such a fate,' added Charley.

'Two no much older than you, Oliver,' said the Dodger. 'How old is you?'

'Twelve years,' said Oliver.

'Of age,' replied the Dodger. 'Subject ta the full force and effect of 'er majesty's law.'

'Charley's got it right,' said Fagin. 'Best to work 'ard to avoid 'er majesty tak'n any interest in you.'

These statements went far towards reassuring Oliver that his two new friends were, in fact, not only industrious, but careful to stay within the unsympathetic lines of the law.

When the breakfast was cleared away; the merry old gentleman and the two boys played at a very curious and uncommon game, which was performed in this way. The merry old gentleman, placing a snuffbox in one pocket of his trousers, a note-case in the other, and a watch in his waistcoat pocket, with a guard chain round his neck, and sticking a mock diamond pin in his shirt, buttoned his coat tight round him, and putting his spectacle case and handkerchief in his pockets, trotted up and down the room with a cane, in imitation of the manner in which old gentlemen walk about the streets any hour of the day. Sometimes he stopped at the fireplace, and sometimes at the door, making believe that he was staring with all his might into shop windows. At such times he would look constantly round him, for fear of thieves, and would keep slapping all his pockets in turn, to see that he hadn't lost anything, in such a very funny and natural manner, that Oliver laughed till the tears ran down his face. All this time the two boys followed him closely about; getting out of his sight so nimbly, every time he turned round, that it was impossible to follow their motions. At last the Dodger trod upon his toes, or ran upon his boot accidently, while Charley Bates stumbled up against him from behind; and in that one moment they took from him, with the most extraordinary rapidity, snuffbox, note-case, watch, guard chain, shirt-pin, handkerchief, and even the spectacle case. If the old gentleman felt a hand in any one of his pockets, he cried out where it was; and then the game began all over again.

When this game had been played a great many times, a couple of young ladies stopped by to see Fagin; one of whom was named Betsy, and the other Nancy. They were both good looking young women, and Nancy was regarded by all as being pretty. They wore a good deal of hair, not very neatly turned up behind, and were rather untidy about the shoes and stockings. They both had considerable colour on their faces—having had liberally applied lipstick, mascara, blush, and other cosmetics—which made them look quite hearty. Being remarkably free and agreeable in their manners, Oliver thought them to be very nice girls indeed; and there is no doubt that they were. It was readily apparent that Betsy and Nancy had come to repay some debt owing to Fagin, as they each handed him some money which he graciously accepted.

The visitors stopped a long time. Spirits were produced, in consequence of one of the young ladies complaining of a coldness within her; and the conversation took a very convivial and improving turn. At length Charley Bates expressed his opinion that it was time to pad the hoof. This, it occurred to Oliver, must be French for going out; for directly afterwards, the Dodger, Charley, and the two young ladies went away together. 'There, my dear,' said Fagin. 'That's a pleasant life, isn't it? They have gone out for the day.'

'Have they done work, sir?' inquired Oliver.

'Yes,' said Fagin, 'that is, unless they should unexpectedly come across any, when they are out; and they won't neglect it, if they do, my dear—depend upon it. Make 'em your models, my dear—make 'em your models,' he said, tapping the fire-shovel on the hearth to add force to his words; 'do everything they bid you, and take their advice in all matters—especially the Dodger's, my dear. He'll be a great man himself, and will make you one too, if you take pattern by him.—Is my handkerchief hanging out of my pocket, my dear?' asked the old man, stopping short.

'Yes, sir,' said Oliver.

'See if you can take it out, without my feeling it; as you saw them do, when we were at play this morning.'

Oliver held up the bottom of the pocket with one hand, as he had seen the Dodger hold it, and drew the handkerchief lightly out of it with the other.

'Is it gone?' cried Fagin.

'Here it is, sir,' said Oliver, proudly, showing it in his hand.

'You're a clever boy, my dear,' said the playful old gentleman, patting Oliver on the head approvingly. 'I never saw a sharper lad. Here's a shilling for you. If you go on, in this way, you'll be the greatest man of the time. And now come here, and I'll show you how to take the marks out of the handkerchiefs.'

Oliver wondered what picking the old gentleman's pocket in play, had to do with his chances of being a great man. But, thinking that Fagin, being so much his senior, must know best, he followed him quietly to the table, and was soon deeply involved in his new study.

Chapter 10
An Incident in Clerkenwell

For many days Oliver remained in the old man's room, picking monogram letters out of silk handkerchiefs (of which a great number were brought home), and sometimes taking part in the game already described, which the two boys and Fagin played regularly every morning. At length he began to languish for fresh air, and took many occasions to earnestly entreat the old gentleman to allow him to go out to work with his two companions.

Oliver was rendered more anxious to be actively employed, by what he had seen of the stern morality of the old gentleman's character. Whenever the Dodger or Charley Bates came home at night empty-handed, he would expound with great vehemence on the misery of idle and lazy habits, and would enforce upon them the necessity of an active life, by sending them to bed without their supper. On one occasion, indeed, he even went so far as to knock them both down a flight of stairs; but this was carrying out his virtuous precepts to an unusual extent.

One particular morning, when he awoke feeling oddly closed-in, Oliver resolved to obtain the permission he so eagerly sought from Fagin; to leave the confines of the house, and to go off to work with Jack and Charley.

'I'm feeling poorly this morning,' complained Oliver to Fagin. 'I should think that taking some air would put me right.' This was not entirely contrived as Oliver honestly felt somewhat ill and sincerely thought that a little exercise might to restore his vigour.

'Feeling poorly are we?' answered Fagin. 'In want of air, are we?'

'Yes, sir,' said Oliver. 'You've been so kind and generous to me; I'm much obliged to you. Wouldn't it be of benefit to you to put another boy to work, sir?'

'That it would,' replied Fagin, 'provid'n the boy has sharp eyes and a quiet tongue.'

At length Fagin acquiesced to Oliver's earnest pleadings, and, perhaps with some misgivings, consented to his going off to work. There had been no handkerchiefs to work upon for two or three days, and the dinners had been rather meagre. Perhaps these were reasons for the old gentleman giving his assent; but, whether they were or no, he told Oliver he might go, and placed him under the joint guardianship of Charley Bates and his friend the Dodger.

The three boys sallied out; the Dodger with his coat-sleeves tucked up, and his hat cocked, as usual; Master Bates sauntering along with his hands in his pockets; and Oliver between them wondering where they were going, and what branch of manufacture he would be instructed in first.

The pace at which they went, was such a very lazy, ill-looking saunter, that Oliver soon began to think his companions were going to deceive the old gentleman, by not going to work at all. The Dodger had a playful propensity, too, of pulling the caps from the heads of small boys and tossing them away; while Charley Bates exhibited some very loose notions concerning the rights of property, by pilfering diverse apples and onions from stalls along the roadsides, and thrusting them into pockets which were so surprisingly capacious, that they seemed to undermine his whole suit of clothes in every direction.

'When will we arrive at our place of employment?' queried Oliver of Jack and Charley.

'My covey,' laughed Charley, 'are ya blind?'

'We is at work,' explained the Dodger. 'We relieve people of those things that weigh 'em down.'

'We's snatchers,' added Charley, 'pickpockets.'

'Ain't you 'fraid of the gallows?' asked Oliver, incredulously.

'Naw,' replied the Dodger. 'Ain't nobody been scragged for pickpocketing since eighteen—eighteen.'

'Watch us,' said Charley. 'We's the best Fagin ever had.'

This statement was punctuated by a very mysterious change of behaviour on the part of the Dodger. They were just emerging from a narrow court not far from the open square in Clerkenwell, which is yet called, by some strange perversion of terms, 'The Green,' when the Dodger made a sudden stop, and, laying his finger on his lip, drew his companions back again, with the greatest caution and circumspection.

'What's the matter?' demanded Oliver.

'Hush!' replied the Dodger. 'Do you see that old cove at the bookstall?'

'The old gentleman over the way?' said Oliver. 'Yes, I see him.'

'He'll do,' said the Dodger.

'A prime plant,' observed Master Charley Bates.

Oliver looked from one to the other with the greatest surprise; but he was not permitted to make any inquiries, for the two boys walked stealthily across the road, and slunk close behind the old gentleman towards whom his attention had been directed. Oliver walked a few paces after them, and, not knowing whether to advance or retire, stood looking on in silent amazement.

The old gentleman was a very respectable looking personage, with a powdered head and gold spectacles. He was dressed in a bottle-green coat with a black velvet collar, wore white trousers, and carried a smart bamboo cane under his arm. He had taken up a book from the stall, and there he stood, reading away as hard as if he were in his elbow chair in his own study. It is very possible that he fancied himself there, indeed; for it was plain, from his utter abstraction, that he saw not the bookstall, nor the street, nor the boys, nor, in short, anything but the book itself, which he was reading straight through, turning over the leaf when he got to the bottom of a page, beginning at the top line of the next one, and going regularly on, with the greatest interest and eagerness.

Oliver stood a few paces off, looking on with his eyes as wide open as they could possibly go, to see the Dodger plunge his hand into the old gentleman's pocket, and draw from thence a handkerchief; to see him hand the same to Charley Bates; and finally to behold them both running away round the corner at full speed!

In an instant the whole mystery of the handkerchiefs, and the watches, and the jewels, and the old man, rushed upon the boy's mind and was made abundantly clear. He stood for a moment, with the blood so tingling through all his veins that he felt as if he were in a burning fire. Then, confused and thrilled and frightened, he took to his heels, and, not knowing what he did, made off as fast as he could lay his feet to the ground.

This was all done in a minute's space. In the very instant when Oliver began to run, the old gentleman, putting his hand to his pocket, and missing his handkerchief, turned sharply round. Seeing a boy scudding away at such a rapid pace, he very naturally concluded him to be the perpetrator; and, shouting 'Stop thief!' with all his might, made off after him, book in hand.

But the old gentleman was not the only person who raised the hue-and-cry. The Dodger and Master Bates, unwilling to attract public attention by running down the open street, had merely retired into the very first doorway around the corner. They no sooner heard the cry, and saw Oliver running, than, guessing exactly how the matter stood, they issued forth with great promptitude, and shouting 'Stop thief!' too, joined in the pursuit like good citizens.

Although Oliver had been brought up by philosophers, he was not theoretically acquainted with the beautiful axiom that self-preservation is the first law of nature. If he had been, perhaps he would have been prepared for this. Not being prepared, however, it alarmed him the more; so away he went like the wind, with the old gentleman and the two boys roaring and shouting behind him.

'Stop thief! Stop thief!' There is a magic in the sound. The tradesman leaves his counter, and the carman his wagon; the butcher throws down his tray, the baker his basket, the milkman his pail, the errand-boy his parcels, the school-boy his marbles, the labourer his pickaxe, and the child his toy. Away they run, pell-mell, helter-skelter, slap-dash; tearing, yelling, screaming, knocking down the passengers as they turn the corners, rousing up the dogs, and astonishing the fowls; and streets, squares, and courts, re-echo with the sound.

'Stop thief! Stop thief!' The cry is taken up by a hundred voices, and the crowd accumulates at every turning. Away they fly, splashing through the mud, and rattling along the pavement. Up go the windows, out run the people, onward bear the mob, a whole audience deserting a Punch and Judy show in the very thickest of the plot, and, joining the rushing throng, swell the shout, and lend fresh vigour to the cry, 'Stop thief! Stop thief!'

'Stop thief! Stop thief!' There is a passion *for hunting something* deeply implanted in the human breast. One wretched breathless child, panting with exhaustion, terror in his looks, agony in his eyes, large drops of perspiration streaming down his face, strains every nerve to make headway beyond his pursuers; and as they follow on his track, and gain upon him every instant, they hail his decreasing strength with still louder shouts, and whoop and scream for joy. 'Stop thief!' Ay, stop him for God's sake, were it only in mercy!

Stopped at last! A clever blow! He is down upon the pavement, and the crowd eagerly gathers round him, each new comer jostling and struggling with the others to catch a glimpse. 'Stand aside!' 'Give him a little air!' 'Nonsense! he don't deserve it.' 'Where's the gentleman?' 'Here he is, coming down the street.' 'Make room there for the gentleman!' 'Is this the boy, sir!'

'Yes.'

Oliver lay, covered with mud and dust, and bleeding from the mouth, looking wildly round upon the heap of faces that surrounded him, when the old gentleman was officiously dragged and pushed into the circle by the foremost of the pursuers.

'Yes,' said the gentleman, 'I am afraid it is the boy.'

'Afraid!' murmured the crowd. 'That's a good 'un!'

'Poor fellow!' said the gentleman, 'he has hurt himself.'

'*I* did that, sir,' said a great lubberly fellow, stepping forward; 'and preciously I cut my knuckle agin' his mouth. I stopped him, sir.'

The fellow touched his hat with a grin, expecting something for his pains; but the old gentleman, eyeing him with an expression of dislike, looked anxiously around, as if he contemplated running away himself, which it is very possible he might have attempted to do, and thus have afforded another chase, had a police officer not (who is generally the last person to arrive in such cases) at that moment made his way through the crowd, and seized Oliver by the collar.

'Come, get up,' said the officer, roughly.

'It wasn't me, indeed, sir. Indeed, indeed, it was two other boys,' said Oliver, clasping his hands passionately, and looking round. 'They are here somewhere.'

'Oh, no, they ain't,' said the officer. He meant this to be ironical, but it was true besides, for the Dodger and Charley Bates had filed off down the first convenient alley they came to. 'Come, get up!'

'Don't hurt him,' said the old gentleman, compassionately.

'Oh, no, I won't hurt him,' replied the officer, tearing his jacket half off his back, in proof thereof. 'Come, I know you; it won't do. Will you stand upon your legs, you young devil?'

Oliver, who could hardly stand, made an effort to raise himself on his feet, and was at once lugged along the streets by his jacket-collar at a rapid pace. The gentleman walked on with them by the officer's side; and as many of the crowd as could achieve the feat got a little ahead, and stared back at Oliver from time to time. The boys shouted in triumph; and on they went.

Chapter 11
Magistrate's Court

The offence had been committed within the district, and indeed within the immediate neighbourhood, of a very notorious metropolitan police station. The crowd had only the satisfaction of accompanying Oliver through two or three streets, and down a place called Mutton Hill, when he was led beneath a low archway, and up a dirty court, into this dispensary of summary justice, by the back way. It was a small paved yard into which they turned; and here they encountered a stout man with a bunch of whiskers on his face and a bunch of keys in his hand.

'What's the matter now?' asked the man carelessly.

'A young hanky-hunter,' replied the officer who had Oliver in charge.

'Are you the party that's been robbed, sir?' inquired the man with the keys.

'Yes, I am,' replied the old gentleman, 'but I am not sure that this boy actually took the handkerchief. I—I would rather not press the case.'

'Must go before the magistrate now, sir,' replied the man. 'His worship will be disengaged in half a minute. Now, young gallows!'

This was an invitation for Oliver to enter through a door which he unlocked as he spoke, and which led into a stone cell. Here he was searched, and nothing being found upon him, locked up.

This cell was in shape and size something like a coal-cellar, only not so light. It was most intolerably dirty; for it was Monday morning, and it had been tenanted by six drunken people who had been locked up since Saturday night. But this is little. In our police stations men and women are every night confined on the most trivial *charges*—the word is worth noting—in dungeons, compared to which those in Newgate Prison, occupied by the most atrocious felons, tried, found guilty, and under sentence of death, are palaces. Let anyone who doubts this, compare the two.

The old gentleman looked almost as rueful as Oliver when the key grated in the lock. He turned with a sigh to the book which had been the innocent cause of all this disturbance.

'There is something in that boy's face,' said the old gentleman to himself as he walked slowly away, tapping his chin with the cover of the book, in a thoughtful manner—'something that touches and interests me. *Can he be innocent?* He looked like—like -,' exclaimed the old gentleman, halting very abruptly, and staring up into the sky,—'Bless my soul!—where have I seen something like that look before?'

After musing for some minutes, the old gentleman walked, with the same meditative face, into a back anteroom opening from the yard; and there, retiring into a corner, called up before his mind's eye a vast amphitheatre of faces over which a dusky curtain had hung for many years. 'No,' said the old gentleman, shaking his head; 'it must be imagination.'

He wandered over them again. He had called them into view, and it was not easy to replace the shroud that had so long concealed them. There were the faces of friends and foes, and of many that had been almost strangers, peering intrusively from the crowd; there were the faces of young and blooming girls that were now old women; there were faces that the grave had changed and closed upon, but which the mind, superior to its power, still dressed in their old freshness and beauty, calling back the lustre of the eyes, the brightness of the smile, the beaming of the soul through its mask of clay, and whispering of beauty beyond the tomb, changed but to be heightened, and taken from earth only to be set up as a light to shed a soft and gentle glow upon the path to Heaven.

But the old gentleman could recall no one countenance of which Oliver's features bore a trace. So he heaved a sigh over the recollections he had awakened; and being, happily for himself, an absent minded old gentleman, buried them again in the pages of the musty book.

He was roused by a touch on the shoulder, and a request from the man with the keys to follow him into the station. He closed his book hastily, and was at once ushered into the imposing presence of the renowned Mr. Fang.

Court was held in a front parlour, with a panelled wall. Mr. Fang sat behind a desk, at the upper end; and on one side the room was a sort of wooden pen in which poor little Oliver was already deposited; taking in with some trepidation the awfulness of the scene.

Mr. Fang was a lean, long-backed, stiff-necked, middle-sized man, with no great quantity of hair and what he had growing on the back and sides of his head. His face was stern and much flushed. If he were really not in the habit of drinking rather more than what was exactly good for him, he might have brought action against his countenance for libel, and have recovered heavy damages.

The old gentleman bowed respectfully, and, advancing to the magistrate's desk, deposited his calling card thereon. Suiting his words to the action he said, 'That is my name and address, sir.' He then withdrew a pace or two; and, with another polite and gentlemanly inclination of his head waited to be questioned.

Now, it so happened that Mr. Fang was at that moment perusing a leading article in a newspaper of the morning, adverting to some recent decision of his, and commending him, for the three hundred and fiftieth time, to the special and particular notice of the Secretary of State for the

Home Department. He was out of temper when he looked up with an angry scowl.

'Who are you?' asked Mr. Fang.

The old gentleman pointed with some surprise to his calling card.

'Officers!' shouted Mr. Fang, tossing the card contemptuously onto the floor, 'who is this fellow?'

'My name, sir,' said the old gentleman, speaking like a gentleman, 'my name, sir, is Brownlow. Permit me to inquire the name of the magistrate who offers a gratuitous and unprovoked insult to a respectable person, under the protection of the bench.' Saying this, Mr. Brownlow looked around the room as if in search of some person who would afford him the required information.

'Officer!' shouted Mr. Fang, throwing the newspaper to one side, 'what's this fellow charged with?'

'He's not charged at all, your worship,' replied the officer. 'He appears against this boy, your worship.'

His worship knew this perfectly well, but it was a good annoyance, and a safe one.

'Appears against the boy, does he?' said Mr. Fang, surveying Mr. Brownlow contemptuously from head to foot. 'Swear him!'

'Before I am sworn, I must beg to say one word,' said Mr. Brownlow, 'and that is, that I really never, without actual experience, could have believed -'

'Hold your tongue, sir!' said Mr. Fang, peremptorily.

'I will not, sir!' replied the old gentleman.

'Hold your tongue this instant, or I'll have you turned out of the station!' said Mr. Fang. 'You're an insolent, impertinent fellow. How dare you bully a magistrate!'

'What!' exclaimed the old gentleman, reddening.

'Swear this person!' said Fang to the clerk. 'I'll not hear another word. Swear him!'

Mr. Brownlow's indignation was greatly roused, but, reflecting perhaps that he might only injure the boy by giving vent to it, he suppressed his feelings and submitted to be sworn at once.

'Now,' said Fang, 'what's the charge against this boy? What have you got to say, sir?'

'I was standing at a bookstall -' Mr. Brownlow began.

'Hold your tongue, sir,' said Mr. Fang. 'Policeman! Where's the policeman? Here, swear this policeman. Now, policeman, what is this?'

The policeman, with becoming humility, related how he had taken the charge; how he had searched Oliver, and found nothing on his person; and how that was all he knew about it.

'Are there any witnesses?' inquired Mr. Fang.

'None, your worship,' replied the policeman.

Mr. Fang sat silent for some minutes; and then, turning round to the prosecutor, said with towering passion:

'Do you mean to state what your complaint against this boy is, fellow, or do you not? You have been sworn. Now if you stand there refusing to give evidence, I'll punish you for disrespect to the bench; I will, by -'

By what, or by whom, nobody knows; for the clerk and jailor coughed very loud, just at the right moment; and the former dropped a heavy book upon the floor, thus preventing the word from being heard—accidently, of course.

With many interruptions, and repeated insults, Mr. Brownlow contrived to state his case; observing that, in the surprise of the moment, he had run after the boy because he had seen him running away; and expressing his hope that, if the magistrate should believe him, although not actually the thief, to be connected with the thieves, he would deal as leniently with him as justice would allow.

'He has been hurt already,' said the old gentleman in conclusion. 'And I fear,' he added, with great energy, looking towards the bar, 'I really fear that he is ill.'

'Oh, yes, I dare say!' said Mr. Fang, with a sneer. 'Come, none of your tricks here, you young vagabond; they won't do. What's your name?'

Oliver tried to reply, but his tongue failed him. He was deadly pale, and the whole place seemed to be turning round and round.

'What's your name, you hardened scoundrel?' demanded Mr. Fang. 'Officer, what's his name?'

This was addressed to a bluff old fellow, in a striped waistcoat, who was standing by the bar. He bent over Oliver, and repeated the inquiry; but finding him really incapable of understanding the question, and knowing that his not replying would only infuriate the magistrate the more, and add to the severity of his sentence; he hazarded a guess.

'He says his name's Mark White, your worship,' said the kind-hearted thief-catcher.

'Oh, he won't speak out, won't he?' said Fang. 'Very well, very well. Where does he live?'

'Where he can, your worship,' replied the officer; again pretending to receive Oliver's answer.

'Has he any parents?' inquired Mr. Fang.

'He says they died in his infancy, your worship,' replied the officer, hazarding the usual reply.

At this point of the inquiry Oliver raised his head, and, looking around with imploring eyes, murmured a feeble request for a draught of water.

'Stuff and nonsense!' said Mr. Fang. 'Don't try to make a fool of me.'

'I think he really is ill, your worship,' remonstrated the officer.

'I know better,' said Mr. Fang.

'Take care of him, officer,' said the old gentleman, raising his hands instinctively; 'he'll fall down.'

'Stand away, officer,' cried Fang; 'let him, if he likes.'

Oliver availed himself of the kind permission, and fell to the floor. The men in the room looked at each other, but no one dared to stir.

'I knew he was shamming,' said Fang, as if this were incontestable proof of the fact. 'Let him lie there; he'll soon be tired of that.'

'How do you propose to deal with the case, sir?' inquired the clerk in a low voice.

'Summarily,' replied Mr. Fang. 'He stands committed for three months—hard labour of course. Clear the room.'

The door was opened for this purpose, and a couple of men were preparing to carry the insensible boy to his cell; when an elderly man of decent but poor appearance, clad in an old suit of black, rushed hastily into the room, and advanced towards the bench.

'Stop, stop! Don't take him away! For Heaven's sake stop a moment!' cried the new-comer, breathless with haste.

Although the presiding magistrate in such a court as this exercises a summary and arbitrary power over the liberties, the good name, the character, almost the lives of Her Majesty's subjects, especially of the poorer class; and although, within such walls, enough fantastic tricks are daily played to make the angels blind with weeping; they are closed to the public, save through the medium of the daily press. Mr. Fang was consequently not a little indignant to see an unbidden guest enter in such irreverent disorder.

'What is this? Who is this? Turn this man out. Clear the room!' cried Mr. Fang.

'I *will* speak!' cried the man. 'I will not be turned out. I saw it all. I keep the bookstall. I demand to be sworn. I will not be put down. Mr. Fang, you must hear me. You must not refuse, sir.'

The man was right. His manner was bold and determined, and the matter was growing rather too serious to be hushed up.

'Swear the fellow,' growled Mr. Fang, with very ill grace. 'Now, man, what have you got to say?'

'This,' said the man: 'I saw three boys—two others and the prisoner here—loitering on the opposite side of the way, when this gentleman was reading. The robbery was committed by another boy. I saw it done; and I saw that this boy was perfectly amazed and stupefied by it.' Having by this time recovered a little breath, the worthy bookstall keeper proceeded to relate, in a more coherent manner, the exact circumstances of the robbery.

'Why didn't you come here before?' asked Fang, after a pause.

'I hadn't a soul to mind the shop,' replied the man. 'Everybody who could have helped me, had joined in the pursuit. I could get nobody till five minutes ago; and I've run here all the way.'

'The prosecutor was reading, was he?' inquired Fang, after another pause.

'Yes,' replied the man. 'The very book he has in his hand.'

'Oh, that book, eh?' said Fang. 'Is it paid for?'

'No, it is not,' replied the man, with a smile.

'Dear me, I forgot all about it!' exclaimed the absent old gentleman, innocently.

'A nice person to prefer a charge against a poor boy!' said Fang, with a comical effort to look humane. 'I consider, sir, that you have obtained possession of that book under very suspicious and disreputable circumstances; and you may think yourself very fortunate that the owner of the property declines to prosecute. Let this be a lesson to you, my man, or the law will overtake you yet. The boy is discharged. Clear the room!'

'Damn me!' cried the old gentleman, bursting out with the rage he had kept down so long, 'damn me! I'll -'

'Clear the room!' said the magistrate. 'Officers, do you hear? Clear the room!'

The mandate was obeyed, and the indignant Mr. Brownlow was conveyed out, with the now infamous book in one hand and his bamboo cane in the other, in a perfect frenzy of rage and defiance. He reached the yard, and his passion vanished in a moment. Little Oliver Twist lay on his back on the pavement, with his shirt unbuttoned, and his temples bathed with water; his face a deadly white, and a cold tremble convulsing his whole frame.

'Poor boy, poor boy!' said Mr. Brownlow, bending over him and feeling his forehead. 'He has a wicked fever. Call a coach, somebody, pray, directly!'

A coach was obtained, and Oliver having been carefully laid on one seat, the old gentleman got in and sat himself on the other.

'May I accompany you?' asked the bookstall keeper, looking in.

'Bless me, yes, my dear friend,' said Mr. Brownlow, quickly. 'I forgot you. Dear, dear! I have this unhappy book still! Jump in. Poor fellow! There's no time to lose.'

The bookstall keeper got into the coach, and away they drove.

Chapter 12
Mr. Brownlow

The coach rattled away, down Mount Pleasant and up Exmouth Street, over nearly the same ground as that which Oliver had traversed when he first entered London accompanied by the Dodger and, turning a different way when it reached the Angel at Islington, stopped at length before a grand house on a quiet shady street near Pentonville. Here a bed was prepared, without loss of time, in which Mr. Brownlow saw his young charge carefully and comfortably deposited; and here he was tended with a kindness and solicitude that knew no bounds.

But, for many days, Oliver remained insensible to all the goodness of his new friends. The sun rose and sank, and rose and sank again, and many times after that, and still the boy lay stretched on his uneasy bed battling the wasting heat of fever. The worm does not work more surely on the dead body, than does this slow creeping fire upon the living frame.

He awoke at last from what seemed to have been a long and troubled dream. Summoning all of his strength, he raised his head up off the bed and looked anxiously around.

'What room is this? Where have I been brought to?' asked Oliver. 'This is not the place I went to sleep in. Am I in Heaven?'

He uttered these words to no one in particular, but they were overheard at once. The curtain at the bed's head was hastily drawn back by a motherly old lady, very neatly and precisely dressed, who had risen quickly from the armchair in which she had been sitting nearby doing needle-work.

'Hush, my dear,' said the old lady softly. 'You must be very quiet, or you will be ill again; and you have been very bad,—as bad as bad could be, pretty nigh. Lie down again; there's a dear!' With those words, the old lady very gently placed Oliver's head upon the pillow, and, smoothing back his hair from his forehead, looked so kindly and loving at his face that he could not help placing his hand in hers, and drawing it round his neck.

'Save us!' said the old lady, with tears in her eyes. 'What a strong boy you are! What would your mother feel if she had sat by you as I have, and could see you now!'

'Perhaps she does see me,' whispered Oliver, folding his hands together; 'perhaps she has sat by me. I almost feel as if she had.'

'That was the fever, my dear,' said the old lady, mildly.

'I suppose it was,' replied Oliver, 'because Heaven is a long way off; and they are too happy there to come down to the bedside of a poor boy.

But if she knew I was ill she must have pitied me, even there; for she was very ill herself before she died. She can't know anything about me though,' added Oliver, after a moment's silence. 'If she had seen me so, it would have made her sorrowful; and her face has always looked sweet and happy when I have dreamt of her.'

The old lady made no reply to this, but wiping her eyes first, and her spectacles, which lay on the counterpane, afterwards, as if they were part and parcel of those features, brought some cool tea for Oliver to drink; and then, patting him on the cheek, told him he must lie very quiet, or he would be ill again.

'Where am I? Who, if I may ask, are you?' asked Oliver. 'You have been very kind.'

'You are in Mr. Brownlow's house,' said the lady. 'I am Mr. Brownlow's housekeeper.'

So Oliver kept very still; partly because he was anxious to obey the kind old lady in all things; and partly, to tell the truth, because he was completely exhausted with what he had already said. He soon fell into a gentle doze, from which he was awakened by the light of a candle, which, being brought near the bed, showed him a gentleman with a very large and loud-ticking gold watch in his hand, who felt his pulse, and said that he was a great deal better.

'You *are* a great deal better, are you not, my boy?' said the doctor.

'Yes, thank you, sir,' replied Oliver.

'Yes, I know you are,' said the doctor. 'You're hungry too, ain't you?'

'No, sir,' answered Oliver.

'Hem!' said the doctor. 'No, I know you're not. He is not hungry, Mrs. Bedwin,' said the doctor, looking very wise.

The old lady made a respectful inclination of the head, which seemed to say that she thought the doctor was a very clever man. The doctor appeared to hold the same opinion himself.

'You feel sleepy, don't you, my dear?' said the doctor.

'No, sir,' replied Oliver.

'No,' said the doctor, with a very shrewd and satisfied look. 'You're not sleepy. Nor thirsty. Are you?'

'Yes, sir, rather thirsty,' answered Oliver.

'Just as I expected, Mrs. Bedwin,' said the doctor. 'It's very natural that he should be thirsty. You may give him a little tea, ma'am, and some dry toast without any butter. Orange slices, if you have one, will give him strength. Don't keep him too warm, ma'am; but be careful that you don't let him be too cold—will you have the goodness?'

The old lady dropped a curtsey. The doctor, after tasting the cool tea, and expressing a qualified approval thereof, hurried away, his boots creaking in a very important and wealthy manner as he went downstairs.

Oliver dozed off again, soon after this. When he awoke, it was nearly twelve o'clock. The old lady tenderly bade him goodnight shortly afterwards, and left him in the charge of a fat old woman who had just come; bringing with her, in a little bundle, a small Prayer Book and a large nightcap. Putting the latter on her head and the former on the table, the old woman, after telling Oliver that she had come to sit up with him, drew her chair close to the fire and went off into a series of short naps, chequered at frequent intervals with sundry tumblings forward, and diverse moans and chokings. These, however, had no worse effect than causing her to rub her nose very hard, and then fall asleep again.

And thus the night crept slowly on. Oliver lay awake for some time, counting the little circles of light which the reflection of the light-shade threw upon the ceiling, or tracing with his languid eyes the intricate pattern on the wallpaper. The darkness and the deep stillness of the room were very solemn; as they brought into the boy's mind the thought that death had been hovering there, for many days and nights, and might yet fill it with the gloom and dread of his awful presence.

Gradually he fell into that deep tranquil sleep which ease from recent suffering alone imparts, that calm and peaceful rest which it is painful to wake from. Who, if this were death, would be roused again to all the struggles and turmoil of life; to all its cares for the present; its anxieties for the future; and, more than all, its weary recollections of the past!

It had been bright day for hours when Oliver opened his eyes, and when he did so he felt cheerful and happy. The crisis of the disease was safely past. He belonged to the world again.

In three days' time he was able to sit in an easy chair, well propped up with pillows; and, as he was still too weak to walk, Mrs. Bedwin had him carried downstairs into the little housekeeper's room, which belonged to her, where, having sat him up by the fireside, the good old lady sat herself down too, in a state of considerable delight at seeing him so much better.

'You're very, very kind to me, ma'am,' said Oliver.

'Well, never you mind that, my dear,' said the old lady. 'That's got nothing to do with your broth, and it's full time you had it for the doctor says Mr. Brownlow may come in to see you this morning; and we must get up our best looks, because the better we look the more he'll be pleased.' And with this, the old lady applied herself to warming up in a little saucepan a basin full of broth; strong enough to furnish an ample dinner, when reduced to the regulation strength, for three hundred and fifty paupers at the very lowest computation.

Mrs. Bedwin, satisfied that he felt comfortable, salted and broke bits of toasted bread into the broth, with all the bustle befitting so solemn a preparation. Oliver ate it all with extraordinary expedition, and had scarcely swallowed the last spoonful when there came a soft tap at the door. 'Come in,' said the old lady; and in walked Mr. Brownlow.

The old gentleman came in as brisk as need be, and Oliver, looking very worn and shadowy from sickness, made an attempt to stand up out of respect to his benefactor, which terminated in his sinking back into the chair again. Raising his spectacles on his forehead and thrusting his hands behind his back, Brownlow bent over to take a good long look at Oliver. The gentleman's countenance underwent a very great variety of odd contortions. The fact is, if the truth must be told, that Mr. Brownlow's heart was large enough for any six ordinary gentlemen of humane disposition. He felt a welling up of relief and pity and pride that seemed to lodge in his vocal cords.

'Poor boy, poor boy!' said Mr. Brownlow, clearing his throat. 'I'm rather hoarse this morning, Mrs. Bedwin. I'm afraid I have caught cold.'

'I hope not, sir,' said Mrs. Bedwin. 'Everything you have had, has been well aired, sir.'

'I don't know, Bedwin. I don't know,' said Mr. Brownlow; 'I rather think I had a damp napkin at dinner time yesterday; but never mind that. How do you feel, my dear?'

'Very happy, sir,' replied Oliver. 'And very grateful indeed, sir, for your goodness to me.'

'Good boy,' said Mr. Brownlow, stoutly. 'Have you given him any nourishment, Bedwin? Any slops, eh?'

'He has just had a basin of beautiful strong broth, sir,' replied Mrs. Bedwin, drawing herself up slightly and laying strong emphasis on the last word, to intimate that between slops, and broth well compounded, there existed no affinity or connection whatsoever.

'Ugh!' said Mr. Brownlow, with a slight shudder; 'a couple of glasses of port wine would have done him a great deal more good. Wouldn't they, Mark White, eh?'

'My name is Oliver, sir,' replied the boy with a look of great astonishment.

'Oliver?' retorted Mr. Brownlow. 'Oliver what? Oliver White, eh?'

'No, sir, Twist—Oliver Twist.'

'Odd name!' stated the old gentleman. 'What made you tell the magistrate your name was White?'

'I never told him so, sir,' returned Oliver in amazement.

This sounded so like a falsehood that the old gentleman looked somewhat sternly at Oliver's face. It was, however, impossible to doubt him; there was truth in every lineament of his face.

'Some mistake,' said Mr. Brownlow. Although his motive for looking steadily at Oliver no longer existed; the old idea of the resemblance between his features and some familiar face came upon him so strongly that he could not withdraw his gaze.

'I hope you are not angry with me, sir?' said Oliver, raising his eyes earnestly.

'No, no, of course not,' said Mr. Brownlow, with less conviction than he may have intended. 'Eat heartily, gain your strength, and I will call upon you anon once you feel strong again.'

There is little reason to expand upon how Oliver endeavoured to obey these undemanding orders, which affords the narrative an opportunity of relieving the reader from suspense on behalf of the two young pupils of the Merry Old Gentleman; and of recording:—

That when the Dodger and his accomplished friend Master Bates joined in the hue-and-cry which was raised at Oliver's heels in consequence of their executing an illegal conveyance of Mr. Brownlow's personal property, as has already been described, they were motivated by a very laudable and becoming regard for themselves; and forasmuch as the freedom of the subject and the liberty of the individual are among the first and proudest boasts of a true-hearted Englishman, so I need hardly beg the reader to observe that this action should tend to exalt them in the opinion of all public and patriotic men, in almost as great a degree as this strong proof of their anxiety for their own preservation and safety goes to corroborate and confirm the little code of laws which certain profound and sound-judging philosophers have laid down as the mainsprings of all of Nature's deeds and actions: the said philosophers very wisely reducing the good lady's proceedings to matters of maxim and theory, and, by a very neat and pretty compliment to her exalted wisdom and understanding, putting entirely out of sight any considerations of heart or generous impulse and feeling. For these are matters totally beneath a female who is acknowledged by universal admission to be far above the numerous little foibles and weaknesses of her sex.

If I wanted any further proof of the strictly philosophical nature of the conduct of these young gentlemen in their very delicate predicament, I should at once find it in the fact (also recorded in a foregoing part of this narrative) of their quitting the pursuit when the general attention was fixed upon Oliver, and making immediately for their home by the shortest possible cut. For although I do not mean to assert that it is usually the practice of renowned and learned sages to shorten the road to any great conclusion—their course indeed being rather to lengthen the distance by various circumlocutions and discursive staggerings like unto those in which drunken men, under the pressure of a too mighty flow of ideas, are prone to indulge—still I do mean to say, and do say distinctly, that it is the invariable practice of many mighty philosophers, in carrying out their theories, to evince great wisdom and foresight in providing against every possible contingency which can be supposed at all likely to affect themselves. Thus to do a great right, you may do a little wrong; and you may take any means which the end to be attained will justify, the amount of the right or the amount of the wrong, or indeed the distinction between the two, being left entirely to the philosopher concerned, to be settled and determined by his clear, comprehensive, and impartial view of his own particular case.

It was not until the two boys had scoured, with great rapidity, through a most intricate maze of narrow streets and courts, that they ventured to halt beneath a low and dark archway. Having remained silent here just long enough to recover breath to speak, Master Bates uttered an exclamation of amusement and delight, and, bursting into an uncontrollable fit of laughter, flung himself upon a doorstep, and rolled thereon in a transport of mirth.

'What's the matter?' inquired the Dodger.

'Ha! ha! ha!' roared Charley Bates.

'Hold your noise,' remonstrated the Dodger, looking cautiously round. 'Do you want to be grabbed, stupid?'

'I can't help it,' said Charley, 'I can't help it! To see him splitting away at that pace, and cutting round the corners, and knocking up against the posts, and starting on again as if he was made of iron as well as them, and me, with the hankie in my pocket, singing out after him—oh, my eye!' The vivid imagination of Master Bates presented the scene before him in flamboyantly strong colours. As he revelled in this vision, he again rolled upon the door-step, and laughed louder than before.

'What'll Fagin say?' inquired the Dodger; taking advantage of the next interval of breathlessness on the part of his friend to propound the question.

'What?' repeated Charley Bates.

'Ah, what?' said the Dodger.

'Why, what should he say?' inquired Charley, stopping rather suddenly in his merriment; for the Dodger's manner was impressive. 'What should he say?'

Mr. Dawkins whistled for a couple of minutes; then, taking off his hat, scratched his head.

'What do you mean?' asked Charley.

'Toor rul lol loo, gammon and spinnage, the frog he wouldn't, and high cockalorum,' said the Dodger, with a slight sneer on his intellectual countenance.

This was explanatory, but not satisfactory. Master Bates felt it so, and again asked, 'What do you mean?'

The Dodger made no reply; but putting his hat on again, and gathering the skirts of his long-tailed coat under his arm, thrust his tongue into his cheek, slapped the bridge of his nose some half-dozen times in a familiar but expressive manner, and turning on his heel, made his way down the court. Master Bates followed, with a thoughtful countenance.

The noise of footsteps on the creaking stairs, a few minutes after the occurrence of this conversation, roused the merry old gentleman as he sat over the fire with a sausage and a small loaf in his left hand, a pocket-knife in his right, and a pewter pot on the trivet. There was a rascally smile on his face as he turned round, and looking sharply out from under his thick eyebrows, bent his ear towards the door and listened intently.

'Why, how's this?' muttered Fagin, changing his expression. 'Only two of 'em? Where's the third? They can't have got into trouble. Hark!'

The footsteps approached nearer; they reached the landing. The door was slowly opened, and the Dodger and Charley Bates entered, closing it behind them.

Chapter 13
Bill Sikes and Nancy

'Where's Oliver?' asked the furious old miser, rising with a menacing look. 'Where's the boy?'

The young thieves eyed their preceptor as if they were alarmed at his violence, and looked uneasily at each other. But they made no reply.

'What's become of the boy?' asked Fagin, seizing the Dodger tightly by the collar, and threatening him with horrid imprecations. 'Speak out, or I'll throttle you!'

Mr. Fagin looked so very much in earnest that Charley Bates, who deemed it prudent in all cases to be on the safe side, and who conceived it by no means improbable that it might be his turn to be throttled second, dropped upon his knees, and raised a loud, well-sustained, and continuous roar—something between a mad bull and a speaking trumpet.

'Will you speak?' thundered the old man, shaking the Dodger so much that his keeping the big coat on seemed perfectly miraculous.

'Why, the traps have got him, and that's all about it,' said the Dodger, sullenly. 'Come, let go o' me, will you!' With one jerk he swung himself clean out of his big coat, which he left in Fagin's hands, and, snatched up the toasting fork, made a pass at the merry old gentleman's waistcoat; which, if it had taken effect, would have let out a little more merriment than could have been easily replaced in a month or two.

Fagin stepped back in this emergency, with more agility than could have been anticipated in a man of his apparent decrepitude, and, seizing up the pot, prepared to hurl it at his assailant's head. But with Charley Bates, at this very moment, attracting his attention with a perfectly terrific howl, he suddenly altered its destination, and flung it full at that young gentleman still kneeling by the doorway.

'Why, what the blazes is in the wind now!' growled a deep voice. 'Who pitched that 'ere pot at me? It's well it's the beer, and not the pot, as hit me, or I'd have settled somebody. I might have know'd as nobody but that infernal, rich, plundering, thundering old Fagin could afford to throw away any drink but water—and not that, unless he done the Water Company every quarter. Wot's it all about, Fagin? Damn you, if my neck handkerchief ain't lined with beer! Come in, you sneaking varmint; wot are you stopping outside for, as if you was ashamed of your master! Come in!'

The man who growled out these words was a stoutly-built fellow of about five-and-twenty, in a black velveteen coat, very soiled khaki breeches, laced up half boots, and grey cotton stockings, which enclosed a bulky pair of legs, with large swelling calves—the kind of legs that, in such costume, always look in an unfinished and incomplete state without a set of shackles to garnish them. He had a brown hat on his head and a dirty handkerchief round his neck, with the long frayed ends of which he smeared the beer from his face as he spoke. He disclosed, when he had done so, a broad heavy countenance with a beard of three days' growth, and two scowling eyes; one of which displayed various multi-coloured symptoms of having been recently damaged by a blow.

'Come in, d'ye hear?' growled this engaging ruffian.

A white furred dog, with a black patch over one eye, skulked into the room. His face was scratched and torn in twenty different places.

'Why didn't you come in afore?' asked the man. 'You're getting too proud to own me afore company, are you? Lie down Bull's-eye, lie down!'

This command was accompanied with a kick which sent the animal to the other end of the room. He appeared well used to it, however; for he coiled himself up in a corner very quietly, without uttering a sound, and winking his ill-looking eyes twenty times in a minute, appeared to occupy himself with taking a survey of the apartment.

'What are you up to?—Ill-treating the boys, you covetous, avaricious, in-sa-ti-a-ble old fence?' said the young man, seating himself deliberately. 'I wonder they don't murder you! *I* would if I was them. If I'd been your 'prentice, I'd have done it long ago; and—no, I couldn't have sold you afterwards, for you're fit for nothing but keeping as a curiosity of ugliness in a glass bottle, and I suppose they don't blow glass bottles half large enough.'

'Hush! hush! Mr. Sikes,' said the old gentleman, trembling. 'Don't speak so loud!'

'None of your mistering,' replied the ruffian; 'you always mean mischief when you come to that. You know my name; out with it! I shan't disgrace it when the time comes.'

'Well, well, then—Bill,' said Fagin, with abject humility. 'You seem out of humour.'

'Perhaps I am,' replied Sikes. 'I should think *you* was rather out of sorts too, unless you mean as little harm when you throw pewter pots about as you do when you blab and -'

'Are you mad?' asked Fagin, catching the man by the sleeve, and pointing towards the boys.

Mr. Sikes contented himself with tying an imaginary knot under his left ear, and jerking his head over on the right shoulder—a piece of dumb show which the old gentleman appeared to understand perfectly. He then, in duplicitous terms, with which his whole conversation was plentifully besprinkled, but which would be quite unintelligible if they were recorded here, demanded a glass of liquor.

'And mind you don't poison it,' said Mr. Sikes, laying his hat upon the table.

This was said in jest; but if the speaker could have seen the evil leer with which Fagin bit his pale lip as he turned round to the cupboard, he might have thought the caution not wholly unnecessary, or the wish (at all events) to improve upon the distiller's ingenuity not very far from the old gentleman's merry heart.

After swallowing two or three glasses of spirits, Mr. Sikes condescended to take some notice of the young gentlemen; which gracious act led to a conversation in which the cause and manner of Oliver's capture were circumstantially detailed, with such alterations and improvements on the truth that to the Dodger appeared to be most advisable under the circumstances.

'I'm afraid,' said the old man, 'that he may say something which will get us into trouble.'

'That's very likely,' returned Sikes, with a malicious grin. 'You're blowed upon, Fagin.'

'And I'm afraid, you see, added Fagin, speaking as if he had not noticed the interruption; and regarding the other closely as he did so—'I'm afraid that, if the game was up with us, it might be up with a good many more, and that it would come out rather worse for you than it would for me, my dear.'

The man started, and turned fiercely round upon Fagin. But the old gentleman's shoulders were shrugged up to his ears, and his eyes were vacantly staring at the opposite wall.

There was a long pause. Every member of the respectable coterie appeared plunged in his own reflections, not excepting the dog, who, by a certain malicious licking of his lips, seemed to be meditating an attack upon the legs of the first lady or gentleman he might encounter in the streets when he went out.

'Somebody must find out wot's been done by the police,' said Mr. Sikes in a much lower tone than he had taken since he came in.

The old miser nodded assent.

'If he hasn't peached, and is committed, there's no fear till he comes out again,' said Mr. Sikes, 'and then he must be taken care of. You must get hold of him somehow.'

Again Fagin nodded.

The prudence of this line of action, indeed, was obvious; but, unfortunately, there was one very strong objection to its being adopted. This was that the Dodger, and Charley Bates, and Fagin, and Mr. William Sikes, happened, one and all, to entertain a most violent and deeply-rooted antipathy to going near a police station on any ground or pretext whatever.

How long they might have sat and looked at each other in a state of uncertainty not the most pleasant of its kind, it is difficult to guess. It is not necessary to make any guesses on the subject, however; for the sudden entrance of two young ladies, whom Oliver had seen on a former occasion, caused the conversation to flow afresh.

'The very thing!' said Fagin. 'Betsy will go; won't you, my dear?'

'Where?' inquired the young lady.

'Only just up to the station, my dear,' said the old gentleman coaxingly.

It is due to the young lady to say that she did not positively affirm that she would not, but that she merely expressed an emphatic and earnest desire to be 'blessed' if she would; a polite and delicate evasion of the request, which shows the young lady to have been possessed of that natural good breeding which cannot bear to inflict upon a fellow-creature the pain of a direct and pointed refusal.

Fagin's countenance fell. He turned from this young lady, who was gaily, not to say gorgeously attired, in a red gown, green boots, and yellow barrettes in her curly hair, to the other female who was dressed in an equally becoming outfit.

'Nancy, my dear,' said the old man in a soothing manner, 'what do *you* say?'

'That it won't do; so it's no use a-trying it on, Fagin,' replied Nancy.

'What do you mean by that?' said Mr. Sikes, looking up in a surly manner.

'What I say, Bill,' replied the lady collectedly.

'Why, you're just the very person for it,' reasoned Mr. Sikes; 'nobody about here knows anything of you.'

'And as I don't want 'em to, neither,' replied Nancy, in the same composed manner, 'it's rather more no than yes with me, Bill.'

'She'll go, Fagin,' said Sikes.

'No, she won't, Fagin,' said Nancy.

'Yes, she will, Fagin,' said Sikes.

And Mr. Sikes was right. By dint of alternate threats, promises, and bribes, the lady in question was ultimately prevailed upon to undertake the commission. She was not, indeed, withheld by the same considerations as her agreeable friend; for, having recently moved into the neighborhood of Field Lane from the remote but genteel suburb of Ratcliffe, she was not under the same apprehension of being recognised by any of her numerous male acquaintances.

Accordingly, with a clean white apron tied over her gown, and her barrettes tucked up under a straw bonnet—both articles of dress being provided from Fagin's inexhaustible stock—Miss Nancy prepared to issue forth on her errand.

'Stop a minute, my dear,' said the old gentleman, producing a little covered basket. 'Carry that in one hand. It looks more respectable, my dear.'

'Give her a door-key to carry in her t'other one, Fagin,' said Sikes; 'it looks real and genuine like.'

'Yes, yes, my dear, so it does,' said Fagin, hanging a large front door key on the forefinger of the young lady's right hand. 'There; very good! Very good indeed, my dear!' said the old miser, rubbing his hands.

'Oh, my brother! My poor, dear, sweet, innocent little brother!' exclaimed Nancy, bursting into tears, and wringing the little basket and the front door key in an agony of distress. 'What has become of him! Where have they taken him to! Oh, do have pity and tell me what's been done with the dear boy, gentlemen; do, gentlemen, if you please, gentlemen!'

Having uttered those words in a most lamentable and heartbroken tone, to the immeasurable delight of her small audience, Miss Nancy paused, winked to the company, nodded smilingly round, and disappeared.

'Ah, she's a clever girl, my dears,' said Fagin, turning round to his young friends, and shaking his head gravely, as if in mute admonition to them to follow the bright example they had just beheld.

'She's an honour to her sex,' said Mr. Sikes, filling his glass, and smiting the table with his enormous fist. 'Here's her health, and wishing they was all like her!'

While these, and many other praises, were being passed on the accomplished Nancy, that young lady made the best of her way to the police station; whither, notwithstanding a little natural timidity consequent upon walking through the streets alone and unprotected, she arrived at the station in perfect safety shortly afterwards.

Entering by the back way, she tapped softly with the key at one of the cell-doors, and listened. There was no sound within; so she coughed and listened again. Still there was no reply; so she spoke.

'Nolly, dear?' murmured Nancy, in a gentle voice. 'Nolly?'

There was nobody inside but a miserable shoeless criminal, who had been taken up for playing the flute, and who, the offence against society having been clearly proved, had been very properly committed by Mr. Fang to the House of Correction for one month, with the appropriate and amusing remark that since he had so much breath to spare, it would be more wholesomely expended on the treadmill than in a musical instrument. He made no answer, being occupied mentally bewailing the loss of the flute, which had been confiscated for the use of the county; so Nancy passed on to the next cell, and knocked there.

'Well!' cried a faint and feeble voice.

'Is there a young boy here?' inquired Nancy, with a preliminary sob.

'No,' replied the voice; 'God forbid.'

This was a vagrant of sixty-five, who was going to prison for *not* playing the flute—or in other words, for begging in the streets, and doing nothing for his livelihood. In the next cell was another man, who was going to the same prison for hawking tin saucepans without license; thereby doing something for his living, in defiance of the Stamp Office.

But, as neither of these criminals answered to the name of Oliver, or knew anything about him, Nancy made straight up to a bluff officer in a striped waistcoat, and with the most heartfelt weeping and lamentations, rendered more piteous by a prompt and efficient use of the front door key and the little basket, demanded her own dear brother.

'I haven't got him, my dear,' said the officer.

'Where is he?' asked Nancy, in a distracted manner.

'Why, the gentleman's got him,' replied the officer.

'What gentleman? Oh, gracious heavens! What gentleman?' exclaimed Nancy.

In reply to this incoherent questioning, the officer informed the deeply affected sister that a boy had been taken ill in the station, and discharged in consequence of a witness having proved the robbery to have been committed by another boy, not in custody; and that the prosecutor had carried him away in an insensible condition to his own residence, of and concerning which all the informant knew was that it was somewhere in Pentonville, he having heard that place mentioned in the directions to the coachman.

In a dreadful state of doubt and uncertainty the agonised young woman staggered to the gate, and then, exchanging her faltering walk for a swift, steady run, returned by the most devious and complicated route she could think of to the domicile of the old miser.

Mr. Bill Sikes no sooner heard the account of the expedition delivered than he very hastily called up his white dog, and putting on his hat, expeditiously departed, without devoting any time to the formality of wishing the company a good morning.

'We must know where he is, my dears; he must be found,' said Fagin, greatly excited. 'Charley, do nothing but prowl about till you bring home some news of him! Nancy, my dear, I must have him found. I trust to you, my dear—to you and the Artful—for everything!' 'Stay, stay,' added the old man, unlocking a drawer with a shaking hand; 'there's money, my dears. I shall shut up this shop tonight. You'll know where to find me! Don't stop here a minute—not an instant, my dears!'

With these words, he pushed them from the room; and carefully double-locking and barring the door behind them, drew from its place of concealment the box which he had unintentionally disclosed to Oliver. Then he hastily proceeded to dispose of the watches and jewellery beneath his clothing.

A rap at the door startled him in this occupation. 'Who's there?' he cried in a shrill tone.

'Me!' replied the voice of the Dodger, through the keyhole.

'What now?' cried Fagin, impatiently.

'Is he to be kidnapped to the other ken, Nancy asks?' inquired the Dodger.

'Yes,' replied Fagin, 'wherever she lays hands on him. Find him, find him out, that's all. I shall know what to do next; never fear.'

The boy murmured a reply of intelligence, and hurried downstairs after his companions.

'He has not peached so far,' said the old man as he pursued his occupation. 'If he means to blab against us, we may stop his mouth yet.'

Chapter 14
Mr. Griffith

Oliver, under the kind ministrations of Mrs. Bedwin, began to recover from his illness. As the old lady had been so kind to him in his illness, he endeavoured to listen attentively to a great many stories she told him, about an amiable and handsome daughter of hers, who was married to an amiable and handsome man, and lived in the country; and about a son, who was clerk to a merchant in the West Indies; and who was also such a good young man, and wrote such dutiful letters home four times a year, that it brought tears to her eyes to talk about them. When the old lady had expounded a long time on the excellences of her children, and the merits of her good kind husband besides, who had been dead and gone, poor dear soul! just six-and-twenty years, it was time to have tea. After tea she began to teach Oliver cribbage, which he learnt as quickly as she could teach, and at which game they played, with great interest and gravity, until it was time for Oliver to have some warm wine and water, with a slice of dry toast, and then to go to bed.

They were happy days those of Oliver's recovery. Everything was so quiet, and neat, and orderly, everybody so kind and gentle, that after the noise and turbulence in the midst of which he had always lived, it seemed like Heaven itself. He was no sooner strong enough to put his clothes on properly, than Mr. Brownlow caused a complete new suit, and a new cap, and a new pair of shoes, to be provided for him. As Oliver was told that he might do what he liked with the old clothes, he gave them to a servant who had been very kind to him, and asked her to sell them to a rag dealer, and keep the money for herself. This she very readily did; and, as Oliver looked out of the parlour window, and saw the peddler roll them up into his bag and walk away, he felt quite delighted to think that they were safely gone, and that there was now no possible danger of his ever being able to wear them again. They were sad rags, to tell the truth; and Oliver had never had a new suit before.

One evening about a week after Mr. Brownlow's last visit, as Oliver was sitting and talking with Mrs. Bedwin, there came a message down from that gentleman that, if Oliver Twist felt well enough, he should like to see him in his study, and talk to him a little while.

'Bless us, and save us! Wash your face and hands, and let me part your hair nicely for you, child,' said Mrs. Bedwin. 'Dear heart alive! If we had known he would have asked for you, we would have put you in a clean shirt, and made you as smart as a new sixpence!'

Oliver did as the old lady bade him. Although she lamented grievously, meanwhile, that there was not even time to iron his shirt-collar; he looked so handsome, despite his lacking that important personal advantage, that she went so far as to say, looking at him with great complacency from head to foot, that she really didn't think it would have been possible, on the longest notice, to have made much difference in him for the better.

Thus encouraged, Oliver tapped at the study door. On Mr. Brownlow calling for him to come in, he found himself in a back room, quite full of books, with a window looking upon some pleasant little gardens. There was a table drawn up before the window, at which Mr. Brownlow was seated reading. When he saw Oliver, he pushed the book away from him, and told him to come to the table and sit down. Oliver complied, marvelling where the people could be found to read such a great number of books as seemed to have been written to make the world wiser; which is still a marvel to more experienced people than Oliver Twist every day of their lives.

'There are a good many books, are there not, my boy?' said Mr. Brownlow, observing the curiosity with which Oliver surveyed the shelves that reached from the floor to the ceiling.

'A great number, sir,' replied Oliver. 'I never saw so many.'

'You shall read them, if you behave well,' said the old gentleman kindly, 'and you will like that better than looking at the outsides—that is, in some cases, because there *are* books of which the backs and covers are by far the best parts.'

'I suppose they are those heavy ones, sir,' said Oliver, pointing to some large quartos with a good deal of gilding about the binding.

'Not always those,' said the old gentleman, smiling. 'There are other equally heavy ones, though of a much smaller size. How would you like to grow up to be a clever man, and write books, eh?'

'I think I would rather read them, sir,' replied Oliver, cautiously.

'What! wouldn't you like to be a book-writer?' said the old gentleman.

Oliver considered a little while; and at last said that he thought that it would be a much better thing to be a book-seller; upon which the old gentleman laughed heartily, and declared he had said a very good thing; which Oliver felt glad to have done, though he by no means knew what it was.

'Well, well,' said the old gentleman, composing his features. 'Don't be afraid! We won't make an author of you, not while there's an honest trade to be learnt, or brick-making to turn to.'

'Thank you, sir,' said Oliver. At the earnest manner of his reply, the old gentleman laughed again, and said something about a curious instinct, which Oliver, not understanding, paid no very great attention to.

'Now,' said Mr. Brownlow, speaking if possible in a kinder, but at the same time in a much more serious manner, than Oliver had ever known him to assume yet, 'I want you to pay great attention, my boy, to what I am going to say. I shall talk to you without any reserve, because I am sure you are as well able to understand me as many older persons would be.'

'Oh, don't tell you are going to send me away, sir, pray!' exclaimed Oliver, alarmed at the serious tone of the old gentleman's commencement! 'Don't turn me out-of-doors to wander in the streets again. Let me stay here and be a servant. Please don't send me back to the wretched place I came from, sir!'

'My dear child,' said the old gentleman, moved by the sincerity of Oliver's sudden appeal, 'you need not be afraid of my deserting you, unless you give me cause.'

'I never, never will, sir,' interposed Oliver.

'I hope not,' rejoined the old gentleman. 'I do not think you ever will. I have been deceived, before, by those whom I have endeavoured to benefit; but I feel strongly disposed to trust you, nevertheless; and I am more interested in your behalf than I can well account for, even to myself. The persons on whom I have bestowed my dearest love lie deep in their graves; but, although the happiness and delight of my life lie buried there too, I have not made a coffin of my heart, and sealed it up forever from my best affections. Deep affliction has but strengthened and refined them.'

As the old gentleman said this in a low voice, more to himself than to his young companion, and as he remained silent for a short time afterwards, Oliver sat quite still.

'Well, well!' said the old gentleman at length, in a more cheerful tone, 'I only say this because you have a young heart; and knowing that I have suffered great pain and sorrow, you will be more careful, perhaps, not to wound me again. You say you are an orphan, without a friend in the world; all the inquiries I have been able to make, confirm the statement. Let me hear your story—where you come from, who brought you up, and how you got into the company in which I found you. Speak the truth, and you shall not be friendless while I live.'

Oliver's fears checked, he spoke at length, holding little back. He related how he had been brought up at the farm, returned to the workhouse by Mr. Bumble, nearly indentured to Mr. Gamfield the chimney-sweep, indentured to Mr. Sowerberry the undertaker, making his escape, and, finally, being taken in by a jolly bunch of rogues and thieves. Mr. Brownlow didn't inquire into the identity or whereabouts of the rogues and thieves and Oliver didn't feel an immediate need to expound further on the subject.

'Remarkable story!' exclaimed Mr. Brownlow, after Oliver stopped reminiscing. 'Remarkable!'

'I do hope you believe me,' said Oliver. 'You have been so very good to me, I wouldn't fib to you.'

'I expect not,' replied Mr. Brownlow.

Oliver sat mute, feeling rather like an empty vessel, having poured out all of his thoughts and feelings.

'I know what,' Mr. Brownlow continued, 'you could use, I dare say, a little exercise. I would like to take you to meet my good friend and neighbour Mr. Griffith.'

Mr. Brownlow donned suitable visiting clothes and, soon, he and Oliver were out-of-doors walking down the street, around the corner, and through a gate onto the grounds of another grand house. Mr. Brownlow knocked twice sharply on the large front door with the knob of his bamboo cane and then waited patiently. Presently the door opened, and two old long-haired dogs and a middle-aged man servant appeared.

'Good afternoon, Mr. Giles,' said Mr. Brownlow. 'Are there any muffins in the house? My little friend and I have come for tea.'

'Yes, of course, Mr. Brownlow. He's in the library.' replied Mr. Giles. 'I shall announce your arrival and send tea up.'

'Is he coming up?' bellowed a voice from somewhere up the stairs, 'or must I come down?'

'Yes, sir,' replied Mr. Giles, as loudly as he could without actually shouting, 'or, perhaps, no, sir. He asked if there were any muffins in the house. Shall I send tea up with Mr. Brittles?'

'Yes, of course,' replied the voice.

Mr. Brownlow smiled and, turning to Oliver, said that Mr. Griffith was an old friend of his, and that he must not mind his being a little rough in his manners; for he was a worthy creature at bottom, as he had reason to know.

As Mr. Brownlow and Oliver proceeded down the front hallway to the stairs, Oliver stopped to look about at all of the portraits that hung upon the walls.

'Is Mr. Griffith an artist, sir?' inquired Oliver.

'Oh, no,' replied Mr. Brownlow, with a smile. 'He has no talent for painting that I am aware of. He commissioned these portraits of his wife and children.'

'They are lovely people,' observed Oliver.

'Yes, they certainly were,' replied Mr. Brownlow. 'Sadly, they have all died. Like myself, Mr. Griffith has outlived his wife and children.'

Mr. Brownlow and Oliver continued up the stairs and into a large room occupied by a stout old gentleman, rather lame in one leg, supporting himself with a sturdy cane. He was dressed in a blue coat, striped waistcoat, tan-coloured breeches, and gaiters. A pleated shirt frill stuck out from his waistcoat; and a very long steel watch-chain, with nothing but a key at the end, dangled loosely below it. The ends of his white neckerchief were twisted into a ball about the size of an orange. A large broad-brimmed white hat, with the sides turned up with green, sat on the table beside him. The variety of shapes into which his countenance twisted defy description. He had a manner of screwing his head on one side when he spoke; and of looking out of the corners of his eyes at the same time, which irresistibly reminded the beholder of a parrot. In this attitude, he fixed himself, the moment Mr. Brownlow and Oliver made their appearance.

Holding out a small piece of orange peel at arm's length, Mr. Griffith exclaimed, in a growling, discontented voice:

'Look here! Do you see this? Isn't it a most wonderful and extraordinary thing that I can't make my way from one room to the next but I find a piece of this poor surgeon's friend in the hall? I've been lamed by orange peel once, and I know orange peel will be my death, sir! The doctor called upon me not half an hour ago, and, much to his disappointment I am sure, claimed me to be fit as a hippopotamus. He dropped it where I might tread upon it, or I'll be content to eat my hat.'

This was the handsome offer with which Mr. Griffith backed and confirmed nearly every assertion he made; and it was the more singular in his case because, even admitting for the sake of argument the possibility of changing fashion producing edible hats, in the event of one being so disposed, Mr. Griffith's hat, being proportional in size to his generously proportioned head, was a particularly large one. Even a most optimistic man could hardly entertain the hope of being able to get through it at a sitting. His hat covered the better part of the table on which it sat.

'I'll eat my hat, sir,' repeated Mr. Griffith, striking his cane upon the ground.—'Hallo! what's that!' looking at Oliver, and retreating a pace or two.

'This is young Oliver Twist, whom we were speaking about earlier,' said Mr. Brownlow.

Oliver bowed.

'You don't mean to say that's the boy who had the fever, I hope?' said Mr. Griffith, recoiling a little more. 'Wait a minute! Don't speak! Stop!'

continued Mr. Griffith, abruptly losing all dread of the fever in his triumph at the discovery; 'that's the boy who had the orange! If that's not the boy, sir, who had the orange, and threw this bit of peel upon the floor, I'll eat my hat and his too.'

'No, no, he has not had any such opportunity,' said Mr. Brownlow, laughing. 'Come! Put the orange peel to rest; and speak to my young friend.'

'I feel strongly on this subject, sir,' said the irritable old gentleman. 'There's always more or less orange peel on the pavement in our street, and I *know* it's put there by the surgeon's boy at the corner. A young woman stumbled over a bit last night, and fell against my garden railings. Directly, when she got up, I saw her look towards his infernal red lamp advertising his surgery. "Don't go to him," I called out of the window, "he's an assassin! A mantrap!" So he is. If he is not -' Here the irascible old gentleman gave a great knock on the ground with his cane; which was always understood, by his friends, to imply the customary offer, whenever it was not expressed in words. Then, still keeping his cane in his hand, he sat down and squinted at Oliver, who, seeing that he was the object of close inspection, coloured, and bowed again.

'That's the boy, is it?' said Mr. Griffith, at length.

'That's the boy,' confirmed Mr. Brownlow.

'How are you, boy?' asked Mr. Griffith.

'A great deal better, thank you, sir,' replied Oliver.

At this juncture, Brownlow suggested to Oliver that he go downstairs and assist Mr. Giles and Mr. Brittles with the tea and muffins; which task he happily agreed to perform.

'He reminds me of someone, but I cannot think of whom,' stated Mr. Brownlow. 'He is a nice-looking boy, is he not?'

'I don't know,' replied Mr. Griffith, pettishly.

'Don't know?'

'No; I don't know. I never see any difference in boys. I only know two sorts of boys; scrawny boys and beef-faced boys.'

'And which is Oliver?'

'Scrawny. I know a friend who has a beef-faced boy—a fine boy, they call him—with a round head and red cheeks, and glaring eyes; a horrid boy; with a body and limbs that appear to be swelling out of the seams of his clothes; with the voice of a ship's pilot and the appetite of a wolf. I know him! The wretch!'

'Come,' said Mr. Brownlow, 'these are not the characteristics of young Oliver Twist; so he needn't excite your wrath.'

'They are not,' replied Mr. Griffith. 'He may have worse.'

Here, Mr. Brownlow harrumphed; which appeared to afford Mr. Griffith the most exquisite delight.

'He may have worse, I say,' repeated Mr. Griffith. 'Where does he come from? Who is he? What is he? He has had a fever. What of that? Fevers are not peculiar to good people; are they? Bad people have fevers sometimes; haven't they, eh? I knew a man who was hung in Jamaica for murdering his master. He had had a fever six times; he wasn't recommended to mercy on that account. Pooh! Nonsense!'

Now, the fact was, that in the inmost recesses of his own heart, Mr. Griffith was strongly disposed to admit that Oliver's appearance and manner were unusually prepossessing; but he had a strong appetite for contradiction, sharpened on this occasion by the finding of the orange peel; and, inwardly determining that no man should dictate to him whether a boy was good looking or not, he had resolved, from the first, to oppose his friend. When Mr. Brownlow admitted that on no one point of inquiry could he yet return a satisfactory answer, and that he had postponed any investigation into Oliver's previous history; Mr. Griffith chuckled maliciously. And he demanded, with a sneer, whether Mrs. Bedwin was in the habit of counting the silverware at night; because, if she didn't find a tablespoon or two missing some sunshiny morning, why, he would be content to—and so forth.

All this, Mr. Brownlow, although himself somewhat of an impetuous gentleman, knowing his friend's peculiarities, bore with great good humour. He was pleased, however, when Oliver returned accompanied by a younger man servant, Mr. Brittles, to serve tea. Mr. Brownlow graciously expressed his entire approval of the muffins and turned the conversation towards the price of wool and other such weighty matters. Oliver began to feel more at his ease than he had earlier under the fierce old gentleman's glare. Oliver's ease, however, was soon punctured by Mr. Griffith posing the following inquiry of Mr. Brownlow:

'And when are you going to determine at full, the true, and particular account of the life and adventures of Oliver Twist?' asked Griffith of Mr. Brownlow, at the conclusion of the meal; looking sideways at Oliver, as he resumed his subject.

'Soon,' replied Mr. Brownlow. 'I am making arrangements. Your narrative will be corroborated, won't it Oliver'

'Yes, sir,' replied Oliver. He answered with some hesitation, because he was unsettled by Mr. Griffith's looking so hard at him.

'I'll tell you what,' whispered that gentleman to Mr. Brownlow; 'his unlikely tale will not stand up to scrutiny. I saw him hesitate. He is deceiving you, my good friend.'

'I'll swear he is not,' replied Mr. Brownlow, warmly.

'If he is not,' said Mr. Griffith, 'I'll -' and down went the cane.

'I'll answer for that boy's truth with my life!' said Mr. Brownlow, knocking the table.

'And I for his falsehood with my hat!' rejoined Mr. Griffith, knocking the table also.

'We shall see,' said Mr. Brownlow, checking his rising anger.

'We will,' replied Mr. Griffith, with a provoking smile; 'we will.'

As fate would have it, Mr. Giles chanced to bring in, at this moment, a small parcel of books, which Mr. Griffith had that morning requested from the identical same bookstall keeper who has already figured in this history. Having laid them on the table, he prepared to leave the room.

'Stop the book peddler, Mr. Giles!' said Griffith. 'There is something to go back.'

'He has gone, sir,' replied Mr. Giles.

'Call after him,' said Mr. Griffith. 'It's particular. He is a poor man, and they are not yet paid for. There are some books to be taken back, too.'

The front door was opened. Oliver ran one way, and Mr. Brittles ran another, and Mr. Giles stood on the step and yelled for the book seller; but there was no one in sight. Shortly, both Oliver and Mr. Brittles returned, in a breathless state, to report that there were no tidings of him.

'Dear me, I am very sorry for that,' exclaimed Mr. Griffith. 'I particularly wished for those books to be returned tonight.'

'Send Oliver with them,' suggested Mr. Brownlow, 'he will be sure to deliver them safely, I'm sure.'

'Yes; do let me take them, if you please, sir,' said Oliver, wanting to earn Mr. Griffith's trust. 'I'll run all the way, sir.'

Mr. Griffith was about to say that he would not trust Oliver on any account when, with a most malicious smile, he determined he should employ him on this small mission as an opportune means of proving the justice of his suspicions.

'You *shall* go, my dear,' said the old gentleman. 'The books are on a chair by my table. Fetch them down.'

Oliver, delighted to be of use, brought down the books under his arm in a great bustle, and waited, cap in hand, to hear what message he was to take.

'You are to say,' said Mr. Griffith, glancing steadily at Brownlow—'you are to say that you have brought those books back; and that you have come to pay the four pound ten I owe him. This is a five-pound note, so you will have to bring me back ten shillings change.'

'I won't be ten minutes, sir,' said Oliver, eagerly. Having buttoned up the banknote in his jacket pocket, and placed the books carefully under his arm, he made a respectful bow, and left the room. Mr. Giles followed him to the front door, giving him many directions about the nearest way, and the name of the bookseller, and the name of the street, all of which Oliver said he clearly understood. Having superadded many injunctions to be sure and not dilly dally, at length he permitted Oliver to depart.

'Let me see; he'll be back in twenty minutes, at the longest,' said Mr. Brownlow, pulling out his watch, and placing it on the table. 'It will be dark by that time.'

'Oh! you really expect him to come back, do you?' queried Mr. Griffith.

'Don't you?' replied Mr. Brownlow, smiling.

The spirit of contradiction was strong in Mr. Griffith's breast, at the moment; and it was rendered stronger by his friend's confident smile.

'No,' he said, smiting the table with his fist, 'I do not. The boy has a new suit of clothes on his back, a set of valuable books under his arm, and a five pound note in his pocket. He'll join his old friends the thieves, and laugh at us. If ever that boy returns to this house, sir, I'll eat my hat.'

With these words he drew his chair closer to the table; and there the two friends sat, in silent expectation, with the watch between them.

It is worthy of remark, as illustrating the importance we attach to our own judgments, and the pride with which we put forth our most rash and hasty conclusions, that, although Mr. Griffith had no desire to see Mr. Brownlow wounded, and would have been sincerely sorry to see his respected friend duped and deceived, he really did, most earnestly and strongly, hope at that moment that Oliver Twist might not come back.

It grew so dark that the figures on the dial-plate were scarcely discernible; but there the two old gentlemen continued to sit, in silence, with the watch between them.

Chapter 15
The Three Cripples

In the obscure parlour of a low public-house: The Three Cripples, or rather the Cripples, which was the name by which the establishment was familiarly known to its patrons; in the filthiest part of Little Saffron Hill—a dark and gloomy den, where a flaring gas-light burnt all day during the wintertime; and where no ray of sun ever shone in the summer—there sat, brooding over a little pewter measure and a small glass, strongly impregnated with the smell of liquor, a man in a velveteen coat, khaki shorts, half-boots and stockings, whom, even by that dim light no experienced agent of the police would have hesitated to recognise as Mr. William Sikes. At his feet sat his white-coated, red-eyed dog, who occupied himself, alternately, in winking at his master with both eyes at the same time, and in licking a large fresh cut on one side of his mouth which appeared to be the result of some recent conflict.

'Keep quiet, you varmint! Keep quiet!' said Mr. Sikes, suddenly breaking silence. Whether his meditations were so intense as to be disturbed by the dog's winking, or whether his feelings were so wrought upon by his reflections that they required all the relief derivable from kicking an unoffending animal to allay them, is matter for argument and consideration. Whatever was the cause, the effect was a kick and a curse bestowed upon the dog simultaneously.

Dogs are not generally apt to revenge injuries inflicted upon them by their masters; but Mr. Sikes's dog, having faults of temper in common with his owner, and labouring, perhaps, at this moment, under a powerful sense of injury, made no more ado but at once fixed his teeth in one of the half-boots. Having given it a hearty shake, he retired, growling, under a bench; just escaping the pewter measure which Mr. Sikes levelled at his head.

'You would, would you?' said Sikes, seizing a poker in one hand, and deliberately opening with the other a large clasp-knife, which he drew from his pocket. 'Come here, you born devil! Come here! D'ye hear?'

The dog no doubt heard, because Mr. Sikes spoke in the very harshest key of a very harsh voice; but appearing to entertain some unaccountable objection to having his throat cut, he remained where he was, and growled more fiercely than before, at the same time grasping the end of the poker between his teeth and biting at it like a wild beast.

This resistance only infuriated Mr. Sikes the more, who, dropping on his knees, began to assail the animal most furiously. As the dog jumped from right to left, and from left to right, snapping, growling, and barking;

the man thrust, and swore, and struck, and blasphemed. The struggle was reaching a most critical point for one or other when the door suddenly opened, and the dog darted out, leaving Bill Sikes with the poker and the clasp-knife in his hands.

There must always be two parties to a quarrel, says the old adage. Mr. Sikes, being disappointed in the dog's lack of participation, at once transferred his share in the quarrel to the new comer.

'What the devil do you come in-between me and my dog for?' complained Sikes, with a fierce gesture.

'I didn't know, my dear, I didn't know,' replied Fagin, humbly—for the old miser was the new comer.

'Didn't know, you white-livered thief!' growled Sikes. 'Couldn't you hear the noise?'

'Not a sound of it, as I'm a living man, Bill,' replied Fagin.

'Oh no! You hear nothing, you don't,' retorted Sikes, with a fierce sneer. 'Sneaking in and out, so as nobody hears how you come or go! I wish you had been the dog, Fagin, half a minute ago.'

'Why?' inquired the old man with a forced smile.

'Cause the Government, as cares for the lives of such men as you, who hasn't half the pluck of curs, lets a man kill a dog how he likes,' replied Sikes, shutting up the knife with a very expressive look; 'that's why.'

Fagin rubbed his hands, and, sitting down at the table, affected to laugh at the pleasantry of his friend. He was obviously very ill at ease, however.

'Grin away,' said Sikes, replacing the poker, and surveying him with savage contempt—'grin away. You'll never have the laugh at me, though, unless it's behind a nightcap. I've got the upper hand over you, Fagin; and, damn me, I'll keep it. There! If I go, you go; so take care of me.'

'Well, well, my dear,' said the old man, 'I know all that; we—we—have a mutual interest, Bill,—a mutual interest.'

'Humph,' said Sikes, as if he thought the interest lay rather more on Fagin's side than on his. 'Well, what have you got to say to me?'

'It's all passed safe through the melting-pot,' replied Fagin, 'and this is your share. It's rather more than it ought to be, my dear; but as I know you'll do me a good turn another time, and -'

'Stow that humbug,' interposed the robber, impatiently. 'Where is it? Hand over!'

'Yes, yes, Bill; give me time, give me time,' replied Fagin, soothingly. 'Here it is! All safe!' As he spoke, he drew forth an old cotton handkerchief from his breast pocket, and, untying a large knot in one corner, produced a small brown paper packet. Sikes, snatching it from him, hastily opened it, and proceeded to count the sovereigns it contained.

'This is all, is it?' inquired Sikes.

'All,' confirmed Fagin.

'You haven't opened the parcel and swallowed one or two as you come along, have you?' inquired Sikes, suspiciously. 'Don't put on an injured look at the question; you've done it many a time. Jerk the tinkler.'

These words, in plain English, conveyed an injunction to ring the bell. It was answered by a young man, a nephew of Fagin's, who served as a waiter. While still a young man, he was nearly as vile and repulsive in appearance as his uncle.

Bill Sikes merely pointed to the empty measure. Fagin's nephew, perfectly understanding the hint, retired to fill it—previously exchanging a remarkable look with Fagin, who raised his eyes for an instant, as if in expectation of it, and shook his head in reply so slightly that the action would have been almost imperceptible to an observant third person. It was lost upon Sikes, who was stooping at the moment to tie the bootlace which the dog had torn. Possibly, if he had observed the brief interchange of signals, he might have thought that it boded no good to him.

'Is anybody here, Barney?' inquired Fagin of his nephew; speaking, now that that Sikes was looking on, without raising his eyes from the ground.

'Dot a soul,' replied Barney; whose words, whether they came from the heart or not, made their way through his nose.

'Nobody?' inquired Fagin, in a tone of surprise, which perhaps might mean that Barney was at liberty to tell the truth.

'Dobody, but Biss Dadsy,' replied Barney.

'Nancy!' exclaimed Sikes. 'Where? Strike me blind, if I don't honour that 'ere girl, for her native talents.'

'She's bid havid a plate of boiled beef id the bar,' replied Barney.

'Send her here,' said Sikes, pouring out a glass of liquor. 'Send her here.'

Barney looked timidly at Fagin, as if for permission. As his uncle remaining silent, not lifting his eyes from the ground, he retired, and presently returned, ushering in Nancy, who was decorated with the bonnet, apron, basket, and front door key, complete.

'You're on the scent, are you, Nancy?' inquired Sikes, proffering the glass.

'Yes, I am, Bill,' replied the young lady, disposing of its contents; 'and tired enough of it I am, too. The young brat's been ill and confined to bed; and -'

'Ah, Nancy, dear!' said Fagin, looking up.

Now, whether a peculiar contraction of Fagin's eyebrows, and a half-closing of his deeply set eyes, warned Miss Nancy that she was disposed to be too communicative, is not a matter of much importance. The fact is all we need care for here; and the fact is that she suddenly checked herself, and, with several gracious smiles upon Mr. Sikes, turned the conversation to other matters. In about ten minutes' time, Mr. Fagin was seized with a fit of coughing; upon which Nancy pulled her shawl over her shoulders and declared that it was time to go. Mr. Sikes, finding that he was walking a short part of her way himself, expressed his intention of accompanying her. They went away together followed, at a little distant, by the dog who slunk out of a backyard as soon as his master was out of sight.

Fagin thrust his head out of the room door once Sikes had left it, looked after him as he walked up the dark passage. He shook his clenched fist, muttered a deep curse, and then, with a horrible grin, reseated himself at the table where he was soon deeply absorbed in the interesting pages of the local tabloid, the *Hue-and-Cry*.

Meanwhile, Oliver, little dreaming that he was within so very short a distance of merry old Fagin, was on his way to the bookstall. When he got into Clerkenwell, he accidently turned down a by-street which was not exactly along his way; but not discovering his mistake until he had got half-way down it, and knowing it must lead in the right direction, he did not think it worthwhile to turn back, and so marched on, as quickly as he could, with the books under his arm.

He was walking along, thinking how happy and contented he ought to feel, and how much he would give for only one look at poor little Ricky—who, starved and beaten, might be expiring at that very moment—when he was startled by a young woman shouting very loudly, 'Oh, my dear brother!' He had hardly looked up, to see what the matter was, when he was stopped by having a pair of arms thrown tight round him.

'Don't,' cried Oliver, struggling. 'Let go of me. Who is it? What are you stopping me for?'

The only reply to this was a great number of loud lamentations from the young woman who had embraced him, and who had a little basket and a front door key in her hand.

'Oh my gracious!' said the young woman, 'I have found him! Oh! Oliver! Oliver! Oh you naughty boy, to make me suffer such distress on your account! Come home, dear—come. Oh, I've found him! Thank gracious goodness heavens, I've found him!' With these incoherent exclamations the young woman burst into another fit of crying, and got so dreadfully hysterical that a couple of women who came up at the moment asked a butcher's boy with a shiny head of hair, anointed with suet, who was also looking on, whether he didn't think he had better run for the doctor. To which the butcher's boy, who appeared to be of a lounging, not to say indolent disposition, replied that he thought not.

'Oh, no, no, never mind,' said the young woman, grasping Oliver's hand—'I'm better now. Come home directly, you cruel boy! Come!'

'What's the matter, ma'am?' inquired one of the women.

'Oh, ma'am,' replied the young woman, 'he ran away, near a month ago, from his parents, who are hard-working and respectable people, and went and joined a set of thieves and bad characters, and almost broke his mother's heart.'

'Young wretch!' said one woman.

'Go home—do, you little brute,' said the other.

'I'm not,' replied Oliver, greatly alarmed. 'I don't know her. I haven't any sister, or father and mother either. I'm an orphan; I live at Pentonville.'

'Oh, only hear him, how he braves it out!' cried the young woman.

'Why, it's Nancy!' exclaimed Oliver, who now saw her face for the first time, and started back in irrepressible astonishment.

'You see he knows me!' cried Nancy, appealing to the bystanders. 'He can't help himself. Make him come home, there's good people, or he'll kill his dear mother and father, and break my heart!'

'What the devil's this?' said a man, bursting out of a beer shop, with a white dog at his heels; 'young Oliver! Come home to your poor mother, you young dog! Come home directly.'

'Let me go!' demanded Oliver. 'I don't belong to them. I don't know them. Help me!' called Oliver to the onlookers, struggling in the man's powerful grasp.

'Help you!' repeated the man. 'Yes; I'll help you, you young rascal! What books are these? You've been a-stealing 'em, have you? Give 'em here.' With these words, the man tore the volumes from his grasp, and struck him on the head.

'That's right!' cried an onlooker, from a garret window. 'That's the only way of bringing him to his senses!'

'To be sure!' cried a sleepy-faced carpenter, casting an approving look at the garret window.

'It'll do him good!' said the two women.

'And he shall have it, too!' rejoined the man, administering another blow, and seizing Oliver by the collar. 'Come on, you young villain! Here, Bull's-eye! mind him, boy! Mind him!'

Weak with recent illness; stupefied by the blows and the suddenness of the attack, terrified by the fierce growling of the dog, and the brutality of the man, and overpowered by the conviction of the bystanders that he really was the hardened little wretch he was described to be—what could one young child do? Darkness had set in; it was a low neighborhood; no help was near; resistance was futile. In another moment he was dragged into a labyrinth of dark narrow courts, and was forced along them at a pace which rendered the few shouts he dared to give utterance to, wholly unintelligible. It was of little moment, indeed, whether they were intelligible or no, for there was nobody to care for them, had they been ever so plain.

The gas-lamps were lighted; Mrs. Bedwin was waiting anxiously at the open door; the servant had run up the street twenty times to see if there were any traces of Oliver; and still the two old gentlemen sat perseveringly in the dark parlour, with the watch between them.

Chapter 16
Such a Jolly Game

The narrow streets and courts at length terminated in a large open space, scattered about which, were pens for beasts, and other indications of a cattle-market. Sikes slackened his pace when they reached this spot, the girl being quite unable to support any longer the rapid rate at which they had hitherto walked. Turning to Oliver, he roughly commanded him to take hold of Nancy's hand.

'Do you hear?' growled Sikes, as Oliver hesitated and looked round.

They were in a dark corner, quite out of the track of other pedestrians. Oliver saw, but too plainly, that resistance would be of no avail. He held out his hand, which Nancy clasped tight in hers.

'Give me the other,' said Sikes, seizing Oliver's unoccupied hand. 'Here, Bull's-eye!'

The dog looked up, and growled.

'See here, boy!' said Sikes, putting his other hand to Oliver's throat; 'if he speaks ever so soft a word, hold him! D'ye mind!'

The dog growled again; and, licking his lips, eyed Oliver as if he were anxious to attach himself to his windpipe without delay.

'He's as willing as a Christian, strike me blind if he isn't!' said Sikes, regarding the animal with a kind of grim and ferocious approval. 'Now, you know what you've got to expect, master, so call away as quick as you like; the dog will soon stop that game. Get on, young'un!'

Bull's-eye wagged his tail in acknowledgment of this unusually endearing form of speech, and giving vent to another admonitory growl for the benefit of Oliver, led the way onward.

It was Smithfield that they were crossing, although it might have been Grosvenor Square, for anything Oliver knew to the contrary. The night was dark and foggy. The lights in the shops could scarcely struggle through the heavy mist, which thickened every moment and shrouded the streets and houses in gloom, rendering the strange place still stranger in Oliver's eyes, and making his uncertainty the more dismal and depressing.

They had hurried on a few paces, when a deep church-bell struck the hour. With its first stroke, his two conductors stopped, and turned their heads in the direction whence the sound proceeded.

'Eight o' clock, Bill,' said Nancy, when the bell ceased.

'What's the good of telling me that? I can hear it, can't I?' replied Sikes.

'I wonder whether *they* can hear it,' said Nancy.

'Of course they can,' replied Sikes. 'It was Bartlemy time when I was pinched; and there warn't a penny trumpet in the fair as I couldn't hear the squeaking of. After I was locked up for the night, the row and din outside made the thundering old jail so silent, that I could almost have beat my brains out against the iron plates of the door.'

'Poor fellows!' said Nancy, who still had her face turned towards the quarter in which the bell had sounded. 'Oh, Bill, such fine young chaps as them!'

'Yes; that's all you women think of,' answered Sikes. 'Fine young chaps! Well, they're as good as dead, so it don't much matter.'

With this consolation, Mr. Sikes appeared to repress a rising tendency to jealousy; and, clasping Oliver's wrist more firmly, told him to step out again.

'Wait a minute!' said the girl. 'I wouldn't hurry by, if it was you that was coming out to be hung, the next time eight o'clock struck, Bill. I'd walk round and round the place till I dropped, if the snow was on the ground, and I hadn't a shawl to cover me.'

'And what good would that do?' inquired the unsentimental Mr. Sikes. 'Unless you could pitch over a file and twenty yards of good stout rope, you might as well be walking fifty mile off, or not walking at all, for all the good it would do me. Come on, and don't stand preaching there.'

The girl burst into a laugh, drew her shawl more closely round her, and they walked away. But Oliver felt her hand tremble, and looking up at her face as they passed a gas-lamp, saw that it had turned a deadly white.

They walked on, by little-frequented and dirty ways, for a full half-hour—meeting very few people, and those appearing, from their looks, to hold much the same position in society as Mr. Sikes himself. At length they turned into a very filthy narrow street, nearly full of old-clothes shops. The dog running forward, as if conscious that there was no further occasion for his keeping on guard, stopped before the door of a shop that was closed and apparently untenanted. The house was in a ruinous condition; and on the door was nailed a board, intimating that it was to let, which looked as if it had hung there for many years.

'All right,' cried Sikes, glancing cautiously about.

Nancy stopped below the shutters, and Oliver heard the sound of a bell. They crossed to the opposite side of the street, and stood for a few moments under a lamp. A noise, as if a sash window were gently raised, was heard, and soon afterwards the door softly opened. Mr. Sikes then seized the terrified boy by the collar with very little ceremony, and all four were quickly inside the house.

The passage was perfectly dark. They waited while the person who had let them in chained and barred the door.

'Anybody here?' inquired Sikes.

'No,' replied a voice, which Oliver thought he had heard before.

'Is the old 'un here?' asked the robber.

'Yes,' replied the voice, 'and precious down in the mouth he has been. Won't he be glad to see you! Oh, no!'

The style of this reply, as well as the voice which delivered it, was familiar to Oliver's ears; but it was impossible to distinguish even the form of the speaker in the darkness.

'Let's have a glimmer,' said Sikes, 'or we shall go breaking our necks, or treading on the dog. Look after your legs if you do! That's all.'

'Stand still a moment, and I'll get you one,' replied the voice. The receding footsteps of the speaker were heard; and, in another minute, the form of Mr. Jack Dawkins, otherwise the Artful Dodger, appeared. He bore in his right hand a tallow candle stuck at the end of a cleft stick.

The young gentleman frowned upon Oliver with an air of regret, but, turning away, beckoned the visitors to follow him down a flight of stairs. They crossed an empty kitchen; and, opening the door of a low earthy-smelling room, which seemed to have been built in a small back-yard, were received with a shout of laughter.

'Oh my! Oh my!' cried Master Charles Bates, from whose lungs the laughter had proceeded; 'here he is! oh, cry, here he is! Oh, Fagin, look at him! Fagin, do look at him! I can't bear it; it is such a jolly game, I can't bear it. Hold me, somebody, while I laugh it out.'

With this irrepressible ebullition of mirth, Master Bates laid himself flat on the floor, and kicked convulsively for five minutes in an ecstasy of facetious joy. Then jumping to his feet, he snatched the candle from the Dodger, and, advancing to Oliver, viewed him round and round; while Fagin, taking off his nightcap, made a great number of low bows to the bewildered boy. The Artful, meantime, was in a rather taciturn disposition; and, despite the obvious hilarity of the situation that so gripped Charley, not much disposed to gave way to merriment.

'Look at his togs, Fagin!' said Charley, putting the light so close to his new jacket as nearly to set him on fire. 'Look at his togs—superfine cloth, and the heavy-swell cut! Oh, my eye, what a game! And his books, too! Nothing but a gentleman, Fagin!' Charley began to rifle through Oliver's pockets with steady diligence.

'Delighted to see you looking so well, my dear,' said the old man, bowing with mock humility. 'The Artful shall give you another suit, my dear, for fear you should spoil that Sunday one. Why didn't you write, my dear, and say you were coming? We'd have got something warm for supper.'

At this, Master Bates roared again—so loud, that Fagin himself relaxed, and even Sikes smiled; but as Charley drew forth the five pound note at that instant, it is doubtful whether it was the sally or the discovery that awakened his merriment.

'Hallo, what's that?' inquired Sikes, stepping forward as the old miser seized the note. 'That's mine, Fagin.'

'No, no, my dear,' said Fagin. 'Mine, Bill, mine. You shall have the books.'

'If that ain't mine!' said Bill Sikes, putting on his hat with a determined air, 'mine and Nancy's that is; I'll take the boy back again.'

Fagin started. Oliver started too, though for a very different cause; as he hoped that the dispute might really end in his being taken back.

'Come! Hand over, will you?' said Sikes.

'This is hardly fair, Bill—hardly fair, is it, Nancy?' inquired the old gentleman.

'Fair, or not fair,' retorted Sikes, 'hand over, I tell you! Do you think Nancy and me has got nothing else to do with our precious time but to spend it in scouting after, and kidnapping, every young boy as gets grabbed through you? Give it here, you avaricious old skeleton, give it here!'

With this gentle remonstrance Mr. Sikes plucked the note from between Fagin's finger and thumb; and looking the old man coolly in the face, folded it up small, and tied it in his neckerchief.

'That's for our share of the trouble,' said Sikes; 'and not half enough, neither. You may keep the books, if you're fond of reading. If you ain't, sell 'em.'

'They're very pretty,' said Charley Bates, who, with sundry grimaces, had been affecting to read one of the volumes in question; 'beautiful writing, isn't is, Oliver?' At sight of the dismayed look with which Oliver regarded his tormentors, Master Bates, who was blessed with a lively sense of the ludicrous, fell into another ecstasy, more boisterous than the first.

'They belong to the gentleman,' said Oliver, wringing his hands, 'the gentleman who took me into his house, and had me nursed, when I was near dying of the fever. Pray, send them back—send him back the books and money. Keep me here all my life long; but, pray, send them back. He'll think I stole them; the old lady, all of them will think I stole them. Keep me and send them back!'

'The boy's right,' remarked Fagin, looking covertly round, and knitting his shaggy eyebrows into a hard knot. 'You're right, Oliver, you're right; they *will* think you have stolen 'em. Ha! ha!' he chuckled, rubbing his hands, 'it couldn't have happened better if we *had* chosen our time!'

'Of course it couldn't,' replied Sikes; 'I know'd that directly. I seen him coming through Clerkenwell, with the books under his arm. It's all right enough. They're soft-hearted psalm-singers, or they wouldn't have taken him in at all; and they'll ask no questions after him, fearing they should be obliged to prosecute, and so get him lagged. He's safe enough.'

Oliver looked from one to the other while these words were being spoken, as if he were bewildered, but when Bill Sikes concluded he saw his chance: spying the open door, he tore wildly out of the room shouting for help, which made the bare old house echo to the roof.

'Keep back the dog, Bill!' cried Nancy, springing to the door and closing it, just after Fagin and his two pupils darted out in pursuit. 'Keep back the dog; he'll tear the boy to pieces.'

'Serve him right!' cried Sikes, struggling to disengage himself from the girl's grasp. 'Stand off from me, or I'll split your head against the wall.'

'I don't care for that, Bill, I don't care for that,' screamed the girl, struggling violently with the man; 'the child shan't be torn down by the dog, unless you kill me first.'

'Shan't he!' said Sikes, setting his teeth fiercely. 'I'll soon do that, if you don't keep off.'

The housebreaker flung the girl from him to the farthest end of the room, just as Fagin and the two boys returned dragging Oliver between them.

'What's the matter here?' inquired Fagin, looking round.

'The girl's gone mad, I think,' replied Sikes, savagely.

'No, she hasn't,' said Nancy, flushed and breathless from the scuffle—'no, she hasn't, Fagin; don't think it.'

'Then keep quiet, will you?' said the old man, with a threatening look.

'No, I won't do that neither,' replied Nancy, speaking very loud. 'Come! What do you think of that?'

Mr. Fagin was sufficiently well acquainted with the manners and customs of that particular species of humanity to which Nancy belonged, to feel tolerably certain that it would be rather unsafe to prolong any conversation with her at present. With the view of diverting the attention of the company, he turned to Oliver. 'So you wanted to get away, my dear, did you, eh?' said Fagin, taking up a jagged and knotted club which lay in a corner by the fireplace. Oliver made no reply. But he watched the old man's motions, and breathed quickly.

'Wanted to get assistance; called for the police; did you?' sneered Fagin, catching the boy by the arm. 'We'll cure you of that, my young master.'

Fagin inflicted a smart blow on Oliver's shoulders with the club, and was raising it for a second, when the girl, rushing forward, wrested it from his hand. She flung it into the fire with a force that brought some of the glowing coals whirling out into the room.

'I won't stand by and see it done, Fagin,' cried the girl. 'You've got the boy, and what more would you have? Let him be—let him be, or I shall put that mark on some of you, that will bring me to the gallows before my time.'

The girl stamped her foot violently on the floor as she vented this threat; and with her lips compressed, and her hands clenched, looked alternately at Fagin and the other robber, her face quite reddened from the passion of rage into which she had gradually worked herself.

'Why, Nancy!' said the old gentleman, in a soothing tone, after a pause, during which he and Mr. Sikes had stared at one another in a disconcerted manner, 'you,—you're more clever than ever tonight. Ha! ha! my dear, you are acting beautifully.'

'Am I!' said the girl. 'Take care I don't overdo it. You will be the worse for it, Fagin, if I do; and so I tell you in good time to keep clear of me.'

There is something about a roused woman, especially if she adds to all her other strong passions the fierce impulses of recklessness and despair, which few men like to provoke. Fagin saw that it would be hopeless to affect any further mistake regarding the reality of Miss Nancy's rage; and shrinking involuntarily back a few paces, cast a glance, half-imploring and half-cowardly, at Sikes, as if to hint that he was the fittest person to pursue the dialogue.

Mr. Sikes, thus mutely appealed to, and possibly feeling his personal pride and influence interested in the immediate reduction of Miss Nancy to reason, gave utterance to about a couple of score of curses and threats, the rapid production of which reflected great credit on the fertility of his invention. As they produced no visible effect on the object against whom they were discharged, however, he resorted to more tangible arguments.

'What do you mean by this?' said Sikes, backing the inquiry with a very common imprecation concerning the most beautiful of human features, which, if it were heard above, only once out of every fifty thousand times that it is uttered below, would render blindness as common a disorder as measles—'what do you mean by it? Burn my body! Do you know who you are, and what you are?'

'Oh, yes, I know all about it,' replied the girl, laughing hysterically, and shaking her head from side to side, in an unconvincing charade of indifference.

'Well, then, keep quiet,' rejoined Sikes, with a growl like that he was accustomed to use when addressing his dog, 'or I'll quiet you for a good long time to come.'

The girl laughed again, even less composedly than before; and, darting a hasty look at Sikes, turned her face aside and bit her lip till the blood came.

'You're a nice one,' added Sikes, as he surveyed her with a contemptuous air, 'to take up the humane and genteel side! A pretty subject for the child, as you call him, to make a friend of!'

'God Almighty help me, I am!' cried the girl passionately; 'and I wish I had been struck dead in the street, or had changed places with them we passed so near tonight, before I had lent a hand in bringing him here. He's a thief, a liar, a devil, and all that's bad from this night forth. Isn't that enough for the old wretch without blows?'

'Come, come, Sikes,' said Fagin appealing to him in a remonstratory tone, and motioning towards the boys, who were eagerly attentive to all that passed; 'we must have civil words—civil words, Bill.'

'Civil words!' cried the girl, whose passion was frightful to see. 'Civil words, you villain! Yes, you deserve 'em from me. I've worked for you since I was a child not half as old as this!' pointing to Oliver. 'I have been in the same trade, and in the same service, for twelve years since. Don't you know it? Speak out! Don't you know it?'

'Well, well,' replied Fagin, with an attempt at pacification; 'and, if you have, it's your living!'

'Aye, it is!' returned the girl; not speaking, but pouring out the words in one continuous and vehement scream. 'It is my living; and the cold, wet, dirty streets are my home; and you're the wretch that drove me to them long ago, and that'll keep me there, day and night, day and night, till I die!'

'I shall do you a mischief!' interposed the old miser, goaded by these reproaches—'a mischief worse than that, if you say much more!'

The girl said nothing more; but, tearing her hair and dress in a transport of passion, made such a rush at Fagin as would probably have left signal marks of her revenge upon him, had not her wrists been seized by Sikes at the right moment, upon which she made a few ineffectual struggles, and fainted.

'She's all right now,' said Sikes, laying her down in a corner. 'She's uncommon strong in the arms when she's up in this way.'

The old man wiped his forehead, and smiled, as if it was a relief to have the disturbance over; but neither he, nor Sikes, nor the dog, nor the boys, seemed to consider it in any other light than a common occurrence incidental to business.

'It's the worst of having to do with women,' said Fagin, replacing his club; 'but they're clever, and we can't get on, in our line, without 'em. Charley, show Oliver to bed.'

'I suppose he'd better not wear his best clothes tomorrow, Fagin, had he?' inquired Charley Bates.

'Certainly not,' replied Fagin, reciprocating the grin with which Charley put the question.

Master Bates, apparently much delighted with his commission, took a candle, and led Oliver into an adjacent kitchen, where there were two or three of the beds on which he had slept before; and here, with many uncontrollable bursts of laughter, he produced the identical old suit of clothes which Oliver had so much congratulated himself upon leaving off at Mr. Brownlow's. It had been the accidental display of his old garments to Fagin, by the rag dealer who purchased them, which had provided the very first clue received of his whereabouts. 'Take off the smart ones,' said Charley, 'and I'll give 'em to Fagin to take care of. What fun it is!'

Oliver unwillingly complied. Master Bates rolled up the new clothes under his arm and departed from the room, locking the door behind him, leaving Oliver in the dark,.

The noise of Charley's laughter, and the voice of Miss Betsy, who opportunely arrived to throw water over her friend, and perform other feminine offices for the promotion of her recovery, might have kept many people awake under more happy circumstances than those in which Oliver was placed, but he was bruised and weary, and soon fell sound asleep.

Chapter 17
Brownlow Receives a Visitor

It is the custom on the stage, in all good murderous melodramas, to present the tragic and the comic scenes in as regular alternation as the layers of red and white in a side of streaky, well-cured bacon. The hero sinks upon his straw bed, weighed down by fetters and misfortunes; and, in the next scene, his faithful but unconscious squire regales the audience with a comic song. We behold, with throbbing bosoms, the heroine in the grasp of a proud and ruthless baron, her virtue and her life alike in danger, drawing forth her dagger to preserve the one at the cost of the other; and, just as our expectations are wrought up to the highest pitch, a whistle is heard, and we are straightway transported to the great hall of the castle; where a grey-headed steward sings a funny chorus with a funnier body of vassals, who are free in all sorts of places from church vaults to palaces, to roam about in company, carolling perpetually.

Such changes appear absurd; but they are not so unnatural as they might seem at first sight. The transitions in real life from well-spread dinner tables to death-beds, and from mourning attire to holiday garments, are not a whit less startling; only, there, we are busy actors, instead of passive onlookers, which makes a vast difference. The actors in the mimic life in the theatre, are blind to violent transitions and abrupt impulses of passion or feeling, which, presented before the eyes of mere spectators, are at once condemned as outrageous and preposterous.

As the sudden shifting scenes, and rapid changes of time and place, are not only sanctioned in books by long usage, but are by many considered as the great art of authorship—an author's skill in his craft being, by such critics, chiefly estimated with relation to the dilemmas in which he leaves his characters at the end of every chapter—this brief introduction to the present one may perhaps be deemed unnecessary. If so, let it be considered a delicate intimation on the part of the historian that he is going back to the town in which Oliver Twist was born; the reader taking it for granted that there are good and substantial reasons for making the journey, or he would not be invited to proceed upon such an expedition.

Mr. Bumble emerged in the early morning from his place of abode and walked, with portly carriage and commanding steps, up the High Street. He was in the full bloom and pride of beadlehood; his cocked hat and coat were dazzling in the morning sun, and he clutched his cane with the vigorous tenacity of health and power. Mr. Bumble always carried his head high; but this morning it was higher than usual. There was an abstraction in his eye, and an elevation in his air, which might have warned an observant stranger that thoughts were passing in the beadle's mind too great for utterance.

Mr. Bumble stopped not to converse with the small shopkeepers and others who spoke to him, deferentially, as he passed along. He merely returned their salutations with a wave of his hand, and relaxed not in his dignified pace until he reached the farm where Mrs. Mann tended to the infant paupers with parochial care.

'Drat that beadle!' said Mrs. Mann, hearing the well-known shaking at the garden gate. 'If it isn't him at this time in the morning!—Lauk, Mr. Bumble, to think of its being you! Well, it *is* a pleasure, this is! Come into the parlour, sir, please.'

The first sentence was addressed to her helper Mary; and the exclamations of delight were uttered to Mr. Bumble, as the good lady unlocked the garden gate, and showed him, with great attention and respect, into the house. Mr. Bumble and Mrs. Mann stepped over and around the several children on their way into the parlour.

'Mrs. Mann,' said Mr. Bumble; not sitting upon, or dropping himself onto a seat, as any common jackanapes would, but letting himself gradually and slowly down onto a chair; 'Mrs. Mann, ma'am, good morning.'

'Well, and good morning to *you*, sir,' replied Mrs. Mann, with many smiles; 'and hoping you find yourself well, sir!'

'So-so, Mrs. Mann,' replied the beadle. 'A parochial life is not a bed of roses, Mrs. Mann.'

'Ah, that it isn't, indeed, Mr. Bumble,' rejoined the lady. And all the paupers might have chorused the rejoinder with great propriety, if they had heard it.

'A parochial life, ma'am,' continued Mr. Bumble, striking the table with his cane, 'is a life of worry, and vexation, and hardihood; but all public characters, as I may say, must suffer prosecution.'

Mrs. Mann, not very well knowing what the beadle meant, raised her hands with a look of sympathy, and sighed.

'Ah! You may well sigh, Mrs. Mann!' said the beadle.

Finding she had done right, Mrs. Mann sighed again; evidently to the satisfaction of the public character, who, repressing a complacent smile by looking sternly at his cocked hat, said:

'Mrs. Mann, I am going to London.'

'Lauk, Mr. Bumble!' cried Mrs. Mann, starting back.

'To London, ma'am,' resumed the inflexible beadle, 'by coach—I and two paupers, Mrs. Mann! A legal action is a-coming on, about a settlement; and the board has appointed me—me, Mrs. Mann—to dispose of the matter before the quarter-sessions at Clerkenwell. And I very much question,' added Mr. Bumble, drawing himself up, 'whether the Clerken-well Sessions will not find themselves in the wrong box before they have done with me.'

'Oh! you mustn't be too hard upon them, sir,' said Mrs. Mann, coax-ingly.

'The Clerkenwell Sessions have brought it upon themselves, ma'am,' replied Mr. Bumble; 'and if the Clerkenwell Sessions find that they come off rather worse than they expected, the Clerkenwell Sessions have only themselves to thank.'

There was so much determination and depth of purpose about the menacing manner in which Mr. Bumble delivered himself of these words that Mrs. Mann appeared quite awed by them. At length she said:

'You're going by coach, sir? I thought it was always usual to send them paupers in carts.'

'That's when they're ill, Mrs. Mann,' said the beadle. 'We put the sick paupers into open carts in the rainy weather, to prevent their taking cold.'

'Oh!' said Mrs. Mann.

'The opposition coach contracts for these two; and takes them cheap,' said Mr. Bumble. 'They are both in a very low state, and we find it would come two pound cheaper to move 'em than to bury 'em—that is, if we can throw 'em upon another parish, which I think we shall be able to do, if they don't die upon the road to spite us. Ha! ha! ha!'

When Mr. Bumble had laughed a little while, his eyes again encoun-tered the cocked hat; and he became grave. 'We are forgetting business, ma'am,' said the beadle; 'here is your parochial stipend for the month.'

Mr. Bumble produced some silver money rolled up in paper, from his pocketbook; and requested a receipt, which Mrs. Mann wrote out.

'It's very much blotted, sir,' said the matron; 'but it's formal enough, I dare say. Thank you, Mr. Bumble, sir, I am very much obliged to you, I'm sure.'

Mr. Bumble nodded blandly, in acknowledgment of Mrs. Mann's curtsey, and inquired how her inmates were.

'Bless their dear hearts!' said Mrs. Mann with emotion, 'they're as well as can be, the dears! Of course, excepting them two that died last week. And little Ricky.'

'Isn't that boy no better?' inquired Mr. Bumble.

Mrs. Mann shook her head.

'He's an ill-conditioned, wicious, bad-disposed parochial child that,' said Mr. Bumble angrily. 'Where is he?'

'I'll bring him to you in one minute, sir,' replied Mrs. Mann. 'Here, you Ricky!'

After some calling, Ricky was discovered. Having had his face put under the pump, and dried upon Mrs. Mann's gown, he was led into the awful presence of Mr. Bumble the beadle.

The boy was pale and thin, his cheeks were sunken, and his eyes large and bright. The scanty parish dress—the livery of his misery—hung loosely on his feeble body; and his young limbs had wasted away like those of an old man.

Such was the little being who stood trembling beneath Mr. Bumble's glance; not daring to lift his eyes from the floor, and dreading even to hear the beadle's voice.

'Can't you look at the gentleman, you obstinate boy?' said Mrs. Mann.

Ricky meekly raised his eyes, and encountered those of Mr. Bumble.

'What's the matter with you, parochial Ricky?' inquired Mr. Bumble, with well-timed jocularity.

'Nothing, sir,' replied the child faintly.

'I should think not,' said Mrs. Mann, who had of course laughed very much at Mr. Bumble's humour. 'You want for nothing, I'm sure.'

'I should like -' faltered the child.

'Hey-day!' interposed Mr. Mann, 'I suppose you're going to say that you *do* want for something, now? Why, you little wretch -'

'Stop, Mrs. Mann, stop!' said the beadle, raising his hand with a show of authority. 'Like what, sir—eh?'

'I should like,' faltered the child, 'if somebody who can write would put a few words down for me on a piece of paper, and fold it up and seal it, and keep it for me after I am laid in the ground.'

'Why, what does the boy mean?' exclaimed Mr. Bumble, on whom the earnest manner and wan aspect of the boy had made some impression, accustomed as he was to such things. 'What do you mean, sir?'

'I should like,' said the child, 'to leave my goodbyes to Oliver Twist, and to let him know how often I have sat by myself and thought of his wandering about in the dark nights with nobody to help him. And I should like to tell him,' said the child pressing his small hands together, and speaking with great fervour, 'that I was glad to die when I was very young; for, perhaps, if I had lived to be a man, and had grown old, my little sister who is in Heaven might forget me, or be unlike me, and it would be so much happier if we were both children there together.'

Mr. Bumble surveyed the little speaker from head to foot with indescribable astonishment, and, turning to his companion, said, 'They're all in one story, Mrs. Mann. That audacious Oliver has demogalized them all!'

'I couldn't have believed it, sir,' said Mrs. Mann, holding up her hands, and looking malignantly at Ricky. 'I never see such a hardened little wretch!'

'Take him away, ma'am!' said Mr. Bumble imperiously. 'This must be stated to the board, Mrs. Mann.'

'I hope the gentlemen will understand that it isn't my fault, sir?' said Mrs. Mann, whimpering pathetically.

'They shall understand that, ma'am; they shall be acquainted with the true state of the case,' said Mr. Bumble. 'There, take him away. I can't bear the sight of him.'

Ricky was immediately taken away, and locked up in the coal-cellar. Shortly afterwards, Mr. Bumble took himself off to prepare for his journey.

At six o'clock the next morning, Mr. Bumble, having exchanged his cocked hat for a round one, and encasing his person in a blue greatcoat with a cape buttoned to it, took his place on the outside of the coach, accompanied by the criminals whose settlement was disputed; with whom, in due course of time, he arrived in London. He experienced no other crosses on the way than those which originated in the perverse behaviour of the two paupers, who persisted in shivering, and complaining of the cold, in a manner which Mr. Bumble declared caused his teeth to chatter in his head, and made him feel quite uncomfortable, although he had a greatcoat on.

Having disposed of these evil-minded persons for the night, Mr. Bumble sat himself down in the house at which the coach stopped; and took a temperate dinner of steaks, oyster sauce, and porter. After which, putting a glass of hot gin-and-water on the fireplace mantel, he drew his chair to the fire; and, with sundry moral reflections on the too-prevalent sins of discontent and complaining, composed himself to read the paper.

The very first paragraph upon which Mr. Bumble's eye rested was the following advertisement: -

FIVE GUINEAS REWARD

Whereas a young boy, named Oliver Twist, absconded, or was enticed, on Thursday evening last, from his home, at Pentonville; and has not since been heard of. The above reward will be paid to any person who will give such information as will lead to the discovery of the said Oliver Twist, or tend to throw any light upon his previous history, in which the advertiser is, for many reasons, warmly interested.

And then followed a full description of Oliver's dress, person, appearance, and disappearance, with the name and address of Mr. Brownlow at full length.

Mr. Bumble opened his eyes; read the advertisement, slowly and carefully, three times; and in something less than five minutes he was on his way to Pentonville, having actually, in his excitement, left the glass of hot gin-and-water untasted.

'Is Mr. Brownlow at home?' inquired Mr. Bumble of the servant girl who opened the door of a fine home at 23 Park Lane.

To this inquiry the girl returned the not uncommon, but rather evasive reply of 'I don't know, sir; where do you come from?'

Mr. Bumble no sooner uttered Oliver's name, in explanation of his errand, than Mrs. Bedwin, who had been listening at the parlour door, hastened into the passage in a breathless state.

'Come in—come in,' said the old lady; 'I knew we should hear of him. Poor dear! I knew we should! I was certain of it. Bless his heart! I said so all along.'

Having heard this, the worthy old lady hurried back into the parlour again, and, seating herself on a sofa, burst into tears. Meanwhile the girl, who was not quite so susceptible, had run upstairs; and now returned with a request for Mr. Bumble to follow her immediately, which he did.

He was shown into the little back study, where Mr. Brownlow sat with his friend Mr. Griffith, with decanters and glasses before them. The latter gentleman at once burst into the exclamation:

'A beadle! A parish beadle, or I'll eat my hat.'

'Pray don't interrupt just now,' said Mr. Brownlow. 'Take a seat, will you?'

Mr. Bumble sat himself down, quite confounded by the oddity of Mr. Griffith's manner. Mr. Brownlow moved the lamp, so as to obtain an uninterrupted view of the beadle's countenance, and said, with a little impatience:

'Now, sir, you come in consequence of having seen the advertisement?'

'Yes, sir,' said Mr. Bumble.

'And you *are* a beadle, are you not?' inquired Mr. Griffith.

'Yes, gentlemen, I am a parochial beadle,' rejoined Mr. Bumble proudly.

'Of course,' observed Mr. Griffith aside to his friend, 'I knew he was. A beadle all over!'

Mr. Brownlow gently shook his head to impose silence on his friend, and resumed:

'Do you know where this poor boy is now?'

'No more than nobody,' replied Mr. Bumble.

'Well, what *do* you know of him?' inquired the old gentleman. 'Speak out, my friend, if you have anything to say. What *do* you know of him?'

'You don't happen to know any good of him, do you?' said Mr. Griffith, caustically; after an attentive perusal of Mr. Bumble's features.

Mr. Bumble, catching at the inquiry very quickly, shook his head with portentous solemnity.

'You see?' said Mr. Griffith, looking triumphantly at Mr. Brownlow.

Mr. Brownlow looked apprehensively at Mr. Bumble's pursed-up countenance, and requested him to communicate what he knew regarding Oliver, in as few words as possible.

Mr. Bumble put down his hat, unbuttoned his coat, folded his arms, inclined his head in a retrospective manner, and, after a few moments' reflection, commenced his story.

It would be tedious if given in the beadle's words, occupying, as it did, some twenty minutes in the telling; but the sum and substance of it was that Oliver was a foundling, born of low and vicious parents. That he had, from his birth, displayed no better qualities than treachery, ingratitude, and malice. That he had terminated his brief career in the place of his birth, by making a bloody and cowardly attack on an unoffending lad, and running away in the night-time from his master's house. In proof of his really being the person he represented himself to be, Mr. Bumble laid upon the table the papers he had brought to town. Folding his arms again, he then awaited Mr. Brownlow's observations.

'I fear it is all too true,' said the old gentleman sorrowfully, after looking over the papers. 'This is not much for your intelligence' he added, handing Mr. Bumble the promised reward, 'but I would gladly have paid you treble the reward, if it had been favourable to the boy.'

It is not improbable that if Mr. Bumble had been possessed of this information at an earlier period of the interview, he might have imparted a very different colouring to his little history. It was too late to do it now, however; so he shook his head gravely, and, pocketing the five guineas, withdrew.

Mr. Brownlow paced the room to and fro for some minutes, evidently so much disturbed by the beadle's tale, that even Mr. Griffith forbore to vex him further.

At length he stopped, and rang the bell violently. 'Mrs. Bedwin,' said Mr. Brownlow, when the housekeeper appeared, 'that boy, Oliver, is an imposter.'

'It can't be, sir. It cannot be,' said the old lady energetically.

'I tell you he is,' retorted the old gentleman. 'What do you mean by can't be? We have just heard a full account of him from his birth, and he has been a thorough-paced little villain all his life.'

'I never will believe it, sir,' replied the old lady, firmly. 'Never!'

'You old women never believe anything but quack-doctors and lying story-books,' growled Mr. Griffith. 'I knew it all along. Why didn't you take my advice in the beginning? You would have, if he hadn't had a fever, I suppose, eh? He was interesting, wasn't he? Interesting! Bah!' And Mr. Griffith poked the fire with a flourish.

'He was a dear, grateful, gentle child, sir,' retorted Mrs. Bedwin, indignantly. 'I know what children are, sir, and have done these forty years; and people who can't say the same, shouldn't say anything about them. That's my opinion!'

This was a hard hit at Mr. Griffith. As it extorted nothing from that gentleman but a smile, the old lady tossed her head, and smoothed down her apron preparatory to another speech, when she was stopped by Mr. Brownlow.

'Silence!' said the old gentleman, feigning an anger he was far from feeling. 'Never let me hear the boy's name again. I rang to tell you that. Never—never, on any pretence, mind! You may leave the room, Mrs. Bedwin. Remember, I am in earnest.'

There were sad hearts at Mr. Brownlow's that night.

Oliver felt miserable whenever he thought of Mr. Brownlow and Mrs. Bedwin and the generous trust they had placed in him. It was well for him that he could not know what they had heard, or it might have broken him outright.

Chapter 18
A Prig's Life

About noon the next day, when the Dodger and Master Bates had gone out to pursue their customary avocations, Mr. Fagin took the opportunity of reading Oliver a long lecture on the crying sin of ingratitude, of which he clearly demonstrated he had been guilty, to no ordinary extent, in wilfully absenting himself from the society of his anxious friends; and, still more, in endeavouring to escape from them after so much trouble and expense had been incurred in his recovery. Mr. Fagin laid great stress on the fact of his having taken Oliver in, and cherished him, when, without his timely aid, he might have perished with hunger; and he related the dismal and affecting history of a young lad whom, in his philanthropy he had succoured under parallel circumstances, but who, proving unworthy of his confidence, and evincing a desire to communicate with the police, had unfortunately come to be hanged at the Old Bailey one morning. Mr. Fagin did not seek to conceal his share in the catastrophe, but lamented with tears in his eyes that the wrong-headed and treacherous behaviour of the young person in question, had rendered it necessary that he should become the victim of certain evidence for the Crown, which, if it were not precisely true, was indispensably necessary for the safety of him (Mr. Fagin) and a few select friends. Mr. Fagin concluded by drawing a rather disagreeable picture of the discomforts of hanging; and, with great friendliness and politeness of manner, expressed his anxious hopes that he might never be obliged to submit Oliver Twist to that unpleasant operation.

Oliver's blood ran cold as he listened to the old man's words, and comprehended the dark threats conveyed in them. That it was possible for justice itself to confound the innocent with the guilty, when they were in accidental companionship, he knew already; and that deeply-laid plans for the destruction of inconveniently knowing or over-communicative persons had really been devised and carried out by Fagin on more occasions than one, he thought by no means unlikely, when he recollected the general nature of the altercations between that gentleman and Mr. Sikes, which seemed to bear reference to some foregone conspiracy of the kind. As he glanced up, and met Fagin's searching look, he knew that his troubled countenance and uneasy stance were neither unnoticed, nor unrelished by, that wary old gentleman.

The old miser, smiling hideously and patting Oliver on the head, said that if he kept himself quiet and applied himself to business, he saw they would be very good friends yet. Then, taking his hat, and covering himself with an old patched greatcoat, he went out locking the room door behind him.

And so Oliver remained all that day, and for the greater part of many subsequent days—seeing nobody between early morning and late night; and left, during the long hours, to commune with his own thoughts, which, never failing to revert to his kind friends, and the opinion they must long ago have formed of him, were sad indeed.

After the lapse of a week or so, the old man left the room door unlocked, and he was at liberty to wander about the house.

It was a very dirty place. The rooms upstairs had impressive wooden fireplace mantels and large doors, with panelled walls and cornices to the ceiling; which, although they were black with neglect and dust, were ornamented in various ways. From all of these tokens Oliver concluded that a long time ago, before Mr. Fagin was born, it had belonged to better people, and had perhaps been quite bright and handsome, dismal and dreary as it looked now.

Spiders had built their webs in the angles of the walls and ceilings; and sometimes, when Oliver walked softly into a room, the mice would scamper across the floor, and run back terrified to their holes. With these exceptions, there was neither sight nor sound of any living thing; and often, when it grew dark, and he was tired of wandering from room to room, he would crouch in the corner of the passage by the front door, to be as close to living people as he could; and would remain there, listening and counting the hours, until Fagin or the boys returned.

In all the rooms, the mouldering shutters were fast closed, the bars which held them were screwed tight into the wood; the only light which was admitted, stealing its way through round holes at the top, which made the rooms more gloomy, and filled them with strange shadows. There was a back garret window with rusty bars outside, which had no shutter; and out of this Oliver often gazed with a melancholy face for hours together. But nothing was to be observed from it but a confused and crowded mass of housetops, blackened chimneys, and gable-ends. Sometimes, indeed, a grizzly head might be seen, peering over the parapet-wall of a distant house; but it was quickly withdrawn again; and as the window of Oliver's observatory was nailed down, and dimmed with the rain and smoke of years, it was as much as he could do to make out the forms of the different objects beyond, without making any attempt to be seen or heard—which he had as much chance of being as if he had lived inside the ball of St. Paul's Cathedral.

One afternoon, the Dodger and Master Bates being engaged out that evening, the latter-named young gentleman took it into his head to evince some anxiety regarding the decoration of his person (to do him justice, this was by no means an habitual weakness with him); and, with this end and aim, he condescendingly commanded Oliver to assist him in his getting dressed, straightway.

Oliver was but too glad to make himself useful, too happy to have some faces, however bad, to look upon, too desirous to conciliate those about him when he could honestly do so, to throw any objection in the way of this proposal. So he at once expressed his readiness; and, sitting on a chair, while Charley sat upon the table so that he could put his foot in his lap, Oliver applied himself to a process which Master Bates designated as 'japanning his trotter-cases.' This phrase, rendered into plain English, signified cleaning his boots.

Whether it was the sense of freedom and independence which a rational animal may be supposed to feel when he sits on a table in an easy attitude, smoking a pipe, swinging one leg carelessly to and fro, and having his boots cleaned at the same time, without even the past trouble of having taken them off, or the prospective misery of putting them on to disturb his reflections; or whether it was the goodness of the tobacco that soothed Charley's feelings, or the mildness of the beer that mollified his thoughts; he was evidently tinctured, at that moment, with a spice of romance and enthusiasm foreign to his general nature. He looked down on Oliver with a thoughtful countenance, for a brief space; and then raising his head, and heaving a gentle sigh, said, half in abstraction, and half to the Artful Dodger:

'What a pity it is he isn't a prig!'

'Ah!' said the Dodger; 'he don't know what's good for him.'

Charley sighed again, and resumed his pipe; as did Jack. They both smoked, for some seconds, in silence.

'I suppose you don't even know what a prig is?' said Charley, desolately.

'I think I know that,' replied Oliver, looking up. 'It's a the—; you're one, are you not?' inquired Oliver, checking himself.

'I am,' replied Charley. 'I'd scorn to be anything else.' Master Bates straightened his posture and threw back his shoulders after delivering this sentiment, and looked at the Dodger, as if to denote that he would feel obliged by his saying anything to the contrary.

'I am,' repeated Charley. 'So's Jack here. So's Fagin. So's Sikes. So's Nancy. So's Betsy. So we all are, down to the dog. And he's the downiest one of the lot!'

'And the least given to peaching,' added the Dodger. 'He wouldn't so much as bark in a witness box for fear of committing himself—no, not if you tied him up in one, and left him there without chow for a fortnight.'

'Not a bit of it,' observed Charley.

'He's a rum dog. Don't he look fierce at any strange cove that laughs or sings when he's in company?' pursued the Dodger. 'Won't he growl at all, when he hears a fiddle playing? And don't he hate other dogs as ain't of his breed?—Oh, no!'

'He's an out-and-out Christian,' said Charley.

This was merely intended as a tribute to the animal's abilities, but it was an appropriate remark in another sense, if Master Bates had only known it; for there are a good many ladies and gentlemen, claiming to be out-and-out Christians, between whom and Mr. Sikes's dog there exist very strong and singular points of resemblance.

'Well, well,' said the Dodger, recurring to the point from which they had strayed, with that mindfulness of his profession which influenced all his proceedings, 'this hasn't got anything to do with young Green here.'

'No more it has,' said Charley. 'Why don't you put yourself under Fagin, Oliver?'

'And make your fortun' out of hand?' added the Dodger, with a grin.

'And so be able to retire on your property, and do the genteel; as I mean to, in the very next leap-year but four that ever comes, and the forty-second Tuesday in Trinity week,' said Charley Bates.

'I don't like it,' rejoined Oliver, timidly; 'I wish they would let me go. I—I—would rather go.'

'And Fagin would *rather* you not!' rejoined Charley.

Oliver knew this too well; but thinking it might be dangerous to express his feelings more openly, he only sighed, and went on with his boot cleaning.

'Come!' exclaimed the Dodger. 'Why, where's your spirit? Don't you take any pride in yourself? Would you go and stay dependent on your friends?'

'Oh, blow that!' said Master Bates, drawing two or three silk handkerchiefs from his pocket, and tossing them into a basket. 'That's too mean; that is,' he continued with an air of haughty disgust, '*I* couldn't do it.'

'You can leave your friend, though,' said Oliver with a half smile; 'and let him be punished for what you did.'

'For that, I do apologize,' replied the Dodger, with an air of honest regret. 'That was all out of consideration for Fagin, 'cause the traps know that we work together, and he might have got into trouble if we hadn't made our lucky—that was the move, wasn't it, Charley?'

Master Bates nodded assent, and would have spoken; but the recollection of Oliver's flight came so suddenly upon him that the smoke he was inhaling got entangled with a laugh, and went up into his head and down into his throat, and brought on a fit of coughing and stamping about five minutes long.

'Look here!' said the Dodger, drawing forth a handful of shillings and halfpence. 'Here's a jolly life! What's the odds where it comes from? Here, catch hold; there's plenty more where they were took from.'

'You won't, won't you?' observed Charley.

Oliver shook his head in silent agreement.

'Oh, you precious flat! It's naughty, ain't it, Oliver?' taunted Charley Bates, surveying his boots with much satisfaction now that Oliver had polished them. 'Cause, yuh'll come to be scragged, won't yuh?'

'I don't know what that means,' replied Oliver.

'Something in this way, old feller,' explained Charley. As he said it, Master Bates caught up an end of his neckerchief, and holding it erect in the air, dropped his head on his shoulder, and emitted a curious sound through his teeth; thereby indicating, by a lively pantomimic representation, that scragging and hanging were one and the same thing.

'That's what it means,' said Charley. 'Look how he stares, Jack! I never did see such prime company as this 'ere boy; he'll be the death of me, I know he will.' Master Charley Bates, having laughed heartily again, resumed his pipe with tears in his eyes.

'You've been brought up strange,' said the Dodger. 'Fagin will make something of you, though, or you'll be the first boy he ever had that turned out unprofitable. You'd better begin at once; for you'll come to the trade long before you think of it, and you're only losing time, Oliver.'

Master Bates backed this advice with sundry moral admonitions of his own; which, being exhausted, he and his friend Mr. Dawkins launched into a glowing description of the numerous pleasures incidental to the life they led, interspersed with a variety of hints to Oliver that the best thing he could do would be to secure Fagin's favour without more delay, by the means which they themselves had employed to gain it.

'And always put this in your pipe, Nolly,' said the Dodger, as the old man was heard unlocking the door above, 'if you don't take fogels and tickers -'

'What's the good of talking in that way?' interposed Master Bates; 'he don't know what you mean.'

'If you don't take handkerchiefs and watches,' said the Dodger, reducing his conversation to the level of Oliver's capacity, 'some other cove will; so that the coves that lose 'em will be all the worse, and you'll be all the worse too, and nobody a peppercorn's worth the better, except the chaps wot gets them—and you've just as good a right to them as they have.'

'To be sure, to be sure!' said Fagin, who had entered unseen by Oliver. 'There it all lies in a nutshell, my dear—in a nutshell; take the Dodger's word for it. Ha! ha! He understands the catechism of his trade.'

The old man rubbed his hands gleefully together as he corroborated the Dodger's reasoning in these terms; and chuckled with delight at his pupil's proficiency.

The conversation proceeded no farther at this time, for the old man had returned home accompanied by Miss Betsy, and a gentleman whom Oliver had never seen before, but who was accosted by the Dodger as Tom Chitling; and who, having lingered on the stairs to exchange a few gallantries with the lady, now made his appearance.

Mr. Chitling was older in years than the Dodger, having perhaps numbered eighteen winters; but there was a degree of deference in his deportment towards that younger gentleman which seemed to indicate that he felt himself conscious of a slight inferiority in point of genius and professional acquirements. He had small twinkling eyes, and a pock-marked face; wore a fur cap, a dark corduroy jacket, greasy corduroy trousers, and an apron. His wardrobe was, in truth, rather out of repair; but he excused himself to the company by stating that his 'time' was only out an hour before, and that, in consequence of having worn the regimentals for six weeks past, he had not been able to bestow any attention on his private clothes. Mr. Chitling added, with strong marks of irritation, that the new way of fumigating clothes up yonder was infernally unconstitutional, for it burnt holes in them and there was no remedy against the county. The same remark he considered to apply to the regulation mode of cutting hair; which he held to be decidedly unlawful. Mr. Chitling wound up his observations by stating that he had not touched a drop of anything for forty-two mortal long hard-working days; and that he 'wished he might be busted if he warn't as dry as a lime-basket.'

'Where do you think the gentleman has come from, Oliver?' inquired Fagin, with a grin, as the other boys put a bottle of spirits on the table.

'I—I—don't know, sir,' replied Oliver.

'Who's that?' inquired Tom Chitling, casting a contemptuous look at Oliver.

'A young friend of mine, my dear,' replied Fagin.

'He's in luck, then,' said the young man, with a meaningful look at Fagin. 'Never mind where I came from, young'un; you'll find your own way there, soon enough, I'll bet a crown!'

At this sally, the boys laughed. After some more jokes on the same subject, they exchanged a few short whispers with Fagin; and withdrew.

After some words apart between the last comer and Fagin, they drew their chairs towards the fire; and the old man, telling Oliver to come and sit by him, led the conversation to the topics most calculated to interest his hearers. These were, the great advantages of the trade, the proficiency of the Dodger, the amiability of Charley Bates, and the liberality of Fagin himself. At length these subjects displayed signs of being thoroughly exhausted; and Mr. Chitling appeared the same, for the house of correction becomes fatiguing after a week or two. Miss Betsy accordingly withdrew, and left the party to their repose.

From this day, Oliver was seldom left alone, but was placed in almost constant communication with the two boys, who played the old game with the old man every day—whether for their own improvement or Oliver's, Mr. Fagin knew best. At other times the old man would tell them stories of robberies he had committed in his younger days, mixed up with so much that was droll and curious, that Oliver could not help laughing heartily, and showing that he was amused in spite of all his better feelings.

In short, the wily old miser had the boy in his toils; and, having prepared his mind, by solitude and gloom, to prefer any society to the companionship of his own sad thoughts in such a dreary place, he was now slowly instilling into his soul the poison which he hoped would blacken it, and change its hue forever.

Oliver, while as strong minded as any lad of his age and history, was not immune to the enticingly persuasive arguments put forth by his young friends and elderly benefactor. Many a moment found Oliver contemplating the hedonic joys described by Jack and Charley. Nevertheless, whether it was due to a fear of being scragged or loyalty to the good residents of Pentonville—not that it matters as he himself was unsure of whence his impulse sprang—Oliver did not yet care to become a prig.

Chapter 19
Flash Toby Crackit

It was a chilly, damp, windy night, when Fagin, buttoning his greatcoat tight round his shrivelled body, and pulling the collar up over his ears so as to completely obscure the lower part of his face, emerged from his den. He paused on the step as the door was locked and chained behind him; and having listened while the boys made all secure, and until their retreating footsteps were no longer audible, slunk down the street as quickly as he could.

The house to which Oliver had been conveyed was in the neighborhood of Whitechapel. Mr. Fagin stopped for an instant at the corner of the street, and, glancing suspiciously round, crossed the road, and struck off in the direction of the Spitalfields.

The mud lay thick upon the stones, and a black mist hung over the streets; the rain fell sluggishly down; and everything felt cold and clammy to the touch. It seemed that the night befitted such a being as the old miser to be abroad. As he glided stealthily along, creeping beneath the shelter of the walls and doorways, the hideous old man seemed like some loathsome reptile, engendered in the slime and darkness through which he moved, crawling forth, by night in search of some rich offal for a meal.

He kept on his course, through many winding and narrow ways, until he reached Bethnal Green; then, turning suddenly off to the left, he soon became involved in a maze of the mean and dirty streets which abound in that close and densely populated quarter.

Fagin was evidently all too familiar with the ground he traversed to be at all bewildered, either by the darkness of the night, or the intricacies of the way. He hurried through several alleys and streets; and at length turned into one, lighted only by a single lamp at the farther end. At the door of a house in this street he knocked; having exchanged a few muttered words with the person who opened it, he walked upstairs.

A dog growled as he touched the handle of a room door, and a man's voice demanded who was there.

'Only me, Bill; only me, my dear,' said Fagin, looking in.

'Bring in your body then,' said Sikes. 'Lie down, you stupid brute! Don't you know the devil when he's got a greatcoat on?'

Apparently the dog had been somewhat deceived by Mr. Fagin's outer garment; for as the old man unbuttoned it, and threw it over the back of a chair, he retired to the corner from which he had risen, wagging his tail as he went, to show that he was as well satisfied as it was in his nature to be.

'Well!' said Sikes.

'Well, my dear,' replied the old man. 'Ah! Nancy.'

The latter recognition was uttered with just enough of embarrassment to imply a doubt of its reception; for Mr. Fagin and his young friend had not met since she had interfered on behalf of Oliver. All doubts upon the subject, if he had any, were speedily removed by the young lady's behaviour. She took her feet off the fender of the cook stove, pushed back her chair, and bade Fagin draw up his, without saying more about it; for it was a cold night, and no mistake.

'It *is* cold, Nancy dear,' said Fagin, as he warmed his skinny hands over the fire. 'It seems to go right through one,' added the old man, touching his side.

'It must be a piercer, if it finds its way through *your* heart,' said Mr. Sikes. 'Give him something to drink, Nancy. Burn my body, make haste! It's enough to turn a man ill, to see his lean old carcase shivering in that way, like a ugly ghost just rose from the grave.'

Nancy quickly brought a bottle from a cupboard, in which there were many, which, to judge from the diversity of their appearance, were filled with several kinds of liquids. Sikes pouring out a glass of brandy, bade the old miser to drink it off.

'Quite enough, quite, thank ye, Bill,' replied Fagin, putting down the glass after just setting his lips to it.

'What! You're afraid of our getting the better of you, are you?' inquired Sikes, fixing his eyes on the old miser. 'Ugh!'

With a hoarse grunt of contempt, Mr. Sikes seized the glass, and threw the remainder of its contents into the ashes—as a preparatory ceremony to filling it again for himself from the same bottle, which he did at once.

The old man glanced round the room, as his companion tossed down the second glassful; not in idle curiosity, for he had seen it often before, but in a restless and suspicious manner habitual to him. It was a meanly furnished apartment, with nothing but the contents of the closet to induce the belief that its occupier was anything but a working man; and with no more suspicious articles displayed to view than two or three heavy bludgeons which stood in a corner, and a 'life-preserver' that hung over the fireplace mantel.

'There,' said Sikes, smacking his lips, 'now I'm ready.'

'For business?' inquired Fagin.

'For business,' replied Sikes; 'so say what you've got to say.'

'About the crib in Pentonville, Bill?' said Fagin, drawing his chair forward, and speaking in a very low voice.

'Yes. Wot about it?' inquired Sikes.

'Ah! you know what I mean, my dear,' said the old man. 'He knows what I mean, Nancy; don't he?'

'No, he don't,' sneered Mr. Sikes. 'Or he won't, and that's the same thing. Speak out, and call things by their right names; don't sit there, winking and blinking, and talking to me in hints, as if you warn't the very first to have thought about the robbery. Wot d'ye mean?'

'Hush, Bill, hush!' said Fagin, who had in vain attempted to stop this burst of indignation; 'somebody will hear us, my dear—somebody will hear us.'

'Let 'em hear!' said Sikes; 'I don't care.'

But, upon reflection, Mr. Sikes *did* care. He dropped his voice as he said the words, and grew calmer.

'There, there,' said Fagin, coaxingly. 'It was only my caution—nothing more. Now, my dear, about that crib in Pentonville; when is it to be done, Bill, eh?—when is it to be done? Such silverware, my dear, such silverware!' said the old miser, rubbing his hands, and elevating his eyebrows in a rapture of anticipation.

'Not at all,' replied Sikes, coldly.

'Not to be done at all?' echoed Fagin in surprise; leaning back in his chair.

'No, not at all,' rejoined Sikes. 'At least it can't be a put-up job, as we expected.'

'Then it hasn't been properly gone about,' said the old miser, turning red with anger. 'Don't tell me!'

'But I will tell you,' retorted Sikes. 'Who are you, that's not to be told? I tell you that Toby Crackit has been hanging about the place for a fortnight, and he can't get one of the servants in line.'

'Do you mean to tell me, Bill,' said Fagin, softening as the other grew heated, 'that neither of them two servants in the house can be got over?'

'Yes, I do mean to tell you so,' replied Sikes. 'The gentleman of the house has had 'em these twenty years; and if you were to give 'em five hundred pound, they wouldn't be in it.'

'But the women? Do you mean to say, my dear,' remonstrated Fagin, 'that the women can't be persuaded?'

'Not a bit of it,' replied Sikes.

'Not by flash Toby Crackit?' retorted the old man incredulously. 'Think what women are, Bill,'

'No; not even by flash Toby Crackit,' replied Sikes. 'He says he's worn sham whiskers, and a canary waistcoat, the whole blessed time he's been loitering down there, and it's all of no use.'

'He should have tried a mustache and a pair of military trousers, my dear,' said Fagin.

'So he did,' rejoined Sikes, 'and they warn't of no more use than the other plant.'

Mr. Fagin looked befuddled by this information. After ruminating for some minutes with his chin sunk on his breast, he raised his head and said, with a deep sigh, that if flash Toby Crackit reported aright, he feared the scheme was up.

'And yet,' said the old man, dropping his hands on his knees, 'it's a sad thing, my dear, to lose so much when we had set our hearts upon it.'

'So it is,' said Mr. Sikes. 'Worst luck!'

A long silence ensued, during which Fagin was plunged in deep thought, with his face wrinkled into an expression of perfectly demonic villainy. Sikes eyed him furtively from time to time. Nancy, apparently fearful of irritating the housebreaker, sat with her eyes fixed upon the fire, as if she had been deaf to all that passed.

'Fagin,' said Sikes, abruptly breaking the stillness that prevailed; 'is it worth fifty shiners extra, if it's safely done from the outside?'

'Yes,' said the old man, suddenly rousing himself.

'Is it a bargain?' inquired Sikes.

'Yes, my dear, yes,' rejoined the old miser, his eyes glistening, and every muscle in his face working, with the excitement that the inquiry had awakened.

'Then,' said Sikes, thrusting aside the old man's hand with some disdain, 'let it come off as soon as you like. Toby and I were over the garden wall the night afore last, sounding the panels of the doors and shutters. The crib's barred up at night like a jail, but there's one part we can crack, safe and softly.'

'Which is that, Bill?' asked Fagin, eagerly.

'Why,' whispered Sikes, 'as you cross the lawn -'

'Yes, yes?' said the old man, bending his head forward, with his eyes almost starting out of it.

'Umph!' cried Sikes, stopping short, as the girl, scarcely moving her head, looked suddenly round, and pointed for an instant to the old man's face. 'Never mind which part it is. You can't do it without me, I know; but it's best to be on the safe side when one deals with you.'

'As you like, my dear, as you like' replied Fagin. 'Is there no help wanted, but yours and Toby's?'

'None,' said Sikes. 'Cept barkers and a boy. The first we've both got; the second you must find us.'

'A boy!' exclaimed the old man. 'Oh! then it's a panel, eh?'

'Never mind wot it is!' replied Sikes. 'I want a boy, and he musn't be a big 'un. 'Lord!' said Mr. Sikes, reflectively, 'if I'd only got that young boy of Ned, the chimbley-sweeper's! He kept him small on purpose, and let him out by the job. But the father gets lagged; and then the Juvenile Delinquent Society comes, and takes the boy away from a trade where he was earning money, teaches him to read and write, and in time makes a 'prentice of him. And so they go on,' said Mr. Sikes, his wrath rising with the recollection of his wrongs, 'so they go on; and, if they'd got money enough (which it's a Providence they haven't,) we shouldn't have half a dozen boys left in the whole trade in a year or two.'

'No more we should,' acquiesced Fagin, who had been considering during this speech, and had only caught the last sentence. 'Bill!'

'What now?' inquired Sikes.

Fagin nodded his head towards Nancy, who was still gazing at the fire; and intimated, by a sign, that he would have her told to leave the room. Sikes shrugged his shoulders impatiently, as if he thought the precaution unnecessary; but complied, nevertheless, by requesting Miss Nancy to go fetch him a jug of beer from across the street.

'You don't want any beer,' said Nancy, folding her arms, and retaining her seat very composedly.

'I tell you I do!' replied Sikes.

'Nonsense!' rejoined the girl, coolly. 'Go on, Fagin. I know what he's going to say, Bill; he needn't mind me.'

The old man still hesitated. Sikes looked from one to the other in some surprise.

'Why, you don't mind the old girl, do you, Fagin?' he asked at length. 'You've known her long enough to trust her, or the devil's in it. She ain't one to blab. Are you, Nancy?'

'*I* should think not!' replied the young lady, drawing her chair up to the table, and putting her elbows upon it.

'No, no, my dear, I know you're not,' said Fagin; 'but -' and again the old man paused.

'But wot?' inquired Sikes.

'I didn't know whether she mightn't per'aps be out of sorts, you know, my dear, as she was the other night,' replied the old man.

At this confession, Miss Nancy burst into a loud laugh; and, swallowing a glass of brandy, shook her head with an air of defiance, and burst into sundry exclamations of 'Keep the game a-going!' 'Never say die!' and the like. These seemed to have the effect of re-assuring both gentlemen; for the old man nodded his head with a satisfied air, and resumed his seat, as did Mr. Sikes likewise.

'Now, Fagin,' said Nancy, with a laugh, 'tell Bill at once about Oliver!'

'Ha! you're a clever one, my dear; the sharpest girl I ever saw!' said Fagin, patting her on the shoulder. 'It *was* about Oliver I was going to speak, sure enough. Ha! ha! ha!'

'What about him?' demanded Sikes.

'He's the boy for you, my dear,' replied the old man in a hoarse whisper, laying his finger on the side of his nose, and grinning frightfully.

'He!' exclaimed Sikes.

'Have him, Bill!' said Nancy. 'I would, if I was in your place. He mayn't be so much up as any of the others; but that's not what you want, if he's only to open a door for you. Depend upon it, he's a safe one, Bill.'

'I know he is,' rejoined Fagin. 'He's been in good training these last few weeks; and it's time he began to work for his bread. Besides, the others are all too big.'

'Well, he is just the size I want,' said Mr. Sikes, ruminating.

'And he'll do everything you want, Bill, my dear,' interposed the old man; 'he can't help himself. That is—if you frighten him enough.'

'Frighten him!' echoed Sikes. 'It'll be no sham frightening, mind you. If there's anything off about him when we once get into the work, in for a penny, in for a pound. You won't see him alive again, Fagin. Think of that, before you send him. Mark my words!' said the robber, poising a crowbar, which he had drawn from under the bedstead.

'I've thought of it all,' said Fagin with energy. 'I've—I've had my eye upon him, my dears, close—close. Once we let him feel that he is one of us; once we fill his mind with the idea that he has been a thief; then he's ours! Ours for his life. Oho! It couldn't have come about better! The old man crossed his arms upon his breast, and, drawing his head and shoulders into a heap, literally hugged himself for joy.

'Ours!' said Sikes. 'Yours, you mean.'

'Perhaps I do, my dear,' said Fagin, with a shrill chuckle. 'Mine, if you like, Bill.'

'And wot,' said Sikes, scowling fiercely on his agreeable friend, 'wot makes you take so much pains about one chalkfaced kid, when you know there are fifty boys snoozing about Common Garden every night, as you might pick and choose from?'

'Because they're of no use to me, my dear,' replied the old man, with some fervour, 'not worth the taking. Their looks convict 'em when they get into trouble, and I lose 'em all. With this boy, properly managed, my dears, I could do what I couldn't with twenty of them. Besides,' said Fagin, recovering his self-possession, 'he has us now if he could only give us leg-bail again; and he must be in the same boat with us. Never mind how he came there; it's quite enough for my power over him that he was in a robbery—that's all I want. Now, how much better this is, than being obliged to put the poor leetle boy out of the way—which would be dangerous, and we should lose by it besides.'

'When is it to be done?' asked Nancy, stopping some turbulent exclamation on the part of Mr. Sikes, expressive of the disgust with which he received Fagin's affectation for humanity.

'Ah, to be sure,' said Fagin; 'when is it to be done, Bill?'

'I planned with Toby, the night after tomorrow,' rejoined Sikes in a surly voice, 'if he heerd nothing from me to the contrary.'

'Good,' said the old man; 'there's no moon.'

'No,' rejoined Sikes.

'It's all arranged about bringing off the swag, is it?' asked Fagin.

Sikes nodded.

'And about -'

'Oh, ah, it's all planned,' rejoined Sikes, interrupting him. 'Never mind particulars. You'd better bring the boy here tomorrow night, under cover of darkness. Then you hold your tongue, and keep the melting-pot ready, and that's all you'll have to do.'

After some discussion, in which all three took an active part, it was decided that Nancy should return to the old miser's the following evening once the night had set in, and bring Oliver away with her; Fagin craftily observing, that, if he evinced any disinclination to the task, he would be more willing to accompany the girl who had so recently interfered on his behalf, than anybody else. It was also solemnly arranged that poor Oliver should, for the purposes of the contemplated expedition, be unreservedly consigned to the care and custody of Mr. William Sikes; and further, that the said Sikes should deal with him as he thought fit, and should not be held responsible by the old man for any mischance or evil that might be necessary to visit on him; it being understood that, to render the compact in this respect binding, any representations made by Mr. Sikes on his return should be required to be confirmed and corroborated, in all important particulars, by the testimony of flash Toby Crackit.

These preliminaries settled, Mr. Sikes proceeded to drink brandy at a furious rate, and to flourish the crowbar in an alarming manner; bellowing forth, at the same time, some unmusical snatches of song mingled with wild execrations. At length, in a fit of professional enthusiasm, he insisted upon producing his box of housebreaking tools; which he had no sooner stumbled in with, and opened for the purpose of explaining the nature and properties of the various implements it contained, and the peculiar beauties of their construction, than he fell over the box upon the floor and went to sleep where he fell.

'Goodnight, Nancy,' said the old man, muffling himself up as before. 'Goodnight.'

Their eyes met, and Fagin scrutinised her narrowly. There was no flinching about the girl. She was as true and earnest in the matter as Toby Crackit himself would be.

The old man again bade her goodnight; and, bestowing a sly kick upon the prostrate form of Mr. Sikes while her back was turned, groped his way downstairs.

'Always the way!' muttered Fagin to himself as he turned homeward. 'The worst of these women is, that a very little thing serves to call up some long-forgotten feeling; and, the best of them is, that it never lasts. Ha! ha! The man against the child, for a bag of gold!'

Beguiling the time with these pleasant reflections; Mr. Fagin wended his way through mud and mire to his gloomy abode, where the Dodger was sitting up impatiently awaiting his return.

'Is Oliver a-bed? I want to speak to him,' was his first remark as they descended the stairs.

'Hours ago,' replied the Dodger, throwing open a door. 'Here he is!'

The boy was lying fast asleep on a rude bed upon the floor; looking to be, as sleeping children so often do, the quintessence of innocence.

'Not now,' said the old man, turning softly away. 'Tomorrow, tomorrow.'

Chapter 20
Nancy's Advice

When Oliver awoke in the morning, he was a good deal surprised to find that a new pair of shoes, with strong thick soles, had been placed at his bedside, and that his old shoes had been removed. At first, he was pleased with the discovery, hoping that it might be the forerunner of his release; but such thoughts were quickly dispelled, on his sitting down to breakfast along with Fagin, who told him, in a tone and manner which increased his alarm, that he was to be taken to the residence of Bill Sikes that night.

'To—to—stop there, sir?' asked Oliver, anxiously.

'No, no, my dear; not to stop there,' replied the old miser. 'We shouldn't like to lose you. Don't be afraid, Oliver, you shall come back to us again. Ha! ha! ha! We won't be so cruel as to send you away, my dear. Oh no, no!'

The old man, who was stooping over the fire toasting a piece of bread, looked around as he bantered with Oliver thus; and chuckled, as if to show that he knew he would still be very glad to get away if he could.

'I suppose,' said the old man, fixing his eyes on Oliver, 'you want to know what you're going to Bill's for—eh, my dear?'

Oliver coloured, involuntarily, to find that the old thief had been reading his thoughts; but boldly said, 'Yes,' he did want to know.

'Bah!' said the old miser, turning away following a close perusal of the boy's face. 'Wait till Bill tells you.'

Oliver was vexed by Mr. Fagin not expressing any further news on the subject; but he was made wary, by the earnest cunning of Fagin's looks, of making any further inquiries just then. He had no better opportunity; for the old man remained very surly and silent till that night, when he prepared to go abroad.

'You may burn a candle,' said Fagin, putting one upon the table. 'And here's a book for you to read, till they come to fetch you. Goodnight!'

The old man walked to the door, looking over his shoulder at the boy as he went. Suddenly stopping, he called him by his name.

Oliver looked up, and Fagin, pointing to the candle, motioned him to light it. He did so; and as he placed the candle holder upon the table, saw that the old man was gazing fixedly at him, with lowered and contracted brows, from the dark end of the room.

'Take heed, Oliver, take heed!' said the old man, shaking his right hand before him in a warning manner. 'He's a rough man, and thinks nothing of blood when his own is up. Whatever falls out, say nothing;

and do what he bids you. Mind!' Placing a strong emphasis on the last word, he suffered his features gradually to resolve themselves into a ghastly grin, and, nodding his head, left the room.

Oliver leaned his head upon his hands when the old man disappeared, and pondered on the words he had just heard. The more he thought of Mr. Fagin's admonition, the more he was at a loss to divine its real purpose and meaning.

He could think of no bad object to be attained by sending him to Sikes, which would not be equally well answered by his remaining with Fagin. After meditating some time, he concluded that he had been selected to perform some ordinary menial tasks for the housebreaker, until another boy better suited for his purpose could be engaged. He was too well accustomed to suffering, and had suffered too much where he was, to fear the prospect of change very severely. He remained lost in thought for some minutes; and then, with a heavy sigh, moved the candle closer, and taking up the book which the old man had left with him, began to read.

He turned over the pages—carelessly at first; but, lighting on a passage which attracted his attention, he soon became intent upon the volume. It was a history of the lives and trials of great criminals, and the pages were soiled and thumbed with use. Here he read of dreadful crimes that made the blood run cold—of secret murders that had been committed by the lonely wayside, of bodies hidden from the eye of man in deep pits and wells, which would not keep them down, deep as they were, but had yielded them up at last, after many years, and so maddened the murderers with the sight that in their horror they had confessed their guilt, and yelled for the gallows to end their agony. Here, too, he read of men who, lying in their beds in the dead of night, had been tempted (so they said) and led on, by their own bad thoughts, to such dreadful bloodshed that it made the flesh creep and the limbs quail to think of. The terrible descriptions were so real and vivid that the sallow pages seemed to turn red with gore, and the words upon them to be sounded in his ears as if they were whispered, in hollow murmurs, by the spirits of the dead.

In a paroxysm of loathing, the boy closed the book, and thrust it away from him. Then, falling upon his knees, he prayed for Heaven to spare him from such deeds, and rather to will that he should die at once than be reserved for crimes so fearful and appalling. By degrees he grew more calm and besought, in a low voice, that he might be rescued from his present dangers; and that if any aid were to be raised up for a poor outcast boy who had never known the love of kin, it might come to him now when so desolate and deserted.

He was in another place, in mind if not in body, when a grating noise aroused him. 'Who's that!' he called out, starting up, and catching sight of a figure standing by the door. 'Who's there?'

'Me—only me,' replied a tremulous voice.

Oliver raised the candle off the table, and looked towards the door. It was Nancy.

'Put down the light,' said the girl, turning away her head. 'It hurts my eyes.'

Oliver saw that she was very pale, and gently inquired if she were ill. The girl threw herself into a chair, with her back towards him, and wrung her hands, but made no reply.

'God forgive me!' she cried after a while, 'I never thought of this.'

'Has anything happened?' asked Oliver. 'Can I help you? I will if I can. I will, indeed.'

She rocked herself to and fro while breathing deeply, deliberating inhaling and exhaling.

'Nancy!' cried Oliver, 'what is it?'

The girl then beat her hands upon her knees, and stamped her feet upon the ground. Suddenly stopping, she drew her shawl close round her and shivered with cold.

Oliver stirred the fire. Drawing her chair close to it, she sat there, for a little time, without speaking; but at length she raised her head and looked round.

'I don't know what comes over me sometimes,' she said, affecting to busy herself in arranging her dress; 'it's this damp dirty room, I think. Now, Nolly, dear, are you ready?'

'Am I to go with you?' asked Oliver.

'Yes, I have come from Bill,' replied the girl. 'You are to go with me.'

'What for?' asked Oliver, recoiling.

'What for?' echoed the girl, raising her eyes, and averting them again the moment they encountered the boy's face. 'Oh! For no harm.'

'I don't believe it,' said Oliver, who had watched her closely.

'Have it your own way,' rejoined the girl, affecting to laugh. 'For no good, then.'

Oliver could see that he had some power over the girl's better feelings, and, for an instant, thought of appealing to her compassion for his helpless state. But then, the thought darted across his mind that it was barely nine o'clock; and that many people were still in the streets, of whom surely some might be found to give credence to his tale. As this reflection occurred to him, he stepped forward and said, somewhat hastily, that he was ready.

Neither his brief consideration, nor its purport, was lost on his companion. She eyed him narrowly while he spoke; and cast upon him a look of intelligence which sufficiently showed that she guessed what had been passing in his thoughts.

'Hush!' said the girl, stooping over him, and pointing to the door as she looked cautiously round. 'You can't help yourself. I have tried hard for you, but all to no purpose. You are hedged round and round. If ever you are to get loose from here, this is not the time.'

Struck by the energy of her manner, Oliver looked up at her face with great surprise. She seemed to speak the truth; her countenance was white and agitated, and she trembled with earnestness.

'I have saved you from being ill-used once, and I will again, and I do now,' continued the girl aloud; 'for those who would have fetched you, if I had not, would have been far more rough than me. I have promised for your being quiet and silent: if you are not, you will only do harm to yourself and to me too; and perhaps be my death. See here! I have borne all this for you already, as true as God sees me show it.'

She pointed, hastily, to some livid bruises on her neck and arms, and continued with great rapidity:

'Remember this! and don't let me suffer more for you, just now. If I could help you, I would; but I have not the power. They don't mean to harm you; whatever they make you do, is no fault of yours. Hush! every word from you is a blow for me. Give me your hand. Make haste! Your hand!'

She caught the hand which Oliver instinctively placed in hers, and, blowing out the light, drew him after her up the stairs. The front door was opened quickly by someone shrouded in the darkness, and was as quickly closed when they had passed out. A hackney carriage was in waiting. With the same vehemence which she had exhibited in addressing Oliver, the girl pulled him in with her, and drew the curtains close. The driver wanted no directions, but lashed his horse into full speed without the delay of an instant.

The girl still held Oliver fast by the hand, and continued to pour into his ear, the warnings and assurances she had already imparted. All was so quick and hurried that he had scarcely time to recollect where he was, or how he came there, when the carriage stopped at the house to which Fagin's steps had been directed on the previous evening.

For one brief moment Oliver cast a hurried glance along the empty street, and a cry for help hung upon his lips. But the girl's voice was in his ear, beseeching him in such tones of agony to remember her, that he had not the heart to utter it. While he hesitated the opportunity was lost, for he was already in the house, and the door was shut.

'This way,' said the girl, releasing her hold for the first time. 'Bill!'

'Hallo!' replied Sikes, appearing at the head of the stairs, with a candle and his dog. 'Oh! That's the time of day. Come on!'

This was a very strong expression of approval, and an uncommonly hearty welcome, from a person of Mr. Sikes's temperament. Nancy, appearing much gratified thereby, saluted him cordially.

'So you've got the kid,' said Sikes, when they had all reached the room, closing the door as he spoke.

'Yes, here he is,' replied Nancy.

'Did he come quiet?' inquired Sikes.

'Like a lamb,' rejoined Nancy.

'I'm glad to hear it,' said Sikes, looking grimly at Oliver; 'for the sake of his young carcass, as he would otherwise have suffered for it. Come here, young 'un; and let me read you a lecture, which is as well got over at once.'

Thus addressing his new pupil, Mr. Sikes pulled off Oliver's cap and threw it into a corner; and then, taking him by the shoulder, sat himself down by the table, and stood the boy in front of him.

'Now, first; do you know wot this is?' inquired Sikes, taking up a pocket pistol which lay on the table.

Oliver replied in the affirmative.

'Well, then, look here,' continued Sikes. 'This 'ere's powder, that 'ere's a bullet, and this little bit of an old hat is for wadding.'

Oliver murmured his comprehension of the different bodies referred to; and Mr. Sikes proceeded to load the pistol, with great nicety and deliberation.

'Now it's loaded,' said Mr. Sikes, when he had finished.

'Yes, I see it is, sir,' replied Oliver.

'Well,' said the robber, grasping Oliver's wrist, and putting the barrel so close to his temple that they touched; at which moment the boy could not repress a start—'if you speak a word when you're out o' doors with me, except when I speak to you, that bullet will be in your head without notice. So, if you *do* make up your mind to speak without leave, say your prayers first.'

Having bestowed a scowl upon the object of this warning, to increase its effect, Mr. Sikes continued:

'As near as I know, there isn't anybody as would be asking very partickler after you, if you *was* disposed of; so I needn't take this devil-and-all trouble to explain matters to you, if it warn't for you own good. D'ye hear me?'

'The short and the long of what you mean, Bill,' said Nancy, speaking very emphatically, and slightly frowning at Oliver as if to bespeak his serious attention to her words, 'is, that if you're crossed by him in this job you have on hand, you'll prevent his ever telling tales afterwards by shooting him through the head; and will take your chance of swinging for it, as you do for a great many other things in the way of business, every month of your life.'

'That's it!' observed Mr. Sikes, approvingly; 'women can always put things in fewest words. Except when it's blowing up; and then they lengthens it out. And now that he's thoroughly up to it, let's have some supper, and get a in a good long snooze.' It'll be a long night tomorrow.

In pursuance of this request, Nancy quickly laid the cloth, and, disappearing for a few minutes, presently returned with a pot of porter and a dish of sheep's heads; which gave occasion to several pleasant witticisms on the part of Mr. Sikes, founded upon the singular coincidence of the word 'jemmies' being a common name for the dish, and also for the simple, sturdy tool much used in his profession. Indeed, the worthy gentleman, stimulated perhaps by the immediate prospect of being in active service, was in great spirits and good humour; in proof where of it may be here remarked that he humorously drank all the beer at a draught, and did not utter, on a rough calculation, more than fourscore oaths during the whole progress of the meal.

Supper being ended—it may be easily conceived that Oliver had no great appetite for it—Mr. Sikes locked the room door and removed the key. He then disposed of a couple of glasses of spirits and water, and threw himself on the bed, ordering both Nancy and Oliver, with many imprecations in case of failure, to be as quiet as mice and not wake him. Oliver stretched himself out in his clothes, by command of the same authority, on a mattress upon the floor; with Bull's-eye curled up on the floor next to him. The girl sat for some time tending the fire, and occupying herself, perhaps, with thoughts of what might have been.

For a long time Oliver lay awake, thinking it not impossible that Nancy might seek that opportunity of whispering some further advice; but the girl sat brooding over the fire, without moving, save now and then to trim the light. Weary with watching and anxiety, he at length fell asleep.

When he awoke there was dull daylight coming through the window. Sikes was inspecting the contents of a box of tools he had pulled out from under the bed. The table was covered with tea things, and Nancy was busily engaged in preparing breakfast. A heavy rain beat against the window panes, and the sky looked black and cloudy.

After breakfast, Sikes and Nancy deliberated between them as to who would tend to Oliver—and when—over the course of the day. It was determined that Nancy would go to the market that morning to purchase necessary provisions and complete one or two other errands. In the afternoon, following a noontime meal, Sikes would be free to go about town as he pleased; which meant frequenting whichever public-houses seemed most congenial to his mood.

Though short, the time spent in the sole company of Mr. Sikes seemed interminable. Bull's-eye was more companionable. While guarded in what she said, Nancy proved to be more amiable; happy to fill the time talking to Oliver about life at the orphan farm and in the workhouse, and telling amusing stories she recalled about her own life in London. Oliver's questions regarding Fagin and his merry band of boys were gently deflected.

Later in the afternoon Sikes and Bull's-eye returned, and Nancy set out an early supper she had prepared. Bill ate impatiently as he was growing weary of waiting, and proportionately anxious to be on his way.

'Now, then!' growled Sikes, as he finished his meal by downing the last of his beer; 'half-past five! Look sharp boy, we're heading out; for it's late as it is.'

Oliver replied by saying that he was quite ready. Sikes began thrusting various articles into the pockets of his greatcoat, which hung over the back of a chair.

Nancy, scarcely looking at the boy, threw him a handkerchief to tie round his throat; Sikes gave him a large rough cape to button over his shoulders. Thus attired, he gave his hand to the robber, who, merely pausing to show him, with a menacing gesture, that he had that same pistol in a side pocket of his greatcoat, clasped it firmly in his, and, exchanging a farewell with Nancy, led him away with his dog.

Oliver turned, for an instant, when they reached the door, in the hope of meeting a look from the girl. But she had resumed her old seat in front of the fire, and sat, perfectly motionless before it.

Chapter 21
A Cheerless Journey

It was a cheerless hour when Sikes, Oliver, and Bull's-eye ventured out onto the street. While the rain had stopped, storm clouds still darkened the sky. The day had been wet, as large pools of water had collected on the road, and the gutters were overflowing. Only those pedestrians who had sufficient reason to be out-of-doors were on the street. Straggling groups of labourers were returning home from their work. It had been market day: men and women with empty fish-baskets on their heads, donkey-carts no longer laden with vegetables, chaise carts on longer hauling carcasses of meat, and women with empty milk-pails trudged along from whence they had come early that morning. Now and then a stagecoach, covered with mud, rattled briskly by, the driver bestowing, as he passed, an admonitory lash upon his horses to ensure his arriving at the post office not a quarter of a minute after his time. Another busy day in London was drawing to a close.

By the time they had turned onto Bethnal Green Road, dusk had arrived. Many of the street lamps were already lit. The public-houses, with gaslights burning inside, were crowded. By degrees, other shops began to close, and only a few scattered people were met with. Sikes nodded, twice or thrice, to a passing friend; and, resisting as many invitations to take a dram, pressed steadily onward.

'Now, young 'un!' said Sikes, looking up at the clock of a church, 'half-past six! you must step out. Come, don't lag behind already, Lazy-legs!'

Mr. Sikes accompanied this speech with a jerk of his little companion's wrist. Oliver, quickening his pace into a trot, kept up with the long strides of the housebreaker as well as he could. To be sure, while Oliver felt some trepidation being in the unescorted company of such a rough fellow, and much uncertainty about what lay ahead, he also felt a sense of adventure. Being interminably cooped up in Fagin's cramped and musty house had not been agreeable.

The landscape began to change. The houses became larger and, certainly, tidier. After they passed by several grand estates and a number of lovely parks, Sikes abruptly turned off of the main thoroughfare and into a narrow lane leading down a gentle hill. Looking intently forward, Oliver saw that water was just below them, and that they were coming to the foot of a bridge. The lights of a town could be seen at a distance beyond the bridge. Sikes kept straight on, until they were close upon the bridge; then he suddenly veered off the road and down a narrow footpath towards the river bank. 'The water!' thought Oliver, turning sick with fear. 'He has brought me to this lonely, dark place to murder me!'

He was about to disengaged himself from Sikes's sturdy grip, and make a run for his young life, when Oliver saw that they stood before a solitary house, all ruinous and decayed. There was a window on each side of the dilapidated entrance; and one story above; but no light was visible. The house was dark, dismantled, and, to all appearances, uninhabited.

Sikes, with Oliver's hand still in his, softly approached the low porch, and raised the latch. The door yielded to the pressure, and they passed in together. Bull's-eye followed.

'Hallo!' cried a loud, hoarse voice as soon as they set foot in the passage.

'Don't make such a row,' said Sikes, bolting the door. 'Show a glim, Toby.'

'Aha! my pal!' cried the same voice—'a glim, Barney, a glim! Show the gentleman in, Barney. Wake up first, if convenient.'

The speaker appeared to throw a boot-jack, or some such article, at the person he addressed, to rouse him from his slumbers; for the noise of a wooden body, falling violently, was heard; and then an indistinct muttering, as of a man between being asleep and awake.

'Do you hear?' cried the same voice. 'There's Bill Sikes in the passage with nobody to do the civil for him; and you sleeping there, as if you took laudanum with your meals, and nothing stronger. Are you any fresher now, or do you want the iron candlestick to wake you thoroughly?'

A pair of slipshod feet shuffled, hastily, across the bare floor of the room, as this interrogatory was put; and there issued, from a door on the right hand; first, a feeble candle, and next, the form of the same individual who has heretofore been described as labouring under the infirmity of speaking through his nose, and officiating as a waiter at the public-house on Saffron Hill.

'Bister Sikes!' exclaimed Barney, with real or counterfeit joy; 'cub id, sir; cub id.'

'Here! you get on first,' said Sikes, putting Oliver in front of him. 'Quicker! or I shall tread upon your heels.'

Muttering a curse upon his tardiness, Sikes pushed Oliver before him, and they entered a low dark room with a smoky fire, two or three broken chairs, a table, and a couple of very old couches; on one of which, with his legs much higher than his head, a man was reposing at full length, smoking a long clay pipe. He was dressed in a smartly-cut snuff-coloured coat, with large brass buttons; an orange neckerchief; a nicely patterned waistcoat; and khaki breeches. Mr. Crackit (for he it was) could be distinguish from other hard men by the refinement of his features and the brightness of his eyes. He had, however, recently acquired a scar alongside one eye which detracted somewhat from his appearance. He was above average size, and strong in the legs; and, apparently, had much admiration for his own top-boots, which he contemplated, in their elevated situation, with lively satisfaction.

'Bill, my boy!' said this relining figure, turning his head towards the door, 'I'm glad to see you. I was almost afraid you'd given it up, in which case I should have made it a personal venture. Hallo!'

Uttering this exclamation in a tone of great surprise, as his eyes rested on Oliver, Mr. Toby Crackit brought himself into a sitting posture, and demanded who that was.

'The boy. Only the boy!' replied Sikes, drawing a chair towards the fire.

'Wud of Bister Fagid's lads,' exclaimed Barney, with a grin.

'Fagin's, eh!' exclaimed Toby, looking at Oliver. 'What an invaluable boy that'll make, for the old ladies' pockets in chapels! His mug is a fortune' to him.'

'There—there's enough of that,' interposed Sikes, impatiently, and stooping over his recumbent friend, he whispered a few words in his ear; at which Mr. Crackit laughed immensely, and honoured Oliver with a long stare of astonishment.

'I heard of him, I have,' said Toby, keeping his eyes on Oliver.

'Now,' said Sikes, as he resumed his seat, 'if you'll give us something to eat and drink while we're waiting, you'll put some heart in us, or in me, at all events. Sit down by the fire, youngster, and rest yourself; for you'll have to go out with us again tonight, though not very far off.'

Oliver looked at Sikes in mute wonder; and drawing a stool to the fire, sat with his head upon his hands, scarcely knowing where he was, or what was passing around him.

'Here,' said Toby, as Fagin's nephew placed some fragments of food and a bottle upon the table, 'Success to the crack!' He rose to honour the toast; and, carefully depositing his empty pipe in a corner, advanced to the table, filled a glass with spirits, and drank off its contents. Mr. Sikes did the same.

'A drain for the boy,' said Toby, half-filling a wine-glass. 'Down with it, innocence.'

'Indeed,' said Oliver, looking up at the man's face; 'indeed, I -'

'Down with it!' repeated Toby, forcefully. 'Do you think I don't know what's good for you? Tell him to drink it, Bill.'

'He had better!' said Sikes, clapping his hand upon his pocket. 'Burn my body, if he isn't more trouble than a whole family of Dodgers. Drink it, you perverse imp! drink it!'

Frightened by the menacing gestures of the two men, Oliver hastily swallowed the contents of the glass, and immediately fell into a violent fit of coughing, which delighted Toby Crackit and Barney, and even drew a smile from the surly Mr. Sikes. This done, Sikes and Oliver satisfied their appetites.

After his meal, Sikes pulled out a length of sturdy cord and tied one end securely about Oliver's waist; the other end he tied to his own wrist. Next, he withdrew his pistol from one pocket, checked it quickly, and returned it to another pocket. The housebreaker then lay down on a couch and ordered Oliver to lay on the floor next to him.

'Bull's-eye', he said to his dog while pointing at Oliver, 'keep an eye on the boy.' The dog wagged his tail in response, apparently pleased at being assigned such a duty.

Looking rather satisfied with these arrangements, Sikes allowed himself to doze off. Oliver, exhausted from walking so far, soon fell asleep himself. Mr. Crackit resumed his former position and Barney, wrapped in a blanket, stretched himself out on the floor.

They slept, or appeared to sleep, for some time until roused by Toby Crackit jumping up and declaring that it was half-past three o'clock. In an instant, the other two men were on their legs. Sikes pulled the cord attached to Oliver, jerking the boy awake, and then untied it. Soon, all three men were all were actively engaged in busy preparation. Sikes and his companion enveloped their necks and chins in large dark shawls, and drew on their greatcoats; while Barney, opening a cupboard, brought forth several articles, which he hastily crammed into the pockets.

'Barkers for me, Barney,' said Toby Crackit.

'Here they are,' replied Barney, producing a pair of pistols. 'You loaded them yourself.'

'All right!' replied Toby, stowing them away. 'The persuaders?'

'I've got 'em,' replied Sikes.

'Crape, keys, centre-bits, lantern—nothing forgotten?' inquired Toby, fastening a small crowbar to a loop inside the skirt of his coat. 'All right! That's the time of day!'

Bill Sikes looked down and addressed his dog. 'Bull's-eye,' he said, 'you stay here. Keep a sharp eye on Barney there. Keep 'im in line.' The dog lay down in a corner of the room.

'Now, then!' said Sikes, holding out his hand. Oliver, who was completely stupefied by the unwonted exercise, the late hour, and the strong drink which had been forced upon him, put his hand mechanically into that which Sikes extended for the purpose.

'Take his other hand, Toby,' said Sikes. 'Take a look out, Barney.'

Barney went to the door, and returned to announce that all was quiet. The two robbers issued forth with Oliver between them. Barney, having made all fast, rolled himself up as before, and was soon asleep again, as was the dog.

Chapter 22
Oliver Sounds the Alarm

Coincidentally, serendipitous events must occur often enough or there would be no need for such a word. What might seem, to a reader of novels and stories, to be contrived occurrences dropped into plots to draw disjointed narratives into implausible tales, happen daily in the common course of things, and come and go with little notice. Old friends meeting by happenstance. A shop owner requiring the services of a tradesman just as one arrives to purchase one doodad or another. Being two shillings short in one's purse and finding three forgotten in some pocket. Serendipitous events are recorded in this history, as in many others, because, if they had not in fact occurred just as they are faithfully reported herein, there would be no story worth telling. Oliver would simply be another unfortunate orphan, amongst hundreds of nameless orphans, to have been born into and to have died in poverty. It is only due to serendipitous events, and to the concerted efforts of certain well-known characters, that the name Oliver Twist is remembered today.

It was intensely dark when the trio made their way across the bridge and towards the lights, which Oliver had seen earlier that evening, which lay some ways ahead of them. The fog lay heavier in the air than it had earlier in the night. The lights were at no great distance off; and, as they walked pretty briskly, they soon arrived at them.

'Down the back service alley,' ordered Sikes; 'there'll be nobody in the way to see us tonight.'

Toby acquiesced; and they hurried down the alley, which at that late hour was wholly deserted. A dim light shone at intervals from some bedroom window, and the hoarse barking of dogs occasionally broke the silence of the night. But there was nobody abroad, and they had almost cleared the town as the church-bell struck four. After walking a short ways further, they stopped behind a large house surrounded by a wall, to the top of which Toby Crackit, scarcely pausing to take breath, climbed in a twinkling.

'The boy next,' said Toby. 'Hoist him up; I'll catch hold of him.'

Before Oliver had time to look round, Sikes had caught him under the arms; and in three or four seconds he and Toby were standing on the grass on the other side of the wall. Sikes followed directly. Together, they stole cautiously towards the house.

Seeing clearly now that housebreaking and robbery, if not murder, were the objects of the expedition, a cold sweat broke across Oliver's face, his limbs failed him; and he sank to the ground.

'Get up!' murmured Sikes, trembling with rage, and drawing the pistol from his pocket; 'Get up, or I'll strew your brains upon the grass.'

Sikes had cocked the pistol, when Toby struck it from his grasp, and placed his hand over the boy's mouth. 'Hush!' cried Toby to Sikes; 'it won't answer here.'

Toby dragged Oliver towards the house whispering as he went:

'Ye don't remember me, I dare say, but ye did me a small favour once on the road to London and I've now done likewise for yourself. Play your part smartly boy, or I'll do you myself with a crack on the head. That makes no noise, and is quite as certain, and more genteel. Here, Bill, wrench the shutter open. He's game enough now, I'll wager. I've seen older hands look the same way, for a minute or two, on a cold night.'

Sikes, invoking terrific imprecations upon Fagin's head for sending Oliver on such an errand, plied the crowbar—or jemmy—vigorously, but with little noise. After some delay, and some assistance from Toby, the shutter to which he had referred swung open on its hinges.

It was a little lattice window, about five feet and a half above the ground, at the back of the house, which belonged to a scullery, off the kitchen, at the end of a passage. The aperture was so small that the inmates had probably not thought it worthwhile to defend it more securely; but it was large enough to admit a boy of Oliver's size, nevertheless. A very brief exercise of Mr. Sikes's art sufficed to overcome the fastening of the lattice, and it soon stood wide open also.

'Now listen, you young limb,' whispered Sikes, drawing a lantern from his pocket and sliding open the shudder that concealed the light; throwing the glare full on Oliver's face; 'I'm a-going to put you through there. Take this light; go softly along the hallway straight afore you, to the front door; unfasten it, and let us in.'

'There's a bolt at the top you won't be able to reach,' interposed Toby. 'Stand upon one of the hall chairs. There are three there, with a jolly large blue unicorn and gold pitchfork on them, which is the family's arms'

'Keep quiet, can't you?' replied Sikes, with a threatening look. 'The dining room door is open, is it?'

'Wide,' replied Toby, after peeping in to satisfy himself. 'The game of that is, that they always latch it open so that their youngest dog, who's got a bed down here, may walk up and down the passage when he feels wakeful. Ha! ha! Barney 'ticed him away tonight. So neat! The other two mutts are deaf as dead men. Ha! Ha!'

Although Mr. Crackit spoke in a scarcely audible whisper, and laughed without noise, Sikes imperiously commanded him to be silent, and to get to work. Toby complied, by first producing his lantern, and placing it on the ground; then by planting himself firmly with his head against the wall beneath the window, and his hands upon his knees, so as to make a step of his back. This was no sooner done than Sikes, mounting upon him, put Oliver gently through the window with his feet first, and, without leaving hold of his collar, planted him safely on the floor inside.

'Take this lantern,' said Sikes, looking into the room through the window. 'You see the big door afore you down the hallway?'

Oliver murmured, 'Yes.'

'Open it.' Sikes, pointing to the front entrance with his pistol barrel, briefly advised him to take notice that he was within shot all the way, and that if he faltered, he would fall dead that instant.

'It's done in a minute,' said Sikes, in the same low whisper. 'Directly I leave go of you, do your work. Hark!'

Oliver made his way along the aforementioned hallway towards the front entrance; and, as directed, with one hand holding up the lantern, he pulled a hall chair over to the door. He climbed upon the chair and pulled the latch bolt across.

No sooner did the bolt click than the door gently opened, as if under its own impetus, until it came to rest against the chair upon which Oliver still stood. Sikes and Crackit quickly entered the hallway, rushing past Oliver.

Oliver stood on the chair holding the lantern and looked about the house. It had an imposing front hallway with a large staircase leading to the upper floor. A number of paintings hung on the walls. 'Just like Mr. Griffith's house,' thought Oliver. Oliver looked at the closest painting more closely; it was a portrait of a beautiful young woman. Oliver felt a glimmer of recognition; her lovely features seemed rather familiar to him, as if she were an acquaintance or friend of his.

'Mr. Griffith's daughter!' exclaimed Oliver aloud, 'This *is* Mr. Griffith's house!'

In the short time he had to collect his senses, the boy firmly resolved that, whether he died in the attempt or no, he would make an effort to alarm the household. Better a quick and sudden death than to betray his benefactor's best friend. Filled with this idea, Oliver jumped off the chair and ran towards the staircase yelling, 'Wake-up! Wake-up! Sound the alarm. Robbers!'

Two terrified, half-dressed men appeared at the top of the stairs. One brandished a pistol. Seeing this, Oliver then turned around and ran towards the still open door. A shot rang out and Oliver fell to the floor.

Sikes and Crackit rushed out of the dining room towards the front entrance, nearly tripping over Oliver, who was twisting about in agony.

While Sikes jumped over him and continued on past, Crackit stopped and looked down at the boy.

'He's bleeding out!' said Toby.

'Leave him to die!' demanded Sikes, without caring to look back.

Chapter 23
Mrs. Corney Receives a Visitor

The night was bitter cold. The snow lay on the ground, frozen into a hard thick crust, so that only the heaps that had drifted into byways and corners were affected by the sharp wind that howled abroad; which, as if expending increased fury on such prey as it found, caught it savagely up in clouds, and, whirling it into a thousand swirling eddies, scattered it in the air. Bleak, dark, and piercing cold, it was a night for the well housed and fed to draw round a bright fire and thank God they were at home; and for the homeless starving wretch to lay himself down and die. Many hunger-worn outcasts close their eyes in our bare streets, at such times, who, let their crimes have been what they may, can hardly open them in a more bitter world.

Such was the aspect of out-of-doors affairs, when Mrs. Corney, the matron of the workhouse to which our readers have been already introduced as the birthplace of Oliver Twist, sat herself down before a cheerful fire in her own little room, and glanced with no small degree of complacency at a small round table, on which stood a tray of corresponding size, furnished with all necessary materials for the most grateful meal that matrons enjoy. In fact, Mrs. Corney was about to solace herself with a cup of tea and some toast. As she glanced from the table to the fireplace, where the smallest of all possible kettles was singing a small song in a small voice, her inward satisfaction evidently increased—so much so, indeed, that Mrs. Corney smiled.

'Well!' said the matron, leaning her elbow on the table, and looking reflectively at the fire, 'I'm sure we have all of us a great deal to be grateful for! A great deal, if we did but know it. Ah!'

Mrs. Corney shook her head mournfully, as if deploring the mental blindness of those paupers who did not know it; and thrusting a silver spoon (private property) into the inmost recesses of a two-ounce tin tea-caddy, proceeded to make the tea.

How slight a thing will disturb the equanimity of our frail minds! The black teapot, being very small and easily filled, ran over while Mrs. Corney was moralising, and the water slightly scalded Mrs. Corney's hand.

'Drat the pot!' said the worthy matron, setting it down very hastily on the fireplace hob; 'a little stupid thing, that only holds a couple of cups! What use is it of, to anybody? Except,' said Mrs. Corney, pausing, 'except to a poor desolate creature like me. Oh dear!'

With these words, the matron dropped into her chair, and, once more resting her elbow on the table, thought of her solitary fate. The small teapot, and the single cup, had awakened in her mind sad recollections of Mr. Corney (who had not been dead more than five-and-twenty years); and she was overpowered.

'I shall never get another!' said Mrs. Corney, pettishly. 'I shall never get another—like him.'

Whether this remark bore reference to the husband, or the teapot, is uncertain. It might have been the latter; for Mrs. Corney looked at it as she spoke; and took it up afterwards. She had just tasted her first cup, when she was disturbed by a soft tap at the room door.

'Oh, come in with you!' said Mrs. Corney, sharply. 'Some old woman dying, I suppose. They always die when I'm at meals. Don't stand there, letting the cold hallway air in, don't. What's amiss now, eh?'

'Nothing, ma'am, nothing,' replied a man's voice.

'Dear me!' exclaimed the matron, in a much sweeter tone, 'is that Mr. Bumble?'

'At your service, ma'am,' said Mr. Bumble, who had stopped in the hall to rub his shoes clean, and to shake the snow off his coat; and who now made his appearance, bearing the cocked hat in one hand and a bundle in the other. 'Shall I shut the door, ma'am?'

The lady modestly hesitated to reply, lest there should be any impropriety in holding an interview with Mr. Bumble behind closed doors. Mr. Bumble taking advantage of the hesitation, and being very cold himself, shut it without permission.

'Hard weather, Mr. Bumble,' said the matron.

'Hard, indeed, ma'am,' replied the beadle. 'Anti-parochial weather this, ma'am. We have given away, Mrs. Corney, we have given away a matter of twenty loaves and a cheese and a half, this very blessed afternoon; and yet them paupers are not contented.'

'Of course not. When would they be, Mr. Bumble?' said the matron, sipping her tea.

'When, indeed, ma'am!' rejoined Mr. Bumble. 'Why here's one man that, in consideration of his wife and large family, has a loaf and a good pound of cheese, full weight. Is he grateful, ma'am? Is he grateful? Not a copper farthing's worth of it! What does he do, ma'am, but ask for a few coals; if it's only a pocket handkerchief full, he says! Coals! What would he do with coals? Toast his cheese with 'em, and then come back for more. That's the way with these people, ma'am; give 'em an apron full of coals today, and they'll come back for another, the day after tomorrow, as brazen as alabaster.'

The matron expressed her entire concurrence in this intelligible simile, and the beadle went on. 'I never,' said Mr. Bumble, 'see anything like the pitch it's got to. The day afore yesterday, a man—you have been a married woman, ma'am, and I may mention it to you—a man, with hardly a rag upon his back (here Mrs. Corney looked at the floor), goes to our overseer's door when he has got company coming to dinner; and says he must be relieved, Mrs. Corney. As he wouldn't go away, and shocked the company very much, our overseer sent him out a pound of potatoes and half a pint of oatmeal. 'My heart!' says the ungrateful villain, 'what's the use of *this* to me? You might as well give me a pair of iron spectacles!' 'Very good,' says our overseer, taking 'em away again, 'you won't get anything else here.' 'Then I'll die in the streets!' says the vagrant. 'Oh no, you won't,' says our overseer.'

'Ha! ha! That was very good! So like Mr. Grannett, wasn't it?' interposed the matron. 'Well, Mr. Bumble?'

'Well, ma'am,' rejoined the beadle, 'he went away; and he *did* die in the streets. There's an obstinate pauper for you!'

'It beats anything I could have believed,' observed the matron emphatically. 'But don't you think out-of-door relief a very bad thing, anyway, Mr. Bumble? You're a gentleman of experience, and ought to know. Come.'

'Mrs. Corney,' said the beadle, smiling as men smile who are conscious of superior information, 'out-of-door relief, properly managed—properly managed, ma'am—is the parochial safeguard. The great principle of out-of-door relief is to give the paupers exactly what they don't want, and then they get tired of coming.'

'Dear me!' exclaimed Mrs. Corney. 'Well, that is a good one, too!'

'Yes. Betwixt you and me, ma'am,' returned Mr. Bumble, 'that's the great principle; and that's the reason why, if you look at any cases that get into them audacious newspapers, you'll always observe that sick families have been relieved with slices of cheese. That's the rule now, Mrs. Corney, all over the country. But, however,' said the beadle, stopping to unpack his bundle, 'these are official secrets, ma'am; not to be spoken of; except, as I may say, among the parochial officers, such as ourselves. This is the port wine, ma'am,' he said whilst holding up two bottles, 'that the board ordered for the infirmary—real, fresh, genuine port wine; only out of the cask this forenoon; clear as a bell, and no sediment!'

Having held the first bottle up to the light, and shaken it well to test its excellence, Mr. Bumble placed them both on top of a chest of drawers; folded the handkerchief in which they had been wrapped; put it carefully in his pocket, and took up his hat as if to go.

'You'll have a very cold walk, Mr. Bumble,' said the matron.

'It blows, ma'am,' replied Mr. Bumble, turning up his coat-collar, 'enough to cut one's ears off.'

The matron looked, from the little kettle, to the beadle, who was moving towards the door; and as the beadle coughed preparatory to bidding her goodnight, bashfully inquired whether—whether he wouldn't take a cup of tea?

Mr. Bumble instantaneously turned back his collar again, laid his hat and stick upon a chair, and drew another chair up to the table. As he slowly seated himself, he looked at the lady. She fixed her eyes upon the little teapot. Mr. Bumble coughed again, and slightly smiled.

Mrs. Corney rose to get another cup and saucer from the closet. As she sat down, her eyes once again encountered those of the gallant beadle; she coloured, and applied herself to the task of making his tea. Again Mr. Bumble coughed—louder this time than he had coughed yet.

'Sweet? Mr. Bumble?' inquired the matron, taking up the sugar basin.

'Very sweet, indeed, ma'am,' replied Mr. Bumble. He fixed his eyes on Mrs. Corney as he said this; and if ever a beadle looked tender, Mr. Bumble was that beadle at that moment.

The tea was made, and handed in silence. Mr. Bumble, having spread a handkerchief over his knees to prevent the crumbs from sullying the splendour of his breeches, began to eat and drink; varying these amusements, occasionally, by fetching a deep sigh, which, however, had no injurious effect upon his appetite, but, on the contrary, rather seemed to facilitate his operations in the tea and toast department.

'You have a cat, ma'am, I see,' said Mr. Bumble, glancing at one who, in the centre of her family, was basking before the fire; 'and kittens too, I declare!'

'I am so fond of them, Mr. Bumble, you can't think,' replied the matron. 'They're *so* happy, *so* frolicsome, and *so* cheerful, that they are quite the companions for me.'

'Very nice animals, ma'am,' replied Mr. Bumble, approvingly; 'so very domestic.'

'Oh, yes!' rejoined the matron with enthusiasm; 'so fond of their home, too, that it's quite a pleasure, I'm sure.'

'Mrs. Corney, ma'am,' said Mr. Bumble, slowly, and marking the time with his teaspoon, 'I mean to say this, ma'am; that any cat, or kitten, that could live with you, ma'am, and *not* be fond of its home, must be an ass, ma'am.'

'Oh, Mr. Bumble!' remonstrated Mrs. Corney.

'It's of no use disguising facts, ma'am,' said Mr. Bumble, slowly flourishing the teaspoon with a kind of amorous dignity which made him doubly impressive; 'I would drown it myself, with pleasure.'

'Then you're a cruel man,' said the matron vivaciously, as she held out her hand for the beadle's cup; 'and a very hard-hearted man besides.'

'Hard-hearted, ma'am?' said Mr. Bumble, 'hard?' Mr. Bumble resigned his cup without another word; squeezed Mrs. Corney's little finger as she took it; and inflicting two open-handed slaps upon his laced waistcoat, gave a mighty sigh, and hitched his chair a very little morsel farther from the fire.

It was a round table; and as Mrs. Corney and Mr. Bumble had been sitting opposite each other, with no great space between them, and fronting the fire, it will be seen that Mr. Bumble, in receding from the fire, and still keeping at the table, increased the distance between himself and Mrs. Corney; which proceeding some prudent readers will doubtless be disposed to admire, and to consider an act of great heroism on Mr. Bumble's part, he being in some sort tempted by time, place, and opportunity, to give utterance to certain soft nothings, which, however well they may become the lips of the light and thoughtless, do seem immeasurably beneath the dignity of judges of the land, members of parliament, ministers of state, lord mayors, and other great public functionaries, but more particularly beneath the stateliness and gravity of a beadle, who (as is well known) should be the sternest and most inflexible among them all.

Whatever were Mr. Bumble's intentions, however—and no doubt they were of the best—it unfortunately happened, as has been twice before remarked, that the table was a round one; consequently Mr. Bumble, by moving his chair little by little, soon began to diminish the distance between himself and the matron, and, continuing to travel round the outer edge of the circle, brought his chair in time close to that in which the matron was seated. Indeed, the two chairs touched; and when they did so, Mr. Bumble stopped.

Now, if the matron had moved her chair to the right, she would have been scorched by the fire; and if to the left, she must have fallen into Mr. Bumble's arms; so (being a discreet matron, and no doubt foreseeing these consequences at a glance) she remained where she was, and handed Mr. Bumble another cup of tea.

'Hard-hearted, Mrs. Corney?' said Mr. Bumble, stirring his tea, and looking up at the matron's face; 'are *you* hard-hearted, Mrs. Corney?'

'Dear me!' exclaimed the matron, 'what a very curious question from a single man. What can you want to know for, Mr. Bumble?'

The beadle drank his tea to the last drop, finished a piece of toast, whisked the crumbs off his knees, wiped his lips, and deliberately kissed the matron.

'Mr. Bumble!' cried that discreet lady in a whisper; for the fright was so great, that she had quite lost her voice—'Mr. Bumble, I shall scream!' Mr. Bumble made no reply, but in a slow and dignified manner put his arm round the matron's waist.

As the lady had stated her intention of screaming, of course she would have screamed at this additional boldness, but that the exertion was rendered unnecessary by a hasty knocking at the door; which was no sooner heard, than Mr. Bumble darted, with much agility, to the wine bottles, and began dusting them with great violence, while the matron sharply demanded who was there. It is worthy of remark, as a curious physical instance of the efficacy of a sudden surprise in counteracting the effects of extreme fear, that her voice had quite recovered all its official asperity.

'If you please, mistress,' said a withered old female pauper, hideously ugly, putting her head in at the door, 'Old Sally is a-going fast.'

'Well, what's that to me?' angrily demanded the matron. 'I can't keep her alive, can I?'

'No, no, mistress,' replied the old woman, 'nobody can; she's far beyond the reach of help. I've seen a many people die—little babes and great strong men—and I know when death's a-coming, well enough. But she's troubled in her mind; and when the fits are not on her—and that's not often, for she is dying very hard—she says she has got something to tell, which you must hear. She'll never die quiet till you come, mistress.'

At this intelligence, the worthy Mrs. Corney muttered a variety of invectives against old women who couldn't even die without purposely annoying their betters; and muffling herself in a thick shawl which she hastily caught up, briefly requested Mr. Bumble to stay till she came back, lest anything particular should occur, and bidding the messenger to walk fast, and not be all night hobbling up the stairs, she followed her from the room with a very ill grace, scolding all the way.

Mr. Bumble's conduct, on being left to himself, was rather inexplicable. He opened the closet, counted the teaspoons, weighed the sugar-tongs, closely inspected a silver milk-pot to ascertain that it was of the genuine metal; and, having satisfied his curiosity on these points, put on his cocked hat cornerwise, and danced with much gravity four distinct times round the table.

Having gone through this very extraordinary performance, he took off the cocked hat again, and, spreading himself before the fire with his back towards it, seemed to be mentally engaged in taking an exact inventory of the furniture.

Chapter 24
Sally's Trust

It was no unfit messenger of death, who had disturbed the quiet of the matron's room. Her body was bent by age, her limbs trembled with palsy, and her face, distorted into a mumbling leer, resembled more the grotesque shaping of some wild artist's pencil, than the work of Nature's hand.

Alas! How few of Nature's faces are left alone to gladden us with their beauty! The cares, and sorrows, and hungerings of the world change them as they change hearts; and it is only when those passions sleep, and have lost their hold forever, that the troubled clouds pass off, and leave Heaven's surface clear. It is a common thing for the countenances of the dead, even in that fixed and rigid state, to subside into the long-forgotten expression of sleeping infancy, and settle into the very look of early life; so calm, so peaceful do they grow again, that those who knew them in their happy childhood, kneel by the coffin's side in awe, and see an Angel even upon earth.

The old crone tottered along the passages, and up the stairs, muttering some indistinct answers to the chidings of her companion; being at length compelled to pause for breath, she put the light into her matron's hand, and remained behind to follow as she might, while the more nimble superior made her way to the room where the sick woman lay.

It was a bare garret room, with a dim light burning at the farther end. There was another old woman watching by the bed; and the parish apothecary's apprentice was standing by the fire, making a toothpick out of a quill.

'Cold night, Mrs. Corney,' said this young gentleman, as the matron entered.

'Very cold, indeed, sir,' replied the mistress, in her most civil tones, and dropping a curtsey as she spoke.

'You should get better coals out of your contractors,' said the apothecary's deputy, breaking a lump on the top of the fire with the rusty poker; 'these are not at all the sort of thing for a cold night.'

'They're the board's choosing, sir,' rejoined the matron. 'The least they could do, would be to keep us pretty warm, for our places are hard enough.'

The conversation was interrupted here by a moan from the sick woman.

'Oh!' said the young man, turning his face towards the bed, as if he had previously quite forgotten the patient, 'it's all over there, Mrs. Corney.'

'It is, is it, sir?' asked the matron.

'If she lasts a couple of hours, I shall be surprised,' said the apothecary's apprentice, intent upon the toothpick's point. 'It's a breakup of the system altogether. Is she dozing, old lady?'

The attendant stooped over the bed, to ascertain, and nodded in the affirmative.

'Then perhaps she'll go off in that way, if you don't make a row,' said the young man. 'Put the light on the floor—she won't see it there.'

The attendant did as she was told, shaking her head meanwhile, to intimate that the woman would not die so easily. Having done so, she resumed her seat by the side of the other nurse, who had by this time returned. The mistress, with an expression of impatience, wrapped herself in her shawl, and sat at the foot of the bed.

The apothecary's apprentice, having completed the manufacture of the toothpick, planted himself in front of the fire, and made good use of it for ten minutes or so, when apparently growing rather dull, he wished Mrs. Corney joy in her job, and took himself off on tip-toe.

When they had sat in silence for some time, the two old women rose from the bed, and crouching over the fire, held out their withered hands to catch the heat. The flame threw a ghastly light on their shrivelled faces, and made their ugliness appear terrible, as, in this position, they began to converse in a low voice.

'Did she say any more, Anny dear, while I was gone?' inquired the messenger.

'Not a word,' replied the other. 'She plucked and tore at her arms for a little time; but I held her hands, and she soon dropped off. She hasn't much strength in her, so I easily kept her quiet. I ain't so weak for an old woman, although I am on parish allowance; no, no!'

'Did she drink the hot wine the doctor said she was to have?' demanded the first.

'I tried to get it down her,' rejoined the other, 'but her teeth were tightly set, and she clenched the mug so hard that it was as much as I could do to get it back again. So *I* drank it; and it did me good!'

Looking cautiously round, to ascertain that they were not overheard, the two hags cowered nearer to the fire, and chuckled heartily.

'I mind the time,' said the first speaker, 'when Sally would have done the same, and made rare fun of it afterwards.'

'Ay, that she would,' rejoined the other; 'she had a merry heart. A many, many beautiful corpses she laid out, as nice and neat as waxwork. My old eyes have seen them—ay, and these old hands touched them, too; for I have helped her scores of times.'

Stretching forth her trembling fingers as she spoke, the old creature shook them exultingly before her face; and fumbling in her pocket, brought out an old time-discoloured tin snuffbox, from which she shook a few grains into the outstretched palm of her companion, and a few more into her own. While they were thus employed, the matron, who had been impatiently watching for the dying woman to awaken from her stupor, joined them by the fire, and sharply asked how long she was to wait?

'Not long, mistress,' replied the second woman, looking up into her face. 'We have none of us long to wait for Death. Patience, patience! He'll be here soon enough for us all.'

'Hold your tongue, you doting idiot!' said the matron, sternly. 'You, Martha, tell me—has she been in this way before?'

'Often,' answered the first woman.

'But will never be again,' added the second one; 'that is, she'll never wake again but once—and mind, mistress, that won't be for long!'

'Long or short,' said the matron, snappishly, 'she won't find me here when she does wake. And take care, both of you, how you worry me again for nothing. It's no part of my duty to see all the old women in the house die; and I won't—that's more. Mind that, you impudent old harridans. If you make a fool of me again, I'll soon cure you, I warrant you!'

She was bouncing away, when a cry from the two women, who had turned towards the bed, caused her to look round. The patient had raised herself upright, and was stretching her arms towards them.

'Who's that?' Sally cried in a hollow voice.

'Hush, hush!' said one of the women, stooping over her. 'Lie down, lie down!'

'I'll never lie down again alive!' protested Sally, struggling. 'I *will* tell her! Come here! Nearer! Let me whisper in your ear.'

Sally clutched the matron by the arm, and forcing her into a chair by the bedside, was about to speak, when, looking around, she caught sight of the two old women bending forward in the attitude of eager listeners.

'Turn them away,' demand Sally, drowsily. 'Make haste! make haste!'

The two old crones, chiming in together, began pouring out many piteous lamentations that the poor dear was too far gone to know her best friends, and were uttering sundry protestations that they would never leave her, when the superior pushed them from the room, closed the door, and returned to the bedside. On being excluded, the old ladies changed their tone, and cried through the keyhole that old Sally was drunk—which, indeed, was not unlikely, since, in addition to a moderate dose of opium prescribed by the apothecary, she was labouring under the effects of a final taste of gin-and-water which had been previously administered, in the openness of their hearts, by the worthy old ladies themselves.

'Now listen to me,' said the dying woman aloud as if making a great effort to revive one latent spark of energy. 'In this very room—in this very bed—I once nursed a pretty young creetur' that was brought into the house with her feet cut and bruised with walking, and all soiled with dust and blood. She gave birth to a boy, and died. Let me think—what was the year again!'

'Never mind the year,' said the impatient auditor; 'what about her?'

'Ay,' murmured the sick woman, relapsing into her former drowsy state, 'what about her?—what about—I know!' she cried, jumping fiercely up, her face flushed, and her eyes starting from her head—'She gave it to me!'

'Gave you what, for God's sake?' cried Mrs. Corney, with a gesture as if she would call for help.

'*It!*' replied Sally, laying her hand over the other's mouth—'The only thing she had. She wanted clothes to keep her warm, and food to eat; but she had kept it safe, and had it in her bosom. It was gold, I tell you! Rich gold, that might have saved her life!'

'Gold!' echoed the matron, bending eagerly over the woman as she fell back. 'Go on, go on—yes—what of it? Who was the mother? When was it?'

'She charged me to keep it safe,' replied Sally, with a groan, 'depend'n on me as the only woman about her to hold it 'n trust till he came of age!'

'Who?' asked Mrs. Corney. 'Speak!'

'The boy grew so like his mother,' said the dying woman, rambling on, and not heeding the question, 'that I could never forget it when I saw his face. Poor girl! poor girl! She was so young, too! Such a gentle lamb! Wait; there's more to tell. I ain't told you all, have I?'

'No, no,' replied the matron, inclining her head to catch the words, as they came more faintly from the dying woman. 'Be quick, or it may be too late!'

'The mother,' said Sally, making a more violent effort than before; 'his mother, when the pains of death first came upon her, whispered in my ear that if her baby was born alive, and thrived, the day might come when it would not feel so much disgraced to hear its poor young mother named. "And oh, kind Heaven!" she said, "whether it be boy or girl, raise up some friends for it in this troubled world, and take pity upon a lonely, desolate child, abandoned to its mercy!"'

'The boy's name?' demanded the matron.

'He's gone away now; so sudden, so young,' lamented Sally. 'No one knows where.'

'The boy's name?' repeated the matron.

'They *called* him Oliver,' replied the woman, feebly. 'The gold locket is -'

'Yes, yes—what?' cried Mrs. Corney.

'No one else to trust,' whispered Sally.

She was bending eagerly over the woman to hear her reply; but drew back, instinctively, as Sally once again rose, slowly and stiffly, into a sitting posture. Then, clutching for something under her nightshirt with both hands, muttered some indistinct sounds in her throat, and fell lifeless onto the bed.

'Stone dead!' said the matron, as she opened the door to allow the two old crones back into the room to get on with their dreadful duties. 'And nothing to tell, after all,' she added, walking carelessly away.

Chapter 25
Toby Crackit Returns

While these things were passing in the country workhouse, Mr. Fagin sat in the old den—the same from which Oliver had been removed by the girl—brooding over a dull, smoky fire. He held a pair of bellows upon his knee, with which he had apparently been endeavouring to rouse it into more cheerful action; but he had fallen into deep thought, and with his arms folded on them, and his chin resting on his thumbs, fixed his eyes, abstractedly on the rusty bars.

At a table behind him sat the Artful Dodger, Master Charles Bates, and Mr. Chitling, all intent upon a game of whist; the Artful taking the dummy hand against Master Bates and Mr. Chitling playing together. The countenance of the first-named gentleman, peculiarly intelligent at all times, acquired great additional interest from his close observance of the game, and his attentive perusal of Mr. Chitling's hand; upon which, from time to time, as occasion served, he bestowed a variety of earnest glances, wisely regulating his own play by the result of his observations upon his neighbour's cards. It being a cold night, the Dodger wore his hat, as, indeed, was often his custom within doors. He also sustained a clay pipe between his teeth, which he only removed for a brief space when he deemed it necessary to apply for refreshment to a quart pot upon the table, which stood ready filled with gin-and-water for the accommodation of the company.

Master Bates was also attentive to the play; but being of a more excitable nature than his accomplished friend, it was observable that he more frequently applied himself to the gin-and-water, and moreover indulged in many jests and irrelevant remarks, all highly unbecoming a scientific rubber. Indeed, the Artful, presuming upon their close attachment, more than once took occasion to reason gravely with his companion upon these improprieties; all of which remonstrations, Master Bates received in extremely good part, merely requesting his friend to be 'blowed,' or to insert his head in a sack, or replying with some other neatly-turned witticism of a similar kind, the happy application of which excited considerable admiration in the mind of Mr. Chitling. It was remarkable that the latter gentleman and his partner invariably lost; and that this circumstance, so far from angering Master Bates, appeared to afford him the highest amusement, inasmuch as he laughed most uproariously at the end of every deal, and protested that he had never seen such a jolly game in all his born days.

'That's two doubles and the rub,' said Mr. Chitling, with a very long face, as he drew half a crown from his waistcoat pocket. 'I never see such a feller as you, Jack; you win everything. Even when we've good cards, Charley and I can't make nothing of 'em.'

Either the matter or the manner of this remark, which was made very ruefully, delighted Charley Bates so much, that his consequent shout of laughter roused Fagin from his reverie, and induced him to inquire as to what was the matter.

'Matter?' cried Charley. 'I wish you had watched the play. Tommy Chitling hasn't won a point; and I went partners with him against the Artful and dumb.'

'Ay, ay!' said the old man, with a grin, which sufficiently demonstrated that he was at no loss to understand the reason. 'Try 'em again, Tom; try 'em again.'

'No more of it for me, thankee, Fagin,' replied Mr. Chitling; 'I've had enough. That 'ere Dodger has such a run of luck that there's no standin' again' him.'

'Ha! ha! my dear,' replied Fagin, 'you must get up very early in the morning to win against the Dodger.'

'Morning!' said Charley Bates; 'you must keep your boots on over-night, and have a telescope at each eye, and an opera-glass between your shoulders, if you want to come over him.'

Mr. Dawkins received these handsome compliments with much philosophy, and offered to cut any gentleman in company, for the first picture-card, at a shilling at a time. Nobody accepting the challenge, and his pipe being by this time smoked out, he proceeded to amuse himself by sketching a ground-plan of Newgate Prison on the table with the piece of chalk which had served him in lieu of counters, whistling, meantime, with particular musicality.

'How precious dull you are, Tommy!' said the Dodger, stopping short when there had been a long silence, and addressing Mr. Chitling. 'What do you think he's thinking of, Fagin?'

'How should I know, my dear?' replied the old man, looking round as he plied the bellows. 'About his losses, maybe; or the little retirement in the country that he's just left, eh? Ha! ha! Is that it, my dear?'

'Not a bit of it,' replied the Dodger, stopping the subject of discourse as Mr. Chitling was about to reply. 'What do *you* say, Charley?'

'*I* should say,' replied Master Bates, with a grin, 'that he was uncommon sweet upon Betsy. See how he's a-blushing! Oh, my eye! here's a merry-go-rounder! Tommy Chitling's in love! Oh, Fagin! Fagin! what a spree!'

Thoroughly overpowered with the notion of Mr. Chitling being the victim of tender passion, Master Bates threw himself back in his chair with such violence, that he lost his balance and pitched over upon the floor, where (the accident abating nothing of his merriment) he lay at full length until his laugh was over, when he resumed his former position, and began another.

'Never mind him, my dear,' said Fagin, winking at Mr. Dawkins, and giving Master Bates a reproving tap with the nozzle of the bellows. 'Betsy's a fine girl. Stick up to her, Tom. Stick up to her.'

'What I mean to say, Fagin,' replied Mr. Chitling, very red in the face, 'is that it isn't anything to anybody here.'

'No more it is,' replied the old miser; 'Charley will talk. Don't mind him, my dear; don't mind him. Betsy's a fine girl. Do as she bids you, Tom, and you will make your fortune.'

'So I *do* do as she bids me,' replied Mr. Chitling; 'I shouldn't have been milled if it hadn't been for her advice. But it turned out a good job for you; didn't it, Fagin? And what's six weeks of it? It must come some time or another; and why not in the winter time, when you don't want to go out a-walking so much—eh, Fagin?'

'Ah, to be sure, my dear,' replied Fagin.

'You wouldn't mind it again, Tom, would you,' asked the Dodger, winking at Charley and the old man, 'if Bet was all right?'

'I mean to say that I shouldn't,' replied Tom, angrily. 'There, now. Ah! Who'll say as much as that, I should like to know; eh, Fagin?'

'Nobody, my dear,' replied Fagin; 'not a soul, Tom. I don't know one of 'em that would do it besides you; not one of 'em, my dear.'

'I might have got clear off, if I'd peached on her; mightn't I, Fagin?' angrily pursued the poor half-witted dupe. 'A word from me would have done it; wouldn't it, Fagin?'

'To be sure it would, my dear,' replied the old man.

'But I didn't blab it; did I, Fagin?' demanded Tom, pouring question upon question with great volubility.

'No, no, to be sure,' replied Fagin; 'you were too stouthearted for that—a deal too stout, my dear!'

'Perhaps I was,' rejoined Tom, looking round; 'and if I was, what's to laugh at in that, eh, Fagin?'

Mr. Fagin, perceiving that Mr. Chitling was considerably roused, hastened to assure him that nobody was laughing; and to prove the gravity of the company, appealed to Master Bates, the principal offender. But, unfortunately, Charley, in opening his mouth to reply that he was never more serious in his life, was unable to prevent the escape of such a violent roar, that the abused Mr. Chitling, without any preliminary ceremonies, rushed across the room and aimed a blow at the offender, who, being skilful in evading pursuit, ducked to avoid it, and chose his time so well that it lighted on the chest of the Merry Old Gentleman himself, and caused him to stagger to the wall, where he stood panting for breath, while Mr. Chitling looked on with intense dismay.

'Hark!' cried the Dodger at this moment, 'I heard the tinkler.' Catching up the light, he crept softly upstairs.

The bell was rung again, with some impatience, while the party remained in darkness. After a short pause, the Dodger reappeared, and whispered to Fagin mysteriously.

'What!' cried the old man, 'alone?'

The Dodger nodded in the affirmative; and shading the flame of the candle with his hand, gave Charley Bates a private intimation, in dumb show, that he had better not be funny just then. Having performed this friendly office, he fixed his eyes on Fagin's face, and awaited his directions.

The old man bit his yellow fingers, and meditated for some seconds, his face working with agitation the while, as if he dreaded something, and feared to know the worst. At length he raised his head.

'Where is he?' he asked.

The Dodger pointed to the floor above, and made a gesture as if to leave the room.

'Yes,' said Fagin, answering the mute inquiry; 'bring him down.' Hush! Quiet! Charley, Tom, gently! Scarce, scarce!'

This brief direction to Charley Bates and his recent antagonist was softly and immediately obeyed. There was no sound of their whereabouts, when the Dodger descended the stairs, bearing the light in his hand, and followed by a man in a coarse smock-frock, who, after casting a hurried glance round the room, pulled off his hat and a large scarf which had concealed the lower portion of his face—disclosing all haggard, unwashed, and unshorn—the singular features of Toby Crackit.

'How are you, Fagey?' said this worthy, nodding to the old man. 'Pop that scarf away with my hat up on the shelf, Dodger, so that I may know where to find it when I cut out a-here; that's the time of day! You'll be a fine young cracksman afore long now.'

With these words he pulled up the smock-frock, and, winding it around his middle, drew a chair to the fire, and placed his feet upon the hob of the fireplace.

'See there, Fagey,' he said, pointing disconsolately to his top boots; 'not a drop of Day and Martin since you know when—not a bubble of blacking, by—! But don't look at me in that way, man. All in good time.

I can't talk about business until I've eaten; so produce some sustenance, and let's have a quiet fill-out for the first time these three days!'

The old man motioned to the Dodger to place what eatables there were, upon the table; and, seating himself opposite the housebreaker, waited his leisure.

To judge from appearances, Toby was by no means in a hurry to open the conversation. At first, Fagin contented himself with patiently watching his countenance, as if to gain from its expression some clue to the intelligence he brought; but in vain.

He looked tired and worn, but there was the same complacent repose upon his features that they always wore, and through dirt, and beard, and whisker there still shone, unimpaired, the self-satisfied smirk of flash Toby Crackit. Then Fagin, in an agony of impatience, watched every morsel he put into his mouth, pacing up and down the room, meanwhile, in irrepressible excitement. It was all of no use. Toby continued to eat with the utmost outward indifference, until he could eat no more; then, ordering the Dodger out, he closed the door, mixed a glass of spirits and water, and composed himself for talking.

'First and foremost, Fagey,' said Toby.

'Yes, yes!' interposed the old miser, drawing up his chair.

Mr. Crackit stopped to take a draught of spirits and water, and to declare that the gin was excellent, and then, placing his feet against the low fireplace mantel, so as to bring his boots to about the level of his eye, he quietly resumed.

'First and foremost, Fagey,' said the housebreaker, 'how's Bill?'

'What!' screamed Fagin, starting up from his seat.

'Why, you don't mean to say—'began Toby, turning pale.

'Mean!' cried Fagin, stamping furiously on the ground. 'Where are they? Sikes and the boy! Where are they? Where have they been? Where are they hiding? Why have they not been here?'

'The crack failed,' said Toby, faintly.

'I know that,' replied the old man, tearing a newspaper from his pocket and pointing to it. 'What more?'

'He turned on us, the boy did!' explained Toby. 'Alarmed the whole bloody household, he did.'

'Damn!' cried Fagin.

'We cut out straight away,' continued the robber. 'They gave chase. The whole county was awake, and the dogs upon us. They were close upon our heels; every man for himself, or each for the gallows! Me and Bill, we soon parted company.'

'The boy?' asked Fagin.

'They fired and hit the boy,' answered Toby. 'We left him lying where he fell. Alive or dead, that's all I know of him.'

'For your sake and mine,' said Fagin, 'and Bill's, let's pray that he's dead.

'I tell you,' said Toby, 'it was badly planned. Why not have kept him here among the rest, and made a sneaking, snivelling pickpocket of him at once?'

'Only hear him!' exclaimed the old man, shrugging his shoulders.

'Why, do you mean to say you couldn't have done it, if you had chosen?' demanded Toby, sternly. 'Haven't you done it, with other boys, scores of times?'

'He might have become of use to me, but I saw that it was not easy to train him to the business,' replied the old man; 'he was not like other boys in the same circumstances.'

'Curse him, no!' muttered Toby, 'or he would have been a thief, long ago.'

'I had no hold upon him to make him worse,' pursued Fagin, anxiously watching the countenance of his companion. 'His hand was not in it. I had nothing to frighten him with; which we always must have in the beginning, or we labour in vain. What could I do? Send him out with the Dodger and Charley? We had enough of that, my dear. He needed a sense of commitment.'

With that, Fagin donned his greatcoat and, leaving his companion to ponder his thoughts, headed out into the night.

Chapter 26
Fagin Queries Nancy

The old man had gained the street corner before he began to recover from the effect of Crackit's intelligence. He had relaxed nothing of his unusual speed, but was still pressing onward in the same wild and disordered manner, when the sudden dashing past of a carriage, and a boisterous cry from the foot passengers, who saw his danger, drove him back upon the pavement. Avoiding, as much as was possible, all the main streets, and skulking only through the byways and alleys, he at length emerged on Snow Hill. Here he walked even faster than before; nor did he linger until he had again turned into a court, when, as if conscious that he was now in his proper element, he fell into his usual shuffling pace, and seemed to breathe more freely.

Near to the spot at which Snow Hill and Holborn Hill meet there opens, upon the right hand as you come out of the City, a narrow and dismal alley, leading to Saffron Hill. In its filthy shops are exposed for sale huge bunches of second-hand silk handkerchiefs, of all sizes and patterns; for here reside the traders who purchase them from pickpockets. Hundreds of these handkerchiefs hang dangling from pegs outside the windows or flaunting from the door-posts; and the shelves, within, are piled with them. Confined as the limits of Field Lane are, it has its barber, its coffee-shop, its beer-shop, and its fried fish warehouse. It is a commercial colony onto itself—the emporium of petty larceny; visited in early morning and at the coming of dusk by silent merchants, who traffic in dark back-parlours, and who go as strangely as they come. Here the clothes trader, the shoe cobbler, and the rag merchant display their goods, as sign-boards to the petty thief. Here too, stores of old iron and bones, and heaps of mildewy fragments of woollen stuff and linen, rust and rot in the grimy cellars.

It was into this place that Fagin turned. He was well known to the sallow denizens of the lane; for such of them as were on the look-out to buy or sell nodded familiarly as he passed along. He replied to their salutations in the same way; but bestowed no closer recognition until he reached the farther end of the alley, when he stopped to address a salesman of small stature, who had squeezed as much of his person into a child's chair as the chair would hold, and was smoking a pipe at his warehouse door.

'Why, the sight of you, Mr. Fagin, would cure pneumonia!' said this respectable trader, in acknowledgment of the old man's inquiry after his health.

'The neighbourhood was a little too hot, Lively,' said Fagin, elevating his eyebrows, and crossing his hands upon his shoulders.

'Well, I've heerd that complaint of it, once or twice before,' replied the trader; 'but it soon cools down again. Don't you find it so?'

Fagin nodded in the affirmative. Pointing in the direction of Saffron Hill, he inquired whether any one was up yonder tonight.

'At the Cripples?' inquired the man.

The old man nodded.

'Let me see,' pursued the merchant, reflecting. 'Yes, there's some half-dozen of 'em gone in, that I knows.'

'Sikes is not, I suppose?' inquired the old man, with a disappointed countenance.

'I don't think your friend's there,' replied the little man, shaking his head, and looking amazingly sly. 'Have you got anything in my line to-night?'

'Nothing tonight,' said Fagin, turning away.

'Are you going up to the Cripples, Fagin?' cried the little man, calling after him. 'Stop! I don't mind if I have a drop there with you!'

But as Fagin, looking back, waved his hand to intimate that he pre-ferred being alone, and, moreover, as the little man could not very easily disengage himself from the chair, the sign of the Cripples was for a time bereft of the advantage of Mr. Lively's presence. By the time he had got upon his legs the old miser had disappeared; so Mr. Lively, after inef-fectually standing on tip-toe in the hope of catching sight of him, again forced himself into the little chair, and, exchanging a shake of the head with a lady in the opposite shop, in which doubt and mistrust were plain-ly mingled, resumed his pipe with a grave demeanour.

At the Three Cripples, the public-house in which Mr. Sikes and his dog have already figured, merely making a sign to a man at the bar, Fagin walked straight upstairs, and opening the door of a room, and softly in-sinuating himself into the chamber, looked anxiously about, shading his eyes with his hand as if in search of some particular person.

The room was illuminated by two gas-lights; the glare of which was prevented by the barred shutters and closely-drawn curtains of faded red, from being visible outside. The ceiling was blackened, to prevent its colour from being injured by the flaring of the lamps; and the place was so full of dense tobacco smoke, that at first it was scarcely possible to discern anything more. By degrees, however, as some of it cleared away through the open door, an assemblage of heads, as confused as the noises that greeted the ear, could be made out; and as the eye grew more accus-tomed to the scene, the spectator gradually became aware of the presence of a numerous company, male and female, crowded round a long table, at the upper end of which sat the landlord of the Cripples as if the chairman of a meeting.

A professional gentleman, with a bluish nose, and his face tied up for the benefit of a toothache, presided at a jingling piano in a remote corner while a young lady, none other than Mr. Chitling's Betsy, entertained the crowd with a ballad in four verses. Thereafter, at the urging of the landlord, two older women volunteered a duet sung to great applause.

Fagin stepped softly into the room. It was curious to observe some of the faces which stood out prominently from among the group. The landlord himself was a coarse, rough, heavy-built fellow, who, while the songs were proceeding, rolled his eyes hither and thither, and, seeming to give himself up to joviality, had an eye for everything that was done, and an ear for everything that was said—and sharp ones, too. Near him were the singers, women all, receiving with professional indifference the compliments of the company, and applying themselves in turn to a dozen proffered glasses of spirits and water, tendered by their more boisterous admirers, whose countenances, expressive of almost every vice in almost every grade, irresistibly attracted one's attention by their very repulsiveness. Cunning, ferocity, and drunkenness in all its stages were there, in their strongest aspects; and the women—some with the last lingering tinge of their early freshness almost fading as you looked; others with every mark and stamp of their sex utterly beaten out, and presenting but one loathsome blank of profligacy and crime; some mere girls, others but young women, and none past the prime of life—formed the darkest and saddest portion of this dreary picture.

Fagin, troubled by no grave emotions, looked eagerly from face to face while these proceedings were in progress, but apparently without meeting that of which he was in search. Succeeding, at length, in catching the landlord's eye, he beckoned to him slightly, and left the room, as quietly as he had entered it.

'What can I do for you, Mr. Fagin?' inquired the landlord, as he followed him out onto the landing. 'Won't you join us? They'll be delighted, every one of 'em.'

Fagin shook his head impatiently, and asked in a whisper, 'Is Sikes or Nancy here?'

'No,' replied the landlord.

'And no news of Barney?' inquired Fagin.

'None,' replied the landlord. 'He won't stir till it's all safe. Depend on it, they're on the scent down there; and that if he moved, he'd blow upon the thing at once. He's all right enough, Barney is, else I should have heard of him. I'll wager that Barney's managing properly. Give him credit for that.'

'Not a word now,' said Fagin, descending the stairs.

'I say,' said the other, looking over the rails, and speaking in a hoarse whisper; 'what a time this would be for a sell! I've got Phil Barker here, so drunk that a boy might take him!'

'Aha! But it's not Phil Barker's time,' said the old man, looking up. 'There is more to do before we can afford to part with him; so go back to the company, my dear, and tell them to lead merry lives—*while they last.* Ha! ha! ha!'

The landlord reciprocated the old man's laugh, and returned to his guests. Mr. Fagin was no sooner alone than his countenance resumed its former expression of anxiety and thought. After a brief reflection, he called a hackney carriage, and bid the man to drive towards Bethnal Green. He dismissed him within some quarter of a mile of Mr. Sikes's residence, and performed the short remainder of the distance on foot.

'Now,' muttered the old man, as he knocked at the door, 'if there is any deep play here, I shall have it out of you, my girl, cunning as you are.'

'She's in her room,' said a matronly woman sitting by the front door. Fagin crept softly upstairs, and entered it without any previous ceremony.

The girl was alone; lying with her head upon the table, and her hair straggling over it. 'She has been drinking,' thought Fagin, coolly, 'or perhaps she is only miserable.'

The old man turned to close the door, as he made this reflection; the noise thus occasioned, roused the girl. She eyed his crafty face narrowly, as she inquired whether there was any news, and listened to his recital of Toby Crackit's story. When it was concluded, she sank into her former attitude, but spoke not a word. She pushed the candle impatiently away, and once or twice, as she feverishly changed her position, shuffled her feet upon the ground; but this was all.

During this silence the old man looked restlessly about the room, to assure himself that there was no evidence of Sikes having covertly returned. Apparently satisfied with his inspection, he coughed twice or thrice, and made as many efforts to open a conversation; but the girl heeded him no more than if he had been made of stone. At length he made another attempt, and rubbing his hands together, said in his most conciliatory tone:

'And where do you think Bill is now, my dear?'

The girl moaned out some half intelligible reply, that she could not tell, and seemed, from the smothered noise that escaped her, to be crying.

'And the boy, too,' said Fagin, straining his eyes to catch a glimpse of her face. 'Poor leetle child! Shot and left bleeding, Nance; only think!'

'The child,' said the girl, suddenly looking up, 'is better where he is, than among us; and if no harm comes to Bill from it, I hope he lies dead, and that his young bones may rot.'

'What!' cried the old man, in amazement.

'Ay, I do,' returned the girl, meeting his gaze. 'I shall be glad to have him away from my eyes, and to know that the worst is over. I can't bear to have him about me. The sight of him turns me against myself, and all of you.'

'Pooh!' said Fagin, scornfully. 'You're drunk.'

'Am I?' cried the girl, bitterly. 'It's no fault of yours, if I am not! You'd never have me anything else, if you had your will, except now;—the humour doesn't suit you, does it?'

'No!' rejoined the old miser, furiously. 'It does not.'

'Change it, then!' responded the girl, with a laugh.

'Change it!' exclaimed Fagin, exasperated beyond all bounds by his companion's unexpected obstinacy and the vexation of the night. 'I *will* change it! Listen to me, you drab. Listen to me, who, with six words, can strangle Sikes as surely as if I had his bull's throat between my fingers now. If he comes back, and leaves the boy behind to peach—murder him yourself if you would have him escape the hangman. And do it the moment he sets foot in this room, or mind me, it will be too late!'

'What is all this?' cried the girl involuntarily.

'What is it?' pursued Fagin, mad with rage.

Panting for breath, the old man stammered for a word, and in that instant checked the torrent of his wrath, and changed his whole demeanour. A moment before, his clenched hands had grasped the air, his eyes had dilated, and his face grown livid with passion; but now he shrunk into a chair, and, cowering together, trembled with the apprehension of having himself disclosed some hidden villainy. After a short silence, he ventured to look round at his companion. He appeared somewhat reassured, on beholding her in the same listless attitude from which he had first aroused her.

'Nancy, dear!' croaked Fagin, in his usual voice. 'Did you mind me, dear?'

'Don't worry me now, Fagin!' replied the girl, raising her head languidly. 'If Bill has not done it this time, he will another. He has done many a good job for you, and will do many more when he can; and when he can't he won't; so no more about that.'

'Regarding the boy, my dear?' said the miser, rubbing the palms of his hands nervously together.

'The boy must take his chance with the rest,' interrupted Nancy, hastily; 'and I say again, I hope he is dead, and out of harm's way, and out of yours—that is, if Bill comes to no harm. And if Toby got clear off, Bill's pretty sure to be safe; for he's worth two of Toby any time.'

'About what I was saying, my dear,?' observed Fagin, keeping his glistening eye steady upon her.

'You must say it all over again, if it's anything you want me to do,' rejoined Nancy; 'and if it is, you had better wait till tomorrow. You put me up for a minute; but now I'm stupid again.'

Fagin put several other questions, all with the same drift of ascertaining whether the girl had profited by his unguarded hints; but she answered them so readily, and was withal so utterly unmoved by his searching looks, that his original impression of her being more than a trifle in liquor was fully confirmed. Nancy, indeed, was not exempt from a failing which was very common among the old man's female pupils, and in which, in their tender years, they were rather more encouraged than checked. Her disordered appearance, and a wholesale perfume of Geneva which pervaded the apartment, afforded strong confirmatory evidence of the justice of Fagin's supposition; and when, after indulging in the temporary display of violence above described, she subsided, first into dullness, and afterwards into a compound of feelings, under the influence of which she shed tears one minute, and in the next gave utterance to various exclamations of 'Never say die!' and diverse calculations as to what might be the amount of the odds so long as a lady or gentleman was happy, Mr. Fagin, who had had considerable experience of such matters in his time, saw, with great satisfaction, that she was very far gone indeed.

Having eased his mind by this discovery, and having accomplished his twofold object of imparting to the girl what he had that night heard, and of ascertaining, with his own eyes, that Sikes had not returned; Mr. Fagin turned round and walked towards the door, leaving his young friend with her head upon the table.

'If you hear any news of Bill or the boy,' said Fagin, looking back, 'you'll tell me straight away.' Nancy failed to respond. 'Eh, our impulses may differ,' muttered Fagin, 'but our ends correspond.'

Chapter 27
Mr. Bumble's Proposition

As it would be by no means seemly in a humble author to keep so mighty a personage as a beadle waiting, with his back to the fire, and the skirts of his coat gathered up under his arms, until such time as it might suit his pleasure to relieve him; and as it would still less become his station, or his gallantry, to involve in the same neglect a lady on whom that beadle had looked with an eye of tenderness and affection, and in whose ear he had whispered sweet words, which, coming from such a quarter, might well thrill the bosom of maid or matron of whatsoever degree; the historian whose pen traces these words—trusting that he knows his place, and that he entertains a becoming reverence for those upon earth to whom high and important authority is delegated—hastens to pay them that respect which their position demands, and to treat them with all that duteous ceremony which their exalted rank, and (by consequence) great virtues, imperatively claim at his hands. Towards this end, indeed, he had purposed to introduce, in this place, a dissertation touching upon the divine right of beadles, and elucidative of the position that a beadle can do no wrong, which could not fail to have been both pleasurable and profitable to the right-minded reader, but which he is unfortunately compelled, by want of time and space, to postpone to some more convenient and fitting opportunity; on the arrival of which, he will be prepared to show, that a beadle properly constituted—that is to say, a parochial beadle, attached to a parochial workhouse, and attending in his official capacity the parochial church—is, in right and virtue of his office, possessed of all the excellences and best qualities of humanity; and that to none of those excellences can mere companies' beadles, or court-of-law beadles, or even chapel-of-ease beadles (save the last, and they in a very lowly and inferior degree), lay the remotest sustainable claim.

Mr. Bumble had re-counted the teaspoons, reweighed the sugar-tongs, made a closer inspection of the milk-pot, and ascertained to a nicety the exact condition of the furniture, down to the very horse-hair seats of the chairs; and had repeated each process full half a dozen times, before he began to think that it was time for Mrs. Corney to return. Thinking begets thinking; and, as there were no sounds of Mrs. Corney's approach, it occurred to Mr. Bumble that it would be an innocent and virtuous way of spending the time, if he were further to allay his curiosity by a cursory glance at the interior of Mrs. Corney's chest of drawers.

Having listened at the keyhole, to assure himself that nobody was approaching the chamber, Mr. Bumble, beginning at the bottom, proceeded to make himself acquainted with the contents of the three long drawers; which, being filled with various garments of good fashion and texture, carefully preserved between two layers of old newspapers, speckled with dried lavender, seemed to yield him exceeding satisfaction. Arriving, in course of time, at the right-hand corner drawer (in which was the key), and beholding therein a small padlocked box, which, being shaken, gave forth a pleasant sound, as of the chinking of coin, Mr. Bumble returned with a stately walk to the fireplace; and, resuming his old attitude, said, with a grave and determined air, 'I'll do it!' He followed up this remarkable declaration, by shaking his head in a waggish manner for ten minutes, as though he were remonstrating with himself for being such a pleasant dog; and then, he took a view of his legs in profile, with much seeming pleasure and interest.

He was still placidly engaged in this latter survey, when Mrs. Corney, hurrying into the room, threw herself, in a breathless state, on a chair by the fireside, and covering her eyes with one hand, placed the other over her heart, and gasped for breath.

'Mrs. Corney,' said Mr. Bumble, stooping over the matron, 'what is this, ma'am? Has anything happened, ma'am? Pray answer me; I'm on— on -' Mr. Bumble, in his alarm, could not immediately think of the word 'tenterhooks,' so he said, 'broken bottles.'

'Oh, Mr. Bumble!' cried the lady, 'I have been so dreadfully put out!'

'Put out, ma'am!' exclaimed Mr. Bumble; 'who has dared to—? I know!' said Mr. Bumble, checking himself with native majesty, 'this is them wicious paupers!'

'It's dreadful to think of!' said the lady, shuddering.

'Then *don't* think of it, ma'am,' rejoined Mr. Bumble.

'I can't help it,' whimpered the lady.

'Then take something, ma'am,' said Mr. Bumble, soothingly. 'A little of the wine?'

'Not for the world!' replied Mrs. Corney. 'I couldn't—oh! The top shelf in the right-hand corner—oh!' Uttering these words, the good lady pointed distractedly to the cupboard and underwent a convulsion from internal spasms. Mr. Bumble rushed to the closet, and snatching a pint green-glass bottle from the shelf thus incoherently indicated, filled a tea-cup with its contents, and held it to the lady's lips.

'I'm better now,' said Mrs. Corney, falling back after drinking half of it.

Mr. Bumble raised his eyes piously to the ceiling in thankfulness; and, bringing them down again to the brim of the cup, lifted it to his nose.

'Peppermint,' exclaimed Mrs. Corney, in a faint voice, smiling gently at the beadle as she spoke. 'Try it! There's a little—a little something else in it.'

Mr. Bumble tasted the medicine with a doubtful look, smacked his lips, took another taste, and put the cup down empty.

'It's very comforting,' said Mrs. Corney.

'Very much so indeed, ma'am,' said the beadle. As he spoke, he drew a chair beside the matron, and tenderly inquired what had happened to distress her.

'Nothing,' replied Mrs. Corney. 'I am a foolish, excitable, weak creetur.'

'Not weak, ma'am,' retorted Mr. Bumble, drawing his chair a little closer. 'Are you a weak creetur, Mrs. Corney?'

'We are all weak creeturs,' said Mrs. Corney, laying down a general principle.

'So we are,' agreed the beadle.

Nothing was said on either side, for a minute or two afterwards. By the expiration of that time Mr. Bumble had illustrated the proposition by removing his left arm from the back of Mrs. Corney's chair, where it had previously rested, to Mrs. Corney's apron-string, around which it gradually became entwined.

'We are all weak creeturs,' said Mr. Bumble.

Mrs. Corney sighed.

'Don't sigh, Mrs. Corney,' said Mr. Bumble.

'I can't help it,' said Mrs. Corney. And she sighed again.

'This is a very comfortable room, ma'am,' said Mr. Bumble looking around. 'Another room, and this, ma'am, would be a complete thing.'

'It would be too much for one,' murmured the lady.

'But not for two, ma'am,' rejoined Mr. Bumble, in soft accents. 'Eh, Mrs. Corney?'

Mrs. Corney drooped her head, when the beadle said this. The beadle drooped his, to get a view of Mrs. Corney's face. Mrs. Corney, with great propriety, turned her head away, and released her hand to get at her pocket handkerchief; but, insensibly, replaced her hand in one of Mr. Bumble's.

'The board allows you coals, don't they, Mrs. Corney?' inquired the beadle, affectionately pressing her hand.

'And candles,' replied Mrs. Corney, slightly returning the pressure.

'Coals, candles, and house-rent free!' exclaimed Mr. Bumble. 'Oh, Mrs. Corney, what an Angel you are!'

The lady was not proof against this burst of feeling. She sank into Mr.

Bumble's arms; and that gentleman in his agitation, imprinted a passionate kiss upon her chaste nose.

'Such parochial perfection!' exclaimed Mr. Bumble, rapturously. 'You know that Mr. Slout is worse tonight, my fascinator?'

'Yes,' replied Mrs. Corney, bashfully.

'He can't live a week, the doctor says,' pursued Mr. Bumble. 'He is the master of this establishment; his death will cause a wacancy; that wacancy must be filled up. Oh, Mrs. Corney, what a prospect this opens! What an opportunity for a joining of hearts and housekeepings!'

Mrs. Corney sobbed.

'The little word?' said Mr. Bumble, bending over the bashful beauty. 'The one little, little, little word, my blessed Corney?'

'Ye—ye—yes!' sighed out the matron.

'One more,' pursued the beadle; 'compose your darling feelings for only one more. When is it to come off?'

Mrs. Corney twice essayed to speak, and twice failed. At length, summoning up courage, she threw her arms around Mr. Bumble's neck, and said, it might be as soon as ever he pleased, and that he was 'an irresistible duck.' Matters being thus amicably and satisfactorily arranged, the contract was solemnly ratified with another teacupful of the peppermint mixture; which was rendered the more necessary by the flutter and agitation of the lady's spirits. While it was being disposed of, she acquainted Mr. Bumble with the old woman's decease.

'Very good,' said that gentleman, sipping his peppermint. 'I'll call at Sowerberry's as I go home, and tell him to send over tomorrow morning. Was it that as frightened you, love?'

'It wasn't anything particular, dear,' said the lady evasively.

'It must have been something, love,' urged Mr. Bumble. 'Won't you tell your own B.?'

'Not now,' rejoined the lady; 'one of these days. After we're married, dear.'

'After we're married!' exclaimed Mr. Bumble. 'It wasn't any impudence from any of them male paupers as -'

'No, no, love!' interposed the lady, hastily.

'If I thought it was,' continued Mr. Bumble—'if I thought as any one of 'em had dared to lift his wulgar eyes to that lovely countenance -'

'They wouldn't have dared to do it, love,' responded the lady.

'They had better not!' said Mr. Bumble, clenching his fist. 'Let me see any man, parochial or extra-parochial, as would presume to do it, and I can tell you that he wouldn't do it a second time!'

Unembellished by any violence of gesticulation, this might have seemed no very high compliment to the lady's charms; but as Mr. Bumble accompanied the threat with many warlike gestures, she was much touched with this proof of his devotion, and protested, with great admiration, that he was indeed a dove.

The dove then turned up his coat-collar, and put on his cocked hat; and, having exchanged a long and affectionate embrace with his future partner, once again braved the cold wind of the night, merely pausing for a few minutes, in the male paupers' ward, to abuse them a little with the view of satisfying himself that he could fill the office of workhouse master with needful acerbity. Assured of his qualifications, Mr. Bumble left the building with a light heart, and bright visions of his future promotion, which served to occupy his mind until he reached the shop of the undertaker.

Now, Mr. and Mrs. Sowerberry having gone out to tea and supper, and Noah Claypole not being at any time disposed to take upon himself a greater amount of physical exertion than is necessary to a convenient performance of the two functions of eating and drinking, the shop was not closed, although it was past the usual hour for shutting up. Mr. Bumble tapped with his cane on the counter several times; but, attracting no attention, and beholding a light shining through the glass window of the little parlour at the back of the shop, he made bold to peep in and see what was going forward; and when he saw what *was* going forward, he was not a little surprised.

The cloth was laid for supper, and the table was covered with bread and butter, plates and glasses, a porter-pot, and a wine bottle. At the upper end of the table, Mr. Noah Claypole lolled negligently in an easy chair, with his legs thrown over one of the arms, an open clasp knife in one hand, and a mass of buttered bread in the other. Close beside him stood Charlotte, opening oysters from a barrel, which Mr. Claypole condescended to swallow with remarkable avidity. A more than ordinary redness in the region of the young gentleman's nose, and a kind of fixed wink in his right eye, denoted that he was to no slight degree intoxicated; and these symptoms were confirmed by the intense relish with which he took his oysters, for which nothing else but a strong appreciation of their cooling properties, in cases of internal fever, could have sufficiently accounted.

'Here's a delicious fat one, Noah, dear!' said Charlotte; 'try him, do; only this one.'

'What a delicious thing is an oyster!' remarked Mr. Claypole, after he had swallowed it. 'What a pity it is a number of 'em should ever make you feel uncomfortable; isn't it, Charlotte?'

'It's quite a cruelty,' agreed Charlotte.

'So it is,' acquiesced Mr. Claypole. 'Ain't yer fond of oysters?'

'Not overmuch,' replied Charlotte. 'I like to see you eat 'em, Noah dear, better than eating 'em myself.'

'Lor!' said Noah, reflectively; 'how odd!'

'Have another,' said Charlotte. 'Here's one with such a beautiful delicate beard!'

'I can't manage anymore,' said Noah. 'I'm very sorry. Come here, Charlotte, and I'll kiss yer.'

'What?' shouted Mr. Bumble, bursting into the room. 'Say that again, sir.'

Charlotte uttered a scream, and hid her face in her apron. Mr. Claypole, without making any further change in his position than suffering to let both his legs reach the ground, gazed at the beadle in drunken terror.

'Say it again, you wile, audacious fellow!' said Mr. Bumble. 'How dare you mention such a thing, sir? And how dare you to encourage him, you insolent minx? Kiss her!' exclaimed Mr. Bumble, in strong indignation. 'Faugh!'

'I didn't mean to do it!' said Noah, blubbering. 'She's always a-kissing of me, whether I like it or not.'

'Oh, Noah,' cried Charlotte, reproachfully.

'Yer are; yer know yer are!' retorted Noah. 'She's always a-doin' of it, Mr. Bumble, sir; she chucks me under the chin, please, sir; and makes all manner of love!'

'Silence!' cried Mr. Bumble, sternly. 'Take yourself downstairs, ma'am. Noah, you shut up the shop; say another word till your master comes home, at your peril; and when he does come home, tell him that Mr. Bumble said he was to send over a old woman's shell after breakfast tomorrow morning. Do you hear, sir?

Kissing!' cried Mr. Bumble, holding up his hands. 'The sin and wickedness of the lower orders in this parochial district is frightful! If Parliament don't take their abominable courses under consideration, this country's ruined, and the character of the peasantry gone forever!' With these words, the beadle strode, with a lofty and gloomy air, from the undertaker's premises.

And now that we have accompanied Mr. Bumble on his road home, and have made all necessary arrangements for old Sally's funeral, let us set a foot a few inquiries after Oliver Twist, and ascertain whether he be still lying where he was shot?

Chapter 28
An Eventful Morning

Amidst the shouting of men, the barking of dogs, and the smell of spent gun powder, and ignoring Sikes's demand to abandon him; Crackit bent down, picked up Oliver, and threw him over his shoulder as if he were but a sack of flour.

'Hold tight, I've got thee,' said Toby to Oliver.

Then came the loud ringing of a bell, and the sensation of being carried at a rapid pace. As the noises grew confused in the distance, a deadly cold crept over the boy, and Oliver neither saw nor heard anything more.

'How the boy bleeds,' Toby said, to himself; for there was no one about able to hear him,

Crackit ran directly to a neighbouring house he knew well—though the occupants knew not of him; and, having deposited Oliver gently upon the front door step, kicked the door several times with great vigour. Satisfied that the racket would surely alarm all of the occupants, and instigate an investigation, he quickly ran off away from the mounting clamour.

A ways off and heading in the opposite direction, back towards the bridge, the other robber was also trying to increase the distance between himself and the racket. He turned his head, for an instant, looking for Toby—who was nowhere to be seen. There was little to be observed in the mist and darkness, but the shouting of men vibrated through the air; and the barking of neighbourhood dogs, roused by the sound of the alarm bell, resounded in every direction.

'Wolves tear your throats!' muttered Sikes, grinding his teeth. 'I wish Bull's-eye was amongst you; you'd howl the hoarser for it.' Sikes growled forth this imprecation, with the most desperate ferocity that his desperate nature was capable of.

Three men, one leaning heavily on his cane, who had by this time advanced some distance along the road, stopped to take counsel together.

'Ho, ho, there!' cried a tremulous voice in the rear. 'Pincher! Neptune! Come here, come here!'

The elderly dogs, who, in common with their aging master, seemed to have no particular relish for the sport in which they were engaged, readily answered to the command.

'My advice,' said Mr. Griffith, who had called the dogs back, 'is that we immediately go home again.'

'But,' protested Mr. Brittles, 'I shouldn't wish for us to be delinquent in our duties to the law.'

'I am agreeable to the suggestion that we return home,' said Mr. Giles; and who was very pale in the face, and very polite, as frightened men frequently are. 'Our duties lie there, not on the streets.'

'You're not afraid, are you, Mr. Giles?' inquired Mr. Brittles, in an accusatory tone.

'For sure, I ain't,' said Giles.

'You are!' exclaimed Brittles, accusingly.

'That's a falsehood,' said Giles. 'I ask you, who led the way through the gate?'

'I was but a step behind ya,' rejoined Mr. Brittles.

Mr. Griffith brought the dispute to a close, most philosophically. 'I'll tell you what it is, gentlemen,' he said, with a thud of his cane, 'we are all afraid.'

'With all due respect, sir, speak for yourself,' said Mr. Giles indignantly, who was the palest of the party.

'It's natural and proper to be afraid, under such circumstances,' replied Mr. Griffith, 'I am.'

'So am I,' admitted Brittles, not wanting to contradict his master.

These frank admissions softened Mr. Giles who at once owned that *he* was afraid, 'only there's no call to tell a man he is, so, so bounceably.'

With this, they all three faced about, and marched back again with the completest unanimity, until Mr. Brittles (who was encumbered with a large broom) most handsomely insisted on stopping; to make an apology for his hastiness of speech.

'But it's wonderful,' continued Mr. Brittles, 'what a man will do, when his blood is up. I should have committed murder—I know I should—if we'd caught one of them rascals.'

As the other two were impressed with a similar presentiment, and as their blood, like his, had all gone down again; some speculation ensued upon the cause of this sudden change in their temperament.

'I know what it was,' said Mr. Giles; 'it was the gate.'

'I shouldn't wonder if it was,' exclaimed Brittles, catching at the idea.

'You may depend upon it,' said Giles, 'stopping to open the gate stopped the flow of the excitement. I felt all of mine suddenly going away, as I passed through it.'

By a remarkable coincidence, the other two had been visited by the same unpleasant sensation at that same precise moment. It was quite obvious, therefore, that it was the gate; especially as there was no doubt regarding the time at which the change of heart had taken place; all three remembered that they had come in sight of a robber at the very instant of its occurrence.

Encouraging each other with conversation such as this, but keeping very close together, notwithstanding, and looking apprehensively around whenever a fresh gust rattled through the boughs, the three men hurried back to into the house where—with all of the noise and excitement—both the cook and the housemaid awaited them.

Griffith, Giles, and Brittles were pleased to recuperate themselves, after the fatigues and terrors of the night, with tea and sundries, in the kitchen. Not that it was Mr. Griffith's habit to admit to too great a familiarity with his servants, towards whom it was rather his wont to deport himself with a lofty affability, which, while it gratified, could not fail to remind them of his superior position in society. But, death, fires, and burglary make all men equals; so Mr. Griffith sat with his legs stretched out before the cook stove, holding his cane with his left hand, while with his right he illustrated a circumstantial and minute account of the robbery, to which his hearers (but especially the cook and housemaid, who were of the party) listened with breathless interest.

'It was about ten-past four,' said Mr. Griffith, 'or I wouldn't swear that it mightn't have been a little nearer quarter-past , when I woke up, and, turning round in my bed, as it might be so, (here Mr. Griffith turned round in his chair, and pulled a corner of the tablecloth over him to imitate bed covers,) I fancied I heard a noise.'

'What sort of noise?' asked the cook.

'A kind of busting noise,' replied Mr. Griffith, 'or I'll eat my hat.'

At this point of the narrative the cook turned pale, and asked the housemaid to shut the door, who asked Giles, who asked Brittles, who pretended not to hear.

'I heard a noise,' continued Mr. Griffith. 'I said to myself, at first, "This is an illusion, a dream;" and was composing myself off to sleep, when I distinctly heard the noise again.'

The cook and housemaid simultaneously ejaculated 'Lor!' and drew their chairs closer together.

'I heard it now, quite apparent,' continued Mr. Griffith. ' "Somebody," I told myself, "is forcing off a door, or a window. Someone is entering the house for malevolent purposes, for robbery or murder or both, what's to be done?" '

'What did ya do?' asked the housemaid, with her mouth wide open, and her face expressive of the most unmitigated horror.

'I tossed off the covers,' said Griffith, throwing off the tablecloth, and looking very hard at the cook and housemaid, 'got softly out of bed; drew on a pair of -'

'Ladies present, Mr. Griffith,' murmured Giles.

'—Of *shoes*, sir,' said Griffith, turning upon him, and laying great emphasis on the word; 'seized the loaded pistol that always goes upstairs with the plate-basket, and walked on tip-toes towards Mr. Brittles' room. "Brittles," I said, when I had woken him, "don't be frightened." '

'So you did,' confirmed Brittles, in a low voice.

' "We're dead men, I think, Brittles," I said,' continued Griffith; ' "but don't be frightened." '

'*Was* he frightened?' asked the cook.

'Not a bit of it,' replied Mr. Griffith. 'He was as firm—ah! pretty near as firm as I was, or I'll eat my hat.'

'I should have died at once, I'm sure, if it had been me,' observed the housemaid.

'You're a woman,' retorted Brittles, plucking up a little.

'Brittles is right,' said Mr. Giles, nodding his head, approvingly; 'from a woman, nothing else was to be expected.'

'Then we heard shouting!' exclaimed Mr. Griffith.

'As did we all!' confirmed the housemaid, wrapping her arms ever more tightly around herself.

'Brittles and I quickly made our way to the top of the stairs,' declared Griffith. 'I could see one of the robbers, holding a lantern, clear as day.'

'Lor! What's he look like?' asked the cook.

'A big, brawny fellow, with a mean look about him,' answered Mr. Griffith, striking his cane on the floor for emphasis, 'so I shot him, shot him dead!' Mr. Griffith had risen from his seat and raised his pistol so as to illustrate his description with appropriate actions.

'Lor! Where is he?' asked the housemaid, 'this fellow you shot dead?'

'His accomplice picked him up and helped him to run off,' explained Griffith, with little deference given to consistency. 'I saw him go.'

At this point a noise was heard. Mr. Griffith startled violently, in common with the rest of the company, and sat back down on his chair. The cook and housemaid screamed.

'It was just a knock,' said Griffith, assuming perfect serenity. 'Open the front door, somebody.'

Nobody moved.

'It seems a strange sort of a thing, a knock coming so early in the morning,' said Mr. Griffith, surveying the pale faces which surrounded him and looking very blank himself; 'but the door must be opened. Do you hear, somebody?'

Mr. Griffith, as he spoke, looked at Giles; but that able servant, being naturally modest, probably considered himself nobody, and so held that the inquiry could not have any application to him. At all events, he tendered no reply. Mr. Griffith then directed an appealing glance at Brittles; but he had suddenly fallen asleep. The women were out of the question.

'If Mr. Giles would rather open the door, in the presence of witnesses,' said Mr. Griffith, after a short silence, 'I am ready to make one.'

'So I will,' said Brittles, waking up, as suddenly as he had fallen asleep.

Giles capitulated on these terms; and the party being somewhat re-assured by the discovery (made upon throwing open the shutters) that dawn was breaking, made their way to the front entrance, with the dogs in front, and the two women, who were afraid to stay behind, bringing up the rear. By the advice of Mr. Giles, they all talked very loud, to warn any evil disposed person outside, that they were strong in numbers; and by a master stroke of policy, originating in the brain of the same ingenious gentleman, the dogs' tails were well pinched, in the hall, to make them bark savagely.

These precautions having been taken, Mr. Griffith, holding fast to Giles's arm (to prevent his running away, as he pleasantly said), gave the word of command to open the door. Giles obeyed; and the whole group (including Brittles, the cook, the housekeeper, Pincher, and Neptune), peering timorously over each other's shoulders, beheld no more formidable a person than Mr. Brownlow.

'Good morning,' said Mr. Brownlow. 'I am honoured by this splendid greeting.'

'It has been an eventful morning,' said Mr. Griffith, without a tinge of embarrassment.

'So I have gathered,' replied Mr. Brownlow. 'I came calling as early as decency allowed.'

'Come in,' said Mr. Griffith, waving for his friend to step into the house. 'Much has occurred here these past few hours. You won't believe what I have to tell you.'

'I am rather certain of that,' agreed Mr. Brownlow, pleasantly.

Mr. Griffith invited Mr. Brownlow to sit down and began to recount his story, with physical demonstrations when required to emphasize the gravity of the situation. Mr. Brownlow listened with rapt attention, only uttering the odd 'you don't say' and 'my goodness'.

Mr. Griffith concluded, with a thump of his cane, by saying "I never heard of such a thing! So unexpected. In the silence of the night, too. We should be positively dead with the fright.' He was particularly troubled mostly by the fact that the robbery was unexpected, and attempted during the depth of night, as if it were the established custom of gentlemen in the housebreaking profession to transact business at noon, and to make an appointment, by post, a day or two previous.

Mr. Brownlow then asked him if he had yet had an opportunity to survey the scene of the crime.

'No!' exclaimed Mr. Griffith. 'What a marvelous idea! Come, let's take a look round.'

The two gentlemen did not have to venture far to view the most gruesome evidence. A puddle of dark red blood stained the hallway floor a few feet from where they had been sitting and talking.

'My,' said Mr. Brownlow, 'someone bled profusely!'

'Indeed,' replied Mr. Griffith, thoughtfully, 'I am surprised that he was able to run off as quickly as he did.'

The two gentlemen began a tour of all of the ground floor windows and doors. All appeared to be well secured until they entered into the scullery located off of the kitchen. A small, high window was wide open. A closer inspection revealed that the lattice work lay on the ground outside.

'The devils,' extorted Mr. Griffith. 'They came through that window or I'll eat my hat. I heard the scoundrels ripping off the lattice, I did. I shall have to fortify this window much more securely.'

'I shall take a closer look at the security of my own house as well,' said Mr. Brownlow. 'Show me, please,' continued Mr. Brownlow, 'where you were when you fired your shot. I had no that idea you were such a formidable marksman.'

'Ah, yes, upstairs,' said Mr. Griffith as he proceeded towards the staircase.

On the upper floor Mr. Griffith demonstrated how he had risen from his bed, picked up his pistol, made his way to Brittles' room, and quietly spoke to the young man; and how, upon hearing shouting, they had made their way together to the landing at the top of the stairs.

'He was right down there, at the bottom of the stairs,' explained Mr. Griffith, pointing. 'A big brawny fellow. I could hardly miss.'

'A big, brawny fellow you say?' asked Mr. Brownlow.

'Yes, with a vicious look about him,' stated Mr. Griffith, stomping his cane.

'And you fired how many shots?' asked Mr. Brownlow.

'Just the one,' replied Mr. Griffith, 'no need for a second shot.' Besides,' he continued, 'I hadn't time to reload. The scoundrels were out the door before I could do that, lucky for them!'

'Interesting,' said Mr. Brownlow, somewhat distractedly, as he gazed up and down the staircase.

Not yet having had his breakfast, Mr. Brownlow extended his condolences to Mr. Griffith for his misadventure and graciously took his leave.

* * * * *

Now that we have investigated the events that took place at the Griffith residence that fateful morning, let us inquire after young Oliver Twist himself; and ascertain, in particular, as to whether he is dead or alive and, if alive, still lying where Toby Crackit left him.

Some hours earlier Mrs. Bedwin, who was known to be a light sleeper, had been aroused by a hullabaloo taking place a short ways away. She could hear a bell ringing, men shouting, and, of course, dogs barking. Looking out the window, she soon determined that the source of the racket was very likely Mr. Griffith's residence. Knowing that Mr. Brownlow would want to be appraised immediately of anything untoward happening there, Mrs. Bedwin put on her housecoat and slippers with the intention of waking the master of the house. Her mission was, if possible, made all the more urgent by a dreadfully loud banging coming from the front door. By the time she reached his bedroom, even Mr. Brownlow was awake and pulling on his dressing gown.

'What the dickens is that ruckus about, Mrs. Bedwin?' he asked, as they made their way down the stairs.

'Sure I don't know,' replied the housekeeper, 'but it started over Griffith's way.'

'Stay back while I answer the front door,' he commanded, pulling a pistol from a pocket of his housecoat.

Before opening the outside door, Mr. Brownlow peered through a window that provided a view of the front porch. As he could not see anyone standing there, he cautiously opened the door and looked about, but there was no one to be seen in the yard or on the street. He was about to close the door again when he heard a desperate moan, and, looking down, saw a young, badly injured boy lying on the step.

'Oliver!' he cried out while picking up the child.

'Mrs. Bedwin, come directly,' he shouted upon stepping back into the house.

'Oh my! Oh my!' cried Mrs. Bedwin, upon seeing Oliver. 'He's been hurt badly. Come lay him down upon his old bed. Gently now.'

Mr. Brownlow placed Oliver on the bed, and then instructed Mrs. Bedwin to summon the doctor; which she was pleased to do. He stood watch over the boy; praying for his soul should the doctor not arrive in time. Fortunately, the bleeding had slowed considerably, and Oliver was no worse when Mrs. Bedwin and the doctor arrived after a few minutes wait.

'If you would be so kind, Mrs. Bedwin,' said the doctor, 'please bring some hot water and clean linen.'

The doctor began by removing Oliver's clothing, cutting when necessary, and inspecting his body. No injury could be seen until he rolled Oliver over and saw a round, red hole on his back; just beside his left scapula.

'Aha,' said the doctor, 'it could have been worse. 'He has been shot, I dare say, but the ball was stopped by a rib.'

By then Mrs. Bedwin was back with hot water and linens, and proceeded to clean Oliver as best she could while the doctor starting pulling surgical tools and supplies out of his medical bag.

'Who should *ever* want to shoot Oliver?' wondered Mr. Brownlow aloud.

'First off, I will remove the bullet and suture the hole,' explained the doctor as he set to work. 'Then I will apply a poultice. I will return this evening to check on our little patient and to replace the poultice. He should recover well enough in a few days. He will have a sore rib, I dare say, when he wakes up. May even be broken, but not much to do about that.'

'Nothing else you can do for the poor boy?' ask Mrs. Bedwin.

'Perhaps a little bloodletting,' said the doctor. 'I find it helps to cure most maladies.'

'No, that is quite alright," said Mr. Brownlow, forcefully. 'The lad has lost more than enough blood for one day.'

'As you like,' replied the doctor. 'Feed him some strong broth and a little port wine. Give him an orange too. Does wonders for people's health I'm sure.'

The earliest morning sunlight was shining through the mist as the doctor said his goodbyes and made his way onto the street. A few moments later, Mr. Brownlow followed him out of the house and, as has already been recorded, made his way over to his good friend and neighbour's house.

Chapter 29
Oliver's Account

Mr. Brownlow stood looking on for a minute or so, in silence, whilst Mrs. Bedwin glided softly past, and, seating herself on a chair by the bedside, gathered Oliver's hair from his face. As she stooped over him, her tears fell upon his forehead.

The boy stirred, and smiled in his sleep, as though these drops of pity and compassion had awakened some pleasant dream of a love and affection he had never known; as a strain of gentle music, or the rippling of water in a silent place, or the scent of a flower, or even the mention of a familiar word, will sometimes call up dim remembrances of scenes that never were in this life, which vanish like a breath, and which some brief memory from a happier existence, long gone by, would seem to have awakened, for no voluntary exertion of the mind can ever recall them.

Watching over Oliver while he slept, Mr. Brownlow began recounting to Mrs. Bedwin what he had learned from visiting Mr. Griffith early that morning.

'What can this mean?' exclaimed Mrs. Bedwin. 'This poor child can never have been the pupil of robbers!'

'Vice,' said Mr. Brownlow, 'takes up her abode in many temples, and who can say that a fair outside shell cannot enshrine her?'

'But at so early an age?' urged the housekeeper.

'My dear lady,' rejoined Mr. Brownlow, mournfully shaking his head, 'crime, like death, is not confined to the old and withered alone. The youngest and fairest are too often its chosen victims.'

'But can you – oh, sir! can you really believe that this young boy has been the voluntary associate of the worst outcasts of society?' asked Mrs. Bedwin.

Mr. Brownlow shook his head, in a manner which intimated that he feared it was very possible; and observing that they might disturb the patient, led the way into an adjoining room.

'But even if he has been wicked,' pursued the housekeeper, 'think how young he is; think that he may never have known a mother's love, or the comfort of a home, that ill-usage and blows, or the want of bread, may have driven him to herd with men who have forced him to guilt. Mr. Brownlow, for mercy's sake, think of this before you let Mr. Griffith drag this injured child off to a prison, which in any case must be the grave of all of his chances of amendment. Have pity upon him before it is too late!'

'My dear Mrs. Bedwin,' said Mr. Brownlow, gently, 'I have no desire to harm a hair of his head.'

'No?' queried the housekeeper, eagerly.

'No, surely,' said Mr. Brownlow. 'My days are drawing to their close; and may mercy be shown to me as I show it to others! I will do what I can to save him.'

'Oh thank you, thank you,' said the housekeeper, throwing her arms around him.

Removing her arms from around his neck, Mr. Brownlow thought it best to lower her expectations.

'Given what we already know of his history, and given that he had already set foot in Mr. Griffith's house on a previous occasion,' explained Mr. Brownlow, 'it looks very bad for him. The police will soon learn from the good doctor that we are harbouring a wounded juvenile who was shot in the back. Mr. Griffith's low opinion of the boy has, to be sure, been corroborated in every way. I must warn you that it will be difficult to shield Oliver from the consequences of his actions.'

'You must, sir, you must,' pleaded Mrs. Bedwin.

'Let me think, ma'am,' replied Mr. Brownlow, 'let me think.'

Mr. Brownlow thrust his hands into his pockets, and took several turns up and down the room; often stopping and balancing himself on his toes, and frowning frightfully. After various exclamations of 'I've got it now' and 'no, I haven't,' and as many renewals of the walking and frowning, he at length sat down exhausted.

Oliver slept fitfully, often startling and shouting. It was late in the afternoon before he opened his eyes. He tried to sit up immediately, but fell back flinching from the pain.

'Lie still, Oliver,' said Mrs. Bedwin, softly, bending over him. 'You are badly injured and need to rest.'

'How'd I get here?' asked Oliver, wincing in agony.

'How did you get here?" repeated the housekeeper with a kind smile. 'We certainly don't know. We are rather hoping that you could enlighten us when you are feeling stronger.'

Following the doctor's orders, Mrs. Bedwin brought in a bowl of hearty broth, a glass of port wine, and a sliced orange that Mr. Brownlow had purchased that very afternoon. Following the delicious meal she fed to him, Oliver smiled at the housekeeper, and then fell back into a much more contented sleep; not waking again until evening when the good doctor, with a violent yank, ripped off the bandage and poultice to inspect the wound. Oliver shouted with pain.

'I imagine that might have hurt,' said the doctor, with a malicious chuckle.

'There's no need for none of that,' protested Mrs. Bedwin angrily.

'You treat him kindly, like you would any other patient.'

'I'm not in the trade of patching up housebreakers, Mrs. Bedwin,' replied the doctor.

'Mr. Brownlow has instructed that Oliver here is to receive the best of care, sir,' said the housekeeper, 'and I will be happy to let him know if that is not the case.'

'The wound looks good,' said the doctor, matter-of-factly. 'I will apply a new poultice and return in the morning to inspect the patient.'

Mrs. Bedwin fed Oliver some more broth, a little bread and butter, another orange, and bid him pleasant dreams.

'I don't deserve such kindness,' said Oliver, looking up at her, 'I've not earned it.'

'You don't deserve ill treatment neither,' she replied. 'I 'spect that you've had a fair share of that, you have. Now you get some rest. Mr. Brownlow will see you in the morning.'

As it happens, Oliver was already awake and enjoying a little breakfast of tea and toast when the doctor entered his room the next morning. As Mr. Brownlow had given explicit instructions that he was to be present during the good doctor's next visit, Mrs. Bedwin quickly found him.

'How does he look today?' inquired Mr. Brownlow.

'Much better colour, to begin with,' answered the doctor. 'How do you feel, Oliver?'

'Better, sir,' replied Oliver, 'but very sore! Rather like I was gored by a bull, sir.'

'That's your broken rib,' explained the doctor. 'It will heal. Now, I have to inspect your wound. It will hurt, there is no way around that. Mrs. Bedwin, would you care to do the honours. Your gentle hands might lesson the pain.'

Mrs. Bedwin removed the bandage holding the poultice as gently as she could, but Oliver still winced with pain.

'See,' said the doctor, 'I didn't inflict any intentional pain. It can't be avoided.'

'How does it look?' asked Mr. Brownlow. 'Any better?'

'Yes, it is healing as it should,' assured the doctor, 'but we must still apply a poultice to keep out infection for a day or two longer.'

The fourth morning following Oliver's arrival at the Brownlow residence, the doctor declare Oliver's wound to be healing well and in no further need of his attention.

'Time to get him up and about,' said the doctor. 'Lying about in bed will do him more harm than good now.' As it happens, the pain was no longer excruciating and Oliver was happy to comply with the doctor's orders.

'What can I do to assist you, Mrs. Bedwin?' asked Oliver. 'I am much indebted to you and Mr. Brownlow. I feel a great need to repay you for your kindness.'

'There, there,' said the housekeeper. 'Someday I might take you up on that kind offer, but at the moment, Mr. Brownlow has asked that you go up and talk to him. So, off you go now.'

Oliver ascended the stairs, rather cautiously for a twelve year old boy—due to the pain, and walked into Mr. Brownlow's study.

'Good to see you up Oliver,' said Mr. Brownlow, when he entered the room. 'Are you much recovered?'

'Yes, sir, much sir,' said Oliver, 'thank you, sir.'

'I expected as much,' said Mr. Brownlow. 'How is that cracked rib of yours? Can you breathe easily, or does it still pain you?

'It still pains, to be sure, sir,' said Oliver, 'but not so sharply. Not like a knife, more like a bruise. Certainly, I shall avoid laughing as best I can.'

'Ha, ha, very good,' said Mr. Brownlow. 'A gunshot wound is not going to heal overnight. You were lucky, you know; a little higher, a little lower, and we would not be conversing as we are.'

'I do feel lucky, I do, sir,' said Oliver, 'to be back with you and Mrs. Bedwin. While I will never be able to repay you for your kindness and generosity, not in two lifetimes, I should like to do what I can. If you will have me, sir, please put me to work. That way, in some small measure, I might be able to make amends.'

'It is good of you to offer your services, Oliver,' said Mr. Brownlow; 'and someday we may enter into some such arrangement, but not today. Today, I should like to hear your account of how you came to be shot in Mr. Griffith's house.'

'Yes, sir,' said Oliver, 'and I should like to tell you.'

Oliver proceeded to tell Mr. Brownlow, from the perspective of a naive twelve year old boy, all that had happened to him since he was sent on that fateful errand by Mr. Griffith to return a few books to the book dealer: being kidnapped by Nancy and Bill, being locked up by Fagin, being taken by Nancy to Bill, being taken by Bill to the house by the bridge, and, in somewhat more detail, the attempted robbery of Mr. Griffith's house.

Occasionally, on points of interest to him, Mr. Brownlow would gently question Oliver to probe the course of events more deeply and to test his consistency. 'What happened to the books?' 'Was the house to the left or to the right of the bridge?' 'Was it Bill or Toby who put you over the fence?' 'How did you get through the window?' 'Please, tell me again, what happened after you opened the front door?'

Oliver's answer to this last question bears repeating:

'I stood there on the chair holding up a lantern, just looking around, thinking that it all looked familiar with the chairs, the staircase, the paintings, and all. Then I looked at the closest painting and recognized it straight away. It was Mr. Griffith's daughter. She seems familiar somehow. I can't say I'd 'ave been so bold in any other person's house, but I couldn't bear the thought of Mr. Sikes and Crackit robbing Mr. Griffith. I jumped off the chair and ran towards the stairs yelling; calling for everyone to wake up. I saw him, Mr. Griffith that is, at the top of the stairs pointing a pistol; so I turned and ran away. I got hit before I reached the door.'

Mr. Brownlow appeared to be most intrigued by Oliver's account. However, when Oliver was finished telling his story, Mr. Brownlow simply thanked him and said, 'I will be away for the next two days. When I return, we will talk again. Please do whatever Mrs. Bedwin asks of you.'

Chapter 30
Married Life

Mr. Bumble sat in the workhouse parlour, with his eyes moodily fixed on the cheerless fire grate, whence, as it was summer time, no brighter gleam proceeded, than the reflection of certain sickly rays of the sun which were sent back from its cold and shining surface. A paper fly-cage dangled from the ceiling, to which he occasionally raised his eyes in gloomy thought; and, as the heedless insects hovered round the gaudy net-work, Mr. Bumble would heave a deep sigh, while a more gloomy shadow spread over his countenance. Mr. Bumble was meditating. It might be that the insects brought to mind some painful passage in his own past life.

Nor was Mr. Bumble's gloom the only thing calculated to awaken a pleasing melancholy in the bosom of a spectator. There were not wanting other appearances, and those closely connected with his own person, which announced that a great change had taken place in the position of his affairs. The laced coat, and the cocked hat; where were they? He still wore knee-breeches, and dark cotton stockings on his nether limbs; but they were not *the* breeches. The coat was wide-skirted, and in that respect like *the* coat; but, oh, how different! The mighty cocked hat was replaced by a modest round one. Mr. Bumble was no longer a beadle.

There are some promotions in life, which, independent of the more substantial rewards they offer, require peculiar value and dignity from the coats and waistcoats connected with them. A field-marshal has his uniform, a bishop his surplice, a counsellor his silk gown, and a beadle his cocked hat and lace. Strip the bishop of his apron, or the beadle of his cocked hat and lace; what are they? Men. Mere men. Dignity, and even holiness, too, sometimes, are more questions of coat and waistcoat than some people imagine.

Mr. Bumble had married Mrs. Corney, and was master of the workhouse. Another beadle had come into power, and on him the cocked hat, gold-laced coat, and cane had all three descended.

'It is but a fortnight tomorrow that it was done!' said Mr. Bumble, with a sigh. 'It seems an age.'

Mr. Bumble might have meant that he had concentrated a whole existence of happiness into the short space of two weeks; but for the sigh—there was a vast deal of meaning in the sigh.

'I sold myself,' said Mr. Bumble, pursuing the same train of reflection, 'for six teaspoons, a pair of sugar-tongs, and a milk-pot; with a small quantity of second-hand furniture, and twenty pound in money. I went very reasonable. Cheap, dirt cheap!'

'Cheap?' cried a shrill voice in Mr. Bumble's ear; 'you would have been dear at any price; and dear enough I paid for you, Lord above knows that!'

Mr. Bumble turned, and encountered the face of his interesting consort, who, imperfectly comprehending the few words she had overheard of his complaint, had hazarded the foregoing remark at a venture.

'Mrs. Bumble, ma'am!' said Mr. Bumble, with a sentimental sternness.

'Well!' cried the lady.

'Have the goodness to look at me,' said Mr. Bumble, fixing his eyes upon her.

If she stands such an eye as that,' said Mr. Bumble to himself, 'she can stand anything. It is an eye I never knew to fail with paupers; if it fails with her, my power is gone.'

Whether an exceedingly small expansion of eye be sufficient to quell paupers, who, being lightly fed, are in no very high condition; or whether the late Mrs. Corney was particularly proof against eagle glances; are matters of opinion. The matter of fact is that the matron was in no way overpowered by Mr. Bumble's scowl, but, on the contrary, treated it with great disdain, and even raised a laugh thereat, which sounded as though it were genuine.

On hearing this most unexpected sound, Mr. Bumble looked first incredulous, and afterwards amazed. He then relapsed into his former state; nor did he rouse himself until his attention was again awakened by the voice of his partner.

'Are you going to sit there snoring all day?' inquired Mrs. Bumble.

'I am going to sit here as long as I think proper, ma'am,' rejoined Mr. Bumble; 'and although I was *not* snoring, I shall snore, gape, sneeze, laugh, or cry as the humour strikes me, such being my prerogative.'

'Your *prerogative*?' sneered Mrs. Bumble, with ineffable contempt.

'I said the word, ma'am,' said Mr. Bumble. 'The prerogative of a man is to command.'

'And what, in the name of goodness, is the prerogative of a woman?' cried the relict of Mr. Corney, deceased.

'To obey, ma'am,' thundered Mr. Bumble. 'Your late unfortunate husband should have taught you that; and then, perhaps, he might have been alive now. I wish he was, poor man!'

Mrs. Bumble, seeing at a glance that the decisive moment had now arrived, and that a blow struck for the mastership, on one side or other, must necessarily be final and conclusive, no sooner heard this allusion to the dead and gone than she dropped into a chair; and, after screaming loudly that Mr. Bumble was a hard-hearted brute, fell into a paroxysm of tears.

But tears were not the things to find their way to Mr. Bumble's soul; his heart was waterproof. Like washable beaver hats that improve with rain, his nerves were rendered stouter and more vigorous by showers of tears, which, being tokens of weakness, and so tacit admissions of his own power, pleased and exalted him. He eyed his good lady with a look of great satisfaction, and begged, in an encouraging manner, that she should cry her hardest; the exercise being looked upon by the medical profession as being strongly conducive to health.

'It opens the lungs, washes the countenance, exercises the eyes, and softens down the temper,' said Mr. Bumble. 'So cry away.'

As he discharged himself of this pleasantry, Mr. Bumble took his hat from a peg, and putting it on, rather rakishly, on one side, as a man might who felt he had asserted his superiority in a becoming manner, thrust his hands into his pockets, and sauntered towards the door, with much ease and waggishness depicted in his whole appearance.

Now, Mrs. Corney, the workhouse matron, had resorted first to tears because they were rather less troublesome than a manual assault; but she was quite prepared to make trial of the latter mode of proceeding, as Mr. Bumble was not long in discovering.

The first proof he experienced of this fact was conveyed in a hollow sound, immediately succeeded by the sudden flying off of his hat to the opposite end of the room. This preliminary proceeding laying bare his head, the expert lady, clasping him tightly round the throat with one hand, inflicted a shower of blows (dealt with singular vigour and dexterity) upon it with the other. This done, she created a little variety by scratching his face and tearing his hair out; and having, by this time, inflicted as much punishment as she deemed necessary for the offence, she pushed him over a chair, which was luckily well situated for the purpose; and defied him to talk about his prerogative again, if he dared.

'Get up!' said Mrs. Bumble, in a voice of command, 'and take yourself away from here, unless you want me to do something desperate.'

Mr. Bumble rose with a very rueful countenance, wondering much about what something desperate might be; and picking up his hat, looked towards the door.

'Are you going?' demanded Mrs. Bumble.

'Certainly, my dear, certainly,' rejoined Mr. Bumble, making a quicker motion towards the door. 'I didn't intend to—I'm going, my dear! You are so very violent, that really I -'

At this instant, as Mrs. Bumble stepped hastily forward to replace the carpet, which had been kicked up in the scuffle. Mr. Bumble immediately darted out of the room, without bestowing another thought on his unfinished sentence, leaving the late Mrs. Corney in full possession of the field.

Mr. Bumble was fairly taken by surprise, and fairly beaten. He had a decided propensity for bullying; derived no inconsiderable pleasure from the exercise of petty cruelty; and, consequently, was (it is needless to say) a coward. This is by no means a disparagement to his character; for many official personages, who are held in high respect and admiration, exhibit the same character trait. The remark is made, indeed, rather in his favour than otherwise, and with a view of impressing the reader with a just sense of his qualifications for office.

But the measure of his degradation was not yet full. After making a tour of the house, and thinking for the first time that the poor-laws really were too hard on people, and that men who ran away from their wives, leaving them chargeable to the parish, ought, in justice to be visited with no punishment at all, but rather rewarded as meritorious individuals who had suffered much, Mr. Bumble came to a room where some of the female paupers were usually employed in washing the parish linen, and whence the sound of voices in conversation now proceeded.

'Hem!' said Mr. Bumble, summoning up all his native dignity. 'These women at least shall continue to respect my prerogative. Hallo! hallo there! What do you mean by all this noise, you hussies?'

With these words Mr. Bumble opened the door, and walked in with a very fierce and angry manner; which was at once exchanged for a most humiliated and cowering air, as his eyes unexpectedly rested on the form of his lady wife.

'My dear,' said Mr. Bumble, 'I didn't know you were here.'

'Didn't know I was here?' repeated Mrs. Bumble. 'What do *you* do here?'

'I thought they were talking rather too much to be doing their work properly, my dear,' replied Mr. Bumble, glancing distractedly at a couple of old women at the wash-tub, who were comparing notes of admiration at the workhouse master's humility.

'*You* thought they were talking too much?' said Mrs. Bumble. 'What business is it of yours?'

'Why, my dear – ' urged Mr. Bumble submissively.

'What business is it of yours?' demanded Mrs. Bumble again.

'It's very true, you're matron here, my dear,' submitted Mr. Bumble; 'but I thought you mightn't be in the way just then.'

'I'll tell you what, Mr. Bumble,' returned his lady, 'we don't want any of your interference. You're a great deal too fond of poking your nose into things that don't concern you, making everybody in the house laugh, the moment your back is turned, and making yourself look like a fool every hour in the day. Be off! come!'

Mr. Bumble, seeing with excruciating feelings the delight of the two old paupers, who were tittering together most rapturously, hesitated for an instant. Mrs. Bumble, whose patience brooked no delay, caught up a bowl of soapsuds, and motioning him towards the door, ordered him to depart instantly, on pain of receiving the contents upon his portly person.

What could Mr. Bumble do? He looked dejectedly around, and slunk away, and as he reached the door, the titterings of the paupers broke into a shrill chuckle of irrepressible delight. It wanted but this. He was degraded in their eyes; he had lost caste and station before the very paupers; he had fallen from all the height and pomp of beadleship to the lowest depth of the most snubbed henpeckery.

'All in two weeks!' said Mr. Bumble, filled with dismal thoughts. 'Two weeks! Not more than a fortnight ago, I was not only my own master, but everybody else's, so far as the parochial workhouse was concerned, and now—'

It was too much. Mr. Bumble, walking through the hall as in a trance, boxed the ears of the first boy he came across. Feeling somewhat renewed, he walked on to his office.

Chapter 31
Offer of a Just Reward

Making his way from the woman's quarters, past the girl's quarters, the boy's quarters, and, finally, the men's quarter; Mr. Bumble distracted himself by wondering at the marvellous thought and deliberation that went into the planning and construction of the workhouse which had been modeled upon the most scientifically designed of penitentiaries. Parents, of course, were separated from their children, as were husbands from their wives, men from women, and boys from girls. Women had their own sleeping quarters, lavatories, work rooms, and court yard as did the girls, boys, and men. Everyone ate, in closely timed shifts, in a grand—in name only—dining hall next the central kitchen. Women worked at cooking and doing laundry and, when time afforded, spinning and weaving. Girls were taught to knit and spin and weave and, through endless hours of practice, became rather proficient at their trade. Boys mostly picked oakum by unraveling old ropes and cords using spikes. The oakum was then mixed with pine tar to make caulking for ship building. Boys and girls also received a rudimentary education, again in shifts, in a small classroom dedicated to that worthy cause. Men alternated, as demand dictated, between the breaking of rocks into gravel and the crushing of bones into fertilizer; the latter being the preferred occupation as there was always the possibility of sucking the marrow from the bones before crushing them. Elderly paupers were assigned domestic chores such as sweeping, cleaning, and chopping firewood. A small chapel tended to the inmates spiritual instruction, and to the numerous funeral services that were held. While the opening of the workhouse did not, in Mr. Bumble's estimation, lead to an appreciable decrease in the number of paupers seeking charity, as its proponents had claimed it would, Heaven only knew how many more would plague the streets if it had not been built.

When Mr. Bumble arrived at his office, he was taken aback by the presence of a stranger, a gentleman, standing in the hall waiting for him.

'Good afternoon', said the stranger. 'Would you be the master of this benevolent establishment?'

'Yes, I am the master of this workhouse', replied Mr. Bumble, with a rising sense of pride, as he ushered the gentleman into his office. With a wave of his hand, he invited his guest to take a seat. Both men sat down.

'I have seen you before, I think?' said the gentleman. 'We only met for but a few minutes, and you were dressed differently at that time, but I should know you again. You were a beadle once, were you not?'

'I was,' said Mr. Bumble, with some surprise, 'a parochial beadle in this parish.'

'Just so,' rejoined the other, nodding his head. 'It was in that role that I saw you last.'

Mr. Bumble, as the stranger noted, appeared anxious. The inequality in their respective knowledge of one another put Mr. Bumble at a distinct disadvantage.

'Allow me to introduce myself, Mr. Bumble. My name is Mr. Brownlow. I reside in Pentonville, near London. You responded to my advertisement requesting information regarding a young boy.'

'Oh, yes! Oliver Twist,' replied Mr. Bumble, 'I recall our meeting very well, now. I related his life story to you. Did you find him? Is he well? We do miss him here!'

'I am sure you do,' answered Mr. Brownlow.

'You have the same eye to your own interest, that you always had, I doubt not?' resumed the gentleman, looking keenly into Mr. Bumble's eyes, as he raised them in astonishment at the question. 'Don't scruple to answer freely, sir. I know you pretty well, you see.'

'I suppose a married man,' replied Mr. Bumble, 'is not more averse to turning an honest penny when he can, than a single one. Parochial officers are not so well paid that they can afford to refuse any little extra fee when it comes to them in a civil and proper manner.'

Mr. Brownlow smiled and nodded his head again, as if to say he had not mistaken his man.

'Now listen to me,' said Mr. Brownlow, in a serious tone of voice. 'I came to this place today to find you out. I am here to make certain inquiries regarding the birth of Oliver Twist, and, if your answers suffice, I will endeavour to obtain a just reward for you.'

'I would be much obliged to provide you with any and all information in my possession regarding the boy,' offered Mr. Bumble, 'reward or no, but I very much doubt that there is much of value that I can add to what I have already provided to you.'

'I wish to identify his mother', replied Mr. Brownlow. 'Are you able to do that?'

'Oh, that I could,' replied Mr. Bumble. 'To provide poor Oliver with some knowledge of his family would be a very good thing.'

'You have no such records?' asked Mr. Brownlow, incredulously. 'I very much doubt that!'

'Oh, yes, we have such records for most children born within these walls,' answered Mr. Bumble, 'but, unfortunately, I distinctly remember that his sweet mother died anonymously. We never did learn her name. We advertised for his father, but received no intelligence in that regard either.'

'That is unfortunate, indeed,' said Mr. Brownlow. 'However, all is not necessarily lost. I have reason to believe that Oliver's mother was known to me, and I may be able to confirm that fact upon the slightest of evidence.'

'What evidence might suffice?' asked Mr. Bumble, eagerly.

'Carry your memory back—let me see—twelve years, last winter,' suggested the gentleman.

'It's a long time,' said Mr. Bumble. 'Very good. I've done it.'

'The scene: the lying-in room of the workhouse; where pauper women and others bereft of family or friends or means of support are invited to give birth to their newborn children, to be lovingly cared for by your honest staff during their time of need.'

'Yes.'

'Who alive today,' inquired Mr. Brownlow, 'may have had the privilege of attending to Oliver's birth? Is there some nurse or mid-wife, perhaps, whom I might interview?'

'I am afraid that I shall have to disappoint you yet again,' said Mr. Bumble, with honest regret. 'If you had inquired thus but a few weeks earlier, old Sally would have been pleased to talk to you. She attended upon Oliver's birth and always had a soft spot for the boy. She's asked after him many a time. She died a fortnight ago tomorrow. I recall the night all too well.'

'Died?' repeated Mr. Brownlow, in disbelief. 'I am thwarted at every turn. Yet I feel that I am standing at the very precipice of discovery and the least verification will suffice.'

Brownlow looked fixedly at the workhouse master and, although he did not withdraw his eyes for some time afterwards, his stare gradually grew more vacant and abstracted as he became lost in thought. At length he breathed again and, diverting his gaze, rose as if to depart.

But Mr. Bumble was cunning enough, and he at once saw that an opportunity had opened for the lucrative disposal of some secret in the possession of his better-half. He well remembered the night of old Sally's death, the occurrences that had followed that day had given him good reason to recollect it as the occasion on which he had proposed to Mrs. Corney; and although that lady had never confided to him the disclosure to which she had been the solitary witness, he had heard enough to know that it related to something that had occurred during the old woman's attendance, as a workhouse nurse, upon the young mother of Oliver Twist.

Hastily calling this circumstance to mind, he informed Mr. Brownlow, with an air of mystery, that one woman had been closeted with dear old Sally shortly before she died, and that she might be able, he had reason to believe, to throw some light on the subject of his inquiry.

'How can I find her?' inquired the gentleman, thrown off his guard, and plainly showing that his interest (whatever its source) was aroused afresh by this intelligence.

'Only through me,' rejoined Mr. Bumble.

'When? Where?' cried the gentleman, hastily.

'Would tomorrow morning at nine, here in my office, be agreeable?' inquired Bumble.

'Yes, yes indeed,' replied Mr. Brownlow.

The following morning, at precisely nine o'clock, Mr. Brownlow again called upon Mr. Bumble at his office. A woman, roughly his same age, was standing next to him.

'Good morning, Mr. Brownlow,' said Mr. Bumble pleasantly. 'How good to see you again.' Motioning towards the woman, he added, 'this is my wife, Mrs. Bumble, matron of the workhouse.'

'Very pleased to meet you, Mrs. Bumble,' said Mr. Brownlow.

'Pleased to meet you, I'm sure,' replied Mrs. Bumble, with a curtsy.

'As I was telling your husband,' explained Mr. Brownlow, 'I am here to identify Oliver Twist's mother and, if you are able to provide sufficient evidence as to who she was, I will endeavour to obtain a just reward for you.'

'I am sure that my husband has told you that we have no proper record of her name or place of birth,' said the matron.

'He did,' replied Mr. Brownlow. 'However, as I have a name and birthplace in mind, the least corroboration may suffice: an item of clothing, a distinguishing mark; even a casual remark might carry import for my purpose.'

'You are offering to pay for such evidence, my husband tells me,' stated Mrs. Bumble.

'I offered a just reward, but I am willing to pay up front if that is what is required,' said Mr. Brownlow.

'Twenty pounds?' suggested Mr. Bumble.

'Five-and-twenty pounds in gold!' demanded Mrs. Bumble; 'and I will tell you all that I know. Not before.'

'Twenty-five pounds is a steep price to pay when I know not what is being offered,' replied Mr. Brownlow. 'Do you have good reason to believe that your knowledge will satisfy my curiosity?

'Aye, I do,' answered the matron.

Mr. Brownlow pulled out his purse and counted out twenty-five gold sovereigns into the hand of Mrs. Bumble.

'There you go,' said Mr. Brownlow. 'What are you able to tell me?'

'A pauper named Sally attended upon the birth of Oliver Twist,' explained Mrs. Bumble. 'This is well-known within the walls of this workhouse as Sally took a special interest in him. He was raised some three miles away at the children's farm, and she often inquired after him. A fortnight ago, on the very same evening that my good husband here came to me with a proposal of marriage, I was summoned by two old hags to the lying-in room to attend upon Sally who lay dying.'

'Yes,' said Mr. Brownlow, with mounting interest.'

'I was told that Sally wished to speak to me a-fore she died,' continued the matron. 'Upon her deathbed Sally passed along a secret she had kept these past twelve years, whereupon I learned the source of her unusual interest in Oliver's wellbeing. His mother had in her possession a gold locket, an item of such value that it would have paid her way out of penury. Moments before she died, she gave the locket to Sally to hold till Oliver came of age that someday he might know her name.'

'A locket!' exclaimed Mr. Brownlow. 'Where is the locket?

'Mr. Bumble and me sold the locket by weight not a week ago,' she said, 'to a jeweler. Oliver broke his apprenticeship to Mr. Sowerberry, the parochial undertaker, and ran off. His whereabouts were unknown. What little duty I might have had to hold the locket for Oliver was clearly ended by his rash and illegal actions.'

'A locket!' repeated Mr. Brownlow. 'Where is the locket? I must see it.'

'I would be pleased to take you to the jeweler's,' volunteered Mr. Bumble.

'Straight away, my good man,' said Mr. Brownlow, 'straight away!'

The two men left the workhouse and entered into Brownlow's carriage, which stood waiting in the street; Mr. Bumble directed the driver to a neighbouring town several miles away. After instructing the driver to stop in front of a jeweler's shop, the workhouse master led the way inside.

'Good morning, Mr. Foster,' said Mr. Bumble, addressing the proprietor. 'My friend here is interested in that locket that my dear wife brought in last week. Is it still available? I dare say that you might make a quick sale.'

'Certainly, Mr. Bumble,' replied the shop owner. 'An item of that quality does not sell so quickly, not in a small town such as this. I will retrieve it directly.'

Mr. Foster unlocked a heavy door and entered into a backroom.

When he returned momentarily, he first relocked the door and then placed a small velvet pouch on the counter.

'There it is,' said the jeweller, 'an exquisite matrimonial locket.'

Carefully, Mr. Brownlow opened the pouch and retrieved the locket. He walked over to the front window to open the lid and then examined it closely. He appeared to be satisfied with what he saw.

'Mr. Bumble,' said Mr. Brownlow, 'would you be so kind as to step outside? I wish to confer in private with Mr. Foster.'

Taken aback, Mr. Bumble assented to this request and stepped out onto the street. After a few minutes, Brownlow exited the jewellery shop and, without so much as nodding his head to acknowledge Mr. Bumble's presence, climbed into the waiting carriage and drove off; leaving Bumble huffing and stamping his feet in exasperation.

Chapter 32
A Familiar Face

Late in the afternoon, the day following Mr. Brownlow's audience with Mr. and Mrs. Bumble, Oliver was in a little ground floor room at the back of the gentleman's house where he was accustomed to sit and study. It was a pleasant room, with a lattice window; around which were clusters of jasmine and honeysuckle, that crept over the casement, and filled the place with their delicious perfume. It looked into an extensive garden. As the first shades of twilight were beginning to settle upon the earth, Oliver sat at this window, intent upon his books. He had been poring over them for some time; and, as the day had been uncommonly sultry, and he had exerted himself a great deal, it is no disparagement to the authors, whoever they may have been, to say that gradually, and by slow degrees, he fell asleep.

There is a kind of sleep that steals upon us sometimes, which, while it holds the body prisoner, does not free the mind from a sense of things about it, and enables it to ramble at its pleasure. So far as an overpowering heaviness, a prostration of strength, and an utter inability to control our thoughts or power of motion, can be called sleep, this is it; and yet we have a consciousness of all that is going on about us, and if we dream at such a time, words which are really spoken, or sounds which really exist in the moment, accommodate themselves with surprising readiness to our visions, until reality and imagination become so strangely blended that it is afterwards almost a matter of impossibility to separate the two. Nor is this the most striking phenomenon incidental to such a state. It is an undoubted fact, that although our senses of touch and sight be for the time dead, yet our sleeping thoughts, and the visionary scenes that pass before us, will be influenced, and materially influenced, by the *mere silent presence* of someone who may not have been near us when we closed our eyes, and of whose vicinity we have had no waking consciousness.

Oliver was in just such a reverie when he awoke to find that Mrs. Bedwin was, in fact, sitting beside him as he had dreamt.

'Oh good,' she said softly, 'you're awake. Mr. Brownlow has requested that you come and speak to him. Let's get you looking a little less dishevelled.'

A few minutes afterwards, having washed his face and brushed his hair, Oliver stepped into the gentleman's study.

'Ah, Oliver,' said Mr. Brownlow, cheerfully, 'how go your studies?'

'Very well, thank you, sir,' answered Oliver, 'though I sometimes feel that reading is harder work than picking oakum.'

'No doubt, that is sometimes true,' said Mr. Brownlow, 'but well worth the effort, wouldn't you agree?'

Oliver nodded his assent, but could not bring himself to voice that opinion verbally.

'I should like for the two of us to call upon my good friend Mr. Griffith,' continued Mr. Brownlow. 'Would you care to do so?'

'Oh, I shouldn't think so,' said Oliver. 'I don't think Mr. Griffith would want much to see me. I wouldn't want to disturb him more than I have already.'

'Ah,' responded Mr. Brownlow, repressing a chuckle, 'you might be right about that. I do not imagine that Mr. Griffith is sitting in his study hoping that you might call upon him. But pay no heed to that; it will be good for you to face your accuser, and equally good, I might add, for your accuser to face you.'

A few moments later Mr. Brownlow and Oliver were walking to Mr. Griffith's house.

'Now, Oliver,' said Mr. Brownlow, 'I believe that I may have found an honourable way out of this little pickle you find yourself in. The most important thing is for you to answer any questions fully and honestly. Will you do that?'

'Certainly, sir,' said Oliver, 'I will do my best.' Being very much in the habit of being honest, Oliver did not consider this request to be unduly burdensome.

Presently, Mr. Brownlow and his young companion were standing outside of Mr. Griffith's house, whereupon Mr. Brownlow knocked on the door in his customary manner. Shortly thereafter, Mr. Giles opened the door accompanied by Pincher and Neptune who, judging by their snarly greeting, were not pleased to see Oliver. Mr. Giles's own smiling countenance changed when he looked down to see Oliver; yet he still conducted himself with the utmost propriety.

'Good afternoon, Mr. Brownlow, Oliver,' he said, 'please come in. I will inform Mr. Griffith that you are here. He is in the garden.'

'Certainly,' Mr. Giles,' replied Mr. Brownlow, 'thank you.'

'Please sit here,' said Mr. Giles, motioning to the hallway chairs, 'while I determine Mr. Griffith's pleasure. I trust that you will watch the boy.'

As the two of them sat waiting in the front hallway, Oliver looked around the house.

'See,' he said, 'I recognized these chairs, and the stairs, and all of these paintings. 'Specially this one closest to us,' he said pointing. 'Isn't she lovely? I'd know her anywheres, I would.'

"Yes,' agreed Mr. Brownlow. 'Mr. Griffith's daughter Anne was very lovely, both in body and in spirit. It's a pity that he lost her.'

'That's where I was shot' stated Oliver, pointing to a patch of faded red that still stained the hallway floor. 'I remember that I was almost out the door.'

At that moment, Mr. Griffith burst into the hallway.

'What's this?' he shouted. 'The culprit has returned to the scene of his crime. How bold! He was part of this, or I will eat my hat. Someone summon the police! Quickly, before he escapes again. '

'Now, now,' Mr. Griffith, 'Oliver came of his own free will and he has no plans on fleeing, do you Oliver?'

'Oh no, sir!' said Oliver, emphatically.

'He came to apologize for his part in the caper,' explained Mr. Brownlow, 'and, if you wish, to help answer a few mysteries about the course of events that night.'

'What mysteries?' asked Mr. Griffith, suspiciously.

'First things, first,' said Mr. Brownlow. 'Oliver, please apologize to Mr. Griffith.'

'Oh, yes!' said Oliver. 'I do apologize to you, sir, for breaking into your house and opening the front door for those two villains who wanted so to rob you. I am very sorry. It was a horrible, terrible thing that I did.'

'See!' said Mr. Griffith. 'He admits his guilt. Giles! Brittles! Someone! Anyone! Go and fetch the police.'

'Please, Mr. Griffith,' pleaded Mr. Brownlow, firmly, 'there will be lots of time for calling the police. I will do so myself if you are still so inclined, once we have solved those mysteries I mentioned. If Oliver is arrested now, we may never get to the bottom of this. Meanwhile, I will stand as surety to secure his continued attendance.'

'Well,' agreed Mr. Griffith, 'I do like getting to the bottom of things. I suppose we can wait a short time before calling in the authorities. What mysteries are in need solving?'

'Well, to begin with,' said Mr. Brownlow, 'I know that you must be curious as to who you shot.'

'No, I'm not!' stated Mr. Griffith, striking his cane against the floor. 'I shot this young scoundrel Oliver, or I'll eat my hat. The doctor told me straight away the very same day—nay the very same hour—that I was chasing away thieves, that he had removed a bullet from a young boy fitting Oliver's description sojourning at your residence. I have reason to believe that you have been harbouring this fugitive ever since.'

'Yes, yes,' agreed Mr. Brownlow, calmly, 'we found Oliver here lying on our front door step, dying of a gunshot wound, not a minute following the hullabaloo at your house. Our supposition that the two events were related was eventually confirmed. We summoned the doctor immediately and assumed, correctly, that the news would reach you before the morning post. But I dare say that you never shot Oliver.'

'Never shot Oliver!' exclaimed Mr. Griffith, with a particularly vigorous thud of his cane. 'That is preposterous. Who did I shoot if it wasn't this boy? Answer me that!'

'I don't mean to question your marksmanship, nor your integrity,' said Mr. Brownlow, 'but apparently, you failed to shoot anyone.'

'How do you reach that absurd conclusion,' asked Mr. Griffith, 'given the blood stain on the hallway floor and that young villain's gunshot wound?'

'Let us, if you will, recreate the scene of the robbery,' suggested Mr. Brownlow to Mr. Griffith. 'First, remind me, how many shots did you fire?'

'Just the one,' answered Mr. Griffith. 'One shot is all it takes if one is proficient.'

'I agree,' said Mr. Brownlow. 'If you please, go fetch your pistol and stand at the top of the stairs. Oliver, you go stand by that blood stain where you took the bullet.'

In a minute or two Mr. Griffith was standing, pistol in hand, at the top of the stairs. Oliver stood where he had been shot a few days earlier.

'Now, Mr. Griffith,' said Mr. Brownlow in a voice loud enough to carry up the staircase, 'here's your chance to extract the justice you so desire. Please go ahead and shoot Oliver. Oliver, please stand still so as to give Mr. Griffith a steady target to aim at.'

'I can't see him,' complained Mr. Griffith, 'please ask Oliver to step this way a couple of paces so I can get a clear shot.'

'No, I shan't do that,' explained Mr. Brownlow, 'or you might hurt the boy. But, while you are up there, please take a closer look at the ceiling above staircase.'

'What the blazes?' exclaimed Mr. Griffith. 'Where did that hole come from? It wasn't there before, or I'll eat my hat.'

'Please put your pistol safely away and come rejoin us,' requested Mr. Brownlow.

Once Griffith had rejoined Brownlow and Oliver, who felt much relieved at no longer being employed as a target, Brownlow continued exploring the events of that fateful night.

'Now,' Mr. Griffith,' said Mr. Brownlow, 'please recount for Oliver here, what you told me earlier about what transacted the night of the robbery.'

'I heard some commotion downstairs, which woke me up,' said Mr. Griffith. 'I slipped on my shoes and picked up my pistol which I keep on my bedstand for just such purposes. I went to Mr. Brittles' room and woke him. Then we heard shouting. Together, Brittles and I made our way to the stairs. I saw one of the robbers at the base of the stairs and I shot him.'

'If I recall correctly,' said Mr. Brownlow, 'you described the person you saw as being a big, brawny fellow.'

'Yes,' replied Mr. Griffith, 'with a mean look about him.'

'Sikes!' cried out Oliver, 'Bill Sikes! 'He's the one who'd put me through the window.'

'You must concede,' continued Mr. Brownlow, addressing Mr. Griffith, 'that the description of big and brawny hardly applies to my young friend here.'

'Perhaps not,' agreed Mr. Griffith, grudgingly, 'but he's still an admitted vandal. He should be behind bars.'

'We shall come to that,' said Mr. Brownlow, 'but first, do you suppose that it is a common practice for thieves to yell and shout while they prowl around a victim's home?'

'No,' agreed Mr. Griffith, 'that would not be common practice.'

'Oliver, here,' said Mr. Brownlow, 'might enlighten us as to the cause of the shouting and other related matters. Would you be willing to hear him narrate what happened that night?'

'Certainly,' agreed Mr. Griffith, 'not that I would put much faith in the veracity of what he has to say; seeing as robbery is a hanging offence. Criminals will say anything to avoid the noose.'

'Oliver,' said Mr. Brownlow, 'your story is a long one and it is difficult to know where you might begin. I might suggest, if you are agreeable, beginning with what Bill and Toby had to say to you in Mr. Griffith's backyard after the three of you climbed over the wall.'

'Certainly, sir,' replied Oliver.

Oliver went on to describe in some detail how he, under the threat of death from both Sikes and Crackit, was put through a window and how he then proceeded to open the front door. He further described how he came to recognize that it was Mr. Griffith's house and how he resolved to sound the alarm and wake up the residents.

'So,' said Mr. Brownlow, upon Oliver concluding his story, 'it appears that it was Oliver here who you heard shouting and who, at considerable personal risk, saved you from being robbed. It was, very likely, Mr. Sikes whom you saw at the bottom of the stairs and whom you took a shot at. I dare say, however, that you missed hitting him. Unfortunate that, for it was Mr. Sikes who, in keeping with his solemn promise, shot Oliver.'

Mr. Griffith, contrary to his verbose nature, sat quietly, saying nothing.

'So,' continued Mr. Brownlow, 'shall we ask Mr. Giles to summon the police to come and arrest young Oliver? There is evidence enough to sway a jury beyond a reasonable doubt that Oliver did, albeit under considerable duress, break into your house with the intent of effecting a robbery therein.'

Mr. Griffith continued to sit quietly, looking at Oliver.

'Well,' said Mr. Brownlow, 'there is no need for a speedy decision in that regard. There is another mystery that needs resolving.'

'There is?' asked Mr. Griffith, shaking himself out of his stupor.

'Look at the boy,' demanded Mr. Brownlow. 'Does he not look familiar? Does he not remind you of someone? He seemed rather familiar to me ever since I first laid eyes upon him, but I could not determine why I should find him so.'

Mr. Griffith put on his spectacles and took a closer look at Oliver. Such close inspection caused Oliver some embarrassment and he blushed.

'Yes, now that you mention it,' agreed Mr. Griffith, 'he does remind me of someone. But I can't say who.'

'Come,' said Mr. Brownlow, 'take a closer look at the portrait of your daughter Anne.'

'My Lord!' exclaimed Mr. Griffith, 'he couldn't be.'

'Yes, he is,' said Mr. Brownlow, gently. 'Upon hearing Oliver's account of the robbery, I came to understand why he seemed so very familiar to me. Wanting further proof, these past two days I obtained solid evidence that confirms my suspicions.'

'Evidence? What evidence?' demanded Mr. Griffith.

'Do you remember,' asked Mr. Brownlow, 'when Anne became engaged to be married, the gift I gave to her to mark that happy occasion?'

'Yes, of course,' replied Mr. Griffith, 'a pretty golden locket.'

'I only had the happy couple's names engraved on it. I left space for Anne to add the wedding date,' explained Mr. Brownlow as he pulled a small velvet pouch from his pocket and handed it to Mr. Griffith. 'It is tragic that the remaining space was never engraved upon.'

"Aye,' said Mr. Griffith, sadly; inspecting the locket. 'Her fiancé died in the service of Her Majesty just weeks before they could wed.'

'Remind me,' said Mr. Brownlow, 'what became of Anne?'

'She spent an inordinately long time in bereavement, rarely leaving the house,' recalled Mr. Griffith, with growing anger. 'Then, after many weeks, I discovered the reason for such profound and protracted mourning. She was with child, his child,' he said, with a thump of his cane. 'I was, of course, aghast at this revelation and appalled that she would dishonour herself and her family like a common hussy in this fashion. It was untenable that she would continue to reside with us, casting aspersion upon our good name every moment she remained. I bid her farewell and that was the last we heard of her.'

'Oliver, here,' said Mr. Brownlow, quietly, 'is your grandson and your closest relation.'

'My bastard grandson,' retorted Mr. Griffith, cruelly.

'The term you use,' said Mr. Brownlow, sternly, 'is a reproach to those who have long since passed beyond the feeble censure of the world. It reflects disgrace on no one living, except you who use it. Let that pass.'

'Please leave,' said Mr. Griffith, 'and take the boy with you.'

'Mr. Griffith,' pleaded Mr. Brownlow, 'do not harden your heart against this innocent child.'

Without looking at Mr. Brownlow, Mr. Griffith handed the pouch containing the locket to Oliver. 'This is rightfully yours, Oliver,' he said to the boy. 'Now, please leave.'

'Certainly, sir,' said Oliver. 'I am pleased to have met you.'

Chapter 33
An Evil Wind

The evening following Oliver's recovery of his family property, which he now prized above life itself, Mr. William Sikes, awakening from a nap, drowsily growled forth an inquiry as to what time of night it was.

The room in which Mr. Sikes propounded this question was not one of those he had tenanted previous to the Pentonville expedition, although it was in the same quarter of the town, and was situated at no great distance from his former lodgings. He had taken this haunt, after days of lying low by living out-of-doors, when he felt an illness coming over him.

It was not, in appearance, so desirable a habitation as his old quarters, being a mean and badly furnished apartment, of very limited size, lighted only by one small window in the dormer, and abutting on a close and dirty lane. Nor were there wanting other indications of the good gentleman's having gone down in the world as of late; for the scarcity of furniture, and total absence of comfort, together with the disappearance of all such small moveables as spare clothes and linen, bespoke a state of extreme poverty; while the meagre and attenuated condition of Mr. Sikes himself would have fully confirmed these symptoms, if they had stood in any need of corroboration.

The housebreaker was lying on the bed, wrapped in his greatcoat, by way of dressing gown, and displaying a set of features in no degree improved by the cadaverous hue of illness and the addition of a soiled nightcap, and a stiff black beard of a week's growth. His dog sat at the bedside eyeing his master with a wistful look, and pricking his ears and uttering a low growl if some noise in the street, or in the lower part of the house, attracted his attention. Seated by the window, busily engaged in patching an old waistcoat, which formed a portion of the robber's ordinary dress, was a female, so pale and reduced with watching and privation, that one would have had considerable difficulty recognising her as the same Nancy who has already figured in this tale, but for the voice in which she replied to Mr. Sikes's question.

'Not long gone seven,' said the girl. 'How do you feel tonight, Bill?'

'As weak as water,' replied Mr. Sikes, with an imprecation on his eyes and limbs. 'Here; lend us a hand, and let me get off this thundering bed anyhow.'

Illness had not improved Mr. Sikes's temper; for, as the girl raised him up and led him to a chair, he muttered various curses on her awkwardness, and struck her.

'Whining ,are you?' said Sikes. 'Come! Don't stand snivelling there. If you can't do anything better than that, cut off altogether. D'ye hear me?'

'I hear you,' replied the girl, turning her face aside and forcing a laugh. 'What fancy have you got in your head now?'

'Oh! you've thought better of it, have you?' growled Sikes, marking the tears which trembled in her eye. 'All the better for you, you have.'

'Why, you don't mean to say you'd be hard upon me tonight, Bill?' said the girl, laying her hand upon his shoulder.

'No?' cried Mr. Sikes. 'Why not?'

'Such a number of nights,' said the girl, with a touch of woman's tenderness, which communicated something like sweetness of tone even to her voice—'such a number of nights as I've been patient with you, nursing and caring for you, as if you had been a child; and this the first that I've seen you like yourself; you wouldn't have served me as you did just now, if you'd thought of that, would you? Come, come; say you wouldn't.'

'Well, then,' rejoined Mr. Sikes, 'I wouldn't. Why, damn me, now, the girl's whining again!'

'It's nothing,' said the girl, throwing herself into a chair. 'Don't you mind me. It'll soon be over.'

'What'll be over?' demanded Mr. Sikes, in a savage voice. 'What foolery are you up to now, again? Get up, and bustle about, and don't come over me with your woman's nonsense.'

At any other time, this remonstrance, and the tone in which it was delivered, would have had the desired effect; but the girl really being weak and exhausted, dropped her head over the back of the chair, and fainted, before Mr. Sikes could get out a few of the appropriate oaths with which, on similar occasions, he was accustomed to garnish his threats. Not knowing, very well, what to do, in this uncommon emergency—for Miss Nancy's hysterics were usually of that violent kind in which the patient fights and struggles out of without much assistance—Mr. Sikes tried a little blasphemy; and finding that mode of treatment wholly ineffectual, called for assistance.

'What's the matter here, my dear?' said Fagin, looking in.

'Lend a hand to the girl, can't you?' replied Sikes, impatiently. 'Don't stand chattering and grinning at me!'

With an exclamation of surprise, Fagin hastened to the girl's assistance, while Mr. Jack Dawkins (otherwise the Artful Dodger), who had followed his venerable friend into the room, hastily deposited on the floor a bundle with which he was laden, and snatching a bottle from the grasp of Master Charles Bates, who came close at his heels, uncorked it in a twinkling with his teeth, and poured a portion of its contents down the patient's throat, previously taking a taste himself to prevent mistakes.

'Give her a whiff of fresh air with the bellows, Charley,' said Mr. Dawkins; 'and you slap her hands, Fagin, while Bill undoes the petticoats.'

These united restoratives, administered with great energy, especially that department consigned to Master Bates, who appeared to consider his share in the proceedings a piece of unexampled pleasantry, were not long in producing the desired effect. The girl gradually recovered her senses; and, staggering to a chair by the bedside, hid her face upon the pillow, leaving Mr. Sikes to confront the newcomers, in some astonishment at their unexpected appearance.

'Why, what evil wind has blowed you here?' Sikes asked of Fagin.

'No evil wind at all, my dear,' replied Fagin, 'for evil winds blow nobody any good, and I've brought something good with me that you'll be glad to see. Dodger, my dear, open the bundle, and give Bill the little trifles that we spent all our money on this morning.'

In compliance with Mr. Fagin's request, the Artful untied this bundle, which was of large size, and formed of an old tablecloth; and handed the articles it contained, one by one, to Charley Bates, who placed them on the table with various comments on their rarity and excellence.

'Sitch a rabbit pie, Bill,' exclaimed that young gentleman, disclosing to view a huge pasty; 'sitch delicate creeturs, with sitch tender limbs, Bill, that the wery bones melt in your mouth, and there's no occasion to pick 'em; half a pound of seven-and-sixpenny green, so precious strong that if you mix it with boiling water, it'll go nigh to blow the lid of the teapot off; a pound and a half measure of moist sugar that was worked at hard to get it up to sitch a pitch of goodness – oh, yes! Two loaves of bread; pound of fresh butter; piece of double Glo'ster cheese; and, to wind up all, some of the richest hooch you ever lushed!'

Uttering this last laudatory purchase, Master Bates produced, from one of his extensive pockets, a full-sized wine bottle, carefully corked; while Mr. Dawkins, at the same instant, poured out a wineglassful of raw spirits from the bottle he carried, which the invalid tossed down his throat without a moment's hesitation.

'Ah!' said Fagin, rubbing his hands with great satisfaction. 'You'll do, Bill; you'll do now.'

'Do!' exclaimed Mr. Sikes; 'I might have been done for twenty times over afore you'd have done anything to help me. What do you mean by leaving a man in this state all week, you false-hearted vagabond?'

'Only hear him, boys!' said Fagin, shrugging his shoulders. 'And us come to bring him all these beau-ti-ful things.'

'The things is well enough in their way,' observed Mr. Sikes, a little soothed as he glanced over the table; 'but what have you got to say for yourself, why you should leave me here, down in the mouth, health, blunt, and everything else, and take no more notice of me, all this mortal time, than if I was that 'ere dog.—Drive him down, Charley!'

'I never see such a jolly dog as that,' cried Master Bates, doing as he was desired. 'Smelling the grub like an old lady a-going to market! He'd make his fortun' on the stage, that dog would, and revive the drama besides.'

'Hold your din,' cried Sikes, as the dog retreated under the bed, still growling angrily. 'What have you got to say for yourself, you withered old fence, eh? Where yuh been all this time?'

'I was away from London these past few days, my dear, on a plant,' replied the old miser.

'You've left me lying here,' Sikes continued, 'like a sick rat in his hole?'

'I couldn't help it, Bill. I can't go into a long explanation before company; but I couldn't help it, upon my honour.'

'Upon your what?' growled Sikes, with excessive disgust. 'Here! Cut me off a piece of that pie, one of you boys, to take the taste of that out of my mouth, or it'll choke me dead.'

'Don't be out of temper, my dear,' urged Fagin, submissively. 'I have never forgot you, Bill—never once.'

'No? I'll pound it that you haven't,' replied Sikes, with a bitter grin. 'You've been scheming and plotting away, every hour that I have laid here shivering and burning; and Bill was to do this, and Bill was to do that, and Bill was to do it all, dirt cheap, as soon as he got well, and was quite poor enough to want your work. If it hadn't been for the girl, I might have died.'

'There now, Bill,' remonstrated Fagin, eagerly catching at the word. 'If it hadn't been for the girl! Who but poor old Fagin was the means of your having such a handy girl about you?'

'He says true enough there!' said Nancy, coming hastily forward. 'Let him be; let him be.'

Nancy's appearance gave a new turn to the conversation. For the boys, receiving a sly wink from the wary old man, began to ply her with liquor—of which, however, she took very sparingly; while Fagin, offering an unusual flow of spirits, gradually brought Mr. Sikes into a better temper by affecting to regard his threats as a little pleasant banter, and, moreover, by laughing very heartily at one or two rough jokes, which, after repeated applications to the spirit-bottle, he condescended to make.

'Now Bill,' said Fagin, quietly, 'there are matters that we might discuss now that you have returned and are feeling well again. Is there a place to which we might retire where we might speak without, ah, distraction?'

Bill nodded towards the door, and, without more ado, both men quietly made their exit. Nancy and the boys continued in their merry making, until, a few seconds later, the boys found themselves entirely on their own. As Charley and the Dodger were more than content to laugh and joke and enjoy the good food and drink without further company, they paid no heed to this. They scarcely noticed Nancy slipping back into the room moments before Fagin and Sikes returned.

'It's all very well,' said Mr. Sikes, as he strode back into the room; 'but I must have some blunt from you tonight.'

'I haven't a piece of coin about me,' replied Fagin.

'Then you've got lots at home,' retorted Sikes, 'and I must have some from there.'

'Lots!' cried Fagin, holding up is hands. 'I haven't so much as would–'

'I don't know how much you've got, and I dare say you hardly know yourself, as it would take a pretty long time to count it,' said Sikes; 'but I must have some tonight, and that's flat.'

'Well, well,' said Fagin, with a sigh, 'I'll send the Artful round presently.'

'You won't do nothing of the kind,' rejoined Mr. Sikes. 'The Artful's a deal too artful, and would forget to come, or lose his way, or get dodged by traps, and so be perwented, or anything for an excuse, if you put him up to it. Nancy shall go to the ken and fetch it, to make all sure; and I'll lie down and have a snooze while she's gone.'

Upon this suggestion, Fagin looked at Nancy more closely.

'Why, Nance!' exclaimed the old man, starting back as he put down the candle, 'how pale you are again!'

'Pale?' echoed the girl, shading her eyes with her hands, as if to look steadily at him.

'Quite horrible!' confirmed Fagin, insensitively. 'What have you been doing to yourself?'

'Nothing that I know of, except sitting in this close place for I don't know how long and all,' replied the girl carelessly.

'It will be good then," said the old man, 'for you to get away from this stale place for a while.'

After a great deal of haggling and squabbling, Fagin beat down the amount of the required advance from five pounds to three pounds, four shillings, and a sixpence protesting with many solemn declarations that it would only leave him eighteen-pence to keep house with. Mr. Sikes sullenly remarked that if he couldn't get any more he must be content with that. Nancy prepared to accompany her associates home; while the

Dodger and Master Bates put the eatables in the cupboard. Mr. Fagin then, taking leave of his affectionate friend, returned homewards attended by Nancy and the boys. Mr. Sikes, meanwhile, flung himself on the bed, and composed himself to sleep away the time until the young lady's return.

In due course they arrived at Fagin's abode, where they found Toby Crackit and Mr. Chitling intent upon their fifteenth game at cribbage, which it is scarcely necessary to say the latter gentleman lost, and with it his fifteenth and last sixpence, much to the amusement of his young friends. Mr. Crackit, apparently somewhat ashamed at being found relaxing with a gentleman so much his inferior in station and mental endowments, yawned, and inquiring after Sikes, took up his hat to go.

'Damn, I'm as flat as a juryman; and should have gone to sleep, as fast as Newgate, if I hadn't had the good natur' to amuse this youngster. Horrid dull, I'm blessed if he ain't!'

With these and other ejaculations of the same kind, Mr. Toby Crackit swept up his winnings, and crammed them into his waistcoat pocket with a haughty air, as though such small pieces of silver were wholly beneath the consideration of a man of his figure. This done, he swaggered out of the room with so much elegance and gentility that Mr. Chitling, bestowing numerous admiring glances on his legs and boots till they were out of sight, assured the company that he considered his acquaintance cheap at fifteen sixpences an interview, and that he didn't value his losses the snap of his little finger.

'Wot a rum chap you are, Tom!' said Master Bates, highly amused by this declaration.

'Not a bit of it,' replied Mr. Chitling, 'am I, Fagin?'

'A very clever fellow, my dear,' said Fagin, patting him on the shoulder, and winking to his other pupils.

'And Mr. Crackit *is* a heavy swell; ain't he, Fagin?' asked Tom.

'No doubt at all about that, my dear.' replied Fagin.

'And it *is* a creditable thing to have his acquaintance; ain't it, Fagin?' pursued Tom.

'Very much so, indeed, my dear. They're only jealous, Tom, because he won't give it to them.'

'Ah!' cried Tom, triumphantly, 'that's where it is! He has cleaned me out. But I can go and earn some more when I like; can't I, Fagin?'

'To be sure you can, and the sooner you go the better, Tom; so make up your loss at once, and don't lose any more time. Dodger! Charley! It's time you were on the lay. Come! It's near ten, and you've nothing done yet.'

In obedience to this hint, the boys, nodding to Nancy, took up their hats, and left the room, the Dodger and his vivacious friend indulging, as they went, in many witticisms at the expense of Mr. Chitling; in whose conduct, it is but justice to say, there was nothing very conspicuous or peculiar, inasmuch as there are a great number of spirited young bloods upon town who pay a much higher price than Mr. Chitling for being seen in good society, and a great number of fine gentlemen (composing the good society aforesaid) who established their reputation upon very much the same footing as flash Toby Crackit.

'Now,' said Fagin, when they had left the room, 'I'll go and get you that cash, Nancy. This is only the key of a little cupboard where I keep a few odd things the boys get, my dear. I never lock up my money, for I've got none to lock up, my dear—ha! ha! ha! none to lock up. It's a poor trade, Nancy, and no thanks; but I'm fond of seeing the young people about me, and I bear it all—I bear it all.'

'Come!' said Nancy, expressing some impatience with Fagin's dawdling. 'Let me get back to Sikes; that's a dear.' With a sigh for every piece of money, Fagin told the amount into her hand. They parted without more conversation, merely interchanging a 'goodnight.'

When the girl got into the open street she sat down upon a doorstep, and seemed, for a few moments, wholly bewildered and unable to pursue her way. Suddenly, she arose; and hurrying on, in a direction quite opposite to that in which Sikes was awaiting her return, quickened her pace, until it gradually resolved into a violent run. After completely exhausting herself, she stopped to take breath; and, as if suddenly recollecting herself, and deploring her inability to do something she was bent upon, wrung her hands, and burst into tears.

It might be that her tears relieved her, or that she felt the full hopelessness of her condition, but she turned back, and hurrying with nearly as great rapidity in the contrary direction, partly to recover lost time, and partly to keep pace with the violent current of her own thoughts, soon reached the dwelling where she had left the housebreaker.

If she betrayed any agitation, when she presented herself to Mr. Sikes, he did not observe it; for merely inquiring if she had brought the money, and receiving a reply in the affirmative, he uttered a growl of satisfaction, and replacing his head upon the pillow, resumed the slumbers which her arrival had interrupted.

It was fortunate for her that the possession of money occasioned him so much employment the next few days in the way of eating and drinking, and withal had so beneficial an effect in smoothing down the asperities of his temper, that he had neither time nor inclination to be very critical upon her behaviour and deportment. That she had all the abstracted and nervous manner of one who is on the eve of some bold and hazardous step, which has required no common struggle to resolve upon, would have been obvious to the lynx-eyed Fagin, who would most probably have taken alarm at once; but Mr. Sikes, lacking the niceties of discrimination, and being troubled with no more subtle misgivings than those which resolve themselves into a dogged roughness of behaviour towards everybody, and being, furthermore, in an unusually amiable condition, as has already been observed; saw nothing unusual in her de-meanor, and, indeed, troubled himself so little about her, that had her agitation been far more perceptible than it was, it would have been very unlikely to have awakened his suspicions.

Chapter 34
Mr. and Mrs. Bolter

The same evening that Fagin had sought a private interview with Sikes, there advanced towards London, by the Great North Road, two persons, upon whom it is expedient that this history should bestow some attention.

They were a man and woman—or perhaps they would be better described as a male and female; for the former was one of those long-limbed, knock-kneed, shambling, bony people to whom it is difficult to assign any precise age—looking as they do, when they are yet boys, like under-grown men, and when they are almost men, like over-grown boys. The woman was young, but of a robust and hardy make, as she need have been to bear the weight of the heavy bundle which was strapped to her back. Her companion was not encumbered with much luggage, as there merely dangled from a stick which he carried over his shoulder, a small parcel wrapped in a common handkerchief, and apparently light enough. This circumstance, added to the length of his legs, which were of unusual extent, enabled him with much ease to keep some half-dozen paces in advance of his companion, to whom he occasionally turned with an impatient jerk of the head, as if reproaching her tardiness, and urging her to greater exertion.

Thus they had toiled along the dusty road, taking little heed of any object within sight, save when they stepped aside to allow a wider passage for the mail coaches which were whirling out of town, until they passed through Highgate archway, when the foremost traveller stopped, and called impatiently to his companion:

'Come on, can't yer? What a lazybones yer are, Charlotte.'

'It's a heavy load, I can tell you,' said the female, coming up, almost breathless with fatigue.

'Heavy! What are yer talking about? What are yer made for?' rejoined the male traveller, changing his own little bundle as he spoke, to the other shoulder. 'Oh, there yer are, resting again! Well, if yer ain't enough to tire anybody's patience out, I don't know what is!'

'Is it much farther?' asked the woman, resting herself against a bank, and looking up with perspiration streaming from her face.

'Much farther? Yer as good as there,' said the long-legged tramper, pointing out before him. 'Look there! Those are the lights of London.'

'They're a good two mile off, at least,' said the woman despondingly.

'Never mind whether they're two mile off or twenty,' said Noah Claypole, for he it was; 'but get up and come on, or I'll kick yer, and so I give yer notice.'

As Noah's red nose grew redder with anger, and as he crossed the road while speaking, as if fully prepared to put his threat into execution, the woman rose without any further remark, and trudged onward by his side.

'Where do you mean to stop for the night, Noah?' she asked, after they had walked a few hundred yards.

'How should I know?' replied Noah, whose temper had been considerably impaired by walking.

'Near, I hope,' said Charlotte.

'No, not near,' replied Mr. Claypole. 'There! Not near; so don't think it.'

'Why not?'

'When I tell yer that I don't mean to do a thing, that's enough, without any why or because either,' replied Mr. Claypole, with dignity.

'Well, you needn't be so cross,' said his companion.

'A pretty thing it would be, wouldn't it, to go and stop at the very first public-house outside the town, so that Sowerberry, if he come up after us, might poke in his old nose, and have us taken back in a cart with handcuffs on,' said Mr. Claypole in a jeering tone. 'No! I shall go and lose myself among the narrowest streets I can find, and not stop till we come to the very out-of-the-wayest house I can set my eyes on. 'Cod, yer may thanks yer stars I've got a head; for if we hadn't gone at first the wrong road a-purpose, and come back across country, yer'd have been locked up hard and fast a week ago, my lady. And serve yer right for being a fool.'

'I know I ain't as cunning as you are,' replied Charlotte; 'but don't put all the blame on me, and say I should have been locked up. You would have been if I had been, any way.'

'Yer took the money from the till, yer know yer did,' said Mr. Claypole.

'I took it for you, Noah, dear,' rejoined Charlotte.

'Did I keep it?' asked Mr. Claypole.

'No; you trusted in me, and let me carry it like a dear, and so you are,' said the lady, chucking him under the chin, and drawing her arm through his.

This was indeed the case; but as it was not Mr. Claypole's habit to repose a blind and foolish confidence in anybody, it should be observed, in justice to that gentleman, that he had trusted Charlotte to this extent, in order that, if they were pursued, the money might be found on her, which would leave him an opportunity of asserting his utter innocence of any theft, and would greatly facilitate his chances of escape. Of course he entered at this juncture, into no explanation of his motives, and they walked on very lovingly together.

In pursuance of this cautious plan, Mr. Claypole went on without halting until he arrived at the Angel at Islington, where he wisely judged, from the crowd of passengers and numbers of vehicles, that London began in earnest. Just pausing to observe which appeared to be the most crowded streets, and consequently the most to be avoided, he crossed into Saint John's Road, and was soon deep in the obscurity of the intricate and dirty ways which, lying between Gray's Inn Lane and Smithfield, render that part of the town one of the lowest and worst that improvement has left in the midst of London.

Through these streets, Noah Claypole walked, dragging Charlotte after him; now stepping into the gutter to embrace at a glance the whole external character of some small public-house, now jogging on again, as some fancied appearance induced him to believe it too public for his purpose. At length, he stopped in front of one, more humble in appearance and more dirty than any he had yet seen; and, having crossed over and surveyed it from the opposite pavement, graciously announced his intention of putting up there for the night.

'So give us the bundle,' said Noah, unstrapping it from the woman's shoulders, and slinging it over his own; 'and don't yer speak except when yer spoke to. What's the name of the house—t-h-r—three what?'

'Cripples,' said Charlotte.

'Three Cripples,' repeated Noah, 'and a very good sign too. Now then! Keep close at my heels, and come along.' With these injunctions, he pushed the rattling door with his shoulder, and entered the house followed by his companion. There was nobody in the bar but an ugly young waiter, who, with his two elbows on the counter, was reading an old newspaper. He stared very hard at Noah, and Noah stared very hard at him.

If Noah had been attired in his charity-boy's dress, there might have been some reason for the bartender opening his eyes so wide; but as he had discarded the coat and badge, and wore a short smock-frock over his leathers, there seemed no particular reason for his appearance exciting so much attention in a public-house.

'Is this the Three Cripples?' asked Noah.

'That is the dabe of this 'ouse,' replied the bartender.

'A gentleman we met on the road, coming up from the country, recommended us here,' said Noah, nudging Charlotte, perhaps to call her attention to this most ingenious device for attracting respect, and perhaps to warn her to betray no surprise. 'We want to sleep here tonight.'

'I'b dot certaid you cad,' said Barney, who was the attendant gnome; 'but I'll idquire.'

'Show us the tap, and give us a bit of cold meat and a drop of beer while yer inquiring, will yer?' said Noah.

Barney complied by ushering them into a small backroom, and set-ting the requested food before them; having done which, he informed the travellers that they could be lodged that night, and left the amiable couple to their refreshment.

Now, this backroom was immediately behind the bar, and some steps lower, so that any person connected with the house undrawing a small curtain which concealed a single pane of glass fixed in the wall of the last-named apartment, about five feet from its flooring, could not only look down upon any guests in the backroom without any great hazard of being observed (the glass being in a dark angle of the wall, between which and a large upright beam the observer had to thrust himself), but could also, by applying his ear to the partition, ascertain with tolera-ble distinctness their subject of conversation. The landlord of the house had not withdrawn his eye from this spy window for five minutes, and Barney had only just returned from making the communication related above, when Fagin, in the course of his evening's business, came into the bar to inquire after some of his young pupils.

'Hush!' said Barney; 'stradegers id the next roob.'

'Strangers?' repeated the old man in a whisper.

'Ah! Ad rub uds too,' added Barney, nodding in the affirmative. 'Frob the cuttry, but subthig in your way, or I'b bistaked.'

Fagin appeared to receive this communication with great interest. Mounting a stool, he cautiously applied his eye to the pane of glass, from which secret post he could see Mr. Claypole taking cold beef from the dish, and porter from the pot, and administering homeopathic doses of both to Charlotte, who sat patiently by, eating and drinking at his plea-sure.

'Aha!' he whispered, looking round to Barney, 'I like that fellow's looks. He'd be of use to us; he knows how to train the girl already. Don't make as much noise as a mouse, my dear, and let me hear 'em talk—let me hear 'em.'

He again applied his eye to the glass, and turning his ear to the parti-tion, listened attentively, with a subtle and eager look upon his face, that might have appertained to some old goblin.

'So I mean to be a gentleman,' said Mr. Claypole, kicking out his legs, and continuing a conversation, the commencement of which Fagin had arrived too late to hear. 'No more jolly old coffins, Charlotte, but a gen-tleman's life for me; and, if yer like, yer shall be a lady.'

'I should like that well enough, dear,' replied Charlotte; 'but tills ain't to be emptied every day, and people to get clear off after it.'

'Tills be blowed!' said Mr. Claypole; 'there's more things besides tills to be emptied.'

'What do you mean?' asked his companion.

'Pockets, women's purses, houses, mail coaches, banks!' said Mr. Claypole, rising with the porter.

'But you can't do all that, dear,' said Charlotte.

'I shall look out to get into company with them as can,' replied Noah. 'They'll be able to make us useful some way or another. Why, you yourself are worth fifty women; I never see such a precious sly and deceitful creetur as yer can be when I let yer.'

'Lor, how nice it is to hear yer say so!' exclaimed Charlotte, imprinting a kiss upon his ugly face.

'There, that'll do; don't *yer* be too affectionate, in case I'm cross with yer,' said Noah, disengaging himself with great gravity. 'I should like to be the captain of some band, and have the whopping of 'em, and follering 'em about, unbeknown to themselves. That would suit me, if there was good profit; and if we could only get in with some gentleman of this sort, I say it would be cheap at that twenty pound note you've got—especially as we don't very well know how to get rid of it ourselves.'

After expressing this opinion, Mr. Claypole looked into the porter-pot with an aspect of deep wisdom; and having well shaken its contents, nodded condescendingly to Charlotte, and took a draught, wherewith he appeared greatly refreshed. He was meditating another, when the sudden opening of the door, and the appearance of a stranger, interrupted him.

The stranger was Mr. Fagin. And very amiable he looked, and a very low bow he made, as he advanced, and setting himself down at the nearest table, ordered something to drink of the grinning Barney.

'A pleasant night, sir, but cool for the time of year,' said Fagin, rubbing his hands. 'From the country, I see, sir?'

'How do yer see that?' asked Noah Claypole.

'We have not so much dust as that in London,' replied Fagin, pointing from Noah's shoes to those of his companion, and from them to the two bundles.

'Yer a sharp feller,' said Noah. 'Ha! ha! only hear that, Charlotte!'

'Why, one needs be sharp in this town, my dear,' replied the old man, sinking his voice to a confidential whisper; 'and that's the truth.'

Fagin followed up this remark by striking the side of his nose with his right forefinger—a gesture which Noah attempted to imitate, though not with complete success, in consequence of his own nose not being large enough for the purpose. However, Mr. Fagin seemed to interpret the endeavour as expressing a perfect coincidence with his opinion. When Barney reappeared with a bottle of fine liquor; Fagin poured out generous portions, in a friendly manner, for Noah and Charlotte to taste.

'Good stuff that,' observed Mr. Claypole, smacking his lips.

'Dear!' said Fagin. 'A man need be always emptying a till, or a pocket, or a woman's wallet, or a house, or a mail coach, or a bank if he drinks it regularly.'

Mr. Claypole no sooner heard this extract from his own remarks than he fell back in his chair, and looked from the old man to Charlotte with a countenance of ashy paleness and excessive terror.

'Don't mind me, my dear,' said Fagin, drawing his chair closer. 'Ha! ha! it was lucky it was only me that heard you by chance; it was very lucky it was only me.'

'I didn't take it,' stammered Noah, no longer stretching out his legs like an independent gentleman, but coiling them up as well as he could under his chair. 'It was all her doing. Yer've got it now, Charlotte, yer know, yer have.'

'No matter who's got it, or who did it, my dear,' replied Fagin, glancing, nevertheless, with a hawk's eye at the girl and the two bundles; 'I'm in that way myself, and I like you for it.'

'In what way?' asked Mr. Claypole, a little recovering.

'In that way of business,' rejoined Fagin; 'and so are the people of the house. You've hit the right nail upon the head, and are as safe here as you could be. There is not a safer place in all this town than is the Cripples— that is, when I like to make it so. I have taken a fancy to you and the young woman; so I've said the word, and you may make your minds easy.'

Noah Claypole's mind might have been at ease after this assurance, but his body certainly was not; for he shuffled and writhed about, into various uncouth positions, eyeing his new friend meanwhile with mingled fear and suspicion.

'I'll tell you more,' said Fagin, after he had reassured the girl, by dint of friendly nods and muttered encouragements. 'I have got a friend that I think can gratify your darling wish, and put you in the right way, where you can take whatever department of the business you think will suit you best at first, and be taught all the others.'

'Yer speak as if yer were in earnest,' replied Noah.

'What advantage would it be to me to be anything else?' inquired Fagin, shrugging his shoulders. 'Here! Let me have a word with you outside.'

'There's no occasion to trouble ourselves to move,' said Noah, getting his legs by gradual degrees abroad again. 'She'll take the luggage upstairs the while. Charlotte, see to them bundles.'

This mandate, which had been delivered with great majesty, was obeyed without the slightest demur; and Charlotte made the best of her way off with the packages, while Noah held the door open and watched her out.

'She's kept tolerably well under, ain't she?' he asked the stranger, as he resumed his seat, in the tone of a keeper who had tamed some wild animal.

'Quite perfect,' rejoined Fagin, clapping him on the shoulder. 'You're a genius, my dear.'

'Why, I suppose if I wasn't, I shouldn't be here,' replied Noah. 'But, I say, she'll be back if yer lose time.'

'Now, what do you think?' said Fagin. 'If you was to like my friend, could you do better than join him?'

'Is he in a good way of business? That's where it's at!' responded Noah, winking one of his little eyes.

'The top of the tree,' replied the old man, 'employs a power of hands; has the very best society in the profession.'

'Regular town-maders?' asked Mr. Claypole.

'Not a countryman among 'em; and I don't think he'd take you on, even on my recommendation, if he didn't run rather short of assistants just now,' replied Fagin.

'Should I have to hand over?' asked Noah, slapping his breeches pocket.

'It couldn't possibly be done without,' replied Fagin, in a most decided manner. 'Twenty pounds is the going rate.'

'Twenty pounds, though—it's a lot of money!'

'Not when it's in a note you can't get rid of,' retorted Fagin. 'Number and date taken, I suppose? Payment stopped at the Bank? Ah! It's not worth much to him. It'll have to go abroad, and still he couldn't sell it for a great deal in the market.'

'When could I see him?' asked Noah, doubtfully.

'Tomorrow morning.'

'Where?'

'Here.'

'Um!' commented Noah. 'What's the wages?'

'Live like a gentleman—board and lodging, pipes and spirits, free— half of all you earn, and half of all that the young woman earns,' replied Mr. Fagin.

Whether Noah Claypole, whose avarice was remarkably comprehensive, would have acceded even to these glowing terms, had he been a perfectly free agent, is very doubtful; but as he recollected that, in the event of his refusal, it was in the power of his new acquaintance to give him up to justice immediately (and more unlikely things had come to pass), he gradually relented, and said he thought that would suit him.

'But, yer see,' observed Noah, 'as she will be able to do a good deal, I should like to take something very light.'

'A little fancy work?' suggested Fagin.

'Ah! something of that sort,' replied Noah. 'What do you think would suit me now? Something not too trying on the strength, and not very dangerous, you know. That's the sort of thing!'

'I heard you talk of something in the spy way upon the others, my dear,' said the older miser. 'My friend wants somebody who would do that well, very much.'

'Why, I did mention that, and I shouldn't mind turning my hand to it sometimes,' rejoined Mr. Claypole slowly; 'but it wouldn't pay by itself, you know.'

'That's true!' observed the old man, ruminating, or pretending to ruminate. 'No, it might not.'

'What do you think, then?' asked Noah, anxiously regarding him. 'Something in the sneaking way, where it was pretty sure work, and not much more risk than being at home.'

'What do you think of the old ladies?' asked Fagin. 'There's a good deal of money made in snatching their bags and parcels, and running round the corner.'

'Don't they holler out a good deal, and scratch sometimes?' asked Noah, shaking his head. 'I don't think that would answer my purpose. Ain't there any other line open?'

'Stop!' said Fagin, laying his hand on Noah's knee. 'The kinchin lay!'

'What's that?' demanded Mr. Claypole.

'The kinchins, my dear,' said Fagin, 'is the young children that's sent on errands by their mothers, with sixpences and shillings; and the lay is just to take their money away—they've always got it ready in their hands—then knock 'em into the gutter, and walk off very slow, as if there were nothing else the matter but a child fallen down and hurt itself. Ha! ha! ha!'

'Ha! ha!' roared Mr. Claypole, kicking up his legs in an ecstasy. 'Lord, that's the very thing!'

'To be sure it is,' replied Fagin; 'and you can have a few good beats chalked out in Camden Town, and Battle Bridge, and neighborhoods like that, where they're always going on errands, and you can upset as many kinchins as you want, any hour in the day. Ha! ha! ha!'

With this, Fagin poked Mr. Claypole in the side, and they joined in a burst of laughter both long and loud.

'Well, that's all right!' said Noah, when he had recovered himself, and Charlotte had returned. 'What time tomorrow shall we say?'

'Will ten do?' asked Fagin, adding, as Mr. Claypole nodded assent, 'What name shall I tell my good friend.'

'Mr. Bolter,' replied Noah, who had prepared himself for such an emergency. 'Mr. Morris Bolter. This is Mrs. Bolter.'

'Mrs. Bolter's humble servant,' said Fagin, bowing with grotesque politeness. 'I hope I shall know you better very shortly.'

'Do you hear the gentleman, Charlotte?' thundered Mr. Claypole.

'Yes, Noah, dear!' replied Mrs. Bolter, extending her hand.

'She calls me Noah, as a sort of fond way of talking,' said Mr. Morris Bolter, late Claypole, turning to Fagin. 'You understand?'

'Oh yes, I understand—perfectly,' replied Fagin, telling the truth for once. 'Goodnight! Goodnight!'

With many adieus and good wishes, Mr. and Mrs. Bolter made their way upstairs. Bespeaking his good lady's attention, Noah proceeded to enlighten her relative to the arrangement he had made, with all that haughtiness and air of superiority becoming not only a member of the sterner sex, but a gentleman who appreciated the dignity of a special appointment on the kinchin lay, in London and its vicinity.

Fagin sat quietly contemplating the skills, knowledge, and character of his newest associates. Even the want of such could be turned to good use if shrewdly marshalled. A lack of courage compounded by endless greed made Noah an easy mark. Fagin's reverie was soon disturbed by a dramatic entry. Betsy, whose attire suggested that she'd been working the streets, burst through the door.

'There you are!" she exclaimed.

'Betsy, whatever's the matter?' asked Fagin.

'I've news; horrible, terrible news," replied Betsey.

'Go on then," said Fagin, 'spit it out.'

'It's young Master Bates,' said Betsy. 'He' been lagged. I seen him myself being escorted away by two police officers.'

Chapter 35
Charlie Bates in the Dock

'And so it was you that was your own friend, was it?' asked Mr. Claypole, otherwise Bolter, of Fagin after, by virtue of the compact entered into between them, he and Charlotte had moved to Fagin's house. 'Cod, I thought as much last night!'

'Every man's his own friend, my dear,' replied Fagin, with his most insinuating grin; 'he hasn't as good a one as himself, anywhere.'

'Except sometimes,' replied Morris Bolter, assuming the air of a man of the world; 'some people are nobody's enemies but their own, yer know.'

'Don't believe that,' said Fagin. 'When a man's his own enemy, it's only because he's too much his own friend; not because he's careful for everybody but himself. Pooh! pooh! There ain't such a thing in nature.'

'There oughtn't to be, if there is,' replied Mr. Bolter.

'That stands to reason,' replied the old man. 'Some conjurers say that number three is the magic number, and some say it is the number seven. It's neither, my friend, neither—it's number one.'

'Ha! ha!' cried Mr. Bolter. 'Number one forever.'

'In a little community like ours, my dear,' said Fagin, who felt it necessary to qualify this position, 'we have a general number one—that is, you can't consider yourself as number one without considering me too as the same, and all the other young people.'

'Oh, the devil!' exclaimed Mr. Bolter.

'You see,' pursued Fagin, affecting to disregard this interruption, 'we are so mixed up together, and identified in our interests, that it must be so. For instance, it's your object to take care of number one—meaning yourself.'

'Certainly!' replied Mr. Bolter. 'Yer about right there.'

'Well! You can't take care of yourself, number one, without taking care of me, number one.'

'Number two, you mean,' said Mr. Bolter, who was largely endowed with the quality of selfishness.

'No, I don't!' retorted Fagin. 'I'm of the same importance to you, as you are to yourself.'

'I say,' interrupted Mr. Bolter, 'yer a very nice man, and I'm very fond of yer; but we ain't quite so thick together, as all that comes to.'

'Only think,' said Fagin, shrugging his shoulders, and stretching out his hands; 'only consider. You've done what's a very pretty thing, and what I love you for doing; but what at the same time would put the cravat round your throat, that's so very easily tied and so very difficult to unloose—in plain English, the noose!' Mr. Bolter put his hand to his neckerchief, as if he felt it uncomfortably tight, and murmured an assent, qualified in tone but not in substance.

'The gallows,' continued Fagin, 'the gallows, my dear, is an ugly fingerpost, which points out a very short and sharp turning that has stopped many a bold fellow's career on the broad highway. To keep in the easy road, and to keep it at a distance, is object number one with you.'

'Of course it is,' replied Mr. Bolter. 'What do yer talk about such things for?'

'Only to show you my meaning clearly,' said Fagin, raising his eyebrows. 'To be able to do that, you depend upon me. To keep my little business all snug, I depend upon you. The first is your number one, the second my number one. The more you value your number one, the more careful you must be of mine; so we come at last to what I told you at first—that a regard for number one holds us all together, and must do so, unless we would all go to pieces in company.'

'That's true,' rejoined Mr. Bolter, thoughtfully. 'Oh! yer a cunning old codger!'

Mr. Fagin saw, with delight, that this tribute to his powers was no mere compliment, but that he had really impressed his recruit with a sense of his wily genius, which it was most important that he should entertain at the outset of their acquaintance. To strengthen an impression so desirable and useful, he followed up the blow by acquainting him, in some detail, with the magnitude and extent of his operations—blending truth and fiction together, as best served his purpose, and bringing both to bear, with so much art, that Mr. Bolter's respect visibly increased, and became tempered, at the same time, with a degree of wholesome fear, which it was highly desirable to awaken.

'It's this mutual trust we have in each other that consoles me under heavy losses,' said Fagin. 'A good hand; no, a great and worthy hand was taken from me yesterday.'

'You don't mean to say he died?' cried Mr. Bolter.

'No, no,' replied Fagin, 'not so bad as that—not quite so bad.'

'What, I suppose he was -'

'Wanted,' interposed Fagin. 'Yes, he was wanted.'

'Very particular?' inquired Mr. Bolter.

'No,' replied Fagin, 'not very. He was charged with attempting to pick a pocket, and they found a silver snuffbox on him—his own, my dear, his own, for he took snuff himself, and was very fond of it. They remanded him till today, for they thought they knew the owner. Ah! he was worth fifty boxes, and I'd give the price of as many to have him back. You should have known Charley, my dear; you should have known my apprentice Master Charley Bates.'

'Well, but I shall know him, I hope; don't yer think so?' said Mr. Bolter.

'I'm doubtful about it,' replied Fagin, with a sigh. 'If they don't get any fresh evidence, it'll only be a summary conviction, and we shall have him back again after six weeks or so; but, if they do, it's a case of lagging. They know what a clever lad he is; he'll be a lifer. They'll make Master Bates nothing less than a lifer.'

'What do you mean by lagging and a lifer?' demanded Mr. Bolter. 'What's the good of talking in that way to me; why don't yer speak so as I can understand yer?'

Fagin was about to translate these mysterious expressions into the vulgar tongue—and, being interpreted, Mr. Bolter would have been informed that they represented that combination of words, 'transportation for life'—when the dialogue was cut short by the entry of Jack Dawkins, with his hands in his breeches-pockets, and his face presenting a look of woe.

'It's all up, Fagin,' said the Dodger, when he and his new companion had been made known to each other.

'What do you mean?' asked the old miser, with trembling lips.

'They've found the gentleman as owns the box; two or three more's a-coming to 'dentify him; and Master Charley Bates is booked for a passage out to the colonies,' replied the Dodger. 'I must have a full suit for mourning in, Fagin, and a hatband, to visit him in, afore he sets out upon his travels. To think of Charley—lummy Master Charley Bates—going abroad for a common two penny sneeze-box! I never thought he'd a done it under a gold watch and chain, at the lowest. Oh, why didn't he rob some rich old gentleman of all his valuables, and go out as a gentleman, and not like a common prig, without no honour nor glory!'

With this expression of feeling for his unfortunate friend, the Artful Dodger sat himself on the nearest chair with an aspect of chagrin and despondency.

'What do you talk about his having neither honour nor glory for!' exclaimed Fagin, darting an angry look at his pupil. 'Wasn't he always top-drawer among you all? Is there one of you that could touch him or come near him on any scent! *Eh?*'

As the occasion called for less than perfect candour, the Dodger replied, in a voice rendered husky by regret; 'Not one.'

'Then what do you talk of?' asked Fagin, angrily; 'what are you blubbering for?'

'A-cause it isn't on the record, is it?' said the Dodger, chafed into perfect defiance of his venerable friend by the current of his regrets; 'a-cause it can't come out in the indictment; a-cause nobody will never know half of what he was. How will he stand in the Newgate Calendar? P'raps not be there at all. Oh, my eye, my eye, wot a blow it is!'

'Ha! ha!' cried Fagin, extending his right hand, and turning to Mr. Bolter in a fit of chuckling which shook him as though he had the palsy; 'see what a pride they take in their profession, my dear. Ain't it beautiful?'

Mr. Bolter nodded assent; and the old man, after contemplating the grief of Jack Dawkins for some seconds with evident satisfaction, stepped up to that young gentleman and patted him on the shoulder.

'Never mind, Jack,' said Fagin, soothingly; 'it'll come out, it'll be sure to come out. They'll all know what a clever fellow he was; he'll show it himself, and not disgrace his old pals and teachers. Think how young he is too! What a distinction, Jack, to be lagged at his time of life!'

'Well, it is an honour, that is!' said the Dodger, a little consoled.

'He shall have all he wants,' continued the old miser. 'He shall be kept in the Stone Jug, Jack, like a gentleman. Like a gentleman! With his beer every day, and money in his pocket to pitch and toss with, if he can't spend it.'

'No! shall he, though?' cried the Dodger.

'Ay, that he shall,' replied Fagin, 'and we'll have a big-wig, Jack, one that's got the greatest gift of the gab, to carry on his defence; and he shall make a speech for himself too, if he likes; and we'll read it all in the papers—'Master Charley Bates—shrieks of laughter—here the court was convulsed'—eh, Jack, eh?'

'Ha! ha! laughed the Dodger, 'what a lark that would be, wouldn't it, Fagin? I say, how Charley would bother 'em, wouldn't he?'

'Would?' cried Fagin. 'He shall—he will!'

'Ah, to be sure, so he will,' repeated the Dodger, rubbing his hands.

'I think I see him now,' cried the old man, bending his eyes upon his pupil.

'So do I,' cried the Dodger. 'Ha! so do I. I see it all afore me—upon my soul I do, Fagin. What a game! What a regular game! All the big-wigs trying to look solemn, and Master Bates addressing 'em as intimate and comfortable as if he was the judge's own son making a speech after dinner—ha! ha! ha!'

In fact, Mr. Fagin had so well humoured his young friend's somber disposition, that the Artful, who had at first been disposed to consider the imprisoned Charley rather in the light of a victim, now looked upon him as the chief actor in a scene of most uncommon and exquisite humour, and felt quite impatient for the arrival of the time when his old companion should have so favourable an opportunity of displaying his abilities.

'We must know how he gets on today, by some handy means or other,' said Fagin. 'Let me think.'

'Shall I go?' asked the Dodger.

'Not for the world,' replied Fagin. 'Are you mad, my dear, stark mad, that you'd walk into the very place where—No, Jack, no. One is enough to lose at a time.'

'You don't mean to go yourself, I suppose?' inquired the Dodger, with a mischievous grin.

'That wouldn't quite fit,' replied Fagin, shaking his head.

'Then why don't you send this new cove?' asked Jack, laying his hand on Noah's arm. 'Nobody knows him.'

'Why, if he didn't mind -' observed Fagin.

'Mind!' interposed Jack. 'What should *he* have to mind?'

'Really nothing, my dear,' said Fagin, turning to Mr. Bolter, 'really nothing.'

'Oh, I dare say about that, yer know,' observed Noah, backing towards the door, and shaking his head with a kind of sober alarm. 'No, no—none of that. It's not in my department, that ain't.'

'Wot department has he got, Fagin?' inquired the Dodger, surveying Noah's lank form with much disgust. 'The cutting away when there's anything wrong, and the eating of all the vittles when everything's right; is that his branch?'

'Never mind,' retorted Mr. Bolter; 'and don't yer take liberties with yer superiors, little boy, or yer'll find yerself in the wrong shop.'

The Artful Dodger laughed so vehemently at this magnificent threat, that it was some time before Fagin could interpose, and represent to Mr. Bolter that he incurred no possible danger in visiting the police station; that, inasmuch as no account of the little affair in which he had engaged, nor any description of his person, had yet been forwarded to the metropolis, it was very probable that he was not even suspected of having resorted to it for shelter; and that if he were properly disguised, it would be as safe a spot for him to visit as any in London, inasmuch as it would be, of all places, the very last to which he could be supposed likely to resort of his own free will.

Persuaded, in part, by these representations, but overborne in a much greater degree by his fear of Fagin, Mr. Bolter at length consented, with very poor grace, to undertake the expedition. By Fagin's directions, he immediately substituted for his own attire a wagoner's frock, velveteen breeches, and leather leggings, all of which articles the old man had at hand. He was likewise furnished with a felt hat well garnished with turn-pike tickets, and a carter's whip. Thus equipped, he was to saunter into the station, as some country fellow from Covent Garden Market might be supposed to do for the gratification of his curiosity; and as he was as awkward, ungainly, and raw-boned a fellow as need be, Mr. Fagin had no fear but that he would look the part to perfection.

These arrangements completed, he was informed of the necessary signs and tokens by which to recognise Charley, and was conveyed by the Artful Dodger through dark and winding ways to within a very short distance of Bow Street. Having described the precise location of the police station, and accompanied it with copious directions as to how he was to walk straight up the passage, and when he got into the yard to take the door up the steps on the right-hand side, and pull off his hat as he went into the room, Jack Dawkins bade him hurry on alone, and promised to bide his return at the spot of their parting.

Noah Claypole, or Morris Bolter as the reader pleases, promptly followed the directions he had received, which—the Artful being pretty well acquainted with the locality—were so exact that he was able to gain the magisterial presence without asking anyone any question, or meeting with any interruption along the way.

He found himself jostled among a crowd of people, chiefly women, who were huddled together in a dirty frowsy room, at the upper end of which was a raised platform railed off from the rest, with a dock for the prisoners on the left hand against the wall, a box for the witnesses in the middle, and a desk for the magistrates on the right; the awful locality last named being screened off by a partition which concealed the bench from the common gaze, and left the vulgar to imagine (if they could) the full majesty of justice.

There were only a couple of women in the dock, who were nodding to their admiring friends, while the clerk read some depositions to a couple of policemen and a man in plain clothes who leant over the table. A jailer stood reclining against the dock-rail, tapping his nose listlessly with a large key, except when he repressed an undue tendency to conversation among the idlers, by proclaiming silence; or looked sternly up to bid some woman 'Take that baby out,' when the gravity of justice was disturbed by feeble cries, half-smothered in the mother's shawl, from some meagre infant. The room smelt close and unwholesome, the walls were dirt-discoloured, and the ceiling blackened. There was an old smoky bust up on the mantelshelf, and a dusty clock above the dock—the only thing present that seemed to go on as it ought; for depravity, or poverty, or a habitual acquaintance with both, had left a taint on all of the animate matter, hardly less unpleasant than the thick greasy scum coating every inanimate object in the room.

Noah looked eagerly about him for Charley Bates; but although there were several women who would have done very well for that distinguished character's mother or sister, and more than one man who might be supposed to bear a strong resemblance to his father, nobody at all answering the description given to him of Master Bates was to be seen. He waited in a state of much suspense and uncertainty until the women, being committed for trial, went flaunting out; and then was quickly relieved by the appearance of another prisoner who he felt at once could be none other than the object of his visit.

It was indeed Master Charley Bates, who, shuffling into the room with his left hand in his pocket and his hat in his right hand, preceded the jailer, with a rolling gait altogether indescribable, and, taking his place in the dock, requested in an audible voice to know why he was placed in this 'ere disgraceful situation for.

'Hold your tongue, will you?' said the jailer.

'I'm an Englishman, ain't I?' rejoined Charley, 'where are my privileges?'

'You'll get your privileges soon enough,' retorted the jailer, 'and pepper with 'em.'

'We'll see wot the Secretary of State for the Home Affairs has got to say to the beaks, if I don't,' replied Master Bates. 'Now then! Wot is this here business? I shall thank the magistrates to dispose of this here little affair, and not to keep me while they read the newspaper, for I've got an appointment with a genelman in the City, and as I am a man of my word and wery punctual in business matters. He'll go away if I ain't there to my time, and then pr'aps there won't be an action for damages against them as kept me away. Oh, no, certainly not!'

At this point, Charley, with a show of being very particular with a view to the proceedings to be had thereafter, desired the jailer to communicate 'the names of them two fellows as was on the bench,' which so tickled the spectators, that they laughed most heartily. This disconcerted Master Bates for a moment or two as he meant to impress, not amuse.

'Silence there!' cried the jailer.

'What is this?' inquired one of the magistrates.

'A pick-pocketing case, your worship.'

'Has the boy ever been here before?'

'He ought to have been, a many times,' replied the jailer. 'He has been pretty well everywhere else. I know him well, your worship.'

'Oh! you know me, do you?' cried Charley, making note of the statement. 'Wery good. That's a case of deformation of character, anyway.'

Here there was another laugh, and another cry for silence.

'Now then, where are the witnesses?' asked the clerk.

'Ah! that's right,' added Charley. 'Where are they? I should like to see 'em.'

This wish was immediately gratified, for a policeman stepped forward who had seen the prisoner attempt to pick the pocket of an unknown gentleman in a crowd, and indeed had taken a handkerchief there from, which, being a very old one, he deliberately put back again, after trying in on his own countenance. For this reason, he took Charley Bates into custody as soon as he could get near him, and the said Charley Bates upon being searched, had on his person a silver snuffbox, with the owner's name engraved upon the lid. This gentleman had been discovered on reference to the Court Guide, and being then and there present, swore that the snuffbox was his, and that he had missed it on the previous day, the moment he had disengaged himself from the crowd before referred to. He had also noticed a young gentleman in the throng particularly active in making his way about, and that young gentleman was the prisoner before him.

'Have you anything to ask this witness, boy?' asked the magistrate.

'I wouldn't abase myself by descending to hold no conversation with him,' replied Charley.

'Have you anything to say at all?'

'Do you hear his worship ask if you've anything to say?' inquired the jailer, nudging the silent Charley Bates with his elbow.

'I beg your pardon,' said Charley, looking up with an air of abstraction. 'Did you redress yourself to me, my man?'

'I never see such an out-and-out young vagabond, your worship,' observed the officer with a grin. 'Do you mean to say anything, you young shaver?'

'No,' replied Charley, 'not here, for this ain't the shop for justice; besides which, my attorney is a-breakfasting this morning with the Wice President of the House of Commons; but I shall have something to say elsewhere, and so will he, and so will a wery numerous and 'spectable circle of acquaintances as'll make them beaks wish they'd never been born, or that they'd got their footmen to hang 'em up to their own hat-pegs afore they let 'em come out this morning to try it on upon me. I'll -'

'There! He's fully committed!' interposed the clerk. 'Take him away.'

'Come on,' said the jailer.

'Oh, ah! I'll come on,' replied Charley, brushing his hat with the palm of his hand. 'Ah! (to the Bench) it's no use your looking frightened; I won't show you no mercy, not a halfpenny of it. *You'll* pay for this, my fine fellers. I wouldn't be you for anything! I wouldn't go free, now, if you was to fall down on your knees and ask me. Here, carry me off to prison! Take me away!'

With these last words Charley suffered himself to be led off by the collar, threatening, till he got into the yard, to make a parliamentary business of it; and then grinning in the officer's face with great glee and self-approval.

Having seen him locked up by himself in a little cell, Noah made the best of his way back to where he had left the Artful Dodger. After waiting there some time, he was rejoined by that young gentleman, who had prudently abstained from showing himself until he had looked carefully abroad from a snug retreat, and ascertained that his new friend had not been followed by any impertinent person.

The two hastened back together, to bear to Mr. Fagin the animating news that Master Charley Bates was doing full justice to his bringing-up, and establishing for himself a glorious reputation.

Chapter 36
Nancy's Staunch Friend

Adept as she was in all the arts of cunning and dissimulation, the girl Nancy could not wholly conceal the effect that the knowledge she had gained from overhearing Fagin and Sikes had worked upon her mind. She remembered that both the crafty Fagin and the brutal Sikes had often confided to her schemes which had been hidden from all others, in the full confidence that she was trustworthy and beyond the reach of their suspicion. Vile as those schemes were, however, this new plan horrified her. Her mind could not be quieted.

Notwithstanding this, loyalty bound her tightly to old companions. Desperate as they were, and bitter as her feelings were towards Fagin, who had led her, step by step, deeper and deeper down into an abyss of crime and misery from whence there was no escape; still there were times when, even towards him, she felt some relenting, lest her betrayal should bring him within the iron grasp he had so long eluded, and he should fall at last—richly as he merited such a fate—by her hand.

But these were the mere wanderings of a mind unable to wholly detach itself from old associations, although able enough to fix itself steadily on one object, and resolved not to be turned aside by any consideration. Her fear of Sikes was a more powerful inducement to recoil while there was yet time; but she would drop no clue which might lead to his learning of her treachery. What more could she do! She was resolved.

Though all her mental struggles terminated at the same conclusion, they forced themselves upon her again and again, and left their traces too. She grew pale and thin, even within a few days. At times, she took no heed of what was passing before her, or no part in conversations where once she would have been the loudest. At other times she laughed without merriment, and was noisy without cause or meaning. At others – often within a moment afterwards—she sat silent and dejected, brooding with her head upon her hands; while the very effort by which she roused herself told more forcibly than even these indications that she was ill at ease, and that her thoughts were occupied with matters very different and distant from those in the course of discussion by her companions.

It was Sunday night, and the bell of the nearest church struck the hour. Sikes and Fagin were talking, but they paused to listen. The girl looked up from the low seat on which she crouched, and listened too. Seven. 'And getting dark already,' said Sikes, rising to open the blind and look out. Returning to his seat he added, 'A dark and heavy night it is too. A good night for business this.'

'Ah!' replied Fagin. 'What a pity, Bill, my dear, that there's none quite ready to be done.'

'You're right for once,' replied Sikes, gruffly. 'It is a pity, for I'm in the humour too.'

Fagin sighed, and shook his head despondingly.

'We must make up for lost time when we've got things into a good train. That's all I know,' said Sikes.

'That's the way to talk, my dear,' replied Fagin, venturing to pat him on the shoulder. 'It does me good to hear you.'

'Does you good, does it!' cried Sikes. 'Well, so be it.'

'Ha! ha! ha!' laughed Fagin, as if he were relieved by even this concession. 'You're like yourself tonight, Bill. Quite like yourself.'

'I don't feel like myself when you lay that withered old claw on my shoulder, so take it away,' said Sikes, casting off the old miser's hand.

'It make you nervous, Bill,—reminds you of being nabbed, does it?' said Fagin, determined not to be offended.

'Reminds me of being nabbed by the devil,' returned Sikes. 'There never was another man with such a face as yours, unless it was your father, and I suppose *he* is singeing his grizzled beard by this time, unless you came straight from the old 'un without any father at all betwixt you; which I shouldn't wonder at a bit.'

Fagin offered no reply to this compliment, but pulling Sikes by the sleeve, pointed his finger towards Nancy, who had taken advantage of the foregoing conversation to put on her bonnet, and was now leaving the room.

'Hallo!' cried Sikes. 'Nance! Where's a gal going to at this time of night?'

'Not far.'

'What answer's that?' returned Sikes. 'Where are you going?'

'I say, not far.'

'And I say where?' retorted Sikes, 'Do you hear me?'

'I don't know where,' replied the girl.

'Then I do,' said Sikes, more in the spirit of obstinacy than because he had any real objection to the girl going where she liked. 'Nowhere. Sit down.'

'I'm not well. I told you that before,' rejoined the girl. 'I want a breath of air.'

'Put your head out of the winder,' replied Sikes.

'There's not enough there,' said the girl. 'I want it in the street.'

'Then you won't have it,' replied Sikes. With which assurance he rose, locked the door, took the key out, and pulling her bonnet from her head, flung it up on top of an old cabinet. 'There,' said the robber. 'Now stop quietly where you are, will you?'

'It's not such a matter as a bonnet would keep me,' said the girl turning very pale. 'What do you mean, Bill? Do you know what you're doing?'

'Know what I'm—Oh!' cried Sikes, turning to Fagin, 'she's out of her senses, you know, or she daren't talk to me in that way.'

'You'll drive me on to something desperate,' muttered the girl placing both hands upon her breast, as though to keep down by force some violent outbreak. 'Let me go, will you,—this minute—this instant!'

'No!' said Sikes.

'Tell him to let me go, Fagin. He had better. It'll be better for him. Do you hear me?' cried Nancy, stamping her foot upon the ground.

'Hear you!' exclaimed Sikes, turning round in his chair to confront her. 'Aye! And if I hear you for half a minute longer, the dog shall have such a grip on your throat as'll tear some of that screaming voice out. Wot has come over you, you jade! Wot is it?'

'Let me go,' said the girl, with great earnestness; then sitting herself down on the floor, before the door, she said, 'Bill, let me go; you don't know what you are doing. You don't, indeed. For only one hour—do—do!'

'Cut my limbs off one by one!' cried Sikes, seizing her roughly by the arm, 'if I don't think the gal's stark raving mad. Get up.'

'Not till you let me go—not till you let me go—never—never!' screamed the girl. Sikes looked on for a minute, watching his opportunity, and suddenly pinioning her hands, dragged her, struggling and wrestling with him all the way, into a small adjoining room, where he sat himself on a bench, and thrusting her into a chair, held her down by force. She struggled and implored by turns until eight o'clock had struck, and then, wearied and exhausted, ceased to contest the point any further. With a caution, backed by many oaths, to make no more efforts to go out that night, Sikes left her to recover at leisure and rejoined Fagin.

'Whew!' said the housebreaker, wiping the perspiration from his face. 'Wot a precious strange gal that is!'

'You may say that, Bill,' replied Fagin, thoughtfully, 'you may say that.'

'Wot did she take it into her head to go out tonight for, do you think?' asked Sikes. 'Come; you should know her better than me. Wot does it mean?'

'Obstinacy! woman's obstinacy, I suppose, my dear,' replied Fagin, shrugging his shoulders.

'Well, I suppose it is,' growled Sikes. 'I thought I had tamed her, but she's as bad as ever.'

'Worse,' said Fagin thoughtfully. 'I never knew her like this, for such a little cause.'

'Nor I,' said Sikes. 'I think she's got a touch of that fever in her blood yet, and it won't come out—eh?'

'Like enough,' replied Fagin.

'I'll let her a little blood, without troubling the doctor, if she's took that way again,' said Sikes.

Fagin nodded an expressive approval of this mode of treatment.

'She was hanging about me all day, and night too, when I was stretched on my back, and you, like a black-hearted wolf as you are, kept yourself aloof,' said Sikes. 'We was very poor too, all the time, and I think, one way or other, it's worried and fretted her; and that being shut up here so long has made her restless—eh?'

'That's it, my dear,' replied Fagin in a whisper. 'Hush!'

As he uttered these words, the girl herself appeared and resumed her former seat. Her eyes were swollen and red; she rocked herself to and fro, tossed her head, and after a little time, burst out laughing.

'Why, now she's on the other tack!' exclaimed Sikes, turning a look of excessive surprise on his companion.

The old miser nodded to him to take no further notice just then; and, in a few minutes, the girl subsided into her accustomed demeanour. Whispering to Sikes that there was no fear of her relapsing, Fagin took up his hat and bade him goodnight. He paused when he reached the room door, and looking round, asked if somebody would light him down the dark stairs.

'Light him down,' said Sikes, who was filling his pipe. 'It's a pity he should break his neck himself, and disappoint the sight-seers. Show him a light.'

Nancy followed the old man downstairs with a candle. When they reached the passage, he laid his finger on his lip, and drawing close to the girl, said in a whisper:

'What is it, Nancy, dear?'

'What do you mean?' replied the girl, in the same tone.

'The reason for all this,' replied Fagin. 'If *he*'—pointing with his skinny forefinger up the stairs—'is so hard on you (he's a brute, Nance, a brute-beast), why don't you -'

'Well?' said the girl, as Fagin paused, with his mouth almost touching her ear, and his eyes looking into hers.

'No matter just now,' said Fagin, 'we'll talk of this again. You have a friend in me, Nance—a staunch friend. I have the means at hand, quiet and close. If you want revenge on those that treat you like a dog—like a

dog! worse than his dog, for he humours him sometimes—come to me.
I say, come to me. He is a mere hound of the day; but you know me of
old, Nance.'

'Oh, I know you well,' replied the girl, without manifesting the least
emotion. 'Goodnight.'

She shrank back, as Fagin offered to lay his hand on hers, but said
goodnight again, in a steady voice, and, answering his parting look with
a nod of intelligence, closed the door between them.

Fagin walked towards his home, intent upon the thoughts that were
working within his brain. He had conceived the idea—not from what
had just passed though that had tended to confirm him, but slowly and
by degrees—that Nancy, weary of the housebreaker's brutality, had conceived an attachment for some new friend. Her altered manner, her repeated absences from home alone, her comparative indifference to the
interests of the gang for which she had once been so zealous, and, added
to these, her desperate impatience to leave home that night at a particular hour, all favoured the supposition, and rendered it, to him at least,
almost a matter of certainty. The object of this new liking was not among
his myrmidons. He would be a valuable acquisition with such an assis-
tant as Nancy, and must (thus Fagin argued) be secured without delay.

There was another and a darker object to be gained. Sikes knew too
much, and his ruffian taunts had not galled Fagin the less because the
wounds were hidden. The girl must know well that if she shook him
off, she could never be safe from his fury, and that it would be surely
wreaked—to the maiming of limbs, or perhaps the loss of life—on the
object of her more recent fancy. 'With a little persuasion,' thought Fagin,
'what's more likely than that she would consent to poison him? Women
have done such things, and worse, to secure the same object before now.
There would be the dangerous villain—the man I hate—gone; another
secured in his place; and my influence over the girl, with a knowledge of
this crime to back it, unlimited.'

These things passed through the mind of Fagin, during the time
he sat alone in the housebreaker's room; and with them uppermost in
his thoughts, he had taken the opportunity afterwards afforded him of
sounding the girl in the broken hints he threw out at parting. There was
no expression of surprise, no assumption of an inability to understand his
meaning. The girl clearly comprehended it. Her glance at parting showed
that. But perhaps she would recoil from a plot to take the life of Sikes,
and that was one of the chief ends to be attained. 'How,' thought Fagin,
as he crept homeward, 'can I increase my influence with her? What new
power can I acquire?'

Such brains are fertile in expedients. If, without extracting a confession from her, he laid a watch, discovered the object of her altered regard, and threatened to reveal the whole history to Sikes (of whom she stood in no common fear) unless she entered into his designs, could he not secure her compliance?

'I can,' said Fagin, almost aloud. 'She durst not refuse me then. Not for her life, not for her life! I have it all. The means are ready, and shall be set to work. I shall have you yet!'

He cast back a dark look, and a threatening motion of the hand, towards the spot where he had left the bolder villain, and went on his way, busying his bony hands in the folds of his tattered garment, which he wrenched tightly in his grasp, as though there were a hated enemy crushed with every motion of his fingers.

Chapter 37
A Cunning Sneak

The old man was up early the next morning, and waited impatiently for the appearance of his new associate, who, after a delay that seemed interminable, at length presented himself, and commenced a voracious assault on the breakfast.

'Bolter,' said Fagin, drawing up a chair and seating himself opposite Morris Bolter.

'Well, here I am,' returned Noah. 'What's the matter? Don't yer ask me to do anything till I have done eating. That's a great fault in this place. Yer never get time enough over yer meals.'

'You can talk as you eat, can't you?' asked Fagin, irritably, cursing his dear young friend's greediness from the very bottom of his heart.

'Oh yes, I can talk. I get on better when I talk,' said Noah, cutting a monstrous slice of bread. 'Where's Charlotte?'

'Out,' said Fagin. 'I sent her out this morning with another young woman, because I wanted us to be alone.'

'Oh!' said Noah, 'I wish yer'd ordered her to make some buttered toast first. Well. Talk away. Yer won't interrupt me.' There seemed, indeed, no great fear of anything interrupting him, as he had evidently sat down with a determination to do a great deal of business.

'You did well yesterday, my dear,' said Fagin. 'Beautiful! Six shillings and ninepence halfpenny on the very first day! The kinchin lay will be a fortune to you.'

'Don't you forget to add three pint-pots and a milk-can,' said Mr. Bolter.

'No, no, my dear. The pint-pots were great strokes of genius, but the milk-can was a perfect masterpiece.'

'Pretty well, I think, for a beginner,' remarked Mr. Bolter complacently. 'The pots I took off airy railings, and the milk-can was standing by itself outside a public-house. I thought it might get rusty with the rain, or catch cold, yer know. Eh? Ha! ha! ha!'

Fagin affected to laugh very heartily; and Mr. Bolter having had his laugh out, took a series of large bites, which finished his first hunk of bread and butter, and assisted himself to a second.

'I want you, Bolter,' said Fagin, leaning over the table, 'to do a piece of work for me, my dear, that needs great care and caution.'

'I say,' rejoined Bolter, 'don't yer go shoving me into danger, or sending me anymore o' yer police stations. That don't suit me, that don't; and so I tell yer.'

'There's not the smallest danger in it—not the very smallest,' said the old man; 'it's only to dodge a woman.'

'An old woman?' demanded Mr. Bolter.

'A young one,' replied Fagin.

'I can do that pretty well, I know,' said Bolter. 'I was a regular cunning sneak when I was at school. What am I to dodge her for? Not to -'

'Not to do anything, but to tell me where she goes, who she sees, and, if possible, what she says; to remember the street, if it is a street, or the house, if it is a house; and to bring me back all the information you can.'

'What'll yer give me?' asked Noah, setting down his cup, and looking his employer eagerly in the face.

'If you do it well, a pound, my dear. One pound,' said Fagin, wishing to interest him in the scent as much as possible. 'And that's what I never gave yet for any job where there wasn't valuable consideration to be gained.'

'Who is she?' inquired Noah.

'One of us.'

'Oh Lor!' cried Noah, curling up his nose. 'Yer doubtful of her, are yer?'

'She has found out some new friends, my dear, and I must know who they are,' replied Fagin.

'I see,' said Noah. 'Just to have the pleasure of knowing them, if they're respectable people, eh? Ha! ha! ha! I'm your man.'

'I knew you would be,' cried Fagin, elated by the success of his proposal.

'Of course, of course,' replied Noah. 'Where is she? Where am I to wait for her? Where am I to go?'

'All that, my dear, you shall hear from me. I'll point her out at the proper time,' said Fagin. 'You keep ready, and leave the rest to me.'

That night, and the next, and the next again, the spy sat booted and equipped in his carter's dress, ready to turn out at a word from Fagin. Three nights passed—three long weary nights—and on each, Fagin came home with a disappointed face, and briefly intimated that it was not yet time. On the fourth, he returned earlier, and with an exultation he could not conceal.

'She goes abroad tonight,' said Fagin, 'and on the right errand, I'm sure; for the man she is afraid of will be away himself and not expected back much before daybreak. Come with me. Quick!'

Noah started up without saying a word, for the old man was in a state of such intense excitement that it infected him. They left Fagin's abode stealthily, and, hurrying through a labyrinth of streets, arrived at length before a public-house, which Noah recognised as being the same in which he had slept on the night of his arrival in London.

It was just past seven o'clock, and the door was closed. It opened softly on its hinges as Fagin gave a low whistle. They entered, without noise; and the door was closed behind them.

Scarcely venturing to whisper, but substituting dumb show for words, Fagin, and his nephew who had admitted them, pointed out the pane of glass to Noah, and signed to him to climb up and observe the person in the adjoining room.

'Is that the woman?' he asked, scarcely above his breath.

Fagin nodded yes.

'I can't see her face well,' whispered Noah. 'She is looking down, and the candle is behind her.

'Stay there,' whispered Fagin. He signed to Barney, who withdrew. In an instant, the lad entered the adjoining room, and, under the pretence of replacing the candle, moved it to the required position, and, speaking to the girl, caused her to raise her face.

'I see her now,' cried the spy.

'Plainly?' asked the old man.

'I should know her among a thousand,' confirmed Noah.

They hastily descended, as the room door opened, and the girl came out. Fagin drew him behind a small partition which was curtained off, and they held their breaths as she passed within a few feet of their place of concealment, and emerged by the door through which they had entered.

'Hist!' cried the lad who held the door. 'Dow.' Noah exchanged a look with Fagin, and darted out.

'To the left,' whispered the lad; 'take the left had, and keep od the other side.'

He did so; and, by the light of the lamps, saw the girl's retreating figure, already at some distance before him. He advanced as near as he considered prudent, and kept on the opposite side of the street, the better to observe her motions. She looked nervously round, twice or thrice, and stopped once to let two men who were following close behind her, pass on. She seemed to gather courage as she advanced, and to walk with a steadier and firmer step. The spy preserved the same relative distance between them, and followed, with his eye upon her.

Many of the shops were already closing along lanes and avenues through which she tracked her way. She tore along the narrow pavement, elbowing fellow pedestrians from side to side; and, darting almost under the horses' heads, crossed crowded streets where clusters of persons were eagerly watching for an opportunity to do likewise.

'The woman is mad!' said the people, turning to look after her as she rushed away. Noah had trouble keeping pace. He was beginning to think that dodging women was more work than he really needed.

When the two pedestrians reached a wealthier quarter of the town, after a brisk half-hour's walk, the streets were comparatively deserted. Nancy slowed her pace and, and after looking all about her, stopped outside an inn where several hackney coaches lined the street. After exchanging words with one driver, she entered his coach which promptly drove off. Noah, who had stepped into the shadow of an entrance way, was uncertain as to what to do. He was loath to spend his own coin on hiring a coach, as that seemed a rather profligate use of his hard won earnings; but, on the other hand, he was beginning to appreciate the magnitude of the task entrusted to him by Fagin. Failing to follow the girl, when he had ready means, would surely do damage to his reputation as a reliable associate. He ran ahead and climbed up and sat beside the driver of the next coach.

'That there's my wife,' said Noah, pointing ahead, 'who'd got into that coach. She means to give me the slip.'

'She won't get away with that,' said the driver, as he set off quickly down the street.

'Keep back a ways,' added Noah, 'Not trying to impede her none, just wanna know where she's goin'. Understand?'

The driver indicated that he comprehended the situation and slowed his horse down. Noah expressed great surprise and some consternation when, at the next cross roads, Nancy's coach swung right around and headed back directly along the road they had traversed so far by foot. Noah's driver waited a moment or two before turning his coach around in the same direction and then continued to follow at a discreet distance.

It was an hour before Nancy's coach at last came to a stop and, as if controlled by the same driver, Noah's coach stopped likewise; a hundred yards or more back. When he saw the girl stepped out of her coach and onto the quiet streets of Pentonville, Noah paid his driver and climbed down from his bench to continue his pursuit by foot.

He had not far to go. The girl lingered where she had exited from the coach, illuminated by the brilliant light of a gas lamp that shed its light on the front entrance of a grand house. As Noah watched from behind a hedge, half a block away, she loitered for a few minutes on the walkway as though irresolute, and making up her mind whether to advance or retreat, when a clock struck nine times. The sound of the clock determined her, and she stepped up to the door; looked round with an air of incertitude, and then knocked. After a minute or two the door opened.

'What, in Heaven's name,' said an older woman, with an irritated tone, 'could you want at this late hour?'

'To speak to the gentleman of the house,' answered the girl.

'The gentleman of the house?' repeated the older woman, derisively, accompanied by a scornful look. 'I think not.'

'Please, it's of the utmost importance,' said Nancy.

'What name am I to say?' asked Mrs. Bedwin, for it was the Brownlow house to which Nancy had come calling.

'It's of no use saying any,' replied Nancy. 'He knows me not.'

'I very much doubt that the gentleman of this house has any interest in buying what 'er it is you're selling.' said Mrs. Bedwin.

'Please!' rejoined the girl. 'I must see the gentleman. I must.'

'Go!' said Mrs. Bedwin, forcefully. 'None of this. Carry yourself off. I shall not disturb Mr. Brownlow at this late hour for a hussy who will not state her name.'

Mrs. Bedwin went to shut the door when Nancy placed her foot between it and the door jamb, preventing her from doing so.

'I shall make a scene to wake the devil, if you do not concede to my humble request,' said the girl violently; 'Can't you find it in your heart,' she said, 'to convey a simple message for a poor wretch like me?'

'Tell me the nature of your business!' demanded Mrs. Bedwin, sternly.

'It concerns young Oliver,' whispered Nancy.

'Oh my!' exclaimed Mrs. Bedwin. 'My apologies. Do come in. I will let Mr. Brownlow know that you are here.'

Nancy followed Mrs. Bedwin, with trembling limbs, into the sitting room off the front hallway. A lamp hanging from the ceiling lit the room.

Outside, a gangly young man took note of the number on the house as he sauntered by.

Chapter 38
A Simple Creed

The girl's life had been squandered in the streets and among the most noisome of the stews and dens of London, but there was something of the woman's original nature left in her still; and when she heard a step approaching the door by which she had entered, and thought of the wide contrast which the small room would in another moment contain, she felt burdened with a sense of her own deep shame, and shrunk as though she could scarcely bear the presence of him with whom she had sought this interview.

But struggling with these better feelings was pride—the vice of the lowest and most debased creatures no less than of the high and self-assured; the miserable companion of thieves and ruffians, the fallen outcast of low haunts, the associate of the scourings of the jails and hulks living within the shadow of the gallows itself. Even this degraded being felt too proud to betray a feeble gleam of the womanly feeling which she thought a weakness, but which alone connected her with that humanity of which her wasting life had obliterated so many, many traces when still a very child.

She raised her eyes sufficiently to observe that the figure which presented itself was that of a dignified gentleman; and then, bending them towards the ground, she tossed her head with affected carelessness as she said:

'It's a hard matter to get to see you, sir. If I had taken offence, and gone away, as many would have done, you'd have been sorry for it one day, and not without reason, either.'

'I am very sorry if Mrs. Bedwin has behaved harshly towards you,' replied Mr. Brownlow. 'She was but fulfilling her duty to me. Do not think more of that. Kindly, tell me why you wished to see me.'

The kind tone of this answer, the gentle manner, the absence of any accent of haughtiness or displeasure, took the girl completely by surprise, and she burst into tears.

'Oh, Mr. Brownlow!' she said, clasping her hands passionately before her face, 'what is said of you is true! If there were more like you, there would be fewer like me—there would, there would!'

'Sit down,' said Mr. Brownlow, earnestly. 'If you are in poverty or affliction, I shall be truly glad to relieve you if I can,—I shall, indeed. Sit down.'

'Let me stand, sir,' said the girl, still weeping, 'and do not speak to me so kindly till you know me better. It is growing late. Is—is—that door shut?'

'Yes,' said Mr. Brownlow. 'Why?'

'Because,' said the girl, 'I am about to put my life, and the lives of others, in your hands. I am the girl that dragged little Oliver away the night he went out to return a few books.'

'You?' cried Mr. Brownlow, in disbelief.

'I, sir!' replied the girl. 'I am the infamous creature you may have heard of that lives among the thieves, and that never from the first moment I can recollect my eyes and senses opening on London streets have known any better life, or kinder words than you have given me, so help me God! Do not mind shrinking openly from me, sir. I am younger than you would think, to look at me, but I am well used to it. The poorest women fall back, as I make my way along the crowded pavement.'

'What dreadful things you speak of!' said Mr. Brownlow, involuntarily withdrawing from his strange guest.

'Thank Heaven upon your knees, dear sir,' cried the girl, 'that you had friends to care for and keep you in your childhood, and that you were never in the midst of cold, and hunger, and riot, and drunkenness, and—and—something worse than all—as I have been from my cradle. I may use the word, for the alley and the gutter were mine, as they will be my deathbed.'

'I pity you!' said Mr. Brownlow, in a broken voice. 'It wrings my heart to hear you!'

'Heaven bless you for your goodness!' rejoined the girl. 'If you knew what I am sometimes, you would pity me indeed. But I have stolen away from those who would surely murder me, if they knew I had been here, to tell you what I have overheard. Do you know a man named Fagin?'

'No, I have not heard tell of him,' said Mr. Brownlow.

'He knows you,' replied the girl, 'and he knows that Oliver is here. It was by hearing him tell of this place that I found you out. I, suspecting this man, listened in on a private conversation he held with an associate. Fagin had spent a week or so sulking round hereabouts to confirm the boy's fate. Fagin informed Sikes, a most dangerous man, that Oliver was taken into your house the night of the robbery.'

'These men know that?' said Mr. Brownlow, expressing much surprise.

'Yes!' confirmed Nancy. 'These men dishonourable as they are, conduct business upon the strictest of confidences. Any violation of their simple creed is punished by the worst violence. Oliver knows too much which puts all of us, myself included, at considerable risk. He is not trusted to keep our secrets which puts him in great danger.'

'He is safe here,' assured Mr. Brownlow.

'No, he's not!' asserted Nancy, in a solemn tone. 'They are vile and dangerous men. Send him away from here, someplace safe, least till Sikes' blood cools and Fagin's fears subside.'

'I see from your demeanor that you are gravely serious,' replied Mr. Brownlow. 'We will heed your warning.'

'I deeply regret,' said Nancy, 'dragging Oliver into this cesspool when he had a chance of living an upright life. I cannot forgive myself. Please tell him that for me. I must go now.'

'Go?' cried Mr. Brownlow. 'How can you go back? Why do you wish to return to companions you paint in such terrible colors? Stay here to-night. In the morning, I can consigned both you and Oliver to some place of safety without half an hour's delay.'

'I wish to go back,' said the girl. 'I must go back, because—how can I say such things to an innocent gentleman like you?—because among the men I have told you of, there is one, the most desperate amongst them all, that I can't leave; no, not even to be saved from the life I am leading now.'

'You have interfered on this boy's behalf before, saving him from being savaged by a dog,' said Mr. Brownlow. 'Your coming here, at so great a risk, to tell me what you have heard; your manner, which convinces me of the truth of what you say; your evident contrition, and sense of shame; all lead me to believe that you might yet be reclaimed. I may be the first to appeal to you in a voice of empathy and compassion. Do hear my words, and let me save you yet for better things.'

'Sir,' cried the girl, sinking on her knees, you *are* the first that ever blessed me with such words as these, and if I had heard them years ago, they might have turned me from a life of sin and sorrow; but it is too late, it is too late!'

'It is never too late,' said Mr. Brownlow, 'for penitence and atonement.'

'It is!' cried the girl, writhing with the agony assailing her mind. 'I cannot leave him now! I could not be his death.'

'Why should you be?' asked Mr. Brownlow.

'Nothing could save him,' cried the girl. 'If I told others what I have told you, and led to his being taken, he would be sure to die. He is the boldest, and has been so cruel! As bad a life as he has led, I have led a bad life too; there are many of us who have kept the same courses together-er, and I'll not turn upon them, who might—any of them—have turned upon me, but didn't, bad as they are.'

'Is it possible,' cried Mr. Brownlow, 'that for such a man as this, you can resign every future hope, and the certainty of immediate rescue? It is madness.'

'I don't know what it is,' answered the girl. 'I only know that it is so, and not with me alone, but with hundreds of others as bad and wretched as myself. I must go back. Whether it is God's wrath for the wrong I have done, I do not know; but I am drawn back to him through every suffering and ill usage; and I should be, I believe, even if I knew that I was to die by his hand at last.'

'What am I to do?' said Mr. Brownlow. 'I should not let you depart from me thus.'

'You should, sir, and I know you will,' rejoined the girl, rising. 'You will not stop my going because I have trusted in your goodness, and forced no promise from you, as I might have done.'

'Stay another moment,' interposed Mr. Brownlow, as the girl moved hurriedly towards the door. 'Think once again on your own condition, and the opportunity you have of escaping from it. You have a claim on me, not only as the voluntary bearer of this intelligence, but as a woman lost almost beyond redemption. Will you return to this gang of robbers, and to this man, when I can save you? What fascination is it that can take you back, and make you cling to wickedness and misery? Oh! is there no chord in your heart that I can touch? Is there nothing left, to which I can appeal against this terrible infatuation?'

'Understand,' pleaded Nancy; 'when such as I, who have no certain roof but the coffin lid, and no friend in sickness or death but the hospital nurse, set our rotten hearts on any man, and let him fill the place that has been a blank throughout our wretched lives, who can hope to cure us? Pity us, sir—pity us for having only the one feeling of the woman left, and for having that turned, by a heavy judgment, from a comfort and a pride, into a new means of violence and suffering.'

'You will,' said Mr. Brownlow, after a pause, 'take some money from me, which may enable you to live without dishonesty—at all events until we meet again?'

'No!' replied the girl. 'Not a penny. I have not done this for money. Let me have that to think of.'

'Do not close your heart against all my efforts to help you,' said Mr. Brownlow, stepping gently forward.

'You can help me,' she replied, 'and ease my heart, by keeping Oliver safe. Take him away from here to some safe place in the country. Do not, if you care the least for my welfare, go to the authorities. I will surely hang with the rest if you do so.'

'I must serve you by some means,' protested Mr. Brownlow.

'You would serve me best, sir,' replied the girl, wringing her hands, 'if you could take my life at once; for I have felt more grief to think of what

I am tonight than I ever did before, and it would be something not to die in the hell in which I have lived. God bless you, sir, and may he send as much happiness on your head as I have brought shame upon my own!'

Thus speaking, and sobbing aloud, the unhappy creature turned away; while Mr. Brownlow, overpowered by this extraordinary interview, which had more the semblance of a rabid dream than an actual occurrence, sank into a chair, and endeavoured to collect his wandering thoughts.

Chapter 39
Betrayed

It was nearly two hours before daybreak—that time which, in the autumn of the year, may be truly called the dead of night, when the streets are silent and deserted, when even sounds appear to slumber, and profligacy and riot have staggered home to dream,—it was at this still and silent hour that Fagin sat watching in his old lair, with a face so distorted and pale, and eyes so red and bloodshot, that he looked less like a man than like some hideous phantom, moist from the grave, and worried by an evil spirit.

He sat crouching over a cold hearth, wrapped in an old torn coverlet, with his face turned towards a wasting candle that stood upon a table by his side. His right hand was raised to his lips; and, absorbed in thought, he bit his long black nails, disclosing among his toothless gums a few such fangs as should have been a dog's or rat's.

Stretched upon a mattress on the floor lay Noah Claypole, fast asleep. Towards him the old man sometimes directed his eyes for an instant, and then brought them back again to the candle; which with a long-burnt wick drooping almost double, and hot grease falling down in clots upon the table, plainly showed that his thoughts were busy elsewhere.

Indeed they were. Mortification at the overthrow of his notable scheme; hatred of the girl who had dared to converse with strangers; bitter disappointment at the loss of his revenge on Sikes; the fear of detection, and ruin, and death; and a fierce and deadly rage kindled by all,—these were the passionate considerations which, following close upon each other in a rapid and ceaseless whirl, shot through the brain of Fagin, as every evil thought and blackest purpose lay working at his heart.

He sat without changing his attitude in the least, or appearing to take the smallest heed of time, until his quick ear seemed to be attracted by a footstep in the street.

'At last,' he muttered, wiping his dry and fevered mouth. 'At last!'

The bell rang gently as he spoke. He crept upstairs to the door, and presently returned accompanied by a man and a dog. Muffled to the chin, the man carried a bundle under one arm. Sitting down and throwing back his outer coat, the man displayed the burly frame of Sikes.

'There!' he said, laying the bundle on the table. 'Take care of that, and do the most you can with it. It's been trouble enough to get; I ought to have been here three hours ago.'

Fagin laid his hand upon the bundle, and locking it in the cupboard, sat down again without speaking. But he did not take his eyes off the robber for an instant during this action; and now that they sat across from each other, face to face, he looked fixedly at him, with his lips quivering so violently, and his face so altered by the emotions which had mastered him, that the housebreaker involuntarily drew back his chair, and surveyed him with a look of real terror.

'Wot now?' cried Sikes. 'Wot do you look at a man so for?'

Fagin raised his right hand, and shook his trembling forefinger in the air; but his passion was so great, that the power of speech was for the moment gone.

'Damn me!' said Sikes, feeling for his pistol with a look of alarm. 'He's gone mad. I must look to myself here.'

'No, no,' rejoined Fagin, finding his voice. 'It's not—you're not the person, Bill. I've no—no fault to find with you.'

'Oh, you haven't, haven't you?' said Sikes, looking sternly at him, and ostentatiously passing a pistol into a more convenient pocket. 'That's lucky—for one of us. Which one that is, don't matter.'

'I've got that to tell you, Bill,' said Fagin, drawing his chair nearer, 'as will make you worse than me.'

'Aye?' returned the robber with an incredulous air. 'Tell away! Look sharp, or Nance will think I'm lost.'

'Lost!' cried Fagin. 'She has pretty well settled that, in her own mind, already.'

Sikes looked with an aspect of great perplexity into the old man's face, and reading no satisfactory explanation of the riddle there, clenched his coat collar in his huge hand and shook him soundly.

'Speak, will you!' he said; 'or if you don't, it shall be for want of breath. Open your mouth and say wot you've got to say in plain words. Out with it, you thundering old cur, out with it!'

'Suppose that lad that's laying there -' Fagin began, nodding his head towards the boy.

Sikes turned round to where Noah was sleeping, as if he had not previously observed him. 'Well?' he said, resuming his former position.

'Suppose that lad,' pursued Fagin, 'was to peach—to blow upon us all—first seeking out the right folks for the purpose, and then having a meeting with 'em—of his own fancy; not grabbed, trapped, tried, earwigged by the parson, or brought to it on bread and water—but of his own fancy, to please his own taste; stealing out at night to find those most interested against us, and peaching to them. Do you hear me?' cried the old miser, his eyes flashing with rage. 'Suppose he did all this, what then?'

'What then!' replied Sikes; with a tremendous oath. 'If he was left alive till I came by, I'd grind his skull under the iron heel of my boot into as many grains as there are hairs upon his head.'

'What if *I* did it!' cried Fagin, almost in a yell. 'I, that knows so much, and could hang so many besides myself!'

'I don't know,' replied Sikes, clenching his teeth and turning white at the mere suggestion. 'I'd do something in the jail that would get me put in irons; and if I was tried along with you, I'd fall upon you with them in the open court, and beat your brains out afore the people. I should have such strength,' muttered the robber, poising his brawny arm, 'that I could smash your head as if a loaded wagon had gone over it.'

'You would?'

'Would I?' said the housebreaker. 'Try me.'

'If it was Charley, or the Dodger, or Bet, or -'

'I don't care who,' replied Sikes impatiently. 'Whoever it was, I'd serve them the same.'

Fagin looked hard at the robber; and, motioning him to be silent, stooped over the bed on the floor, and shook the sleeper to rouse him. Sikes leaned forward in his chair, looking on with his hands upon his knees, as if wondering much what all this questioning and preparation was to end in.

'Bolter, Bolter!—Poor lad!' said Fagin, looking up with an expression of devilish anticipation, and speaking slowly and with marked emphasis. 'He's tired—tired with watching for her so long—watching for her, Bill.'

'Wot d'ye mean?' asked Sikes, drawing back.

Fagin made no answer, but bending over the sleeper again, hauled him into a sitting posture. When his assumed name had been repeated several times, Noah rubbed his eyes, and, giving a heavy yawn, looked sleepily about him.

'Tell me that again—once again, just for him to hear,' said the old man, pointing to Sikes as he spoke.

'Tell yer what?' asked the sleepy Noah, shaking himself pettishly.

'That about—*Nancy*,' said Fagin, clutching Sikes by the wrist, as if to prevent his leaving the house before he had heard enough. 'You followed her?'

'Yes.'

'To Pentonville?'

'Yes.'

'Where she entered a grand house at 23 Park Lane.'

'So she did.'

'That's the Brownlow house, Bill,' shrieked Fagin, half mad with fury, 'where Oliver is holed up. She's crossed us Bill. She's crossed us!'

'Hell's fire!' cried Sikes, breaking fiercely from the old man. 'Let me go!' Flinging the old man from him, he rushed from the room, and darted, wildly and furiously, up the stairs.

'Bill, Bill!' cried Fagin, following him hastily. 'A word. Only a word.'

The word would not have been exchanged, but that the housebreaker was unable to open the door; on which he was expending fruitless oaths and violence, when the old miser came panting up.

'Let me out,' said Sikes. 'Don't speak to me! It's not safe. Let me out, I say!'

'Hear me speak a word,' rejoined Fagin, laying his hand upon the lock. 'You won't be -'

'Well,' replied the other.

'You won't be too—too—violent, Bill?'

The day was breaking, and there was light enough for the men to see each other's faces. They exchanged one brief glance; there was a fire in the eyes of both which could not be mistaken.

'I mean,' said Fagin, showing that he felt all disguise was now useless, 'not too violent for safety. Be crafty, Bill, and not too bold.'

Sikes made no reply, but, pulling open the door, of which Fagin had turned the lock, dashed into the silent streets.

Those who knew Sikes best, and he was admittedly a difficult man to know, had no doubt that he had murdered before and would do so again upon the least provocation. Sikes himself did little to soften his bloody reputation but, rather, as it served his purposes well, did much to enhance it. Yet truth be told, his reputation thus far had exceeded his deeds. Yet it was also true, as with many a thug, Sikes had begun to believe in his own reputation and acted accordingly.

Without one pause or a moment's consideration; without once turning his head to the right or left, or raising his eyes to the sky, or lowering them to the ground, but looking straight before him with savage resolution—his teeth so tightly compressed that the strained jaw seemed starting through his skin—the robber held on his headlong course, nor muttered a word, nor relaxed a muscle, until he reached his own door. He opened it, softly with a key; strode lightly up the stairs; and entering his own room, double locked the door, and lifting a heavy table against it, drew back the curtain of the bed.

The girl was lying, half-dressed, upon it. He had roused her from her sleep, for she raised herself with a hurried and startled look.

'Get up!' said the man.

'It *is* you, Bill!' said the girl, with an expression of pleasure at his return.

'It is,' was the reply. 'Get up.'

There was a candle burning, but the man hastily drew it from the candle holder, and hurled it under the fire grate. Seeing the faint light of early day without, the girl rose to draw open the curtain.

'Let it be,' said Sikes, thrusting his hand before her. 'There's enough light for wot I've got to do.'

'Bill?' asked the girl, in the low voice of alarm, 'why do you look like that at me?'

The robber sat regarding her, for a few seconds, with dilated nostrils and heaving breast; and then, grasping her by the head and throat, dragged her into the middle of the room, and looking once towards the door, placed his heavy hand upon her mouth.

Wrestling with the strength of mortal fear, Nancy broke free and took hold of him. 'Bill, Bill!' gasped the girl, 'I—I won't scream or cry—not once—hear me—speak to me—tell me what I have done!'

'You know, you she-devil!' returned the robber, suppressing his breath. 'You were watched tonight. I knows where yuh've been.'

'Then spare my life for the love of Heaven, as I spared yours,' rejoined the girl, clinging to him. 'Bill, dear Bill, you cannot have the heart to kill me. Oh! think of all I have given up, only this one night, for you. You *shall* have time to think, and save yourself this crime. I will not loose my hold; you cannot throw me off. Bill, Bill, for dear God's sake, for your own, for mine, stop before you spill my blood! I have been true to you, upon my guilty soul I have!'

The man struggled violently, to release his arms; but those of the girl were clasped round his, and grappling with her as he would, he could not tear them away.

'Bill,' cried the girl, striving to lay her head upon his breast, 'the gentleman told me tonight of a home where I could end my days in solitude and peace. Let me see him again, and beg him, on my knees, to show the same mercy and goodness to you; and let us both leave this dreadful place, and far apart lead better lives, and forget how we have lived, except in prayers, and never see each other any more. It is never too late to repent. He told me so—I feel it now—but we must have time—a little, little time!'

The housebreaker freed one arm, and grasped his pistol. The certainty of immediate detection if he fired flashed across his mind even in the midst of his fury; so he beat it twice with all the force he could summon, upon the upturned face that almost touched his own.

She staggered and fell nearly blinded with the blood that rained down from a deep gash in her forehead; but raising herself, with difficulty, onto her knees and, holding her folded hands as high towards Heaven as her feeble strength would allow, breathed one prayer for mercy to her Maker.

It was a ghastly figure to look upon. The murderer staggering backward to the wall, and shutting out the sight with his hand, seized a heavy club and struck her down.

Chapter 40
Escaping Justice

Of all the bad deeds that, under the cover of darkness, had been committed within London's wide bounds since night hung over it, it was the worst. Of all the horrors that rose with an ill scent upon the morning air, it was the foulest and most cruel.

The sun—the bright sun, that brings back, not light alone, but new life, and hope, and freshness to man—burst upon the crowded city in clear and radiant glory. Through costly coloured glass and paper mended window, through cathedral dome and rotten crevice, it shed its equal ray. It lighted up the room where the murdered woman lay. It did. He tried to shut it out, but it would stream in. If the sight had been a ghastly one in the dull morning, what was it, now, in all that brilliant light!

He had not moved; he had been afraid to stir. There had been a moan and motion of the hand; and, with terror added to rage, he had struck and struck again. Once he threw a rug over it; but it was worse to fancy the eyes, and imagine them moving towards him, than to see them glaring upward, as if watching the reflection of the pool of gore that quivered and danced in the sunlight on the ceiling. He had plucked it off again. And there was the body—mere flesh and blood, no more—but such flesh, and so much blood!

He struck a light, kindled a fire, and thrust the club into it. There was hair upon the end, which blazed and shrunk into a light cinder, and, caught by the air, whirled up the chimney. Even that frightened him, sturdy as he was; but he held the weapon till it broke, and then piled it on the coals to burn away, and smoulder into ashes. He washed himself, and rubbed his clothes; there were spots that would not be removed, so he cut the pieces out, and burnt them. How those stains were dispersed about the room! The very feet of the dog were bloody.

All this time he had, never once, turned his back upon the corpse—no, not for a moment. Such preparations completed, he moved, backwards towards the door; dragging the dog with him, lest he should soil his feet anew and carry out new evidence of the crime into the streets. He shut the door softly, locked it, took the key, and left the house.

He crossed over, and glanced up at the window, to be sure that nothing was visible from the outside. There was the curtain still drawn, which she would have opened to admit the light she never saw again. It lay nearly under there. *He* knew that. God, how the sun poured down upon the very spot!

The glance was instantaneous. It was a relief to have got free of the room. He whistled on the dog, and walked rapidly away. He made his way, as directly as possible, out of London and into the countryside. He wandered over miles and miles of ground, with no particular destination in mind. Morning and noon had passed, and the day was on the wane, and still he rambled about, up and down and round and round, never lingering long at any one place. He had not the courage to purchase a bit of food or drop of drink, though he had not tasted food nor drink for many hours.

It was nine o'clock at night when Mr. Sikes, quite tired out, and his dog limping and lame from the unaccustomed exercise, turned down a hill by the church of a quiet village, and plodding along the little street, crept into a small public-house, whose scanty light had guided them to the spot. There was a fire in the tap-room, and some country-labourers were drinking before it. They made room for the stranger, but he sat down in the furthest corner, and ate and drank alone, or rather with his dog, to whom he cast a morsel of food from time to time.

The conversation of the men assembled here turned upon the neighboring land and farmers; and when those topics were exhausted, upon the age of some old man who had been buried on the previous Sunday—the young men present considering him very old, and the old men present declaring him to have been quite young—not older, one white-haired grandfather said, than he was, with ten or fifteen years of life in him at least, if he had taken care—if he had taken care.

There was nothing to attract attention, or excite alarm in this. The robber, after paying his reckoning, sat silent and unnoticed in his corner, and had almost dropped asleep, when he was half wakened by the noisy entrance of a newcomer.

This was an antic fellow, half-pedlar and half-charlatan, who travelled about the country on foot to vend sharpening stones, plugs and stoppers, razors, wash balls, harness paste, medicine for dogs and horses, cheap perfume, cosmetics, and suchlike wares which he carried in a case slung on his back. His entrance was the signal for various homely jokes with the countrymen, which slackened not until he had made his supper, and opened his box of treasures, when he ingeniously contrived to unite business with amusement.

'And what be that stuff? Good to eat, Harry?' asked a grinning countryman, pointing to some composition cakes in one corner.

'This,' said the fellow, producing one, 'this is the infallible and invaluable composition for removing all sorts of stain, rust, dirt, mildew, spick, speck, spot, or spatter, from silk, satin, linen, cambric, cloth, crape, carpet, merino, muslin, or woollen stuff. Wine stains, fruit stains, beer stains, water stains, paint stains, pitch stains, any stains, all come out at one rub with the infallible and invaluable composition. If a lady stains her honour, she has only need to swallow one cake and she's cured at once—for it's poison. If a gentleman wants to prove his, he has only need to bolt one little square, and he has put it beyond question—for it's quite as satisfactory as a pistol bullet, and a great deal nastier in the flavour, consequently the more credit in taking it. One penny a square. With all these virtues, one penny a square!'

There were two buyers directly, and more of the listeners plainly hesitated. The vendor observing this, increased in loquacity.

'It's all bought up as fast as it can be made,' said the fellow. 'There are fourteen water mills, six steam engines, and a galvanic battery, always a-working upon it, and they can't make it fast enough, though the men work so hard that they die off, and the widows is pensioned directly, with twenty pound a-year for each of the children, and a premium of fifty for twins—One penny a square! Two half-pence is all the same, and four farthings is received with joy. One penny a square! Wine stains, fruit stains, beer stains, water stains, paint stains, pitch stains, mud stains, blood stains! Here is a stain upon the hat of a gentleman in company that I'll take clean out before he can order me a pint of ale.'

'Hah!' cried Sikes, starting up. 'Give that back.'

'I'll take it clean out, sir,' replied the man, winking to the company, 'before you can come across the room to get it. Gentlemen all, observe the dark stain upon this gentleman's hat, no wider than a shilling, but thicker than a half-crown. Whether it is a wine stain, fruit stain, beer stain, water stain, paint stain, pitch stain, mud stain, or blood stain -'

The man got no further, for Sikes, with a hideous imprecation, overthrew the table, and tearing the hat from him, burst out of the house.

With the same perversity of feeling and irresolution that had fastened upon him, despite himself, all day; the murderer, finding that he was not followed, and that they most probably considered him some drunken sullen fellow, turned back up the town. He was getting out of the glare of the lamps of a stagecoach that was standing in the street that he was walking along, when he recognised it as being the mail service from London, and saw that it was in front of a little post office. He almost knew what was to come; but he crossed over anyway and listened.

The guard was standing at the door, waiting for the letter-bag. A man, dressed like a gamekeeper, came up at the moment, and handed him a basket which lay ready on the pavement. 'That's for your people,' said the guard. 'Now, look alive in there, will you. Damn that 'ere bag, it warn't ready night afore last either; this won't do, you know!'

'Anything new up in town, Ben?' asked the gamekeeper, drawing back to the window shutters, the better to admire the horses.

'No, nothing that I knows on,' replied the man, pulling on his gloves. 'Corn's up a little. I heerd talk of a murder, too, down Spitalfields way, but I don't reckon much upon it.'

'Oh, that's quite true,' said a gentleman inside, who was looking out of the window. 'And a dreadful murder it was.'

'Was it, sir?' rejoined the guard, touching his hat. 'Man or woman, pray, sir?'

'A woman,' replied the gentleman, 'it is supposed -'

'Now, Ben,' replied the coachman impatiently.

'Damn that 'ere bag,' said the guard; 'are you going to sleep in there?'

'Coming!' cried the office keeper, running out.

'Coming,' growled the guard. 'Ah, and so's the young woman of property that's going to take a fancy to me, but I don't know when. Here, give hold. All—right!'

The horn sounded a few cheerful notes, and the mail coach was gone.

Sikes remained standing in the street, apparently unmoved by what he had just heard, and agitated by no stronger feeling than a doubt as to where to go. At length he went back again, and took the road which leads from Hatfield to St. Albans.

He went on doggedly; but as he left the town behind him, and plunged into the solitude and darkness of the road, he felt a dread and awe creeping upon him which shook him to the core. Every object before him, substance or shadow, still or moving, took the semblance of some fearful thing; but these fears were nothing compared to the sense that haunted him of that morning's ghastly figure following at his heels. He could trace its shadow in the gloom, supply the smallest item of the outline, and note how stiff and solemn it seemed to stalk along. He could hear its garments rustling in the leaves, and every breath of wind came laden with that last low cry. If he stopped it did the same. If he ran, it followed; not running too—that would have been a relief—but like a corpse endowed with the mere machinery of life, and borne on one slow melancholy wind that never rose or fell.

At times he turned with desperate determination, resolved to beat this phantom off, though it should look him dead; but the hair rose on his head, and his blood stood still, for it had turned with him, and was behind him then. He had kept it before him that morning; but it was behind him now—always. He leaned his back against a bank, and felt that it stood above him, visible against the cold night sky. He threw himself upon the road—on his back upon the road. At his head it stood; silent, erect, and still—a living gravestone, with its epitaph in blood.

Let no man talk of murderers escaping justice, and hint that Providence must sleep. There were twenty score of violent deaths in one long minute of that agony of fear.

There was a shed in a field he passed, that offered shelter for the night. Outside the door were three tall poplar trees, which made it very dark within; and the wind moaned through them with a dismal wail. He *could not* walk on, till daylight came again; so here he stretched himself close to the wall only to undergo a new torture.

For now a vision came before him, as constant and more terrible than that from which he had escaped. Those widely staring eyes, so lustreless and so glassy, that he had better borne to see them than think upon them, appeared in the midst of the darkness—light in themselves, but giving light to nothing. There were but two, but they were everywhere. If he shut out the sight, there came a vision of his abandoned room with every well-known object—some, indeed, that he would have forgotten had he not gone over its contents from memory—each in its accustomed place. The body was in *its* place, and its eyes were as he saw them when he stole away. He got up and rushed out into the field. The figure was behind him. He re-entered the shed, and shrunk down once more. The eyes were there, again, before he had laid himself down.

And here he remained in such terror as none but he can know, trembling in every limb, and the cold sweat starting from every pore, when suddenly there arose upon the night wind the noise of distant shouting, and the roar of voices mingled in alarm and wonder. Any sound of men in that lonely place, even though it conveyed a real cause of alarm, was something to him. He regained his strength and energy at the prospect of personal danger, and, springing to his feet, rushed into the open air.

The broad sky seemed on fire. Rising into the air with showers of sparks, and rolling one above the other, were sheets of flame, lighting the atmosphere for miles round, and driving clouds of smoke in the direction where he stood. The shouts grew louder as new voices swelled the roar, and he could hear the cry of Fire! mingled with the ringing of an alarm bell, the fall of heavy bodies, and the crackling of flames as they twined round some new obstacle, and shot aloft as though refreshed by food. The noise increased as he looked. There were people there—men and women – light, bustle. It was like new life to him. He darted onward—straight, headlong—dashing through brier and brake, and leaping gate and fence as madly as his dog, who careered ahead of him barking loudly.

He came upon the spot. There were half-dressed figures tearing to and fro, some endeavouring to drag the frightened horses from the stables, others driving the cattle from the yard and outbuildings, and others coming laden with tools and supplies from the burning pile, amidst a shower of falling sparks, and the tumbling down of red-hot beams. The apertures, where doors and windows stood an hour ago, disclosed a mass of raging fire; walls rocked and crumbled into the burning well; molten lead and iron poured down, white hot, upon the ground. Women and children shrieked, and men encouraged each other with noisy shouts and cheers. The clanking of the engine pumps, and the spurting and hissing of the water as it fell upon the blazing wood, added to the tremendous roar. He shouted, too, till he was hoarse; and, flying from memory and himself, plunged into the thickest of the throng.

Hither and thither he dived that night; now working at the pumps, and now hurrying through the smoke and flame, but never ceasing to engage himself wherever noise and men were thickest. Up and down the ladders, upon the roofs of buildings, over floors that quaked and trembled with his weight, under the lee of falling bricks and stones, in every part of that great fire was he; but he bore a charmed life, and had neither scratch nor bruise, nor weariness, nor thought, till morning dawned again, and only smoke and blackened ruins remained.

This mad excitement over, there returned, with tenfold force, the dreadful consciousness of his crime. He looked suspiciously about him, for the men were conversing in groups, and he feared to be the subject of their talk. The dog obeyed the significant beck of his finger, and they drew off stealthily together. He passed near an engine where some men were seated, and they called to him to share in their refreshment. He took some bread and meat; and as he drank a draught of beer, heard the firemen, who were from London, talking about the murder. 'He has gone to Birmingham, they say,' said one; 'but they'll have him yet, for the scouts are out, and by tomorrow night there'll be a cry all through the country.'

He hurried off, and walked till he almost dropped upon the ground; then lay down in a lane, and had a long, but broken and uneasy sleep. He wandered on again, irresolute and undecided and oppressed with the fear of another solitary night.

Suddenly, he made the desperate resolution of going back to London.

'There's somebody to speak to there, at all events,' he thought. 'A good hiding place, too. They'll never expect to nab me there, after this country scent. Why can't I lie by for a week or so, and, forcing blunt from Fagin, get abroad to France? Damn me, I'll risk it.'

He acted upon this impulse without delay, and choosing the least frequented roads, began his journey back, resolved to lie concealed within a short distance of the metropolis, and, entering it at dusk by a circuitous route, to proceed straight to that part of it which he had fixed on as his destination.

The dog, though—so well known across London—would betray him. If any description of him were out, it would not be forgotten that the dog was missing, and had probably gone with him. This might lead to his apprehension as he passed along the streets. He resolved to drown him, and walked on, looking about for a pond, picking up a heavy stone and tying it to his handkerchief as he went along.

The animal looked up into his master's face while these preparations were in the making; and, whether his instinct apprehended something of their purpose, or the robber's sidelong look at him was sterner than ordinary, he skulked a little farther behind than usual, and cowered as he came more slowly along.

When his master halted at the brink of a pool, and looked round to call him, he stopped outright. 'Bull's-eye! Do you hear me call? Come here!' commanded Sikes.

The animal came up from the very force of habit, but, as Sikes stooped to attach the handkerchief to his throat, he uttered a low growl and scurried back. 'Come back!' insisted the robber.

The dog wagged his tail, but moved not. Sikes made a running noose, and called him again. The dog advanced, retreated, paused an instant, and then ran away at his hardest speed.

The man whistled again and again, and sat down and waited in the expectation that he would return. But no dog appeared, and at length he resumed his journey.

Chapter 41
Jacob's Island

Near to that part of the Thames on which the church at Rotherhithe abuts, where the buildings on the banks are the dirtiest and the vessels on the river are the blackest with the dust of colliers and the smoke of closely built low-roofed houses, there exists, at the present day, the filthiest, the strangest, the most extraordinary of the many localities that are hidden in London, wholly unknown, even by name, to the great mass of its inhabitants.

To reach this place, the visitor has to penetrate through a maze of close, narrow, and muddy streets, thronged by the roughest and poorest of waterside people, and devoted to the traffic they may be supposed to occasion. The cheapest and least delicate provisions are heaped in the shops; the coarsest and commonest articles of wearing apparel dangle at the salesman's door, and stream from parapets and windows. Jostling with unemployed labourers of the lowest class, ballast heavers, coal whippers, brazen women, ragged children, and the very raff and refuse of the river, he makes his way along with difficulty, assailed by offensive sights and smells from the narrow alleys which branch off on the right and left, and deafened by the clash of ponderous wagons that bear great piles of merchandise from the stacks of warehouses that rise from every corner. Arriving at length in streets remoter and less-frequented than those through which he has passed, he walks beneath tottering house fronts projecting over the pavement, dismantled walls that seem to totter as he passes, chimneys half crushed, half hesitating to fall, windows guarded by rusty iron bars that time and dirt have almost eaten away, and every imaginable sign of desolation and neglect.

In such a neighborhood, beyond Dockhead, in the Borough of Southwark, stands Jacob's Island, surrounded by a muddy ditch, six or eight feet deep and fifteen or twenty wide when the tide is in, once called Mill Pond, but known today as Folly Ditch. It is a creek or inlet from the Thames, and can always be filled at high water by opening the sluices at Lead Mills from which it took its name. At such times a stranger, looking from one of the wooden bridges thrown across it at Mill Lane, will see the inhabitants of the houses on either side lowering from their back doors and windows, buckets, pails, domestic utensils of all kinds, in which to haul the water up; and when his eye is turned from these operations to the houses themselves, his utmost astonishment will be excited by the scene before him. Crazy wooden galleries common to the backs of half a dozen houses, with holes from which to look upon the slime beneath; windows, broken and patched, with poles thrust out, on which to dry the linen that is never there; rooms so small, so filthy, so confined, that the air would seem too tainted even for the dirt and squalor which they shelter; wooden chambers thrusting themselves out above the mud, and threatening to fall into it, as some have done; dirt besmeared walls and decaying foundations; every repulsive lineament of poverty, every loathsome indication of filth, rot, and garbage;—all these ornament the banks of Folly Ditch.

On Jacob's Island, the warehouses are roofless and empty; the walls are crumbling down; the windows are windows no more; the doors are falling into the streets; the chimneys are blackened, but they yield no smoke. Thirty or forty years ago, before losses and lawsuits came upon it, it was a thriving place; but now it is a desolate island indeed. The houses have no owners; they are broken open, and entered upon by those who have the courage; and there they live, and there they die. They must have powerful motives for a secret residence, or be reduced to a destitute condition indeed, those who seek a refuge on Jacob's Island.

In an upper room of one of these houses—a detached house of fair size, ruinous in other respects, but strongly defended at door and window, of which house the back commanded the ditch in the manner already described—there were assembled three men, who, regarding each other every now and then with looks expressive of perplexity and expectation, sat for some time in profound and gloomy silence. One of these was Toby Crackit, another Mr. Chitling, and the third a robber of fifty years, whose nose had been almost beaten in, in some old scuffle, and whose face bore a frightful scar which might probably be traced to the same occasion. This man was a returned transport, from the penal colony of Australia, and his name was Kags.

'I wish,' said Toby turning to Tom Chitling, 'that you had picked out some other crib, when the two old ones got too warm, and had not come here, my fine feller.'

'Why didn't you, blunderhead!' said Kags.

'Well, I thought you'd have been a little more glad to see me than this,' replied Mr. Chitling, with a melancholy air.

'Why, look here, young gentleman,' said Toby, 'when a man keeps himself so very exclusive as I have done, and by that means has a snug house over his head with nobody a prying and smelling about it, it's rather a startling thing to have the honour of a visit from a young gentleman (however respectable and pleasant a person he may be to play cards with at his convenience) circumstanced as you are.'

'Especially,' added Mr. Kags, 'when the exclusive young man has got a friend stopping with him, that's arrived sooner than was expected from foreign parts, and is too modest to want to be presented to the Judges on his return.'

There was a short silence, after which Toby Crackit, seeming to abandon as hopeless any further effort to maintain his usual devil-may-care swagger, turned to Chitling and asked:

'When was Fagin took, then?'

'Just at dinner-time—two o'clock this afternoon. The Artful and I made our lucky up the back chimney. Bolter got into the empty water barrel, head downwards; but his legs were so precious long that they stuck out at the top, and so they took him too.'

'And Betsy?'

'Poor Bet! She went to see the body, to speak to who it was,' replied Chitling, his countenance falling more and more, 'and went off mad, screaming and raving, and beating her head against the boards; so they put a strait-waistcoat on her and took her to the hospital—and there she is.'

'Wot's come of the Artful Dodger?' demanded Kags.

'He hung about, not wanting to come over here afore dark, but he'll be here soon,' replied Chitling. 'There's nowhere else to go to now, for the people at the Cripples are all in custody, and the bar of the ken—I went up there and see it with my own eyes—is filled with traps.'

'This is a smash,' observed Kags, biting his lips. 'There's more than one will go down with this.'

'The court sessions are on,' said Toby. 'If they get the inquest over, and Bolter turns Crown's evidence—as of course he will, from what he's said already—they can prove Fagin an accessory before the fact, and get the trial on by Friday. He'll swing in six days from this, by God!'

It now being dark the shutter was closed, and a candle was placed upon a table. The terrible events of the last two days had made a deep impression on all three men, increased by the danger and uncertainty of their own position. They drew their chairs closer together, starting at every sound. They spoke little, and that in whispers, and were as silent and awe-stricken as if the remains of the murdered woman lay in the next room.

They had sat thus for some time, when suddenly a hurried knocking was heard at the door below.

'The Artful?' asked Kags, looking anxiously around, to check the fear he felt himself.

The knocking came again.

'No, it isn't he,' said Toby, 'he never knocked like that. Crackit went to the window, and shaking all over, drew in his head. There was no need to tell them who it was; his pale face was enough.

'We must let him in,' said Crackit, taking up the candle.

'Isn't there no help for it?' asked Kags, in a hoarse voice.

'None. He *must* come in.'

'Don't leave us in the dark,' said Chitling, taking a candle down from the fireplace mantel, and lighting it, with such a trembling hand that the knocking was repeated twice before he had finished.

Crackit went down to the door, and returned followed by a man with the lower part of his face buried in a handkerchief, and another tied over his head under his hat. He drew them slowly off. Blanched face, sunken eyes, hollow cheeks, beard of three days' growth, wasted flesh, short thick breath—it was the very ghost of Sikes.

He laid his hand upon a chair which stood in the middle of the room, but shuddering as he was about to drop into it, and seeming to glance over his shoulder, dragged it back close to the wall—as close as it would go—and ground it against it—and sat down.

Not a word had been exchanged. He looked from one to another in silence. If an eye were furtively raised and met his, it was instantly averted. When his hollow voice broke the silence, they all three started. They seemed to have never heard its tones before.

'Tonight's paper says that Fagin's took. Is it true, or a lie?'

'True.'

They were silent again.

'Damn you all!' said Sikes, passing his hand across his forehead. 'Have you nothing to say to me?'

There was an uneasy movement among them, but nobody spoke.

'You that keep this house,' said Sikes, turning his face to Crackit, 'do you mean to sell me, or to let me lie here till this hunt is over?'

'You may stop here, if you think it safe,' returned the person addressed, after some hesitation.

Sikes carried his eyes slowly up the wall behind him—rather trying to turn his head than actually doing it—and asked, 'Is—it—the body—is it buried?'

They shook their heads.

'Why isn't it!' he retorted, with the same glance behind him. 'Wot do they keep such ugly things above the ground for?—Who's that knocking?'

Crackit intimated, by a motion of his hand as he left the room, that there was nothing to fear; and came back directly with Jack Dawkins behind him. Sikes sat opposite the door, so that the moment the boy entered the room he encountered his figure.

'Toby,' said the boy falling back, as Sikes turned his eyes towards him, 'why didn't you tell me this downstairs?'

There had been something so tremendous in the shrinking off of the three men, that the wretched man was willing to appease even this lad. Accordingly he got up, and made as though he would shake hands with him.

'Let me go into some other room,' said the boy, retreating still farther.

'Jack!' said Sikes, stepping forward, 'don't you—don't you know me?'

'Don't come nearer me,' answered the Dodger, still retreating, and looking, with horror in his eyes, upon the murderer's face. 'You, you monster!'

The man stopped half-way, and they looked at each other; but Sikes's eyes sunk gradually to the ground.

'Witness you three,' cried the Dodger shaking his clenched fist, and becoming more and more excited as he spoke—'witness you three—I'm not afraid of him—if they come here after him, I'll give him up; I will. I tell you all at once. He may kill me for it if he likes, or if he dares, but if I am here I'll give him up. I'd give him up if he was to be boiled alive. Murderer! Help! If there's the pluck of a man among you three, you'll help me. Murderer! Help! Down with him!'

Pouring out these cries, and accompanying them with violent gesticulation, the boy suddenly threw himself, single-handed, upon the strong man, and in the intensity of his energy, and the abruptness of his action, brought him heavily to the ground.

The three spectators seemed quite stupefied. They offered no interference, and the boy and man rolled on the ground together; the former, heedless of the blows that showered upon him, wrenching his hands tighter and tighter about the murderer's neck, and never ceasing to call for help with all his might.

The contest, however, was too unequal to last long. Sikes had him down, and his knee was on his throat, when Crackit pulled him back with a look of alarm.

'Enough of that,' cried Toby. 'You've enough blood on your hands already, Bill.'

Jack scrambled to the far side of the room, and sat on the floor with his back against the wall; the glare of fury still in his eyes. For the longest moment of a very long day everyone looked at one another, in silence, each wondering to himself how to save his own skin.

In the quiet, a faint scratching could be heard.

'Wot's that?' asked Chitling, to no one in particular.

The scratching sound was heard again.

'Bull's-eye!' shouted the Dodger, laughing maliciously. 'Good, ol' faithful Bull's-eye. Bill's dog, leading the traps right to our door.'

Sikes ran across the room and grabbed the Dodger by the collar.

'Open the door of some place where I can lockup this Hell-babe,' cried Sikes, fiercely; dragging the boy now as easily as if he were an empty sack.'

Kags quickly obliged, opening the door to a closet. Sikes flung the Artful in, bolted it, and turned the key.

'Is the downstairs door fast?' asked Sikes.

'Double-locked and chained,' replied Crackit, who, as with the other two men, still remained quite helpless and bewildered.

'The door panels – are they strong?'

'Lined with sheet iron."

'And the windows too?'

'Yes, and the windows?'

'The tide,' cried the murderer, as he staggered back into the room, and shut the faces out, 'the tide was out as I came up. Give me a rope, a long rope. They'll come from the front. I'll drop into Folly Ditch, and clear off that way. Give me a rope, or I shall do three more murders and kill myself.

The panic stricken men pointed to where such articles were kept. Sikes hastily selected the longest and strongest rope, and hurried up the stairs. He emerged out onto the housetop by way of a small door accessing the roof and planted a board, which he had carried up with him for the purpose, so firmly against the door that it would be matter of great difficulty to open it from the inside. Creeping over the tiles, he looked over the low parapet.

The water was out, and the ditch a bed of mud.

Soon, at the barricaded door, came the sound of banging and shouting. Sikes ignored the clamour being made by Crackit, Chitling, and Kags. He proceeded to fastened one end of the rope tightly and firmly round the chimney, and threw the loose end over the edge. It reached to within twelve feet of the muddy ground. Being no stranger to the use of ropes for climbing; he made his way down the rope as far as it went, and then dropped the final distance. Trudging through the ditch was slow and difficult, given the weight of muck clinging to his boots, but soon he was up and over the far bank.

Across on the other side of the ditch, running to and fro, was his dog. Upon spotting his master making his way over the bank, Bull's-eye ran to nearby Mill Lane Bridge and had soon joined him.

Trapped inside the house, Crackit and the others could now hear shouting, a multitude of angry voices as would have made the boldest quail, making its way ever closer to their house. Then came a loud knocking at the front door.

'It's the police!' declared Kags.

'In the Queen's name,' cried a loud voice, 'open this door.'

The three men looked at one another helplessly. The sound of knocking was replaced by louder, rhythmic thuds.

'They're breaking down the door with a battering ram,' said Toby. 'We've nowhere to run. Sikes has blocked our only escape.'

'I'm surrendering,' said Kags, making his way down the stairs. 'I've done no crime other than coming to visit me homeland. I've seen 'nough of it, I have.'

'I'm for surrendering,' added Chitling, following Kags.

Toby followed Chitling silently, having no reason for staying back.

Chapter 42
A Return to the Workhouse

The events narrated in the last chapter were yet but two days old, when Oliver found himself, at ten o'clock in the morning, in a travelling carriage rolling fast towards his native town with Mr. Brownlow at his side. Each had his own purpose for the journey.

They did not talk much upon the way. The newspaper had been full of stories about the grisly murder and the subsequent arrests. Oliver had talked extensively with Mrs. Bedwin, who was happy to talk day and night about such things; and with Mr. Brownlow, who explained some of the legal niceties the court would take into account with each of the accused. So they travelled on in silence, each reflecting on the course of events that had brought them together, and neither much disposed to give utterance to their thoughts.

While Oliver, under these influences, remained silent while they journeyed towards his birthplace along a route he had never seen, he became talkative once they turned onto the familiar road which he had traversed on foot, a poor houseless, wandering boy, without a friend to help him, or a roof to shelter his head. Suddenly, the whole current of his recollections ran vividly back to old times; awakening a crowd of emotions.

'See there, there!' cried Oliver, eagerly pointing out of the carriage window; 'that's the stile I came over; there are the hedges I crept behind, for fear any one should overtake me and force me back! Yonder is the path across the fields, leading to the old house where I was a little child! Oh, how I look forward to seeing Ricky. I have so much to tell him. He won't believe half of what I have to tell him.'

'You will see him soon enough,' replied Mr. Brownlow, 'and he will have to believe you when you show him the papers.'

'Yes, yes,' said Oliver, emphatically. 'And,' he added more tentatively, 'you'll take him away from here, won't you, and have him clothed and taught, and find him a nice home not far your house where he may grow strong and well, and we can visit?'

Mr. Brownlow merely nodded his assent to this plaintive request; for the boy's earnest manner made it difficult for him to speak.

'You will be kind and good to him,' said Oliver, 'I know you will, for you are to everyone.'

As they approached the town, and at length drove through its narrow streets, Oliver grew somber again. There was Sowerberry's the undertaker's just as it used to be, only smaller and less imposing in appearance than he remembered it; there was the courthouse; there was Gamfield's cart, the very cart he used to have, standing at the old public-house door; there was the workhouse, the dreary prison of his youth, with its dismal windows frowning on the street; there was the same lean porter standing at the gate, at the sight of whom Oliver involuntarily shrunk back; there were scores of faces at the doors and windows that he knew quite well; there was nearly everything as if he had left it but yesterday, untouched by the course of events.

They drove straight to the door of the chief hotel (which Oliver used to stare up at, with awe, and think a mighty palace, but which had somehow fallen off in grandeur and size). There was dinner prepared, and there were bedrooms made ready; everything arranged as if by magic.

The following morning, following a pleasant breakfast, Mr. Brownlow and Oliver made their way to the workhouse where Mr. Brownlow had arranged, by post, a special meeting with the board. As Oliver walked into the workhouse a cold sweat came over him and his legs nearly failed him. Sensing this, Mr. Brownlow held his hand more securely and reminded him to 'be strong.' Oliver took a deep breath and straightened his shoulders. An elderly pauper known to Oliver, but who failed to recognize Oliver in his new suit of clothes, asked them their business and, upon being so informed, led them to the board room.

Oliver recognized all of the assembled gentlemen; there had been but one change in membership since he first stood before the board on the occasion of his twelve birthday. Mr. Bumble had taken the place of Mr. Slout as master of the workhouse. Slowly at first, but with increasing speed as members conferred with one another, the board members came to recognize the young boy who stood before them. Mr. Brownlow and Oliver bowed towards the members of the board. Mr. Bumble was the first to speak.

'Do my eyes deceive me?' cried Mr. Bumble, with ill-feigned enthusiasm, 'or is that little Oliver? Oh! O-li-ver, if you know'd how I've been a-grieving for you -'

'Hold your tongue, fool,' murmured the gentleman still wearing a white waistcoat.

'Isn't nature,' remonstrated the workhouse master. 'Can't I be supposed to feel—I as brought him up parochially—when I see him a-standing here with a gentleman of the very affablest description? I always loved that boy as if he'd been my—my—my own grandfather,' said Mr. Bumble, halting for an appropriate comparison. 'Master Oliver, my dear, you remember Mr. Slout? Ah! he went to heaven some weeks ago, in an oak coffin with plated handles, Oliver.'

'Come, sir,' said the red faced Mr. Limbkins, who still occupied the highchair, tartly; 'suppress your feelings.'

'I will do my endeavours, sir,' replied Mr. Bumble. 'How do you do, sir? It is good to see you once again. I hope you've been well.'

This salutation was addressed to Mr. Brownlow, who had stepped forward to address the board. Ignoring Mr. Bumble, Brownlow quickly reviewed his reasons for requesting a meeting with the board.

'Gentlemen,' he said, 'I appear before you on two orders of business. The first is that I should like to assume custody and guardianship of a young inmate of yours who goes by the name Ricky. I trust that you would be happily released from the financial burden you incur in caring for him.'

The board members looked askance at one another for a moment or two before the chairman addressed Mr. Bumble.

'Mr. Bumble,' he said, 'I don't recall hearing of that young lad Ricky recently. Is he still resident at the children's asylum?'

Mr. Bumble hesitated a moment before answering, 'No, sir, he no longer resides there.'

'Then where does he reside?' continued the same gentleman.

Mr. Bumble hesitated again before answering, 'He's dead, sir. He died a month ago.'

Upon hearing this sad news, Oliver began to tear up. It was all he could do to stop himself from sobbing.

'Would you like a different boy?' asked the gentleman in the white waistcoat, in a helpful tone of voice. 'We have lots.'

Mr. Brownlow declined to respond to that suggestion.

'Gentlemen,' said Mr. Brownlow, 'my other purpose for appearing before you is to report certain facts within my personal knowledge regarding two individuals in your employ.'

'Go ahead,' replied the chairman.

'First, I would like to confirm,' continued Mr. Brownlow, ' that while few of those who enter these walls have much in the way of worldly possessions, the laws governing personal property still apply, do they not? One pauper could not, say, take a shirt or pair of shoes from another with impunity.'

'Yes, of course,' responded the chairman.

'And the law governing trusts,' said Mr. Brownlow, 'it too applies within these walls.'

'All of the laws of the land apply within these walls, sir,' stated chairman impatiently. 'We are not sovereign onto ourselves. Please come to your point.'

'Oliver's mother, Miss Anne Griffith,' said Mr. Brownlow, had a gold locket in her possession when she took refuge in this charitable institution. I have knowledge of the locket as it was I who gave it to her.'

Mr. Brownlow interrupted his address to the board for a moment to retrieve a small velvet pouch from his pocket. He extracted the locket from the pouch and handed it to Mr. Limbkins to inspect. After a careful inspection of the precious item, the chairman passed the locket to the board member sitting to his left. One by one each member inspected the locket. Once the locket had been passed around the entire table the chairman handed it back to Mr. Brownlow. Mr. Brownlow placed the locket back into the velvet pouch and gave it to Oliver.

'Upon giving birth to her son, who stands before you today,' continued Mr. Brownlow, 'knowing that she was dying, Anne gave the locket to her nurse—a pauper woman named Sally—to hold in trust until Oliver came of age. Sally, though poverty stricken herself, honoured that trust for some twelve years until her own death.'

At this point in Mr. Brownlow's speech, an observant spectator would have notice that Mr. Bumble was becoming rather agitated.

'Upon her own death bed,' continued Mr. Brownlow, 'Sally gave the locket to the only person she knew who might reasonably be expected to honour the trust; the matron of this workhouse, Mrs. Corney, now Bumble. Mr. and Mrs. Bumble promptly broke the trust created by a dying mother, and kept by a pauper woman, and sold the locket. I have with me the signed declaration of the jeweller to whom it was sold.'

'This is a serious accusation,' said the chairman. 'What do you have to say in your defence Mr. Bumble? Is this true?'

'I never touched the locket,' protested Mr. Bumble. 'It was never in my possession.'

'As master of the workhouse, a position of trust I need not add,' said Mr. Brownlow, 'you knowingly acquiesced in the sale of property being held in trust for Oliver Twist.'

'He had run off,' stated Mr. Bumble, 'no one knew his whereabouts.'

'Running off, at the age of twelve,' said Mr. Brownlow, 'does not terminate such a trust.'

'I hope,' said Mr. Bumble, looking about him with great ruefulness, 'I hope that this unfortunate little circumstance will not deprive me of my parochial office? It was all Mrs. Corney's, I mean Mrs. Bumble's, doing.'

'That is no excuse,' replied Mr. Brownlow. 'You were present on the occasion of the sale of the trinket, and, indeed, are the more guilty of the two, in the eyes of the law; for the law supposes that your wife acts under your direction.'

'If the law supposes that,' said Mr. Bumble, squeezing his hat emphatically in both hands, 'the law is an ass—an idiot. If that's the eye of the law, the law is a bachelor; and the worst I wish for the law is, that his eyes may be opened by experience—by experience.'

Mr. Brownlow turned to address the board again.

'It is, of course, for you the board to decide upon the question of Mr. and Mrs. Bumble's continued employment,' stated Mr. Brownlow. 'You may employ known thieves if you choose. If it were up to me, however, neither the master nor the matron of this workhouse would secure a position of trust again. Good day gentlemen.'

With that, Mr. Brownlow took Oliver's hand and the two of them walked out of the room.

Epilogue

The fortunes of those who have figured in this tale are nearly closed. The little that remains for their historian to relate is told in few and simple words.

Mr. and Mrs. Bumble received the just reward to which Mr. Brownlow had earlier alluded. Quickly deprived of their situations, they were gradually reduced to great indigence and misery, and finally became paupers in that very same workhouse in which they had once lorded it over others. Mr. Bumble has been heard to say, that in this reverse and degradation, he has not even the spirit to be thankful for being separated from his wife.

Mr. Griffith, who saw less and less of his old friend and neighbour Mr. Brownlow, died a few years following the events narrated herein. In his last will and testament he provided modestly for the support of Mr. Giles and Mr. Brittles and bequeathed the bulk of his estate, which was considerable, to a cousin living somewhere in Saxony.

Someone matching Mr. Sikes' description was seen roaming the countryside of Normandy with a white dog. It is said that he joined a band of roving mercenaries, and eventually found his way to Morocco. However, it is also said that he signed on as crew aboard a ship bound for Tahiti.

Flash Toby Crackit was found guilty of breaking and entering upon Mr. Griffith's house. He would have been sentenced to hang at Newgate except for the testimony of a young boy who testified as to how Mr. Crackit had saved his life, twice, at considerable risk to his own. Mr. Crackit was transported to the colonies; Tasmania as it were. There, in the small town of Hobart, he stumbled upon Master Charley Bates; whilst scouting out the same mark. The two convicts set upon a plan to raise, by various dubious means, just enough capital to purchase a small sheep station, and, over the years, they prospered. Charley met and married a sweet young lass and, as a father to nine children in need of education, established the first school in the district. Crackit was elected town mayor for two terms in succession.

Mr. Noah Claypole, receiving a free pardon from the Crown in consequence of being admitted approver against Fagin. Deciding that his profession not altogether as safe a one as he could wish for, he was, for some little time, at a loss for the means of a livelihood not burdened with too much work. After some consideration, he went into business as an Informer, in which calling he realises a genteel subsistence. His plan is to walk out once a week during church time attended by Charlotte in respectable attire. The lady faints away at the doors of charitable publicans, and the gentleman being accommodated with three penny worth of brandy to restore her, lays an information next day, and pockets half the penalty. Sometimes Mr. Claypole faints himself, but the result is the same.

Fagin, as predicted by Crackit, was found guilty of being an accessory to murder before the fact and sentenced to be hanged by the neck until dead. This sentence was to be executed at Newgate not a week following his arrest. Sadly, as most of his friends and colleagues were also incarcerated, only one brave soul came to visit and console him prior to his hanging day. As was usual, a crowd of several hundred came to watch the spectacle as a spot of free entertainment. They were sorely disappointed when, at the allotted hour, Fagin failed to appear. A thorough search of the penitentiary was conducted, but he was not to be found.

Soon after the ruckus on Jacob's Island subsided and the house had grown quiet, Jack Dawkins—aptly known as the Artful Dodger—broke free from the closet in which Sikes had shut him up. He lingered there a couple of days before visiting an old friend and mentor then residing at Newgate. He then struck out on his own for the countryside. Appalled by Sikes's crime, he fell into a train of deep reflection as to whether an honest livelihood might not, after all, be the best. Arriving at the conclusion that it certainly was, he turned his back upon the scenes of the past, and resolved to strike out in some new sphere of action. He struggled hard, and suffered much for some time; but, having an amiable disposition and a good purpose, he succeeded in finding honest, if strenuous, employment—brick-making.

Several weeks following the events recorded above, Oliver was wandering through a nearby park in a rather miserable mood. This confused him as he had no reason for feeling dejected as his life had never been so pleasant. Mr. Brownlow had adopted him as his son and was supervising his education. Mrs. Bedwin provided all of the mothering a boy of twelve needed, and then some. Oliver himself failed to identify the cause of his melancholy; loneliness. While his circumstances had often been dreadful, he had always enjoyed the company of children his own age; Mr. Brownlow and Mrs. Bedwin together could not provide the companionship he craved. Oliver was absent mindedly kicking a small stone along the path when he heard a familiar voice call out to him.

'Hullo, my covey! What's the row?'

Oliver very nearly burst with joy upon hearing these friendly words.

'Jack!' cried Oliver, 'what are you doing here?'

"I've come to see my dearest friend Oliver,' said the Dodger, 'to ensure that he's well, an 'appy, an stay'n ahead of the traps.'

Oliver doubted that this was the whole truth and nothing but the truth, given his propensities, but there was no doubt that Dawkins looked happy to see him.

'How are you?' asked Oliver. 'Where are you staying? Do you want for anything?'

'I'm fine,' said the Dodger, 'but not so fine as yurself. Found yurself a right plush situwation, you 'ave.'

The two boys fell into step with one another as they became reacquainted. Dawkins told Oliver all about the events on Jacob's Island and Oliver informed him about his own adventures. After an hour or more of talking, Oliver noted that it was time for him to return home for tea.

'You must join me!' said Oliver, with unconcealed excitement. 'Mrs. Bedwin's such a love; she'd take to you faster than snakes to grass. And Mr. Brownlow, he likes everyone, far as I can tell.'

Dawkins was wary of entering into such fine society, but was eventually persuaded by Oliver. It was remarkable to see the Dodger struck nearly dumb by the grandeur of the Brownlow residence, and by the gracious welcome he received. It is questionable as to whether Mrs. Bedwin took to the Dodger quite as readily as she took to snakes, but, following Mr. Brownlow's lead, she treated him kindly. Mr. Brownlow was soon impressed by Dawkins's cheerful demeanor and quick presence of mind. It was Brownlow who asked him if he might like to join Oliver in his studies.

'That's a right plumy idear,' replied Dawkins. And so it was.

Afterword

Revising a much-loved novel is inherently controversial, but there are times when it can revive a classic. I was about to 'recommend' that my teenage children read *Oliver Twist*, when I decided that it would be wise for me to first reread it myself. As expected, I found it to be a beautifully written and engaging novel until about halfway through when, to my surprise, it turned pedantic and dull.

There are, in my opinion, three problems with *Oliver Twist*. First of all, the book is notoriously anti-Semitic. Secondly, Oliver is a surprisingly passive, often tearful, character who is seldom the author of his own destiny. Thirdly, the plot revolves around Oliver's illegitimate birth, and much of the book is taken up by his step-brother Monk and the self-righteous Maylie family. Young readers today would not appreciate the cruel social consequences of being an unwed mother in Victorian England.

As *Oliver Twist* is now in the public domain, I decided to revise it. It was a fairly simple matter to remove the anti-Semitism and to transform Oliver into a stronger character. Extracting Monk, the Maylie family, and the plot in which they are entwined was a rather more challenging, but an entirely enjoyable endeavour. Every chapter and almost every page required careful revision to create a new story line.

Essentially, I set out to preserve everything that makes *Oliver Twist* fun and adventurous, and take out everything that is objectionable or tedious. The revised book is twenty-five percent shorter than the original and, I trust, a better read.

Trevor Schindeler

www.ingramcontent.com/pod-product-compliance
Lightning Source LLC
Chambersburg PA
CBHW021134110726
47900CB00002B/345